PRAISE FOR THE NICK CHESTER SERIES

'Plenty of action, some well-wrought characterisation and nice evocations of the Marlborough Sounds make for a good solid Kiwi book.' *New Zealand Listener*

'The characters work, the plot is cleverly executed and the sense of place is visceral. There's touches of humour and self-inflicted jeopardy which are perfectly justifiable … an absolute stand-out book …' *Australian Crime Fiction*

'… a terrific read!' *Fullers Bookshop*

'Hard to put down. *Marlborough Man* is crime fiction at its best.' *The Australian*

'A well written, tension-filled and accurate portrait of a man struggling with his past …' *Otago Daily Times*

'… crime writing has never been better. [Five stars]' *Kuttners Choice*

'*Marlborough Man* is an unrelenting, incredibly readable book that will hold you through a whole day … Carter has paced this novel brilliantly, and when Nick Chester's nightmare moment arrives, the crescendo is breathtaking.' *Bookoccino*

'… a roller coaster ride of false leads and red herrings … Carter draws the reader to his characters, flaws and all …' *Fremantle Herald*

'… [New Zealand is] vividly described, in both a beautiful yet haunting way …' *Dircksey*

'What makes a great thriller is nerve-wracking plotting, rich atmospheric settings, and complex characters – *Marlborough Man* has the lot …' *Kiwi Crime*

'This is a cracker of a novel, pacey and sharp … compelling from start to finish. Highly recommended …' *Landfall Review Online*

'Carter is a first-class wordsmith with a particular talent for authentic dialogue. The novel's setting wholly embraces the people and action, and the overall effect is powerful and persuasive.' *Ngaio Marsh Award judges*

'The crime aspects of the novel are well handled, with dogged police work inching the team ever closer to catching the killer. But it is the human aspects of the story that make you understand the characters and care about them.' *New Zealand Review of Books Pukapuka Aotearoa*

'This is a story of perversion and vengeance, made more gripping by the fact that it is set in one of the most beautiful places on earth … It is a fascinating mix that only a skilled writer should attempt. Alan Carter succeeds admirably.' *Queensland Reviewers Collective*

'Carter's laconic style and small-town chills are excellently placed to ease you into a long winter in front of the fire.' *Readings*

'*Marlborough Man* weaves local politics, culture and crime into a story that is gripping and at times brimming with Kiwi humour. The scenery, so beautifully described, could almost be a character in the story.' *Writing WA*

First published 2020 by
FREMANTLE PRESS

Reprinted 2020.

Fremantle Press Inc. trading as Fremantle Press
PO Box 158, North Fremantle, Western Australia, 6159
fremantlepress.com.au

Cover photographs from unsplash.com, istockphoto.com.au and shutterstock.com.
Cover design by Nada Backovic, nadabackovic.com

 A catalogue record for this book is available from the National Library of Australia

ISBN 9781925816815 (paperback)
ISBN 9781760990039 (ebook)

 |

Fremantle Press is supported by the Western Australian State Government through the Department of Cultural Industries, Tourism and Sport.

Publication of this title was assisted by the Commonwealth Government through Creative Australia, its arts funding and advisory body.

Fremantle Press respectfully acknowledges the Whadjuk people of the Noongar nation as the Traditional Owners and Custodians of the land where we work in Walyalup.

ALAN CARTER
DOOM CREEK

FREMANTLE PRESS

Alan Carter was born in Sunderland, UK. He immigrated to Australia in 1991 and now lives in splendid semi-rural semi-isolation south of Hobart, Tasmania. In his spare time he follows the black line up and down the local swimming pool or drags on his wetsuit and braves the icy waters of the D'Entrecasteaux Channel. He is the author of seven previous novels: the Fremantle-set DS Cato Kwong series *Prime Cut* (winner of the Ned Kelly Award for Best First Fiction), *Getting Warmer*, *Bad Seed* and *Heaven Sent*. His New Zealand-set *Marlborough Man*, featuring Sergeant Nick Chester, won the Ngaio Marsh Award for Best Novel. Its sequel is *Doom Creek*.

For Kath

PROLOGUE

A predator-free New Zealand? What a great idea. A Utopian vision requiring the kind of focus and resources you'd need to put a man back on the moon. Where there's a will there's a way – but is there the will? How many rats, stoats, weasels, possums, feral cats would need to die? How many stars are there in the sky? Still, all he can do is his bit, here in this slice of Eden, once a week, regular as clockwork. Tramping deep into the native bush around Pelorus Bridge to check and reset the traps, do a body count, and try against the odds to save a tiny native long-tailed bat from extinction – even if it is the ugliest little bastard you ever saw.

Bob checks his map. Follow the pink ribbons and there should be a set of possum, rat and stoat traps over to the right. He's done this countless times but sometimes his old eyes and mind deceive him: Alzheimer's or just a trick of the ever-changing light? God, it's beautiful in here. Yes, there's the constant throb of tourist and other traffic across the bridge along with the more distant roar of chainsaws on the adjoining pine plantation over the hill. But close your ears, open your eyes, and it's a dappled Rivendell of vivid mosses and ancient rimu; another world. Plus it gets him out of the house, breathing fresh air, staving off his dotage and the old worries that sometimes slink in.

Except the air isn't so fresh. You can smell a garrotted possum, a crushed rat or stoat from metres away. Something stinks today for sure. Ripe as. He can hear flies buzzing too; it must be a relatively fresh feast. Up ahead he sees a clearing, the tell-tale yellow of the wasp-bait box on a black beech tree, the blue funnel of a possum trap. Nothing hanging from it. The smell must be in one of the wooden boxes, the rat and stoat traps maybe.

Bob stumbles. Foot caught in a gnarly vine, aggravating the tendons from that snap when he fell downstairs last year. Old bones refusing to fully heal, muscles and sinew stubbornly resisting the mend. His nostrils flare. Stoat or rat? That's a big smell for such a wee creature. The wind rustles the leaves and ferns and a black humming cloud lifts and settles again on the far side of a totara tree. He realises he's been holding his breath, not from the smell but from something more primal. Fear has crept under the skin and taken hold like the delicate fungi on dead bark. The emerald shimmer dims as cumulus covers the sun. Bob reaches the clearing, moss sponging and twigs cracking under his hiking boots. He edges around the totara to get a better look.

The body is sitting propped against the tree as if just taking a rest; held in place by a rope around the neck and around the tree trunk. A deer. Female, he's guessing, blanketed by flies and maggots. Liquids, dark and viscous, have seeped out – the face and front are open to the world. Bob fights the urge to spew but it's not like he hasn't come across such a scene before.

A rustle and crunch behind him. Ferns lift and a figure steps through in backwoods gear.

'You?' Where there's a will there really is a way. Of course there is. There always was and would be. Bob waves his hand sadly at the deer corpse. 'Poor bugger's come a cropper.'

'Shame,' says the visitor, nodding.

Count the seconds. A sob of anguish. 'Oh, God.' Then a sound somewhere between a thump and a cough. Barely enough to disturb the blowflies.

1.

The river is in fine form this Thursday morning, bubbling through the gorge and catching the green of the surrounding pine plantations. I even saw a trout yesterday in the deep part of the pool. Imagine that. Some days it's so clear you can see a bloody fish three hundred metres away through your window. Especially when you have a telescopic sight.

I'm locked on the centre of the man's back. He hasn't realised he's been spotted. Broad shoulders, he's an easy target. My finger curls on the trigger. One squeeze and he's gone. The river will carry him down to the Sounds and out with the tide. They keep on coming and I have to keep on sending them away. Otherwise it'll never stop.

'You can't shoot him, Nick.' Vanessa nudges me with her hip and plants a mug of coffee at my elbow. 'He's got resource consent from the council.'

'Fucking goldminers. Why don't they just piss off and leave us alone?'

'Two days a week, September to April. Even then the river needs to be low enough for him to get in with his dredge. It's rained most weekends since.' She pats my knee. 'It's just his silly hobby. One more week to go and that's it until spring. Relax, pet.'

Ever since a Canadian company discovered a significant deposit of the yellow stuff down near the pub eighteen months ago, gold fever has returned to the valley after a hundred and fifty years. Men, and it usually is men, from all walks of life but with the same greedy gleam in the eye knock at our door regularly. With friendly smiles they ask if it's okay to use our path to access the river to pan and fossick, to park their utes in our driveway, to store their dredging and excavation gear in our shed. Mate?

No. It's not. I'm beginning to see *Deliverance* from the point of view of the hillbillies. And then their smile slips and it's clear they never wanted to be your friend in the first place.

'Chancers and users the lot of them.'

'You better get to work, grumble-bum. You're obsessing again.' Vanessa swallows the rest of her coffee. 'Paulie!' she yells. 'Time to go.'

Vanessa's teaching at Havelock Primary but it's her turn to get Paulie to his high school twenty k's west in the opposite direction. Early starts all round but Vanessa is loving it and Paulie seems happy enough.

'Lunch?' he says, peering into his school bag anxiously.

'No, I couldn't be bothered today, sweetie. See what you can scrounge from the other kids.'

'Mum!'

'Joke. You. In the car. Now.' She leans over and kisses me, slips her tongue between my lips. 'Have a nice day.'

I promise to try. Paulie has found his ham roll and a banana. He gives me a thumbs up and heads for the door.

Through the window I see the miner has pulled on a wetsuit and started up the dredge. A souped-up lawnmower hum fills the gorge and drowns out the river and bird sounds. A plume of grey sludge blossoms from the infernal machine and clouds the pristine waters.

Driving down the Wakamarina valley road I pass more and more logging sites. As usual it's yin and yang: paradise around one corner, Mordor the next. I read somewhere recently a description of New Zealand as being like a beautiful woman with a ravaging cancer. Not sure what that's supposed to mean, cancer is nasty, whether you're beautiful or not. Maybe it's saying that the beauty is dangerously deceptive and by the time we all recognise the symptoms, it'll be too late. The trees planted a generation ago as a tax break are ready to be chopped down now. It's like that right across the top of South Island – several million more tonnes of topsoil waiting to be washed away by the coming winter rains – an environmental perfect storm in the making. Sometimes you think you're getting used to the carnage, other days you know you're not. And those hundred-percent pure rivers we promise in the tourism ads turn out to be swimming with *E. coli* and other bacteria. Even our own shimmering Wakamarina harbours mercury deep under the rocks from the gold rush days. All these time bombs, ticking away.

Maybe we should have accepted the offer last year from that Russian guy in his helicopter. Sold up while the selling was good. But we were in love with the place, we were safe and happy and our enemies had been vanquished. I heard that Andrei bought another property further down the valley instead, an old hunting lodge-cum-resort that only a fool or a shady mafia-linked oligarch would waste money on. The Lodge is back on the market a year later. Poor old Andrei is in prison in Siberia awaiting a corruption trial cooked up by the authorities. Maybe he shouldn't have said those things on Twitter about the president.

In range, passing the Trout Hotel, my mobile goes. It's Constable Latifa Rapata, wondering what's keeping me. 'Ten minutes,' I say. 'Something up?'

'Some bloke here wants to make a fillum, Sarge.'

'Film?'

'Yeah, he's …' a lowering of decibels. 'Pākehā. Dressed like he's from Auckland or Wellington, or somewhere.'

'And you need me to deal with it?'

'What do I know about fillums? See you in ten.'

When I get to the police station – a weatherboard shack with two desks, a photocopier and a big fibreglass mussel shell on the roof to show we're part of the community – he's there to greet me. He does indeed have a certain metropolitan look about him: hipster beard, tight suit, manbag, shiny sharp shoes. Behind him Latifa crosses her eyes, pokes her top teeth over her bottom lip and does a weird little dance.

'Mr Devon Cornish, Sarge. He's a fillum director from Wellington.'

'Producer, actually.' He offers me a business card.

'How can we help?' I try not to catch Latifa's mischievous eye as she disappears behind the partition.

'As I explained to your colleague, this is a heads-up that we'll be filming in this area for a few days next week.'

'And?'

'And it's a feature film, set in the gold rush. Did you know about those murders that happened around here back then?'

'The Doom Creek murders in the mid-1800s. Five prospectors ambushed by bandits in remote hill country for a few bucks. Yeah, I read about it once.'

'That's it – and the movie is called *Doom Creek*, and guess who's going to be in it.'

'Thrill me.' He rattles off a name and I'm none the wiser.

'Greg from *Shortland Street*?'

I shake my head, no, I'm not a follower of NZ soapies. 'Still not sure why you're telling me. You don't need my permission to film. You need the landowner, or government department, whatever.'

'There is something you could help with, and we've already run it past your district commander in Nelson.'

Marianne Keegan – newly promoted, following Ford's retirement – thanks for the tip-off, Marianne. Not. 'Go on.'

'We're hoping you can assist us with traffic management.'

A distant Latifa-like snort.

'Traffic?'

'We need to keep modern cars out of the frame – think *Braveheart* and the panel vans – and there's still quite a few head up that way. We'll have our own team directing people away but we need your presence in case anybody makes a fuss.'

'We do have proper jobs to do here, Mr Cornish. This isn't a priority.'

He pulls a sheet of paper out of his manbag and hands it to me. It's a letter from Commander Marianne to him saying she'll be delighted to offer my assistance to his bloody film.

'I understand you live up the Wakamarina valley, Sergeant?'

'Says who?'

An embarrassed cough from the other side of the partition.

'We'll be filming just up the road from you at Butchers Flat. Should be a nice quick commute to work for you on those days.' He stands up and offers his hand. 'Until next Tuesday. Eight a.m.' Shoulders his bag. 'Sharp.'

By midmorning I've had it with Latifa calling me 'Best Boy' and 'Key Grip' and head to the bakery to grab a pie and a coffee while she zooms out on to SH6 to nail some speeders. Autumn is a beautiful time of year. The weather can be crisp and fine and it's worth enjoying ahead of the winter chill. The tourists have moved on and the town quietens down, which means less work for us cops but slower business for the shops and cafés and for the tourist boats out on the Marlborough Sounds. It's a good time of year for Devon Cornish to be shooting his film, fewer people in the way, accommodation vacancies in town for his cast and crew, and the promise of calm weather for the next few weeks. I order my coffee and find a table, make a call to DC Keegan at Nelson HQ.

'Morning, Nick. Nice to hear from you.'

She has the power to sack me and knows most of my secrets, in and out of bed. It seeps through her slightly mocking, faintly Scouse-accented voice. Or maybe that's just my imagination.

'I've had a film producer in my office this morning.'

'Oh, Devon. I know him from Wellington. Friend of a friend. Real mover and shaker.'

'A heads-up would have been nice.'

'Didn't you get my email? Bugger. Server's been playing up the last couple of days.'

She isn't lying. It had been a godsend not getting all those OHS circulars and requests for stats and timesheets.

'Playing Lollipop Man is a waste of my talents and hourly rate. Crime does still happen over here you know.'

'I'm sure Constable Rapata will be able to cope. Your face is better known in that valley of yours now. They'll be putty in your hands. Plus you get a lie-in and an early finish. Win-win?'

A hidden agenda, no doubt, but I can't be arsed uncovering it. Probably some old-chums network in Wellington, favours owed, backs scratched. 'If anything more urgent comes up, I'm out of there.'

'Absolutely, Nick. You're in charge.' Some voices in the background, a muffling of the mouthpiece. 'Make sure you drop by next time you're in town. Be good to catch up.'

No time soon, I'm thinking. The permanent move from Wellington to Nelson killed off her shaky marriage. I can't afford to let mine go the same way.

My coffee has arrived so I sit back and enjoy the view. According to the tourist brochures, Havelock is the greenshell mussel capital of the world. The restaurants all serve mussels. There's one, The Mussel Pot, specialising in variations on the theme, with a dozen big fibreglass mussels on the roof so you don't mistake it. Across the road another mussel statue has appeared, two metres high and riding an outboard-powered surfboard. Why? Don't ask me. I'm thinking we might be at a thematic tipping point here; we've reached peak mussel. There's a commotion at the counter behind me, raised voices.

'What's this?'

'It's a cup.'

'Polystyrene? You don't have any crockery?'

'It saves on washing up.'

I find American accents grating at the best of times. Maybe it was all those TV sitcoms we used to watch, with the shouting and canned laughter. Loud, aggressive Americans really piss me off. Even if, like now, they might have a point.

'They aren't recyclable. It all goes into landfill. Your sign says "Organic Fair Trade Coffee" and you serve it to me in this shit? What's the goddamn point of that?'

'No need to get offensive.' Then, as an apparent afterthought, 'Sir.'

A loud thump on the counter. 'Who's in charge here?'

'Me, mate. Not you.'

Time to take a wander over. Janeen behind the counter, barely taller than Frodo, is squaring for a fight. I step in with a smile, tap on the display cabinet. 'Giz a date scone as well, would you, Janeen?'

She glares at me. 'In a sec, I'm busy with this f… fella.'

What the American doesn't realise is that Janeen is capable of ramming his head through the glass cabinet window before he knows what day it is. I've seen her do it, and had to arrest her. She's on a good-behaviour bond and can't afford to stuff it up with three anklebiters at home. I turn to the customer. He's not very big but he has a dangerous light in his eye which you usually associate with religion, drugs, or alcohol.

'Nice day.'

'Butt out, pal. Your uniform means nothing to me.'

Uh-oh. 'I think we need to calm things down a bit, mate. It's a lot of fuss to make over a polystyrene cup.'

He turns square to face me. 'Like I said. Butt out.'

'Leave the premises now, sir. Walk away.'

'And don't forget your coffee,' says Janeen. 'It's takeaway. Chuck it in the bin when you're finished. We don't like litter louts around here.'

I turn to her. 'Shut it.'

That's when he sucker punches me high in the gut. The air leaves me and the day turns bad. I'm lying on the floor, not sure which to do first, vomit or gasp for oxygen. He leans down over me. 'Keep out of my way.' Then he pours his organic Fair Trade coffee on my chest and walks out. Luckily, during the time they've taken to argue, the coffee has cooled a tad.

'Who was that?'

My breath has returned. Janeen is mopping my uniform shirt with a sponge scourer but seems to be making things worse. 'Should've let me deck him, Nick. Stayed out of it.'

I stand and look out the door, up and down the main street. 'Which way did he go?'

A few patrons take breaks from their pies and sausage rolls to thumb west in the general direction of Nelson.

'Gunna arrest him or what?' Janeen hands me the sponge to finish it off.

'Was he in a vehicle?' I'm still dazed and winded. In shock at the absurdity of it all. Floored over a polystyrene coffee cup? Really?

'Motorbike. Harley,' says a young bloke I've picked up for speeding many times. He swallows whatever he was chewing. 'Black it was. New. Flash as.'

I call Latifa and give her the details and we put the word out to our Nelson colleagues from over the Whangamoa Saddle to head this way and look out for him.

'Don't worry,' says Latifa. 'If he gets as far as the ranges we'll have him.'

'Plenty of turn-offs before then.'

'Most of them dead ends.' She closes the call and I head out of the bakery to get the car.

'Wait,' says Janeen. 'You didn't finish your coffee.'

'Another time.'

'Still want that date scone you ordered?'

'No, thanks.'

We meet up with our Tasman colleagues at the halfway point, Rai Valley – it was a one-horse town but the horse bolted years ago. It's clear that the biker has turned off a side road somewhere between Havelock and here. I'd already done detours down the side streets and down by the marina. Nobody I spoke to had seen him.

'So where?' I say, uselessly.

'New bike, he wouldn't want to take it anywhere too rough, would he?' says Latifa, and the Nelson boys nod knowingly. 'So maybe we can narrow it down to the sealed roads.'

We divide them up between us and head back to our vehicles. 'Nobody takes him alone. If you spot him, call it in and wait for back-up.'

'Think he warrants AOS?' says a Nelson constable, name of Blakiston.

Armed Offenders Squad? I think about it a moment. 'He's a scrapper for sure, but batons and tasers should be enough. Bit of pepper spray.'

Latifa looks like she relishes the prospect.

The Nelson lads will cover the area between Rai Valley and Pelorus Bridge and we take the rest between there and Havelock.

'He could be back out and on his way east by now,' I say glumly. 'I've stuffed up. Shouldn't have let him get the better of me in the first place.'

'Chill, Sarge. It wasn't your fault, you're not as young as you used to be.' Latifa checks an incoming message on her mobile. Her face softens, so it must be her fiancé, Daniel the Boy Racer – nice enough lad but hell on wheels. 'We'll get him, if not this time then the next.'

Latifa takes the ten-kilometre section between Havelock and Canvastown, me the rest. We agree to regroup halfway at the Trout Hotel. After two hours of back roads and doorknocks, it's well past lunchtime and I'm regretting not getting that scone at the bakery. Being midweek, the Trout is predictably quiet. Come to that, it doesn't really liven up at the weekend either.

'Usual, Nick?' says the proprietor like he only saw me yesterday instead of two months ago.

'On duty. Ginger beer'd be good. Got any food?'

He thumbs at the menu board on the wall behind him. 'But the kitchen's closed.'

I check my watch. 'One-thirty?' He shrugs. 'Packet of crisps then. Salt and vinegar.'

'Good choice.' He turns to my colleague. 'Latifa?'

'Same, thanks.'

I ask him if he's seen an American on a big flash Harley.

'Brandon? Yeah, he'll be up at the Lodge. Saw him go by a few hours ago.'

'I thought the Lodge was on the market?'

'Not anymore.' He taps his nose. 'Got my finger on the pulse.'

We're out the door. 'Your car?' I say, knowing Latifa's has the shotgun in the boot.

Behind us a shout. 'Sixteen bucks for the drinks and chippies. I'll put it on your tab, Nick.'

The Lodge is halfway up the valley opposite an open paddock with a couple of horses grazing. There was never a For Sale sign outside, it's too expensive to warrant it. Anybody wanting to live here wouldn't be a casual drive-by. The gates are new. Big, strong, and shut. Our Nelson colleagues are on the way. ETA five minutes.

'Climb over?' says Latifa.

'There's a bell.' I press it.

Nothing. Press it again.

'Yeah?'

I jump. Has he crept up behind me? Brace for another sucker punch. 'Up here. Tree to your left.' I see it now. A camera and a small speaker.

'Police,' says Latifa. 'Open up, we want to talk to you.'

'What about?'

'Assault.'

'Get lost.'

'Open up or we'll be back with armed officers to break down your gates and arrest you.'

'This is private property.'

'We'll bring a warrant.'

'Yeah, do that.'

Latifa isn't used to being talked to like this.

The Nelson lads roll up. Blakiston admires the tall gates. 'Tawa. Good hard wood, inset with steel. Impressive.'

Latifa looks at me. 'Who is this Brandon fella?'

'Some Yank with a short fuse.'

The tree says, 'I heard that.'

'I don't know who the hell you think you are but you're digging yourself into a big hole.' Latifa shakes an admonishing finger. 'You assaulted a police officer and you need to let us in or come out and talk to us. We're not going away.'

A snigger, a click and the gates slowly swing open. I tell the Nelson guys to wait here and be ready for anything. Latifa and I get back in the car and roll up the steep driveway. There's what looks like a gatekeeper's cabin just a short way up the drive, immaculately kept lawns with a mix of native and imported shrubs and trees. Finally, at the top of the hill, a hexagonal pine lodge with floor to ceiling windows, lots of aerials on the roof, and some outhouses nearby. The surrounding slopes have recently been logged to hell and back. The contrast is stark, a manicured luxury resort nestled amidst such desolation.

'Rancho Weirdo,' mutters Latifa.

We mount the half-dozen steps to a long wide verandah, and the front door opens. It's the man who floored me in the bakery. He holds a hand up. 'That's close enough.'

Latifa shakes her head. 'I don't think you get it, mister. We're here to arrest you. Turn around, face the wall, hands behind your back.'

'You're making a big mistake.'

I draw my baton. 'Do as she says.'

Latifa has unclipped her taser. 'Three seconds.'

He smiles, raises his hands and turns around. 'What's your name, sister? I like you.'

Latifa puts the cuffs on him, kicks his feet apart, presses him down to his knees. 'What's your name? Brandon what?'

He breathes in slowly and deeply. 'You smell nice.'

She takes the canister of pepper spray off her belt and empties it into his face. 'How's your sense of smell now, dickhead?'

He lies there on his pine verandah. Eyes streaming, face burning, and still smiling. Chuckling even. 'I can see we're going to get along real well, sister.'

2.

'His name is Brandon Cunningham from Shitsville, South Dakota.' Latifa's got this cloudy look in her eyes like she's picked up a bug of some kind. She scrolls down the screen. 'Here on an Entrepreneur Business Visa. He's got a lot of money behind him, stumped up two million to put into a tourism venture out on the Sounds.'

'What kind?'

'Doing up the old farmstead across from Maud Island. An adult wellbeing retreat, according to the visa application.' She shakes her head. 'Māhana. Who does he think he is?'

I don't get the cultural reference and assume Latifa is just cursing in Māori. 'He doesn't strike me as the wellbeing type.' My gut is still tender from that punch.

'Creep, if you ask me.'

'And he can afford to fly a lawyer in from Wellington.'

'That place of his up the Wakamarina. Big house for such a little man.' Latifa logs off the system. 'What's he really doing here?'

'Let's ask him when the lawyer arrives.'

We're camped fifty k's south-east, over at Blenheim, the nearest police station with cells. Cunningham has been checked out at Wairau Hospital down the road from the cop shop and his eyes no longer sting. The Blenheim area commander is taking an interest and wants to know if I need any help. One of his detectives in the room, maybe?

'Should be fine, sir. It's a minor assault charge. I don't feel the need to pursue the matter but I'd like to counsel him about his conduct.'

'He assaulted you, in front of witnesses. We don't normally let people get away with that kind of thing. Bad for morale and PR.'

'Maybe some latitude now will save us a whole lot of time and trouble in the longer run. His flash lawyer could tie us up for months. A cautionary word from me might curb any future excesses.'

'Your call, Nick. His brief has been in my ear before she hopped on the plane. He's obviously connected. Watch yourself.'

'Will do.'

By the time the lawyer arrives it's early evening. Daylight saving went out a few weeks ago, the nights are closing in and it'll be dark by the time I get back to the farm. I've let Vanessa know and she'll be keeping my plate and the bed warm. Latifa and I grabbed a sandwich at the café over the road just as it was closing. We're fuelled and ready.

'Mr Cunningham seems to have sustained injuries to his eyes from capsicum spray.' The lawyer's name is Helen Kostakidis and she usually represents either bikies or bankers. She's a class act: part school principal, part eminent surgeon, part cage fighter.

Brandon shakes his head. 'It was an accident. The officer was just showing me her little toy and it went off.' He smiles at Latifa. 'No real harm done. That right, darlin'?'

'Constable Rapata to you.'

'Pretty name.'

'There's also the matter of the assault on myself by Mr Cunningham.' I lean in. 'Unprovoked and witnessed.'

The lawyer looks up from her notepad. 'Do you have the witness statements, Sergeant? Names?'

'I can have, within twenty-four hours.'

'Perhaps we can all go home then,' says Kostakidis. 'And come back tomorrow?'

'Or we can advise Mr Cunningham that this is not how we do things here in New Zealand. This is not South Dakota. Rich man, poor man, the law treats everybody as equal.'

Cunningham grins. 'You think that, buddy? You really think that?'

Latifa gives me a sideways glance. I'm guessing she's with Brandon on this point. 'It's the principle that drives me, Mr Cunningham. I'm prepared to let the matter drop because I don't need the paperwork. But you need to keep your nose clean, mate, or you're going to get yourself into a lot of trouble.'

Kostakidis turns to Cunningham. 'I think the sergeant is being very generous and pragmatic. Perhaps an apology would go some way?'

Brandon offers his hand. 'Sorry, man. No hard feelings?'

I shake it briefly. 'What's your business here, Mr Cunningham? It doesn't seem like your kind of town?'

'What's my kind of town?'

'Backwoods. Banjo country. Cops in your pocket. Everything up for grabs.'

'No need for rudeness, Sergeant.' Kostakidis is packing her briefcase. 'All settled and friends again. Right?'

Cunningham stands. 'Backwoods, huh?' Eyes the posters on the wall: firewood thefts, hunting infringements, wanted druggies. 'Looks like I got me a home from home.' Another glance at Latifa. 'And I'm working on winning over the local constabulary.'

I really want to floor him with my baton. Empty another canister of spray in his face. Or even just shoot him. 'So what is your business here?'

'Wellbeing.' He grins. 'Now ain't that something we could all do with?'

Driving back up the valley road, I see the gates are closed at the Lodge. When I dropped Latifa off at her house in Havelock it was plain that Cunningham had got under her skin.

'You okay?' I said.

'Yep. He's not the first creep that tried to psych me out. A good hot shower, a cuddle with Daniel, a cuppa tea and Netflix and he'll be history.'

But I've never seen her look so … What? Not like Latifa.

Cunningham is a jerk but hopefully he's smart enough not to rile us. Whatever nefarious business he's up to, he'd be a fool to have us sniffing around unnecessarily.

At home, the lights are on. Paulie is in bed and Vanessa is preparing for the next day's teaching. Twenty-five kids, five levels of ability, half-a-dozen subjects. She'll be at it until midnight. An absent-minded peck on the cheek in greeting.

'Dinner's in the fridge. Spag bol. Shove it in the microwave. Good day?'

'Got punched out by a psycho and given a shit babysitting job by my superiors. You?'

'Same. But the punch missed and he hit a chair instead. Cried the rest of the morning.' She closes one file and opens another. The microwave dings. 'Which psycho?' she asks over the top of her specs. The glasses are a new thing, they suit her. Sometimes she keeps them on while we're bonking and it adds to the frisson.

'Neighbour down the road. American. Living in the Lodge.'

'Andrei's old place? I've seen vehicles coming and going from there recently. Thought somebody must have moved in.'

'You never mentioned.'

A shrug. 'Valley gossip isn't my thing. I already know too much about people's private lives through school.'

'Fair enough.'

'Big lad is he?'

'Not really. Lucky punch.'

'You arrest him?'

'No.'

'Why not?'

'Least said soonest mended?'

'That's not like you.'

I suck in a stray strand of spaghetti. 'I think he's one of those people who thrives on conflict. He's rich, has a posh lawyer, never gives up because he wants to win. Mr Entitlement. Life's too short. I'm not going to give him the pleasure.'

'There are kids like that in my class.'

'Yep, and now we've got one as a neighbour.' I fail to stifle a yawn. My head feels thick and heavy, the light too bright. A Panadol should fix it. 'See you in bed.'

'I'll be up there in an hour or two to ravish you. Be ready.'

I'd better shape up then.

Friday. Latifa and I take turns to patrol SH6 for miscreants. It's another beautiful, crisp April day and nobody seems to be doing anything overly stupid. On the news the new Labor-led government is promising to fix up many of the social problems neglected by the previous one. It's ambitious and may well turn out to be just spin and tosh but it makes a nice change hearing about good intentions. By contrast the news from across the pond, in both directions, is the usual game of spite and malice. I begin to understand now why the Kiwis will never let the matter of the underarm bowling incident drop, even after thirty-odd years. It's the Aussies to a T. Would you be so desperate to win a game of cricket that you'd bowl an unhittable ball along the ground like you're delivering to a toddler? Yep, pathetic and mean-spirited, like the state of Aussie politics these days.

Dog-whistling flat-earthers the lot of them. As for the Americans, don't get me started. A nation of Brandon Cunninghams: attention-seeking self-centred brats. Or maybe that's just the president. Each whim and tantrum pushing us all closer to extinction. I'm being self-righteous and obsessing again. How about some music? Brian FM. Talking Heads. 'Road to Nowhere'. Perfect.

My phone goes. Latifa. 'You nearby, Sarge?'

'Shoe fence. Five minutes away. Why?'

'Got a situation at the Havelock Hotel.'

'Situation?'

'One fella dangling another over the balcony. Threatening to drop him.'

'It's only a few metres.'

'On his head.'

'See you soon.'

I recognise them both immediately. One is Bruce Gelder, the dredge miner I had in my telescopic sights yesterday morning. The other is a hobbyist gold fossicker called Doug. He's the one dangling by his heels. Latifa rolls her eyes in greeting. 'Would have zapped him myself, Sarge, but I didn't want him to lose his grip.'

'I told him a thousand times,' the dredge miner says. 'Keep off my claim.'

'Bring him back over the railing, Bruce.' I hold up a placating hand. 'No need for anyone to get hurt.'

A muffled voice from the dangling man. 'Panning's allowed anywhere, you moron. Claim or not.'

'He's stealing my gold.'

'What gold, you fucking idiot,' says an old-timer from behind a pot of Speights at the bar. 'There's none there. They dug it all up last century.'

'You couldn't find your dick in your daks,' says Bruce. 'Shut the fuck up.'

Unclip my taser. 'Bring Doug back up over the railing, Bruce.'

Bruce gives Doug a last shake. 'Keep off my claim. Final warning.' And hauls him back to safety.

'Piss off, jerk,' says Doug, straightening his clothes and hair. He brushes past me. 'Arrest him and throw away the key.'

Handcuffing Bruce is strangely comforting. It's the next best thing to taking him out with a sniper's rifle. 'You and I need to have a chat.'

Back over the road to the cop shop. While Latifa logs the incident I sit

Bruce down at my desk and explain the charges to him. He can expect a summons in the next few weeks.

'That's not fair.'

'You endangered Doug's life. If you'd dropped him, that would have been it.'

'Bastard's head is thicker than that. Anyway I've got a licence, he hasn't.'

'It's a licence to dredge, not a licence to kill. And it's not exclusive. Amateur panners are allowed anywhere. You don't need me to explain the rules to you.'

'Every day I dredge, he's straight in after I leave. Parasite. That's my gold.'

'Have you found anything there yet?'

'No. Just needs a good rain to flush it down.'

'Those people who found the gold behind the pub last year. They're experts. They used science. Put a lot of money into it. Doesn't mean the whole valley is back to being El Dorado.'

'Science? What would you know?' he says. 'You opposed my excavator.'

'That's because I don't want an industrial site on that river.'

'Nimby. Go back where you came from.'

I hand him the paperwork. 'See you in court. Stay out of trouble and leave Doug alone.'

'Conflict of interest, that's what you have. No justice here.'

'Go away, Bruce,' says Latifa from behind her partition. 'You bore me.'

'This is a conspiracy.'

After he's gone we put the kettle on. 'Gold does funny things to people doesn't it?' I muse over my steaming tea.

'Accentuates the dick factor for sure.'

Let's get off the subject of fools and gold. 'How's Daniel?'

'Good, he's heading down to Christchurch for a few days. His mum's birthday.'

'You guys set a wedding date yet?'

'Not yet, sometime in spring maybe.'

'He's a lucky man.' I raise my cup in salute.

'That's what I keep telling him.' She drains her mug, stares into the depths of it.

'Everything okay?'

'Yep.' Back to the desk. A scan of her computer screen. 'What should we do now? Timesheets or crime stats analysis?'

'Maybe some community policing?'

'Bakery again? Bring me back a sausage roll, Sarge. I'll hold the fort.'

The rest of the day is a combination of more traffic duty on SH6, showing our faces around town, paperwork, and delivering a petty summons or two. By five I'm on my way back up the winding valley road. Just beyond the cluster of houses near the pub, a mastiff runs onto the road and starts trying to attack the car. It's mad and won't get out of the way. The dog belongs to a family that seem to subsist on welfare and the proceeds of firewood thefts, poaching and petty drug deals. They also have regular loud and late parties, which I've been called out to close down now and again. They're not particularly malicious, just thoughtless and useless. The neighbours hate them, dubbing them the Von Crapps. A teenage girl runs out onto the road.

'Winston! Cut it out! Get back inside.'

I wind my window down. 'Thanks, Shanille. See you got a new tatt.'

She tilts her head so I can read what's on her neck. *Heaven on a Stick.* Nice.

'Not gonna put him in the pound are ya?'

'Be good if you could keep your gate shut. Safer for everybody. And Winston.'

'Yeah nah.'

Another time, I guess. 'See you.'

Another four k's up, my distant neighbour Charlie Evans waves me down. All these people out on the road. It's like downtown Auckland today. He's got a For Sale sign outside his chicken and alpaca farm but he's not going anywhere soon. The sign has been there for six months. I slow to a stop and step out for a stretch.

'Charlie? How's it going?'

He scratches his white beard, slaps at a sandfly. 'Same old, same old.'

'No offers yet?'

'Nah. And with winter on the way I can't see any coming.'

'Still managing without Denzel?' The young bloke who was helping him out as part of a restorative justice program to make up for a crossbowed alpaca. He recently signed up at the tech college in Blenheim. Training to be a bricklayer.

'Pretty much. I'm gradually selling off the livestock. Living off mine and

Beattie's savings. That cruise she always wanted never happened.'

Charlie has been a widower for over a year now and it still shows. 'You should come up to ours for a feed sometime. How about next weekend?'

'Thanks, Nick. I'll give you a call, eh? Fix a time.'

He won't. We have this conversation every time we meet and neither of us follows through. He hesitates.

'Something troubling you, Charlie?'

'Those people who've moved into the Lodge.'

'People? There was only one when I was up there yesterday.'

A shake of the head. 'Two vanloads went past today. Minibuses.'

'How do you know where they were going?'

'They stopped and bailed me up. All had the same accent. Howdy-doody and all that. Pretty aggressive bunch.'

'What was their problem?'

A shrug. 'Didn't like my face, I suppose.'

'What'd they say?'

'Nothing specific. Just taking the piss. Treating me like a hillbilly. Maybe they'd been drinking, I don't know.'

'Want me to have a word?'

He squints at the falling sun. 'Wouldn't be a good start to things, me dobbing them in for something so minor. Their north-east perimeter borders me.' He turns to the logged hill behind him which is showing signs of regrowth. 'The other side of that rise.' Waves it away. 'Not worth it. Feuds spark out of nowhere in this valley and can burn for decades.'

'All the same. You don't have to put up with being bullied.'

He puts his hand on my shoulder. 'Good as gold, Nick.'

3.

There's nothing quite so dull as a film set. A lot of people standing around for a long time: lights, cameras, et cetera, the cast in their gold-rush costumes smoking, drinking coffee. The director consulting with her cameraman. Devon Cornish studying his phone. He'll be lucky, the chances of a signal here are next to zilch even with a sat-phone. I've been surplus to requirements since I arrived. A couple of NMIT film school students on placement have kept the sparse Tuesday morning traffic away and pretty much all of those asked have been cool about it, dazzled by the glamour of the film set and the chance to spot stars. Butchers Flat is transformed into the old Doom Creek goldfield. The level campground was perfect for establishing a mini set of ramshackle gold-rush huts and the surrounding hills, vegetation and rushing river are a stunning backdrop. It's an idealised version of course. Tidied-up, firm-jawed, white-teethed. By contrast, the black-and-white pictures in the history books show hard, bitter, disappointed faces and a trashed environment. We're living in the age of anti-history. The lessons have been staring us in the face for decades, if not centuries, but we're more averse than ever to heeding them. The weather has stayed perfect. Check my watch: ten thirty. Another six hours to go, and I'm bored shitless. Nothing has happened in town over the weekend. Bruce and Doug haven't argued about mining claims. Brandon Cunningham hasn't bullied anyone. Everybody has been driving carefully. But even by the standards of the last few days, today is low-octane stuff.

Except I woke up this morning with blood on my hands.

'What's that?' asked Vanessa, noticing the crimson smears on the bedsheets. 'Been fighting again?' My recent bout of even shorter temper has been noted. It's not me. It just seems that lately there's so many more dickheads around.

'Nothing serious,' I lied. 'Scuffle in the pub. Manager asked me to sort it. Fell and grazed my knuckles in the process.'

'That'll account for the tear in your shirt, then.'

I heard the washing machine click into spin and the floorboards began to shudder. 'What time is it?'

'Time to get up. Paulie and I are off now, we let you sleep 'cause you got in so late.'

'Cheers.'

'You were on a late start anyway, weren't you? Up at the film set?'

'Right.' We kissed our goodbyes. 'See you tonight, pet.'

'Maybe you could empty the machine when it finishes? Hang the washing out?'

'Sure.'

Vanessa and Paulie left and I hopped in the shower. Maybe the jet of water would clear my head and tell me what happened last night. But no. Everything is still a blank.

'Should have brought a book.'

Thomas Hemi has appeared at my shoulder. His is the last house in the valley, just up the hill from here. He and his family live a mostly self-sufficient life: a bountiful vegie garden and orchard, free-ranging hens, sheep, the occasional feral pig and deer shot by him and his two boys, and sales of legitimately obtained firewood to help pay the utility and council bills. They're kind of the opposite of the Von Crapps. Hemi's not quite off the grid but near as dammit. There's a valley rumour that he's got a supply of dynamite to blow Deep Creek bridge when the balloon goes up. The idea is the zombies won't make it across the abyss. That's a worry, because my house is on his side of the bridge and I haven't worked out which team I'm supporting. He's wielding a copy of *The Road* by Cormac McCarthy. That'd be right.

'Enjoying it?'

'Bit bleak but the Apocalypse can be, I suppose. Surprised you're hanging around here, Nick. Nothing better to do?'

'Not really. Hoping they'll call me up as an extra.'

'Too clean cut. No chance.'

He's decked out in a collarless shirt artfully smeared with grime. 'You got a gig then?'

'Craggy-faced shocked miner number three. I'm on soon apparently.'

He points at one of the young actors being doused in red liquid. 'My oldest boy, Jaxon. He's about to be found dead and I've got to look suitably disturbed from a distance.'

'You up to it?'

'For two hundred bucks a day, I can give you Shakespeare, mate.'

A call goes out on the megaphone.

'I think you're on.'

Thomas hands me his book for safekeeping, picks up a shovel and heads for his position.

I catch Devon Cornish's eye and head his way. 'Looks like things are under control here, I'll be heading off soon.'

He checks his watch. 'Still a bit to go, yet. Can't see us finishing here until the end of the afternoon when the light changes.'

I'm not your fucking employee. 'All the same. No cars to bother you. You don't need me here.'

Doof, doof, doof. I spoke too soon. A mule all-terrain vehicle is coming down the track: painted camo, a driver and three passengers matching the paintwork. I recognise one of them as Brandon Cunningham.

The director throws a tantrum at the interruption and tells a minion to sort it. Everybody stops what they are doing and looks over as the buggy draws up at a cordon tape manned by a sallow youth who will be no match for Cunningham. I wander over. The rap music is deafening and none of the people in the ATV look like they're enjoying it either.

'Want to turn that down? Or off would be better.'

'Officer Chester,' says Cunningham, lowering the volume. 'Didn't know you were in the movie business?'

'As you can see they're trying to do some work here …'

'Work? That what you call it?' The driver beside Cunningham chuckles; he's twenty years younger with the same wiry menace.

In the back seat, two bigger men are squashed together in the narrow space. One is hairy, the other less so. In the cargo tray behind them there are four hunting rifles: Bushmaster semi-automatics.

'You have permits for those?'

'Sure.'

'Show me.'

They hand them over.

'Satisfied?' says Cunningham after a moment.

Thomas Hemi has joined me. He introduces himself and offers his hand to all the ATV guys for shaking. None of them takes up the offer except Cunningham who attempts a squeeze.

'Oooh,' says Hemi, mock hurt. 'That's a strong grip, fella.' He nods at the guns. 'After a pig?'

The big hairy dude in the back laughs. 'Something like that.'

'Good luck,' says Thomas. 'I think I got the last one yesterday. Won't be any around for a few days now, I reckon.'

'Expert, huh?' says the guy in the back.

'Grew up around here. Our people have walked these parts for a long, long time. Didn't catch your name, mate. I'm Thomas. You'd be …?'

Cunningham interrupts. 'Thank you, Mr Hemi. We'll try our luck anyway. The good Lord is sure to provide.' He nudges the driver, and the engine kicks back into life. A three-point-turn and they bounce back up the steep hill with the music on full.

Devon Cornish puts in an appearance. 'Thanks for dealing with that. I didn't like the look of them.'

'No problem.'

He speaks some words of *te reo* Māori to Thomas, nods and smiles at us both, and walks off.

'What'd he say?'

'Dunno, these city Pākehā think we all speak the language. Mine's schoolboy at best.' The megaphone starts up again. 'Better get back to my spot.' He thumbs back up the hill at the retreating mule and the doof music. 'They the new mob at the Lodge?'

'Yep.'

'Yanks.'

'Apparently.'

Thomas lifts his chin. 'Thousands of them running over here since their country went to the dogs.'

'Weird isn't it? And they seem exactly the kind of guys who would have voted that way and welcomed it with open arms.'

'Made their bed but not prepared to lie in it, eh? S'pose it's smart to keep your options open.'

'Doom Creek is a good name for a survivalist bolthole.'

A shake of the head. 'They've even got that wrong. It's nothing to do with doom at all. It's the shape of the rocks up there. Domes. Or "dooms", as the Scots surveyor called them. I tell you, mate.' Friendly finger prod to my chest. 'People and their funny accents, can get you into all sorts of trouble. Mark my words.'

The megaphone. 'Places everybody!'

Thomas pats himself down. 'How do I look?'

I study him. 'Like a valley hick about to be startled by something terrible.'

'I think you're projecting, bro.'

By lunchtime, I'm out of there. If they can get a signal on their sat-phones they'll call me should Cunningham and his friends return. I don't think he will. As far as I can see, he pushes and backs off, pushes and backs off. As if announcing to everybody that he's around and he's trouble. An empty aimless disruptor, kind of like his president. Not particularly interested in winning people over. He's got his core group around him and that's all he wants or needs. That's okay if you mind your own business. But he seems intent on pissing us off. Such attention-seeking doesn't go down well in these parts.

'Is it a wrap, already?' Latifa has just come through the door after a session out on SH6. She checks the clock on the wall. 'You creative types. No staying power.'

'Had lunch yet?'

She hasn't, so we adjourn to the bakery.

'Hey, Latifa,' says Janeen. 'Hope you're looking after this old fella. Not as fast on his feet as he used to be.' She shadow-boxes, winks at me, then clacks the coffee into the machine and grabs a mug from the rack.

'What's with the china?' I say. 'Somebody prick your conscience?'

'I read up on it. He was right, that Yank. Complete tosser, but right. Don't need all those cups going straight into landfill. Not enough room.'

'What about the water in the dishwasher?' Latifa points out. 'Isn't that a waste?'

'Recycle it onto the garden out back. And it's a low-consumption model anyway.' She hands me my mug.

'Almost worth taking that punch for.' We return to the table with my coffee and Latifa's L&P. Janeen delivers my lamb pie and Latifa's ham wrap and retreats behind her counter.

'Any tickets on SH6?' I ask Latifa.

A shake of the head. 'All sweet.'

'Daniel back from Christchurch yet?'

'Nah, his mum's poorly. He's staying there for the week.'

'Serious?'

'Don't think so. She's probably putting it on to keep him there a bit longer. Can understand the temptation.' Another bite. 'So how was it up on the film set?'

'Lot of standing around. Doesn't seem so glamorous up close.'

'Devon whatsisname let you off early?'

'Nothing happening that needs me. Well, apart from Cunningham turning up.'

'What'd he want?'

'The usual. Bad boy attention.'

'Did he get it?'

'No, he left pretty quickly. Thomas Hemi made his presence felt.'

'Thomas?'

'He's an extra in the film.'

Latifa takes a gulp of L&P. 'Thomas is one fella they shouldn't mess with.'

'Tough?'

'As. He keeps pretty much to himself. Don't see him around the marae or at any community gatherings. He was never one for that kind of thing; not for a long while anyway. People talk about him as the great leader they'll never have.'

'Each to his own, I guess.'

'So what'd he say to scare Cunningham off?'

'Nothing really. Just shook hands and introduced himself.'

She nods. 'Mana.'

'What?'

'Think Jedi mind tricks and double it.'

'I thought you said he was never one for that kind of thing?'

'If you've got it, you've got it. Whether you want it or not.'

The afternoon is routine until I get a call from Vanessa who's just got back home with Paulie. 'I think the water pump is broken.'

Bugger. And I'm not the handiest of blokes. 'You've checked the power switch? Turned it off and on again?'

'Yep. And turned all the outhouse taps on and off in case there was an air bubble. Usual routine. The tank shouldn't be out of water, we've had big rain every other week for yonks.'

'Want me to call the plumber?'

'Nah, I can do that. I'll just try the pump power switch one more time.'

Two minutes later she phones back.

'Somebody shot a hole in the bottom of our water tank.'

'Shit.' The valley is a stray bullet kinda place. Hunters and dickheads and sometimes an unsubtle combination of both. You get used to it. 'I'll pick some stuff up from the marine shop to plug it and get the fire brigade guy out to give us a top-up from his water truck.' I check my watch. 'See you in about twenty.'

'Better bring some water bottles from the Four Square to see us through until the morning.'

'Will do.'

Driving back up the valley road with my supplies of emergency water and resin for the leak, I'm thinking dark thoughts. Sure it could just be an accident; a stray hunter's bullet. The Roar is still on, the optimum deer-hunting time, and the valley has been echoing even more than usual with the crack of rifle fire. But I've decided it's Brandon Cunningham and his gang. Driving past the Lodge I imagine him sitting watching me go by through that little camera on his tree and having a good laugh.

Later. I promise.

Vanessa is flustered and Paulie is out of sorts. He doesn't like it when things don't go to plan. I know the feeling. He looks at the slab of twenty-four water bottles I've brought home. 'I can't shower with that.'

'They're for drinking, mate.'

'What about my shower?'

'Armpits and goolies tonight, love,' says Vanessa. 'We'll go to the pool in Blenheim if it's still not sorted out tomorrow.'

'No shower?'

'Not tonight.'

He looks at all the water bottles again. 'All that plastic, Dad. Should be ashamed of yourself.'

I frown and he breaks into a giggle. He's getting good at winding me up with a straight face. In the remaining daylight hours I do my best to plug the hole in the tank and Marvin the water guy has promised he'll be up with the fire truck first thing in the morning to give us a refill. The evening passes as they often do these days, with Paulie trying to find ways of delaying his bedtime, Vanessa preparing a mountain of school work for the next day, and me looking out the window at the changing light in the valley, brooding and conjuring up new demons for vanquishing. Tonight I feel the sting of my grazed knuckles and search my memory for those lost hours. There's a dull throb at my temples, I've had a few of those lately.

'These things happen, love.' Vanessa peels apart two sticky pages in a student notebook. 'It's just a leaky tank, not the end of the world.'

4.

On the way down the valley the next morning it's tempting to call in on Cunningham and ask about the water tank. But to what effect? All he has to do is say no, it wasn't him. I'm not going to be able to go all forensic on him with something this flimsy and trivial. Apply some resin and a fifty dollar top-up and move on. The bullet is probably sitting in the bottom of the tank but I can't be arsed retrieving it. Still, Cunningham does need a shot across his bow. He doesn't seem to have heeded the first warning.

Charlie Evans flags me down outside his gate. There's a bullet hole in his For Sale sign. I obviously didn't get the memo advising us about National Stray Bullet Awareness Week. Still it's not an uncommon sight: most of the No Hunting, No Dogs, Keep Out, and speed limit signs have been shot up too. It's the valley version of right to reply. Has it been extended to water tanks now?

I nod at his sign. 'Somebody doesn't want you to go?'

He smiles. 'I'll be here until hell freezes over. About that dinner invitation?'

'Yeah?'

'This weekend work for you?'

Wonders never cease. 'Sure. How about Saturday?'

'Need me to bring anything?'

'Just yourself.' I point to the bullet hole. 'And your secret admirer if you want.'

We agree a time and I'm back on my way. Well, well. Since his wife died Charlie's become even more of a hermit. Maybe there's light at the end of his long dark tunnel of grief after all. Once in mobile range I message Vanessa to give her a heads-up and let her know I'll organise the menu. Marvin passes me in the water truck with a finger wave. He doesn't need us around to do what he does and I've left the fifty in an envelope in our mailbox.

As I'm pulling up in my parking spot outside the cop shop Latifa barges out the door, mobile to her ear, gesturing for me to follow. She starts running down the street, heading for the Four Square. Not another chops in the shorts job, I'm thinking. The stats continue to hold up; Marlborough remains the NZ capital for meat shoplifting. But she doesn't go in the main entrance, she heads instead for the coldroom at the back with me close behind. The door is already open and the manager is waiting for us. Ashen.

'In there.'

A bare strip of light illuminates the scene. Shelves lined with joints of meat, bags of fish, frozen pre-packed vegetables. Ice creams. Our breath turns to steam as we survey the scene. Sitting upright, strapped to a plastic chair placed on a wooden pallet is the body of a man. Frozen stiff. He has terrible injuries: cuts, burns, gougings. Missing parts.

'It's Bruce,' says Latifa.

Indeed it is.

Bruce Gelder, the miner who dredges the river below me.

Dead, as I had wished so many times.

'He didn't die quickly.' District Commander Keegan has driven the seventy-odd kilometres over the hills from Nelson HQ and is taking a keen interest. Can't blame her, bloody murder is always more compelling than budget submissions.

'Looks like it,' I agree.

'The coldroom distorts things forensically but the body wasn't here at close of business last night.'

'So, the window is between six-thirty yesterday evening and just after eight-thirty today.'

A cordon has been placed around the Four Square, and anybody needing groceries will have to drive for at least forty minutes to find them. That's not going down well with some locals, and Latifa is on the verge of using her taser to reinforce the point. A handful of detectives are interviewing staff and customers who were there when it was called in. Somebody is in charge of collating any CCTV in the immediate vicinity. A forensic team photographs, marks, and sifts. Uniforms drafted in from Blenheim, Picton and Nelson are doorknocking up and down the main street and I've been helping out with that for the last hour or two until the boss called me aside.

Keegan lights up a ciggie and runs a hand through her new tinted elfin haircut. 'Bruce Gelder. You say you know him?'

'Not well. Had run-ins with him.'

'Run-ins. Arrests, you mean?'

'No. He has a mining claim on the river below my house. I opposed his resource consent application.'

'Motive,' she smiles, through a wreath of blue smoke. 'Just need to pin means and opportunity on you and we're home and dry.'

'Motive won't stick, I kind of won.'

'Any other suspects come to mind or are you it?'

'Gelder was dangling a bloke by his legs over the pub balcony a few days ago. Could have a word with him if you like.'

'Do so.'

'I'll give the details to your detectives.'

'No, you do it, Nick. I trust you. Pity you didn't take up that offer to move over to the Ds when I got this job.'

'The quiet life suits me.'

'Like hell it does. Anyway, detective or not, I'm seconding you to the investigating team.' She summons a bloke in a suit. Will Maxwell's a hefty redhead you wouldn't want to face in a rugby scrum. Last time we met we were looking into the untimely death of a young fella who'd had his skull stoved in with a claw hammer. 'Will's in charge. You know each other of course.'

'Yep,' he says and we shake hands.

'Nick's with you. Use him well.'

'Boss.'

'Maybe you can go and find your dangler, Nick, while I chat with Will here.'

Dismissed, I head up the road to the Havelock Hotel, a favourite haunt of Doug the Dangler. Barely eleven o'clock and he's there at the bar nursing a Speights; he gives me half a nod.

'Nick.'

'Got time for a word, Doug?'

'I'll check my diary.'

'Where've you been since about six last night?'

'Here or at home. Why?'

'Anyone vouch for that?'

'All the people who were here when I was. Only me at home so you'll have to take my word. Again, why?' Hasn't he noticed all the cops out on the street? Or the other pub patrons rubbernecking out the window? He lazily thumbs in the general direction. 'This what all the fuss is about out there?'

'Yes. So can you give me exact times, when you were at home, when you were here, who saw you?'

'I was here from about four yesterday afternoon to closing, around nine. Ask her.' Finger wave at the bartender. 'She'll remember who else was here, fucked if I can, usual suspects I suppose.' A smoker's cough. 'That what I am, a suspect? What for?'

'Something serious. So you went home, which way did you go, anybody see you?'

A shrug. 'Might have, but I seem to be invisible these days. Perks of old age.' He describes his route home. He got there, made a cup of tea, did the crossword in the paper, went to bed around eleven. 'Woke up, had a piss, some brekky, finished off the crossword, came here.'

'What time?'

'About half an hour ago.' He lifts his glass to the bartender. 'That right, Rose? Half an hour?'

'Yeah.' She pours his refill. 'Confess, Doug. You killed him, didn't you?'

'Killed who?'

'God knows but there wouldn't be that many cops out there for a shoplifting.'

It's one of the things I'm beginning to like about folk around here. At least half of them haven't a shred of curiosity about other people's business.

Doug looks at me. 'Somebody got killed?'

'Yes.'

'And you think I might have something to do with it. So I must know them, yeah?'

'Possibly.'

'Fuck's sake, Nick. Give us a name.'

'Sorry, I can't. Yet.' I hand Doug my card. 'We'll need to speak to you again, soon. Don't leave the country.'

'He doesn't even leave the barstool most days,' says Rose.

I'm pretty confident of eliminating him from my enquiries, but you never know.

Detective Senior Sergeant Will Maxwell has established an incident management centre at the Havelock town hall and DC Keegan has gone back to Nelson. It's midafternoon and already desks, chairs, phones and computer lines have been set up plus whiteboards and there are tea and coffee facilities in the kitchen out back behind the stage. I'm impressed by the rapid transformation. The last time I was here two elderly women purporting to be sisters put on a mock opera about the harsh life of a beautiful young shucker from the mussel factory. You had to be there to really appreciate it. It's a majestic old hall, with deep-red brocade stage curtains, ornate woodwork, built with the proceeds of gold mining and logging and maintained now with the proceeds of aquaculture, tourism and council rates. The big gold mining and logging money tends to disappear straight overseas these days. This place has seen it all: political meetings, shows, ceilidhs, country dances, even a hospital ward for the 1918 flu pandemic. And now it's a murder room.

'Bruce Gelder. Thirty-three years old. Home address in Grove. Out on the Sounds on the road between Havelock and Picton,' he clarifies for those draft-ins less familiar with the local geography. 'Married with two children, a toddler and a bub.' Maxwell points to the crime-scene photo of a man strapped to a chair, covered in blood and ice. 'He's due for a post-mortem tomorrow morning in Nelson but as we can already see, somebody has gone to town on him.' He scans the room. 'Who and why?'

One of his junior colleagues puts up her hand. 'One fella told me he reckoned the town cop did it.'

'Which one?' says Latifa icily.

'Your boss,' is the curt reply. I focus on her lanyard. Gemma. Ponytail. Clear skin. No messing.

Heads turn my way, some ooohs and tsk-tsks.

'Confess, confess,' says somebody.

Maxwell damps down the mirth. 'This is your chance to clear your name, Nick.'

'Not without a lawyer. Meantime I've talked to the other prime suspect, Doug Freeman, who had a run-in with the deceased a couple of days ago. He's an old soak and I can't see him being capable but you probably need to have a formal chat with him to sort out his alibis, or lack thereof.'

I hand the details over and Maxwell pushes on. 'No cameras in the coldroom but we're going through the CCTV from the main store. There are only meant to be a couple of keyholders who could have had access and known the alarm code but the alarm has been stuffed for over a year now and wasn't active. In reality there's a number of spare keys out there or with transient casual staff over the years who have lost their set. That kind of thing.'

'Welcome to Havelock,' says Latifa.

'How come the body wasn't discovered until after eight this morning? The shop opens by seven thirty,' says Gemma. 'Don't they need stuff out of the coldroom before that?'

'Not today,' says Maxwell. 'No restocking needed as it was a quiet day yesterday.' He indicates one of the gruesome photos. 'The chair doesn't belong to Four Square. The killer brought his own.'

'How did he get Bruce to sit down on it?' asks Latifa. 'He never struck me as the compliant type. And he could handle himself.'

'Maybe we're looking at more than one perp?' says Gemma.

'Maybe the PM will tell us,' says Maxwell.

Doorknocks and local enquiries will continue: staff and patron interviews at the Four Square, CCTV, forensics. Friends, family, colleagues, associates of the deceased. Bank accounts. Personal life. Secret life. Gelder was a self-employed tradesman, a plumber. He'd have got around a bit, mixed high and low. Maxwell has at his disposal around a dozen detectives and that is likely to increase over the coming days. A similar number of uniforms will be added once Keegan has done some bean-counting back in Nelson. Maxwell calls me to one side as the room clears.

'Jokes aside, you didn't do him, did you?'

'No.'

'Keegan told me you had a beef with him about mining or something?'

'Resource consent. I won. No motive to kill him. She knows this.'

'Yeah, yeah, but Gemma's already heard the jungle drums and your name is in the mix. There'll be more of that as the days unfold. I need to know your side of it, formal if necessary, to cover our arses.'

My knuckles are tingling and I'm aware of a bruisy tenderness behind my right ear. 'Feel free. Happy to talk on the record and provide my alibis. Give my DNA, have my laundry checked. Go for your life.'

'Thanks, Nick. I'll get Gemma to do the formalities with you.'

'Waste of time and resources but be my guest. Does this mean I'm on the team or not?'

'Keegan wants you in, so as soon as we've ticked the boxes then it's a yes. But perhaps not at the centre of things?'

'Let me know when you're ready.'

'Any thoughts on who could have done this?'

'Besides me? No. The state of the corpse, whoever they were they've either got general anger management issues or this is one hell of a grudge.'

He grins. 'Stuff of life in the Wakamarina. Sure it wasn't you?'

The sun is long gone by the time I head back up the valley. There's been no word from the film set so it's assumed that Brandon Cunningham and his cronies stayed away. Passing Charlie Evans' place, I remember the dinner invitation this coming Saturday. Four days should be time enough for me to come up with a menu and do the necessary shopping for it, although perhaps not at the Four Square. If, as Maxwell has alluded, I'm not going to be at the centre of things on the murder enquiry, then it should be plain sailing, especially as Latifa has the routine shift this weekend and will be on call.

Bruce Gelder.

Confession time. I'm not overly saddened by his demise. He was a pushy and abrasive character. Still, one wouldn't wish that kind of death on anyone, even him. Would one?

Music thumps out of the Lodge as I drive past. The same crap they were playing in the ATV. Rap and hip-hop? Here's me chalking them up as country and western fans. As potential psychos go, they're the only ones that come to mind lately but it would be a bit too convenient for them to have killed Gelder. Still, it would be one way of getting them kicked out of the valley.

'You're early,' says Vanessa with a passing peck on the lips. 'I heard about the commotion in town. Didn't expect you for a few hours yet.'

'You heard who it was?'

'No.'

'Bruce Gelder. The man I was aiming my gun at the other day.'

'Wow, careful what you wish for. Who, apart from you, would want to kill him?'

'We don't know yet but it was nasty.'

She shushes me. 'Paulie's still awake. He's got news for you.'

I poke my head around his door frame. 'What's happening?'

He wasn't expecting me, he's got earphones in and is playing a spelling game on his iPad. He reluctantly halts the screen. 'What?'

'Mum said you had some news?'

'Oh yeah, got a new friend at school.'

It hasn't been so easy for Paulie being uprooted from his home town of Sunderland when we had to go into hiding on the other side of the world. Living with Down Syndrome, even relatively high-functioning, also presents certain challenges for making friends, particularly in a small rural community like this.

'Great,' I say. 'What's his name?'

'Mim. Miranda. She's a girl.'

'Have you mentioned her before?'

'No.'

'New to school?'

'Don't think so.'

'Cool. Nice is she?'

'Nice?' He thinks about it for a moment. 'S'pose so.'

That's about as much as he wants to give away. I can tell the game beckons and leave him to it. 'Ten more minutes then teeth, pee, and lights out.'

'Mum said fifteen.'

'Fifteen it is then.'

Back in the kitchen Vanessa hands me a reheated bowl of chilli con carne. 'I see Gary's back.'

Gary used to rent a cabin from us across the driveway; now he's built his own in what used to be our far paddock but which is now his, bought and paid for. He goes out on the trawlers from Nelson, three weeks on and two off – give or take, according to the season.

'Any gossip from his end?' The chilli tastes good.

'He's got a new girlfriend in Nelson. Hurt his hand out on the boats, it's all bandaged up. Nothing permanent.'

'I'll drop over and say hello before leaving in the morning.'

Vanessa heads for her pile of marking. 'Oh, one other thing. He was out of water. Somebody shot a hole in his tank too.'

5.

Thursday morning finds me sitting in an interview room at Blenheim cop shop being grilled by Gemma and a male colleague who looks like he should still be at school. I've been cautioned and have waived my rights to a lawyer and a union rep.

'You sure about that?' says Gemma.

'Let's get on with it, eh?'

Before leaving home I called over to see Gary. He still carries himself tentatively since his left shoulder muscle was badly shredded by Marty Stringfellow's knife last year. Marty – an enforcer for a Geordie gangster I once knew – now there was a bloke you could imagine doing those terrible things in the Four Square coldroom. But Marty's alibied up – dead over a year now. Gary showed me the water tank.

'Same as ours.' I crouched down to look closer. 'Holed low to get maximum leakage.'

'Deliberate, then?'

'Most acts of vandalism are.' We studied the angles, lines of sight for both our tanks. 'Over the river, high up on the hill. Had to be.'

'Fuckwits.'

I gave him my spare resin for the repairs and the number for Marvin the water guy. 'All good otherwise?'

'Good as gold.'

'Quiet without Richie around.' Gary's black mastiff was taken out by a logging truck just last month.

'Not much time for hunting these days. But you never know, might get another.'

Gemma coughs politely to start the ball rolling. Scrolls through her iPad while Wonder Boy riffles a hard copy file in front of him and readies his pen and notebook.

'So we need to account for your movements between about six on Tuesday evening and early Wednesday morning. Can you map it out for us?'

I do. The Wednesday is fine: Charlie Evans and Latifa can alibi me for the hour or so preceding the body being found, Vanessa and Paulie will vouch for me being around at breakfast time, and Vanessa will confirm me being in bed with her all night. Tuesday evening I was home, fixing water tanks and being domestic. But the day before that, Monday evening, is a problem.

'Finished my shift on Tuesday at around four. I was summoned home because there was a leak in our water tank. I left early as there was nothing going on and we closed up the office.'

'We, being you and Constable Rapata?'

'Yes.'

'Then where did you go? Straight home?'

'Pretty much.' I give her the details. What a breeze.

'How about the day before that, Sergeant?' says Gemma. 'Monday?'

Shit.

'Why? I thought the timeframe was Tuesday into Wednesday?'

'We talked to Gelder's wife. She hadn't seen him since Monday. He said he was going off to do some dredging on his claim.'

Gelder had this shack along the road a few k's. He got the block really cheap, levelled it and put up some kit-build granny flat in a day. It's got good access to the river and is round a sharp river bend, so any noise is muffled and any activity is out of sight. I'm convinced he's not been keeping to the terms of the resource consent. I'm sure I've heard the dredge going on days he's not allowed, starting earlier or going later than he should. Maybe I'm paranoid, hearing things. Wrong. Vanessa wants me to let it go. 'Out of sight, out of mind, Nick. For fuck's sake, get a life.'

'Apparently he sometimes sleeps over in his shack, a man-cave type thing.' Gemma does a swipe on her iPad and looks up. 'So nobody had seen him for a full forty hours or so.'

A big show of concentrating. 'Monday. Routine day. Constable Rapata will vouch for that. Close of business I went to the Four Square, got some bits and pieces. That should be on the CCTV. Just before they closed for the day.'

'Then?'

'Called in at the Trout at Canvastown, said hello to a few people, had a cider.'

'Then?'

'I stopped off just outside the Lodge, halfway up the valley road towards home.'

Wonder Boy makes a note of the property number I give him.

'Why?' says Gemma. 'And for how long?'

'I'd had a run-in with a fella that lived there. American.'

'So many run-ins lately. Gelder, and now this guy.'

'It goes with the job.'

'Seems to go with yours, for sure. What was special about this one?'

I smile ruefully. 'He managed to drop me one day last week. I'm not used to that. Been fretting about it. Obsessing.'

'In what way?'

'Replaying it in my head. How it could have gone. Should have gone. You know how it is.'

No. By the look of them, they don't.

She nods at my hands. 'Your knuckles. Been in the wars? Looks recent.'

'Line of duty, again.'

She makes a note. 'This American assaulted you last week. Did you charge him?'

'No.'

'Why not?'

'Decided to have a word instead.'

Some scrolling through iPads, accessing the database. Wonder Boy looks up. 'This would be the Brandon Cunningham arrest?'

'Yes.'

He reads the report. 'Released with a caution. End of story?'

'It seems not,' says Gemma. 'So you called in on him on Monday evening?'

'No, I didn't call in. Just sat outside in the car.'

'For how long?'

'Half an hour maybe?'

'And then where, home?'

'Yes.'

'What time was this?'

'It would be getting on for eight by then.'

'And home for the rest of the night?'

I nod. Now I just need Vanessa to back up my lies.

'There was a needle mark in Gelder's neck. He was drugged before they strapped him to the chair.'

'They?' I lift my eyes from my phone screen. Been trying to get hold of Vanessa but to no avail.

'The pathologist and our forensics crew are now of the opinion that there are at least two killers.' Maxwell has called me in to his office, a former dressing room behind the stage. On the strength of my statement to Gemma he seems happy enough to assign me a specific role in his team. 'There are gloved handprints on parts of his body, bruises if you like. Two sets, one bigger than the other. And forensics have identified two sets of fresh footprints, with blood smears to indicate how fresh, again one lot bigger than the other.'

'Anything else?'

'They went at him with secateurs, a corkscrew, knives, a broken bottle, blowtorch.'

'Ugh.'

'Eyes, ears, nose, fingers. All up for grabs. But the fatal stroke once they'd had their fun was a knife across the throat.'

'Sweet release, I suppose.'

Maxwell nods. 'Glad you're out of the frame, Nick. Thing like this would be bad for PR. Right, let's give you a job.'

'Great. I assume Latifa will get support to make up for my absence?'

He frowns. 'Shouldn't be an issue. I was thinking some routine enquiries by you to lighten the load for our full-time investigators. Even do it from your own desk up there. Should be able to juggle that with your usual duties, right?'

Sure, not forgetting my vital role as Lollipop Man at the film set. 'Is that what Keegan had in mind?'

'I know she thinks highly of you, Nick.' A pause to let the double-entendre sink in. It seems our tempestuous fling last year is an open secret. 'But this is my investigation.'

'Absolutely.'

'We've got a list of plumbing jobs Gelder's been doing the last few months. Maybe you can follow up on them with a few phone calls, visits if needs be, see if he's been overcharging or doing bodgy work.'

'Seriously?'

'No telling what might trigger these things. Diligence, mate. Crossing the i's and dotting the t's. Foundation of all good detecting, you know that.'

He hands me the list and sends me on my way.

Back in our little cop shop, Latifa is fuming. 'Who does she think she is?'

'Who?'

'Gemma Jeez-I'm-Great.'

'What now?'

There follows a long tirade featuring words like patronising, condescending, some *te reo* that's new to me. The gist is that Latifa has offered her services to the investigation and Gemma, as 2-I-C, has rebuffed her. 'She was the year above me at MGC.'

'You went to Marlborough Girls College?'

'Yeah, course I did. Why wouldn't I?'

No reason. It turns out that Gemma got to be head girl instead of Latifa's best friend who was, in Latifa's view, far more deserving and it's been daggers drawn ever since. We're talking nearly a decade here.

'What are you smiling at?' she snaps.

'I'm glad you're human and grudge-bearing just like me.'

'Just like you? God forbid.' She flicks on her computer to check the incident log. 'So you got on the investigation, big shot. What have they got you doing?'

'Routine stuff.'

A grunt. 'Another crash on the Whangamoa overnight: two dead. A drowning up at Tennyson Inlet. Bloke dived off a jetty after a skinful and didn't check the tides. Three reports of vandalism up your way.'

'Vandalism?'

'Somebody shooting at water tanks. Usual hillbilly high jinks.'

I log in and check them out for myself. Three properties a little further down the valley, between the six and nine kilometre marks. Then there's us and Gary. 'Five water tanks shot out.'

'Five? It says three.'

I explain to Latifa and she asks why I never reported it. 'Report what? Some trigger-happy dickhead in the valley?'

'But now we're looking at a pattern. A serial offender.'

She's right and it needs to be nipped in the bud. 'Want to run with it?'

'What?' she says, flushed with mock delight. 'A case pour moi? All of my own? Oh, my!'

Ignore the sarcasm. 'Anything else of interest?'

'Apart from the body in the Four Square, no.'

That reminds me to get on to the list of Gelder's plumbing jobs. Vanessa returns my call, it must be lunchtime. My rumbling stomach confirms it. 'You rang?'

With Latifa in the room it's best not to ask Vanessa if she can provide me with a false alibi. 'No big issue, it'll wait until I get home tonight.'

'So you just called to say you love me, is that right?'

'Absolutely.'

'Go on then.'

'What?'

'Say it.'

Latifa is pretending not to listen.

'I love you.'

'That's nice. Love you too. See you tonight.'

I put my phone away.

'Sweet,' says Latifa, sourly.

Allowing for travel time, the plumbing jobs average six a day for the last month. That's around a hundred and twenty jobs all up. Some are return visits to the same property but it's still over a hundred enquiries. And if this doesn't bring any results, Maxwell might well extend the timeframe just to keep me occupied. Why doesn't he want me in a more useful and central role? Maybe I'm just surplus to requirements and he's going through the motions for Keegan's sake. By now Gelder's name has been released, we've all seen his family crying on the TV news, and the people I phone are wondering what the hell the standard of his plumbing has to do with his grisly death. Most folks are suitably shocked and respectful and nobody has a bad word to say about him. There's the odd joker.

'Mate, the laundry tap still drips so I just had to take the fucker out. Lol.'

Through the window, dark clouds are rolling in from the north-west. There's a few rain spots on the glass and the director of *Doom Creek* is probably pulling her hair out at the prospect of another interrupted filming day. I'm about a third of the way through my list with nothing to show. Then we feel it. Latifa looks up at the same time. A shudder and a jolt, like a big truck just went by – but it didn't.

Earthquake.

'Four and a half, five maybe?' says Latifa. 'Hasn't been one of them for a few weeks.' We check the Geonet website, it's a six point two out in Cook Strait. 'Didn't feel that strong.'

But it's been enough to trigger a couple of car and shop alarms. Heads are poking around doors, looking up and down the street. A few shrugs and back inside. The landline goes.

'Sergeant Chester?' It's Devon Cornish, from the film set. 'Hello? Are you there?' His voice sounds delayed, echoing. Then again it would, it's being bounced off a satellite somewhere in space.

'Yes.'

'You'd better come up here.'

'Is Cunningham back?'

'No, there's been a landslide.' I can hear other noises now. Screams. Yells. 'People hurt …' Interference, dropout. 'Some … body … dead.'

6.

We arrive at Butchers Flat just ahead of the ambulances and the emergency services volunteers. A big old man pine has come down, demolishing the toilet block and the catering caravan. There are people trapped inside, we are told. Some land has slipped down to the river, taking a couple of crew cars with it. Latifa summons the able-bodied to help bring order to the scene. It's eerily quiet, the chaotic screams and yelling heard earlier down the phone have subsided. The crushed caravan is the priority. Devon Cornish and Thomas Hemi are among the throng and Hemi seems to be holding up a tree single-handedly.

'We've got her,' says Devon.

We help pull a young woman out from under a section of tree. It looks like her shoulder is dislocated, otherwise she'll be okay.

Hemi rests his burden, he's barely raised a sweat. 'There's one more under there, the caterer fella.'

The emergency services team coordinator steps up. 'We'll take it from here.' Hemi shrugs, accepts a pat on the shoulder and a cup of tea from someone's thermos.

'How many hurt?' I ask, noticing a couple of walking wounded at the far end of the campground. 'Any serious?'

'No,' says Devon. 'Mainly cuts and bruises, twisted ankles. Sorry, I think I might have overreacted on the phone.'

'Hardly. You mentioned a body, a death?'

'Not one of ours. It looks like it's been here a while.' He nods for me to follow. 'Over here.'

Where the old man pine toppled, a whole pile of earth came with it. And a body. Well half a one actually, from the waist up. It certainly has been there a while, it seems to be nearer to skeleton than corpse, but with a layer of tattered dried skin and remnants of sinew. Flies and other insects are taking a shine to it and we need to do something.

'Anybody got a tarp?'

'Got something better,' says a recently arrived paramedic. 'Body bag do you? Brought some spare, just in case.'

'Perfect.'

He brings one over and we ease the half-body into the bag. The paramedic spots it first where hair and skin has peeled away from the skull. 'That looks like a bullet hole to me.'

The emergency services team have managed to free the caterer. A toppled bar fridge snapped his ankle and his wrist but he'll live. The ambulances have shipped out with those who need extra care and the surviving crew and cast are on their way home for the day. Nobody has asked for trauma counselling but it's available if they want. They've been given a helpline number to call if certain shock symptoms develop. The half-body is on its way to the mortuary. So far we haven't found the other half. All in all it's been quite a day for Devon Cornish but he remains philosophical.

'Luckily we'd done most of the shooting we needed to do. We can always come back later for some pickups with a second unit. Insurance should cover the blowout.'

This must be how film producers think, not unlike police HQ bean counters: how disasters impact the bottom line. Thomas Hemi is among the last to leave. 'Heroic effort there, Thomas. You're a star.'

'Wasn't the whole tree, I just rolled that big branch that's all.'

'Still pretty impressive.'

Hemi lifts his shoulders. 'Pity they've finished. Could get a taste for that film lark.' He stifles a yawn. 'I hear there's been a few water tanks shot out up and down the valley?'

'Yep.'

'Add mine to the list. Must've happened overnight.'

'Bugger.'

'Yeah. And I never heard a thing.'

'Slept through?'

'Not me. I wake up when the birds are clearing their throats. I reckon your shooter's using a silencer.'

It's late afternoon by the time I can leave. The emergency volunteers will tidy up the debris and arrange for the cars to be lifted out of the river. Rather than go back to the office I opt to go straight home. Another migraine throbs at the back of my skull. I used to get them often when I was younger but less so these days. Well until recently anyway. The plumbing list can wait until tomorrow and Latifa has added Hemi's water tank to her investigative caseload.

Vanessa is hosing the vegies as I pull up. 'You're early.' We smooch and I bring her up to speed on the happenings at Butchers Flat. She nods. 'I felt the rumble but didn't think it amounted to much. Saw the ambulances zooming out of Havelock. Assumed it was a crash on the highway.'

'There was this old body there too, uncovered by the landslip.'

'How old?'

'Decades maybe? Haven't a clue.'

She grabs an armful of greenery. 'Vegie quiche do you for dinner?'

'Great, I'll help you chop.' I look around. 'Paulie inside?'

'No, he's having a few hours at Mim's after school. I'll pick him up later.'

'His new friend? Where does she live?'

'A farm between here and Pelorus, near Daltons Bridge.'

Fifteen klicks or so. 'It's great he's making some connections. Is she special needs too?'

'Nah. Straight as.'

I punch her playfully on the arm. 'Sounding more and more Kiwi all the time.'

'There's still a good hour or so before we need to pick him up.' She runs a damp courgette up my forearm. 'Any thoughts?'

'I'll pop a Panadol and be right with you.'

'You okay?'

'A bit of a headache. It's nothing.'

She pouts. 'Is that your version of "Not tonight Josephine"?'

'Perish the thought.'

Rain arrives in the evening and it'll be good for the river, the land, and the water tanks. Particularly those which have been recently holed. Hopefully Thomas has managed to fix his so he can reap full benefit.

Paulie is full of himself, it's a long while since he got invited over to anybody's house. 'Mim's got a horse called Bella. And a TV in her room,' he adds pointedly.

'Better than the other way round.'

He frowns at me. 'That's stupid, Dad.'

'Been at the school a while?'

'Started this year I think. Yeah.'

'Where was she before she came here?'

'That a cop question, Dad?'

'No, it's a dad question, son.' I turn my reading lamp on him and go mock serious. 'Answer. Now.'

'Nelson, I think. Yeah, Nelson.'

'Parents fancied a country change, eh?'

'It's just her and her mum, and grandad.'

'Nice people?'

Vanessa looks up from her marking. 'Mum seems nice enough. Mim's a livewire.'

'Grandad?'

'He was out.'

Back to Paulie. 'So is Mim coming over here anytime?'

'Can she?'

Vanessa and I check with each other. 'Sure. Of course.'

'Great, I'll ask tomorrow.'

I nod. 'What about that earthquake today. Feel it?'

'Yeah.' He wobbles a bit and crosses his eyes. 'Whoaw.'

'Time for bed, Paulie,' says Vanessa.

I'm not far from turning in myself. 'You going late with the books again?'

''Fraid so,' says Vanessa. 'Besides, I've already had my evil way with you.'

'Mum!' says Paulie from the bathroom through a mouthful of toothpaste. 'Yuck!'

She glances up from her books and catches my eye. 'Should be done with this in an hour. Any chance of dessert?'

Friday morning – another week rolls around to its end. The rain has washed through and the sun is back out. The wind got up in the night and there's debris on the valley road: branches, gravel and stuff. Waterfalls have sprung up in roadside gullies. Window down, the place smells fresh and clean and everywhere is a deeper shade of green. The Lodge gates are shut and all is quiet. That suits me.

Havelock is just coming awake, putting on its best tourist village display. Locals greeting each other, children skipping to school, dogs being walked, honest down-to-earth folk going about their business. But Latifa is in a foul mood when I arrive at the cop shop.

'Morning,' I say brightly.

'Yeah.'

'How's things?'

'Daniel's staying down Christchurch another week because of his mum, and somebody scratched the paintwork on my car.'

'The work one?'

'No, mine. They can do what they like to the work one.'

'Deliberate?'

'Looks like it. They did a nice little pattern on my bonnet. A dick. Oversized as usual.'

'Bugger.'

'And I didn't get much sleep last night.'

'Need a coffee from the shop?'

'I'll come with you.'

We lock up, turn the sign to closed, and walk a block down to the bakery. Latifa adds a bacon sandwich to her coffee order and we take a seat by the window. Her mood seems unshakeable.

'Anything else bothering you?'

'Somebody was creeping through the yard last night. Same people who vandalised the car I expect.'

'Kids?'

'Havelock doesn't really have any bad kids, like bad-bad. And then my mobile kept going off in the night. Unknown number.'

'Should have turned it off.'

'Can't. I was on call.'

'Any idea who's behind it?'

The coffee arrives and she takes refuge behind hers. 'That Yank is the only nutcase I've had bother with lately.'

'We'll need evidence, given how lawyered up Cunningham is.'

'I know.' She attacks her bacon sandwich. I'm wishing I'd given in to temptation and got one too.

An idea occurs to me. 'That camera he has on his tree. Maybe we can set one up too. If it is him and he comes back, then bingo. If it isn't then we'll know who to go after.'

'Okay.' She brightens. 'I'll organise it.' Changes the subject. 'Any news on the Mummy?'

'The body's not that old. No, nothing yet. How about the water-tank shooter?'

'After Thomas's tip-off about the silencer, I contacted that bloke near Rai Valley who makes his own.'

There's a retired hydrologist who knows all you need to know about how water moves underground, has set up his own wi-fi system in an area that doesn't have any, and is an expert marksman. In his spare time he crafts his own silencers and sells them to hunters to supplement his pension. I think he might be writing a book too. No, really.

'What'd he say?'

'He insists it couldn't be one of his because he doesn't sell them to dickheads. Besides he reckons they couldn't afford his – artisan, handmade. Bespoke, he said.'

'What if it's a cashed-up dickhead?'

'Much as I'd like to blame Cunningham for everything that's happening right now, I'm not sure it's diligent police work. You should be setting me a better example, Sarge.'

I drain my coffee. 'I checked out the line of sight for the shootings on Gary's and my tanks. What with the trees and angles and whatever you can narrow it down to a small area on that hill over the river.' I bring a map up on my phone and show her.

'You reckon we need to climb that steep hill for what? Spent cartridges, abandoned signed confessions?'

'Diligent police work, Constable. And who's this "we"? It's your case, remember?'

'I knew it was going to be one of those days.'

Back to the list of Bruce Gelder's plumbing jobs until midmorning, then DSS Maxwell summons me to the murder room in the town hall for an update. The Four Square is still shut and communal mutiny is in the air.

'Heard you had some dramas up the valley yesterday. The landslip?'

'No serious injuries. Just an old body that was unearthed.'

He nods. 'Keegan's added it to my caseload. Like I haven't got enough on my plate. How's your plumbing list going?'

'Slowly. It's a waste of time.'

A half-grin. 'It was designed to be. Look I'm not gonna piss around anymore. Drop it for now. I need you to run with this cold case. You up for it?'

'Sure.'

'First things first.' He checks his watch. 'Hightail it to Nelson and you should be just in time for the post-mortem.'

'Is it just me or do I get any help?'

'On an as-needs basis. Let me know after the PM, okay?'

And so it's SH6 over the Whangamoa Saddle to Nelson. Winding through the logged hills, around the hairpin bends with the usual impatient roadsters up my tail, completely unfazed by the 'Police' markings on my car. At one point I flick on the top lights and pull over one particularly annoying dipstick for a talking-to. Five minutes later and a 'who cares' shrug, and he's on his way.

The pathologist is a middle-aged man I've never met before and he's already started his examination. According to my paperwork his name is Professor Bardawi. He's bemused by my uniform as he was expecting a plain-clothes detective.

'I've been seconded to the investigation and was first on the scene when the body was unearthed. I can email you my resumé later if you like?'

'No need. You have a trustworthy face.' Photographs and measurements have been taken. 'He was probably around one hundred and eighty-five centimetres. Maybe once we find the other half we can join him together and confirm that but I'd like to think I'm right.'

'Sounds good to me.'

A report will follow, he tells me, but I'm taking my own notes anyway. 'Age?'

'Anywhere from thirty to sixty. I'll try to narrow it down with a few tests later today.' He brings the magnifier in on its retractable arm. 'You already saw the hole in the head, I believe?'

'Yes. Bullet?'

'I'd say so. There's a corresponding entry hole behind and lower down.' He shows me.

'The exit hole was on top of the skull, above the forehead. That's a pretty extreme angle?'

'Not if he's kneeling in front of you with his head bowed.'

'An execution?'

'I've seen a few. Until twelve years ago I lived in Iraq.'

'Anything else?'

He looks up. 'In a hurry? You only just arrived.' A nod and murmur towards his assistant. 'What looks like ligature markings around the neck. Not sure about that, with the state of putrefaction. Again though, hangings and garrottings are not unfamiliar to me.'

Strangled and shot? I grab a seat and listen and learn.

The rest of the preliminary examination suggested a well-nourished victim with no signs of disease or traces of narcotics or other notable substances. He had died sometime in the last three to five years but Bardawi would need to do further tests to be more accurate. By the end of the examination, the professor was prepared to tighten the age range to the higher bracket.

'So forty-five to sixty-five?'

'Yes. I'll update you in my report in the next few days. I have a number of more urgent and recent cases to deal with, including the poor fellow in the supermarket storeroom who needs further examination. Strange goings on. Is there something in the water over there in Havelock?'

Probably. Outside, there's a message from Vanessa on my mobile. She sounds pissed off. *I've had this Gemma police woman in the staff room asking me to confirm your whereabouts on Monday and Tuesday evening. What's going on?*

So much else happening: earthquakes, bodies, you get the drift. I call her back. 'Sorry, meant to tell you yesterday.'

'Why's she checking up on you?'

'Because of my history with Gelder over the mining.'

'You're a suspect in his murder? Seriously?'

'It's a due diligence thing to make sure I can't be seen to have a conflict of interest in the investigation. Just a formality, a rubber stamp.'

'So where were you on Monday night? I was in bed by the time you got home. Assumed you were working. Gemma says not. She says you told her you were back home by mid-evening. Asked me to confirm it.'

'Did you?'

'You want me to lie for you? Provide a false alibi?'

'I'll explain when I get home.'

'You do that.'

It's midafternoon heading back over the mountains and I've offered to collect Paulie on the way, to save Vanessa the journey and to try to make some amends for enmeshing her in my web of fibs. Before leaving Nelson I dropped by HQ to ask DC Keegan for some help with the donkey work on my Mummy enquiry: a trainee detective, probationary constable, civilian, even a year twelve student placement; whatever. Her office smelled of expensive perfume and sneaky cigarettes.

'Executed you say?'

'According to Professor Bardawi.'

'Organised crime then?'

'Or somebody who watches a lot of nasty movies.'

'Both even.' She glanced at her computer and her fingers moved across the keyboard. 'I'll see what I can do.' A sniff. 'That offer remains open, Nick. There's a job for you over here in the detectives.'

'Thanks, appreciate it. But travel time's an issue and I need to be around to share Paulie with Vanessa. And to be honest I'm getting a taste for the simple life.'

She lifted her eyes from the screen. 'Somebody tortured to death in your local supermarket and a possible gangland execution at the nearest campsite. How's the simple life going?'

Not to mention a water-tank sniper and some American crazies moving in down the road. 'Famine or feast.'

'Have it your way. The execution-style killing is ringing bells for me but not for this region. I'll do some digging.'

'Don't forget my donkey.'

'Leave it with me.'

Paulie's at the school gate when I pull up. He's with a girl who is probably his new friend Mim. He introduces her and we shake hands formally.

'This is Dad. He's a cop.'

'Yeah,' she says. 'You told me.' There's a worldly spark to her eyes, a knowingness beyond her years. I can't help wondering what she sees in Paulie.

'How are you settling in to your new school?'

'New?'

'Started this year, that right?'

A nod. 'Great,' she says. 'My old one was very strict.'

'Making lots of new friends?'

'A few, I suppose. Paul's nice. He makes me laugh.'

'Makes me laugh too.' Paulie is looking a bit agitated. Too much scrutiny, I'm guessing. 'Is your mum picking you up, Mim?'

A shake of the head. 'Grandad. He should be here soon.'

'We'll wait until he arrives. Make sure you're okay.'

'No need.'

'No problem, we aren't in a hurry. Are we, Paulie?'

'It's Paul, Dad. I'm not a kid anymore.'

'Really. There's no need,' Mim steps back nervously.

A ute draws up, dusty, seen better times. An older man at the wheel: late sixties, early seventies maybe. Weather-burnished and tough, like most of them are in these parts. He notices my uniform, the police car. 'What's the problem?'

'No problem.' I offer a hand for shaking. 'Just picking my son up from school. He's in the same class as your granddaughter.'

'Right. Good.' He tells Mim to hop in. 'Gotta be going.'

'Nick,' I say, still holding out the hand. 'And you are?'

A thin smile and a brief firm grip. 'Pleased to meet you.'

'See you Monday, Mim,' says Paulie. Sorry. Make that Paul.

She gives him a wave as perfunctory as her grandad's handshake. 'Bye.'

They crunch the gravel and do a U-turn. 'Michael,' says Paulie.

'What?'

'His name's Michael.'

At home there's a frostiness in the air. Best not to go back into the cop shop and I phone Latifa to that effect.

'I'll do some research from here. Everything okay at your end?'

'Yep. Sweet.'

Paulie is in front of the TV with a healthy afternoon snack and Vanessa is in front of me wanting to know what the hell is going on. Where was I on Monday night?

'Outside the Lodge for a while, obsessing about the guy that hit me.'

'That rings true. Then where?'

'More of the same but down at Gelder's shack on that block he bought.'

'Why? Hadn't we finished with him? We got the ruling we wanted, didn't we?'

'He's not sticking to it. Wasn't.'

'He *was*, where it mattered, within our field of vision and hearing. Who cares what he might do further downriver, Nick? For fuck's sake.'

'Rules and regs, that's what they're there for.'

'When it suits you. What were you doing at his shack anyway?'

'Nosing around.'

'What were you hoping to prove?'

'I don't know. Just, anything.'

'Until nearly midnight? It's not that big a shack.'

'He came back. Caught me.' I find myself rubbing the sore spot behind my ear. She lifts my hand away and sees now the lump that was hidden by my hair. Notices again the knuckles of my right fist, inflamed.

'Jesus, Nick. What have you done?'

The truth is, I can't remember.

7.

Vanessa did lie for me, even before she heard my side of it. She believes me, believes that I really don't remember. Now she wants me to get checked out by a doctor.

'Erratic behaviour. Memory loss. Could be warning signs of a stroke, could be anything.' Vanessa's mam had a stroke recently and Vanessa's been thinking about that a bit lately.

The erratic behaviour isn't a recent development, to be fair. Some would say it's always been my MO. 'But what if I did kill him?'

She's doubtful. 'I can see you punching somebody's lights out but I can't see you torturing anybody. Not without good reason. Either way, for me the priority is getting you looked at.'

'But ...'

'But nothing. Or I withdraw my alibi and they can lock you up.'

'Well if you put it like that.'

It's too late to phone for an appointment now, so first thing Monday. Look busy. Help get dinner ready, give the goats and chooks their tea, check the water tank isn't leaking. So far, so good. Vanessa keeps glancing at me out of the corner of her eye. She's worried and who could blame her? Have I or have I not been responsible for Gelder's death? Have I or have I not got some scary neurological problem going on? Rather than brood about strokes, aneurysms and prison sentences, maybe it's time to change the subject.

'I met Mim's grandad today, when I was picking Paulie up.'

'Paul,' Paulie reminds me from his corner of the room. 'And his name's Michael.'

'Yeah?' says Vanessa.

'Classic Kiwi farmer. Cards close to his chest, reserves any warmth until he's met you at least thirty times.'

Vanessa nods. 'Paulie, did you invite Mim over yet?'

'Yeah, she's going to ask her grandad.'

'Why him? Doesn't mum get a say?'

He shrugs. 'Michael does the driving.'

Fair point.

After dinner it's on to the computer to make up for my early finish by doing a search on where the Mummy might have come from. Log in to the police missing persons database as a starting point. Dead three to five years, Bardawi had said. Male, aged fortyish to sixtyish. I plug in the few scraps of information available.

More candidates than you can point a stick at.

Maybe try narrowing it to people reported missing from this region? It's a starting point but there's no reason why they couldn't be from anywhere in NZ or in the world for that matter. Still, I give it a go and it immediately narrows down to a couple of dozen men from the top of the South Island of that age range reported missing during that timeframe. Some have been outdoor tramper types and have probably fallen down a remote gully or old mineshaft or been taken by a swollen river or king tide. Some had a history of alcohol and/or drug abuse so that probably rules them out as no significant trace was found on the dried-up corpse. Some maybe wanted to just take themselves off the grid. The top of the South, with its thousands of kilometres of fjord-like coastline, hidden coves and dead-end valleys, is a good place to hunker down. Speaking from experience, it can and does work, for a while at least.

Maybe seven or eight pique my interest and even though my research strategy is far from comprehensive (having left out everybody else in New Zealand and the rest of the world) I make them my immediate priority. If nothing else, I might be able to exclude them from my further enquiries. Criminal convictions or associations are a helpful marker. In New Zealand anyway, if not in Iraq, the majority of people who find themselves being shot in the back of the head while kneeling have probably kept very bad company and might have even had it coming. Sure there will be exceptions but they'll be rare. Five on the list fit the bad company bill but I can immediately exclude two gang members with violent histories because it is clear from their photos that barely an inch of them remains uninked. Bardawi found no traces of tattooing in his examination of the parchment shreds remaining on the skeleton. Of the other three, one is an accountant who helped gangsters cook their books, one a lawyer who helped them stay out on the streets and in business. The last one didn't seem like a bad person but he had looked to defend his values and his patch of ground and had come up against types who would eat him alive and barely raise a belch.

My semi-mummified half-corpse could be any of these men or none of them.

The weekend was delightfully uneventful: chickens, goats, chores, a walk along the river. Charlie Evans came around for dinner on Saturday. He's lost without Beattie and his mind is turning towards a house in suburbia where he can forget about farm work and curl up and die.

'Sooner the better,' he murmured over his glass of red.

To be honest we couldn't wait to shuffle him out the door. After a while you tire of other people's grief. Is that callous? Maybe, but we find ourselves rationing our compassion these days. Change the subject. 'How's Denzel? See much of him?'

'Pops round now and then. Think he might have a beau.'

'Great. Happy then?'

'S'pose somebody has to be.'

So much for changing the subject. 'The new fella working out well?' Charlie has hired a bloke from Vanuatu to help out around the farm. There's a bunch of islanders sharing a house down behind the pub near the Von Crapps. These guys subsist on seasonal farm and vineyard labouring. They work hard and keep themselves to themselves, not that that stops the odd neighbour from just not liking the colour of their skin.

'Israel? Yeah, he's good, reliable. Pretty handy. Not much of a conversationalist though.'

Two of a kind then.

'Know anything about fences, Nick?' Charlie said in a moment of outgoing lucidity.

'In what regard?'

'Their legal status. I assumed it was all cut and dried. Fences mark boundaries of ownership. Right?'

'I would have thought so.'

'Those Americans bulldozed a section of mine. Moved it back thirty metres onto my land. Left it to me to put it back up again.'

'When?'

'This morning. First thing. Now there's a big mound of earth curving around. It's their new firing range.'

'Firing range?'

'Are machine guns allowed in New Zealand? They were blasting away with them all afternoon.'

First thing Monday, I organise a doctor's appointment for the end of the afternoon and arrange for a police inspection of the Lodge and their gun collection. Latifa comes through the door looking exhausted again.

'More bumps in the night?'

She nods. 'And the phone again. Both nights, all weekend.'

Should have told her to leave it off. Insisted. 'I'll take the on-call shifts for the next few nights.' I wave away her protests. 'The camera? Is that happening?'

'The guy's coming round this morning to set it up.'

'Did you run a trace on the mystery caller?'

'No, I was waiting until Monday. Thought it all might just fade away.'

'Get the techs onto it. This is harassment.'

She yawns. 'Okay. The camera guy will probably call in here first. Give him the spare key if he needs access inside. I'm off.'

'Where?'

'Got a mountain to climb. The mysterious case of the leaking water tanks.'

'It can wait if you're too stuffed.'

'Fresh air will do me good.'

'Got your personal alarm?'

The Wakamarina, like many parts of New Zealand, has blind and deaf spots where mobiles and police radios won't get a signal. The best you can hope for is that the personal emergency beacon will work. She pats the tab on her vest. 'It's a walk up and down a hill and a five-minute look around, Sarge. A complete waste of time as ordered by my superior officer who lacks sound judgement in most matters but whom it is my solemn duty to obey.'

'Whom? Still studying the law books then.'

'If I'm not back by lunchtime, release the hounds.'

Back to my Mummy candidates. Accountant David Archer, a forty-six-year-old married man with two kids, was reported missing by his wife three and a half years ago. He had failed to return to their bayside Atawhai home just outside of Nelson. The file shows a concrete and glass cube sitting halfway up the hill with no doubt a stunning view of the water and the distant hills of the Abel Tasman National Park. The cube was worth a cool two million dollars, which wasn't bad for a bloke who had no connection to the major accounting firms or any clients from big multinational corporations. But, according to the police Financial Intelligence Unit based in Wellington, he was helping to launder money for a company fronting for a local chapter of an outlaw bikie gang, which in turn was channelling funds for the national organisation. The details are there on the database but I was never good at maths at school and I'm happy to be convinced that it was both complex and lucrative. Until a police task force decided to take an interest in Archer and apply pressure to him about his private life. He was on the verge of spilling the evidential beans on his clients' money trail. Then one day soon after, he never came home, and Mrs Archer found she could no longer afford to pay the mortgage on the Atawhai house because the insurers were unprepared to pay out on a bloke yet to be proven dead. A mysterious crossbow attack on the family dog also helped nudge her and the kids out of town. The property was sold for a song to another company linked to Archer's shadowy clients. Cash, of course.

Candidate number two. Stephen Jones, aged fifty-three, lawyer, father of two adult sons, but divorced and living with his long-time companion at the time of his disappearance four years ago. His lover, Bryce, didn't report him missing until six days after the event because he was known to often go off for days after a row, of which there were many in their tempestuous relationship. There was nothing particularly complex or suspiciously lucrative about Jones' relationship with his clients. He was a good criminal lawyer, a fox with twelve chickens he was fond of saying. Jones was able to get a well-known Nelson identity off a wounding charge even when the incident was caught on two CCTV cameras and half a dozen smartphones. He was master of the slicing quip, devastating put-down, and forensic dismantling of the prosecution case. The media loved his flamboyance and his witty sound bites. With Jones advocating on your behalf you developed Teflon-coatability. He'd have made enemies all over the place: cops failing to secure a hard-worked-for and sure-fire conviction, rape victims trashed in the witness box, you name it. But he could just as easily have put a client offside. He knew all their secrets and had recently signed a publishing deal for his memoir – *A Fox with Twelve Chickens*. Would he have been indiscreet? Maybe somebody feared so.

Lastly, and saddest of all, Karel Havelka. At sixty-two he was at the outer range of the professor's age estimate on the victim but, according to the file, Karel was fit and active and might have physically passed for a younger man. Karel, an emigrant from the former Czechoslovakia, was living in semi-retirement in Springlands, a suburb of Blenheim, when he went missing about five years ago. He was a keen tramper and swimmer and volunteered with an environmental group, a homeless charity, and a disability transport service. He balanced that with part-time work from a home office as a telecommunications consultant, coming up with solutions to broadband dead zones in the Marlborough Sounds. But he was a meddler. He was often complaining to the council about instances he observed out in the Sounds or among his neighbours in Springlands where somebody was breaching the rules. Maybe it was his upbringing in then Communist Czechoslovakia where informing on your neighbour was a viable career path. Reading the file, it's obvious he's a bit like me: can't stand to see people getting away with not doing the right thing: resource consents, noisy parties, boy racers, barking dogs. The list goes on and I feel your pain, Karel. But at some point it's all got out of hand. An argument and altercation in the street late one night; a boy racer doing skiddies. Some pushing and shoving. The kid pulls a knife and Karel – a champion boxer in the Czech army, his wife would later tell the police – gets his punch in first. The kid falls, hits his head on the kerb and goes into a coma. Six weeks later life support is switched off and Karel's assault charge is upgraded to manslaughter, although he is still allowed out on bail as he is not regarded as a flight risk. He never gets to stand trial, disappearing within a week of the charge being laid. He'd punched the wrong kid: the teenage son of a local gang leader.

Three candidates for my half-body. And where is the other half? Butchers Flat is now blocked off as a crime scene with the assistance of conservation department rangers. Whether anything useful will be found after three to five years we don't know but the other half of the corpse would be a good start. Or a bullet casing. Some ID on the victim and the perpetrator. Professor Bardawi is extracting whatever DNA he can and running it through the system. Maybe it will match with one of my three candidates. Or maybe my skeleton isn't even reported missing from its closet.

My stomach gurgles and, checking the clock, I see it's heading for lunchtime. Latifa should be back soon. Flick the sign on the door and go in search of a sandwich. Outside the bakery a ute pulls up. Thomas Hemi. He's been in the wars.

'What happened to you?'

He fingers a nasty cut over his eye, eases himself gingerly out from behind the wheel. 'Nothing I can't deal with.'

'Don't want any feuds around here. Too much on my plate already.'

'Buy me a cuppa tea?'

'Sure. Anything to eat?'

He scans the display cabinet. 'Cheese scone?'

I put the orders in and join him at my favourite window table. 'Something tells me this isn't a chance encounter. Am I right?'

He tries a grin but his bottom lip is split. 'Saw Latifa this morning heading up the hill. She told me to talk to you.'

The order arrives. I pour and we settle in. 'Fire away.'

'Those blokes at the Lodge are up to something.'

'Are they the ones who did this to you?'

'Like I said, nothing I can't deal with. I don't go telling tales.'

'All the same, Thomas, here we are sitting and talking.'

'A punch-up is nothing. But they're planning something bigger.'

'Like what?'

'Ever read the scriptures, Nick?'

'Nah, can't say I'm a believer.'

'Neither am I, used to be but not anymore. I've read them.'

'And?'

'Those guys in the Lodge believe all that shit. The Rapture, Armageddon, Apocalypse, Second Coming, all that.'

'They wouldn't be alone. New Zealand has its fair share of religious freaks. There's some up and down either side of the valley. Even rumours about you. Each to their own, I say.'

'But they're not are they?'

'What?'

'To their own. They're not just moving in to the area, they're seizing it like it's the Promised Land.'

'What makes you think that?'

It's the first time I've seen him look vulnerable. Scared even. 'I don't know, but they're fucking relentless, man. One bloke quoting from the Bible and speaking in tongues while his mates stomp the shit out of you. And all to a Bob Marley soundtrack.'

The Marley track? 'Exodus'. Thomas goes his not so merry way with my promise and warning in his ears. No feuds. If he wants to respond to what must have been a systematic beating at the hands of Cunningham and his stooges, he needs to do it officially and make a complaint. In turn I will bring in the big guns if that's what it takes to rein these people in. But it has to stay within the rules; rules are all we have left.

'That's the thing,' says Thomas, climbing back into his ute. 'If you believe in the End Times, like these jokers do, then the only rules are the ones you write yourself.'

It feels like that often these days. Like the rules have changed or even no longer count. By one o'clock I'm getting antsy sitting at my desk scrolling through circulars and other electronic Head Office guff and by quarter to two I'm worried. Latifa should have been back long since. I've tried contacting her on radio and mobile. Nothing. So it's in the patrol car and out to the Trout Hotel in Canvastown in record time. The police helicopter and the Marlborough–Nelson rescue chopper are on alert; if Latifa has fallen or been injured in some way, we need to act quickly. The rescue helicopter is busy collecting a mountain biker off the Queen Charlotte Track, a weekly occurrence at certain times of the year. Laurie, the coffee van guy outside the Trout, tells me he saw Latifa head up the other side of the river on Tapps Road a good four hours ago.

'And she didn't come back out?'

'Nah, I'd have noticed.'

Tapps Road, running parallel to Wakamarina Road, follows the river but on the far side. It's much rougher and unsealed most of the way. After a few kilometres it's blocked off for forestry by a padlocked barrier. Latifa had organised to collect a spare key and lock up behind her going in and coming out. Not having time for such niceties I snap the padlock, chuck the boltcutters on the passenger seat and shoot through. The track weaves through sections of logged, and yet to be logged, plantation land. Both are eerie in their own way, lifeless and alien. Along the way, there is evidence of wild pigs: mounds of earth and trampled undergrowth. And of hunters too, ATV tracks and discarded collateral kill. Latifa's car is parked in a clearing at the corner of which is a walking track that will take her up the hill opposite Gary's and my water tanks. The car is locked. I open it with my spare key and check the boot. She's taken her pistol but left the shotgun.

'Latifa?'

No answer. Collect the shottie and ratchet it. If she got lost, or stuck, or injured, why hasn't she activated her alarm? Starting the climb up the track, it gets pretty steep pretty quick and I'm having to stop often to catch my breath. My thighs are burning and I'm sweating. From here on in, surely she should be in earshot.

'Latifa?'

Climbing higher, the dark dead world of pines gives way to native vegetation and trees. Almost immediately there's more bird life and noise, sun and breeze. But it's also more overgrown outside the management of forestry. Vines snake across the track, and in the end the trail disappears and it's a matter of wading through whatever spaces show themselves.

'Latifa?'

Looking back down the hill through gaps in the trees and the vegetation, I can see the red roof of my house, the top of my green water tank and, over to the left, Gary's tin roof. She has to be near, has to be in hearing distance.

'Latifa, it's me. Where are you? You okay?'

There's nothing to show which direction she took. No track. No trampled or broken bushes. All I can go from is the line of sight back down the hill, that sweet spot where you can see both the bottom of my water tank and Gary's, and take them both out from the one position. So that's the direction I choose, checking my view down the hill, edging towards that spot. It's becoming more and more dense, tangled, hard to move through. How the hell did Latifa do it? Or the shooter for that matter?

Just over to the left, there seems to be more light, more space. And a noise. Stop, strain to hear it again.

A groan, strangled, gasping.

Breaking my way through to the clearing, I can't see anything. The noise again. Then I see it. A tree with a wire, some legs, blood. Arms flailing. Latifa is curled around the base of the trunk. Face covered in blood, her eyes are bulging, she's caught in a snare meant for a large animal; a pig or deer. The cord is strong thick aircraft wire, the type that moves parts around in the wings and elsewhere and gives you the confidence to keep buying those air tickets. It's killing Latifa. The more she struggles, the tighter it gets. She can't speak, the snare is too tight around her neck.

I try to calm her. My knife won't cut through this. I need the boltcutters from the car but she'll be dead by the time I get there and back again. Latifa's hands are free, why didn't she trigger her alarm? Then I see it's been snipped cleanly from her uniform. This is no accident.

Latifa hisses in agony. Face and lips turning blue. I try to examine how the snare is working, see if there's a way of loosening it without cutting through. A bolt and washer lock, beyond the ken of the average wild beast, and beyond Latifa's reach, but if I can unscrew that then we're in business. She grips my arm. Panic in her eyes.

The washer is screwed tight and my hands are sweaty. Latifa is dying while I fumble with these bits of metal.

'Hold on,' I plead. 'Just hold on.'

The light is fading from her, like when the sun slips behind the mountain in winter. Her grip on my arm loosens.

'Hold on.'

Bit by bit, it's coming. Moments later Latifa is disentangled and breathing freely again. A drink from my water bottle, some deep steadying breaths.

'What happened?'

Another gulp. Her lower lip trembles. More deep breaths. 'I got hit from behind, side of the head. Next I know I'm trussed to a tree with this thing around my neck.'

'Can you describe the attacker?'

Another pause. 'He wore a ski mask. About four, five centimetres shorter than you, similar build. He had a handgun. Held it to my head. Right-handed.'

'Did he say anything?'

'Nothing.'

'Clothing. Smell. Anything particular? A way of moving?'

'Cigarette breath.' She describes generic dark outdoors tramper gear. Macpac labels.

'Hands?'

'Average size. Gloved. But thin gloves, like cyclists wear.'

'And he cut away your alarm.'

'Yes.' She lowers her gaze. 'Felt me up. Dirty bastard.'

'Anything else?'

'No. He left when he heard you shouting down the hill.'

He's not long gone but still he could be anywhere. I'm not game to leave Latifa to go looking for him in that dense tangle of bush. We discuss bringing the chopper in. Latifa doesn't want to. She's able to walk back to the vehicle. The blood on her face is superficial from when she fell after the first blow. She doesn't want to cause a fuss.

'He left you to die.'

Fiercely back at me. 'You think I don't know that?'

'How did he know you'd be up here?'

She shrugs. 'Saw me come this way? Followed me?'

'So he knew where you were going and why.'

'He's our water-tank shooter?'

'Not your average hick playing at target practice.'

Latifa sips again from the water bottle. 'What's his point?'

My mind returns to my encounter with Thomas earlier. This attack on Latifa has Cunningham written all over it. En route and back in mobile range I call DS Will Maxwell to see if he can spare some uniforms from the murder enquiry to come and collect Latifa's car while I take her down to the hospital in Blenheim for a check-up.

'Sure,' he says when I explain why. 'Know who's behind it?'

'Got some ideas.' The gist follows.

'We need to nail them to the floor. Bastards.'

'Proof might be a problem.'

'Worry about that later, Nick.'

It's tempting but rules are rules. Aren't they? It's a promise I made to myself, and Vanessa, after my flouting of them put my own son in peril not so long ago. Except Brandon Cunningham seems to be making up his own. Driving back from Blenheim after Latifa's been checked and had her cuts and abrasions cleaned up, I realise I've forgotten my own appointment with the Havelock GP and now they'll be closed for the day.

'So where to from here?' Latifa is playing cool and tough but the look in her eyes tells me she's unmoored, caught in the undertow. I hate seeing her like this.

'Let's get you home.'

Face it. There was never a hope in hell of me keeping my promise to Vanessa. Bugger the rules. I broke them when I paid a visit to Gelder's shack to snoop around and I'm already in grief because of that. Now Cunningham is sequestering land and, according to Charlie Evans, firing machine guns in rural NZ, and I think he's behind the attacks on Latifa and Thomas, and the water-tank snipings.

To hell with him. If he's looking for trouble, he's found it.

8.

Neither DC Keegan nor the Blenheim Commander are prepared to authorise the deployment of the Armed Offenders Squad on Cunningham at the Lodge.

'There's no proof, Nick. His lawyer will scream blue murder if we go in with the ninjas.'

'What about the machine guns?'

'Are you sure your old farmer friend isn't imagining things? Some of those rapid-fire semi-automatics can sound scary but they are still legal.'

'What are civilians doing with weapons like that?'

'Ask the politicians and gun lobby. The fact remains.'

Static and hiss. Is it the mobile reception or my state of mind? 'The land stealing, Charlie's broken fence?'

'That's a civil matter, Nick.'

She's right, I know that. 'Cunningham's playing us for fools. He can't be allowed to get away with attacking one of our own.'

'If it was him.' Keegan cups her hand over the phone and sends someone away. 'Look, what happened to Rapata was an outrage, but we have to do this by the book. Gather evidence, by all means we can invite Cunningham in for another conversation, but we do this right or we don't do it at all.'

The investigation into the attack on Latifa is to be run out of Nelson. To be fair it's probably a good idea; my eyes are clouded by red mist and Will Maxwell has enough to contend with. 'Is there any intelligence on Cunningham we need to know of? Surely he's come to the attention of the US authorities?'

'I'll ask around. In the meantime you need to stay calm, keep an open mind, and let us investigate the assault on Latifa diligently.'

The insistent beep of call waiting. I sign off and let her take it. There's been a sprinkle of rain overnight and the breeze is fresh with pine and salt. It's low tide and the mudflats shimmer in the weak sunlight. Leaving home this morning, Vanessa was unhappy about my missed medical appointment and worried, both for me and Latifa.

'Whatever's out there, it's toxic.'

The doctor is not due back in town until tomorrow but I've secured a replacement appointment and promise to be at this one. It's first thing so there's less chance of me being waylaid. Latifa has been ordered to take leave for a few days. She didn't want to, and fiancé Daniel is not due back until the weekend. Has she even told him about the attack? Rather than go nuts on her own at home, she's gone to stay with a friend near the marae. Steve from Traffic is helping me out and he's on SH6 doing what he does best.

There's no end of things to be getting on with. I could be working my way through the list of plumbing jobs Bruce Gelder did before he died. Or looking into the identity of my half-corpse from Butchers Flat. Or signing up for Occ Health and Safety seminars and collating local crime stats to feed to the volume crime intelligence bods. But all I want to do is beat the crap out of Brandon Cunningham and send him packing.

Intelligence.

Maybe I can do some of my own intel gathering while waiting for official word from DC Keegan. Plugging in his name and pressing 'search', I find a plethora of American Brandon Cunninghams on Facebook, Twitter, Instagam, LinkedIn, college sports, real estate and so on. I check the images for him but his pic doesn't show up. Apply a few more filters, some racial and geographical profiling.

Still nothing. He stays off social media. He doesn't get himself in the papers. How does somebody who, over here at least, revels in getting in people's faces manage to keep his own off the internet? I'm going to have to be patient and wait for DC Keegan to come up with the kind of stuff you don't find on Google.

And then something does catch my eye. The search engine has picked up the 'Brandon' and 'Cunningham' parts but because they appear as a hyphenised surname the story is way down on page six of the matches. The *Argus Leader*, Sioux Falls, South Dakota: Gerald Brandon-Cunningham bids farewell to his colleagues in Minnehaha County Sheriff's Office. Deputy Brandon-Cunningham was leaving to spend more time with his family, in particular his teenage daughter who was recently diagnosed with leukaemia. Sheriff Davis wished his deputy well and hoped the Lord would bless him and his family at this tragic and difficult time. Thoughts and prayers et cetera. And there he is, my Brandon Cunningham, shaking hands sombrely with Sheriff Davis at the leaving do. A daughter with leukaemia: the last thing I expected or wanted was to be feeling any sympathy for the bastard.

That's it. As far as I can see he doesn't appear before or since. It's a remarkable achievement in this day and age. Some disgraced celebrities would pay a fortune to disappear from the internet like that. Is that what's happened? Has he been professionally wiped from cyber history with the *Argus Leader* story a missed speck of dust? If so, why? Or perhaps he really is just a nobody who managed to never get noticed. No, I don't buy it. The internet is full of nobodies, people make a lucrative career out of it. Nowadays you have to work hard to avoid getting noticed.

The news about his daughter has blunted the flint of my anger. The need to beat his brains out is less urgent. Maybe I can wait for more information, for more evidence. Forensics have the snare which almost garrotted Latifa, and have taken casts of foot and tyre prints in the vicinity. I can sit and wait for them and for DC Keegan's intel probe. Maybe the Nelson Ds will do it all for me.

To take my mind off it, I go back to the Mummy and an email waiting for me from Professor Bardawi. The DNA matches that of Karel Havelka, the semi-retired do-gooding meddler from Blenheim. Specimens of the missing man's DNA had been taken from a comb and toothbrush when he disappeared. I'm going to have to visit his widow to give her the news.

Since Karel Havelka went missing his wife, now widow, has developed early onset dementia and lives in a nursing home just down the road from their house in Springlands, Blenheim. It's a cruisy forty-minute drive from Havelock south and east through rolling green hills, cow pasture and vineyards. Maria Havelka is a striking looking woman, a picture of health and wellbeing, the kind you see on ads for retirement funds and Rhine cruises. Immaculately dressed, she's made up as if she's heading out to afternoon tea with friends. But she isn't going anywhere and she hasn't a clue who I'm talking about.

'Karel?'

'Your husband, Mrs Havelka.'

'Who?'

'Maybe if you come back tomorrow morning.' The nurse checks her watch. 'She's sometimes better first thing, after her medication.'

'Do I know you?' Mrs Havelka is peering closely at me.

I smile. 'I'll pop back tomorrow.'

'Karel was always tilting at windmills. I knew it would get him into trouble one day.' Her eyes fill with tears. 'He's dead, isn't he?'

She's back with us, but for how long? 'I'm sorry.'

'That Māori boy. The father. Was it him?'

'We don't know.'

'When are they coming?'

'When are who coming?'

'My daughter and her husband. We're going out to lunch.' It's half past three. As far as I know from the records, her daughter lives in Dunedin, the other end of the South Island.

The nurse gives me a signal that time's up. 'They might have been delayed, Maria. I'll check.'

Maria Havelka sits up straight in her chair and shakes my hand demurely in farewell.

'Does the daughter visit often?' I ask the nurse on our way back down the corridor.

'Never.'

The professor's full report is in my inbox on my return. Havelka was executed with a single shot through the back of the head as he was kneeling. His body was then cut in half with a chainsaw.

'The ligature marks?' I ask over the phone.

'They're real. As to where they fit into the chain of events? I'm unable to say.'

There are also traces of seed pods and other vegetation on the body which, according to the flora expert, suggest he was killed somewhere else and then dumped at Butchers Flat.

'Any suggestions where?'

'She believes that some of the specimens are only likely to be found within the reserve at Pelorus Bridge or maybe from other national parks in the region, say Kahurangi or Nelson Lakes.'

'That's a big area.'

'Can't be any more specific at this stage.'

'Thanks, Professor.'

I trot down the road to the Gelder murder room in the town hall to bring DSS Maxwell up to speed. He's dishing out jobs to his core team as I head his way. Gemma gives me a look which I'm unable to read right now.

'Poor bastard,' says Maxwell when I'm through. 'So we need to talk to that boy's dad again.' He checks his notes. 'Morgan Hopu.'

We know from the record he was interviewed at the time of Havelka's disappearance but, as anticipated, he was lawyered up and gave us nothing. 'Not going to be easy to pin this on him after all this time.'

'Chin up, Nick. As my mum used to say, where there's a Will there's a way.'

He's uncharacteristically upbeat. I take a punt. 'Progress with Gelder?'

'Of sorts.'

'Care to share?'

'Traces under the fingernails, the few he had left anyway. He put up a struggle.'

'Any matches?'

'Not yet.'

No, I'm thinking. There won't be unless and until you get samples from me. 'Anything else?'

'Keep you posted.'

Guessing from his smug look there's quite a bit else but he's holding it close. 'I might need somebody with me when I go and see Morgan Hopu. Anybody spare?'

'Take Gemma with you. She's keen to see how you work.'

Back home by just after six-thirty. I've arranged to visit Morgan Hopu at his lawyer's offices in Nelson tomorrow after my doctor's appointment. Gemma will take us from Havelock in her car.

'Everything okay, like with the doc?' she'd enquired.

'Purely routine. Meet you outside the town hall here at nine.'

Vanessa asks about my day as we crack open a local pinot noir so I give her the gist.

'How's Latifa bearing up?'

'Brave face but she's rattled. Anyone would be.'

'And you don't know who did it?'

'I have my suspicions.'

'Look where that got you with Gelder. Don't go off half-cocked, Nick. You made us a promise.'

Paulie wanders in from feeding the chooks. 'What promise?'

'Not to get you a puppy for your birthday. You know I hate dogs.'

'Not funny, Mum. Can Mim sleep over Saturday?'

'Sleep over?' Vanessa and I lock eyes. 'I thought you were just going to invite her for an after-school play?'

'Sleep over's better.'

'Is her grandad okay with that?'

'Michael? Yeah. Sure.'

'And her mum?' asks Vanessa.

'Of course!'

'So what did you have in mind?'

'You make yummy food. We watch videos, eat pizza.' A shrug. 'Sleep over.'

'Got it all worked out haven't you?'

'Pancakes for brekky. Ice cream, blueberries.'

'Her grandad and mum aren't able to share the drop-off or pickup duties with us?'

'Sheesh, Dad. Want me to have friends or not?'

Vanessa smothers a giggle.

'Yes, but …'

'But nothing. They prob'ly have stuff to do.' He gives me a warning frown. 'Important stuff.'

Well that settles it.

Later, with Paulie in bed, Vanessa snuggles up to me on the couch.

'I suppose it's nice that Mim's folks are happy to pack her off to our place for a night?'

'Of course it is,' I say. 'It's just what Paulie needs. Isn't it?'

'I hope it's not some cruel game. I read a thing recently about these disgusting guys who were competing to bed the ugliest girls. Preying on their need for affection, for acceptance. People can be … I don't know.'

'They're only kids, maybe we should take it at face value?'

'There's some twisted kids out there, age no barrier.'

'Jeez, I thought cops had a bad attitude to humanity.'

'They do. Especially you.' She punches my arm. 'Okay, maybe it is a pretty yucky thought.' Stroking my arm where she hit it. 'Any funny turns today? Forgetfulness, whatever?'

'No. All good. And I'm seeing the doc first thing.'

'Want me to come? It's just round the corner from school. I could organise cover.'

'No need. It'll be fine.'

'Yeah, you're right.' She doesn't sound convinced.

'Really. It will.'

'Cuppa tea?'

'Sure.'

I see her reflection in the kitchen window as she flicks on the kettle. Staring blankly out into the dark night.

9.

The doctor is very English, a home counties accent but not overly posh. I can imagine her playing hockey with extra determination to compensate for her perceived lack of good breeding. She seems businesslike and capable and this isn't going to be an easy run.

'So tell me what happened.'

Are doctors like priests? Is the Hippocratic Oath the same as the Sacrament of Confession? Can you spill all and count on them to hold your secrets dear? Perhaps not. 'I was at work, I'm a police officer …'

'That accounts for the uniform,' she says with a half-smile.

'Yes, right. I was carrying out a routine property search.'

'This was when?'

I give her the date and an approximate time. 'And I must have slipped on something, banged my head.'

'Where?'

'In this shed …'

'I meant where on your head.'

'Oh. Here.'

She inspects it. 'Nothing much more than a bump now. Skin isn't broken. Doesn't appear serious but we can have it X-rayed or scanned.'

'And that's all I can remember until the following morning.'

'Complete blank?'

'Yes,' I lie.

'But you remembered your name, your way home, your family, all of those things?'

'Yes.'

'And you've had no similar symptoms since?'

'No.'

'Have you been under any particular stress lately?'

'No more than usual.'

'How's your sex life?'

'Fine, thanks.'

'Active, vigorous?'

'Sometimes.'

A few more questions. How many fingers is she holding up. Three. What day is it today? Wednesday. A torch shone in both eyes. Walk up and down and stand on one leg. Asking about the diet and alcohol consumption.

'We'll arrange some blood tests and a CT scan.'

'That sounds serious.'

'Routine.' She says it the way I describe enquiries into people I intend to nail. 'It sounds like TGA – transient global amnesia – not uncommon and sometimes you hear no more of it. It can be brought on by stress, vigorous sexual activity, a fall or blow to the head, sudden immersion in cold water, things like that. The scan will tell us more and I'd like to check your cholesterol levels in case you're thinking of having a stroke.' She taps at her keyboard and gives me a slip of paper and a dismissing smile.

'That's it?'

'Get the blood tests done, the addresses are on the back of that form. We'll send you an appointment for the scan and a follow-up chat with a neurologist.'

'Neurologist?'

'They're better at reading CT scan results than I am.'

Gemma is waiting outside in her Holden Commodore as I get to the town hall. She winds down the window. 'You right to go?'

Not waiting for an answer she starts the car so I hop in and buckle up. 'Morning.'

'Everything okay?'

'Just a check-up. The older you get, the longer they take.' It's nippy in the car and she's got the fan going full blast. 'Hot flush?' I enquire. 'You seem so young.'

'Just been for a run.'

As we head along SH6 west of Havelock, the tide is low and swamp birds peck at the Pelorus Sound mud. White clouds hang on the hills. It's going to be another glorious day. There's a companionable silence as the kilometres tick down passing Canvastown. My mind floats over several neurologically catastrophic scenarios.

'So what do you know about Morgan Hopu?' Gemma turns the aircon down a notch from Antarctic to Invercargill.

'Not much.' We're crossing Pelorus Bridge. Tourists are taking selfies with a backdrop of the gorge, the exquisite river and the rock pools. Was it somewhere in among that small oasis of native bush that Karel Havelka met his death? 'The file suggests a bog-standard bikie hoodlum with the usual tattoos and charge sheet.'

'A changed man since his son's death, apparently.'

'Getting your pound of flesh from the fella who did it would probably help dim the hurt. Utu, I think they call it.'

'Has Constable Rapata been educating you?'

A sideways glance. I'm not sure I like her tone. 'So you've read Hopu's file and the background on Havelka. How do you want to play this?'

'The boss told me to take a back seat. You're in charge, he says. A hotshot from way back.'

'His words?'

'More or less.' Gemma slows for some road works. A grader smoothing out the over-used alternate route after the Kaikoura earthquake that blocked one of the main north–south arteries. 'What if Hopu just says nah, wasn't me?'

'He probably will and he probably won't be lying. He could get any of a dozen of his eager young lieutenants to do the job.'

Gemma finger waves at the all-clear from the road works traffic guy. 'So maybe this is a waste of time?'

'Tell that to Mrs Havelka.'

'From what I hear she's forgotten she ever had a husband.'

Gemma must have been doing her homework.

'The least we can do is have the conversation with him,' I tell her. 'Tick the boxes.'

'That's the spirit.'

'What?'

'Maxwell said you'd make a good detective.'

Morgan Hopu is smaller than I expected but the resemblance is immediately apparent.

'Are you related to Thomas Hemi?'

'My baby half-brother.' He releases my hand from a bruising grip. 'Different dads. How do you know him?'

'He's my neighbour. Give or take a few kilometres.'

'He was always the smart kid, bit religious there for a while. Some of us get God, others get *Goodfellas*.' He laughs, it's an open, honest chortle. 'Thomas went his way, I went mine. Sometimes we catch up; Christmas, weddings, hangis, tangis.'

Facial moko aside, he's dressed like any businessman, and sharper than his lawyer, who could do with a bit more grooming. Morgan acts respectful and charming to Gemma and we all take our seats around a boardroom table. The room is decorated with paintings of colonial occupation and endeavour. It's unclear whether they're there to reassure and impress Pākehā clients or as some private joke of Morgan's. Maybe both. Gemma puts her phone on record and asks if that's okay.

'No,' says Morgan's lawyer. 'Sorry.'

That's fine, I'm thinking, this is a waste of time anyway. 'But we will take notes,' I say.

Gemma flips open a pad, frowning in a way that suggests the lawyer is going to get his wheels clamped sometime soon. 'We found the body of Karel Havelka a few days ago.'

Morgan acts like the name doesn't ring a bell. Then he allows it to. 'Really? Foul play suspected?'

'Yes.'

'Terrible shame. Wife must be devastated.'

In her own way she is, she's clearly had her grief already and it must have sent her into early dementia. 'I was wondering if you could cast any light on the matter?'

'Light?' says Morgan. 'I gave a statement at the time. I was unable to help then and nothing has changed.'

'At the time you made repeated and witnessed threats against his life. You said you were going to make him pay.'

'The angry words of a bereaved father. Doesn't mean I carried them through.'

'But if anyone was capable of doing so it would be you.'

'I object to your …'

Morgan pats his lawyer's arm. 'Possibly. But the fact is, I didn't.'

And that's all he needs to keep saying until and unless we get some hard evidence.

'Only half of the body was found. It would be closure and some comfort for the family if we could recover all the remains so he can be properly laid to rest.'

'Half?' says Hopu. 'That's barbaric. Who'd do something like that?'

'You're unable to help us?'

'Wish I could, mate.'

I leave him my card. 'If you think of anything get in touch.'

'Will do.' He spins the card on the table then pockets it. 'Say hello to Thomas from me.'

Back over the ranges and around the high hairpin bends. The wind has risen and tugs the car towards the occasional precipice.

'That was a waste of time and petrol.' Gemma brakes suddenly to deter a tailgater. 'Back off, loser,' she snarls at the rear-view.

'But not unexpected.'

'What's your next move?'

'The boffins reckon Havelka was killed elsewhere, traces of native plants on him that you only find in nature reserves and national parks these days.'

'He volunteered on some conservation thing at Pelorus Bridge. Save the bats or whatever.'

'Maybe we should drop in on the way back?'

'You're in charge.'

When we get there we find the ranger's office shut. The café owner tells us he's on leave and anyway the bat volunteers are coordinated out of someone's house in Nelson. 'But feel free to take a look out back if you want.'

Out back in a lean-to shed there's an array of rusty medieval-looking trapping equipment, jars of dried-up peanut butter, and an old fridge with soft apples on one shelf and what looks like beef jerky on another. Gemma wrinkles her nose. 'Smells like a crime scene.'

There's a name and a mobile number scrawled on a grubby whiteboard. I make a note and we hit the road back to Havelock.

'You're remarkably well-informed about this case considering you were only seconded to it late yesterday.'

Gemma squints into the rear-view at another tailgater. 'How do you mean?'

'Havelka's widow being ga-ga, Karel volunteering to save the bats. Not bad for somebody who was going to take the back seat.'

'I reviewed the case last night. I was keen to impress you.'

'Why?'

'DC Keegan reckons you're worth impressing.' I give her my poker face. If there's a subtext, she's hiding it well. 'Girls night out, every month. Informal mentorship over a few vodkas.'

'I don't recall seeing any information about Mrs Havelka or the bat project on the database.'

'I asked around. It's what detectives do. Why are you still in uniform, Nick?'

'That's my business.'

'Your wife is very loyal.'

'I think you need to step back a bit.'

'I did this course on body language a few months back. I don't think lying comes naturally to Vanessa, does it?'

'Meaning?'

'Monday night. You weren't home when you said you were. She's covering for you.'

'You've got quite an imagination. Need to watch that in detective work.'

We pull up outside the town hall and I start to walk up the street to my office. Gemma zaps the car with her key fob. 'You won't object to providing a DNA sample to help us eliminate you from our enquiries?'

'Be my guest.'

'I'll be there with a swab in twenty minutes once I've brought Maxwell up to speed. Put the kettle on. Tea, white with one.'

Latifa is waiting for me. In civvies, as she should be, she's still got the rest of the week off.

'Couldn't stay away?'

'Look.' She spins her laptop screen my way. Grainy night images: two figures creeping around the side of the police house, Latifa's home, checking windows and doors, urinating against a wall, leisurely, taking their time.

'When was this?'

'Last night. Got a notification on my mobile. Came in to check it out.'

'Recognise them?'

She freezes a frame. Zooms in. One of the young men startled by a sudden noise turns his head and his face is caught fully by the camera. 'Jaxon Hemi.'

'Thomas's boy?'

'Pay him a visit?'

'S'pose so. Can you call ahead and check his whereabouts?' Latifa gets on the phone as Gemma comes through the door with her DNA swab kit. We retire to the kitchen where I explain the cuppa will have to wait. She takes the sample, a curiously intimate affair, up close and staring into my eyes as she pokes the white stick in my mouth. Her warm breath caresses my cheek and it's not unpleasant.

'Thanks,' she says finally.

'My pleasure.'

She smiles. 'Mine too. Maxwell wants to know what you plan next with Havelka.'

Behind Gemma, Latifa summons me with a lift of the chin.

'I'll work on a strategy this afternoon. Fill him in later.'

'And the plumbing jobs?'

'In hand.' I gesture at her DNA kit. 'When can I expect to hear?'

'We'll come knocking. Trust me.'

Back up the valley. Out the front of the Lodge there's a couple of vans, a digger, people standing around drinking and smoking. Latifa's hands grip the steering wheel tighter.

'Pity it wasn't them. Would have given us an excuse to go in there.'

'Maybe the two things aren't connected. The prowling and the attack on you.'

'Maybe.'

'You going okay?'

'Yep.'

'What's the latest with Daniel?'

'Back this weekend.' A smile. 'Can't wait.'

'I bet.' As we pass our place I'm feeling flat. The logging is creeping further up the valley and goldminers are sniffing like blowflies around a wound. The Lodge is developing a permanent bad smell too. It feels like we're living in a poisoned paradise. It's tempting to cut and run but I can't for the life of me think where to. And what would Vanessa and Paulie say? They need stability and here's me tapping into my flight instinct again.

'What's Jaxon playing at?' Latifa changes gear crossing Dead Horse Creek. An oncoming camper van nearly cleans us up taking the sharp bend too close. 'Dickhead!' yells Latifa through her open window. She gets the finger in reply.

'Probably best to let me ask the questions when we get there, okay?'

'Whatever.'

It's a steep driveway up to Thomas Hemi's farm. The fences either side are sturdy and the whole place is well-maintained, orderly. He's seen and heard us coming and is waiting on his front verandah, Jaxon by his side. The young bloke is a chip off the old block; strong physique, ready smile, no doubt a heartbreaker in the making.

We all shake hands. Thomas seems to be still carrying himself carefully after the beating, and the bruises are colouring nicely. Ruth, his wife, appears from the kitchen door and stands proprietorially behind her son. Good genes all round. They're a handsome family.

'Jaxon, can we have a word?'

'What's this about?' asks Ruth.

'Police business,' says Latifa. 'We can do it down the station if he likes?'

The two women face off, dark glares at three metres.

'No need,' I say smiling. 'Just a chat. You okay with that, Jaxon?'

'Yeah.'

'Want me to sit in?' asks Thomas.

'Jaxon is only sixteen and entitled to have an adult present,' Ruth says.

'We know. That okay with you, Jaxon? Want Dad to sit in?'

A nervous squint. 'Okay.'

We adjourn to a bench picnic table along the wide verandah. Ruth leaves us with a glower. Thomas offers us a concoction of Dettol and baby oil to keep the sandflies away as we settle in. He notices the abrasions on Latifa's face, the scar on her neck. 'What happened to you?'

'My job. What happened to you?'

'My business.'

I slide a photo printout from the security footage across the table. 'That you, Jaxon?'

He shrugs. 'Yeah.'

'Midnight, last night. Can you explain what you were doing on private police property in Havelock at that time?'

'Police property?'

'It's the official police house,' said Latifa. 'My home.'

'Yeah?' said Jaxon.

'You told us you were staying with a mate near the marae,' said Thomas. 'You shouldn't lie to me, boy.'

I tap the photo. 'So what were you doing?'

'Lookin' around, needed a piss.'

'There's public toilets less than fifty metres away.'

'Locked by then and I couldn't wait.'

Thomas Hemi isn't impressed. 'Stop bein' a dickhead, Jax. Answer the man.'

'We thought there might be something worth liftin'. Somebody in the pub said the place had been empty a few days.'

'Stealing?' says Thomas. 'You wanted to steal something?'

'My mate did. I was just along for the laugh.'

'Which mate?'

'Nobody you know.'

'Which mate?'

A sigh. 'Young guy from the Lodge. Yank. New at school.'

Thomas puts a large hand on his son's chin and turns it his way for full attention. 'What you doin' hanging out with idiots like that? And what you doin' in the pub? You're underage. Jeez, Jax.'

'Not much else to do round here.'

'Which guy from the Lodge?' I ask. 'Name?'

'Mel. Look we didn't take anything. The place was locked up, nothing to steal. We just looked around that's all.'

'Mel who?' says Latifa.

A shrug. 'Just Mel.'

'What about the other nights?' I name the dates.

'Don't know what you're talking about. Only went there once.'

'So where did you stay last night?' asks Thomas.

'At Mel's. Plenty of room there. His uncle drove us to school this morning.'

'The phone calls?' says Latifa.

'What phone calls?'

'Do you have a mobile?'

'Yeah, but it doesn't work up here, only in town.'

He puts it in Latifa's snapping fingers. 'You'll get it back when we're finished.'

'Anything else?' asks Thomas.

'Given what happened to you, I'd be advising Jaxon to keep away from anybody connected with the Lodge.' I turn to the lad. 'Seriously.'

'Sorry to drag you all the way up here for nothing, officers.' Thomas thumbs over his shoulder. 'Jaxon. Inside.'

'Believe him?' Latifa asks on the drive back down the valley. It's late afternoon now. The sun has slipped behind the hill near our place and there's a nip in the air. It'd make sense to be just dropped off at my gate but my car's still in town and it all gets a bit complicated. Besides, Latifa needs to talk.

'I think so. I don't think Thomas has raised a thief. Dickhead maybe but I'm prepared to put it down to his age.'

'Yeah, s'pose. The Lodge again, eh?'

'Jax and Mel don't seem to be connected to the phone calls and other prowlings.'

'Not Jaxon anyway. I checked his mobile number, it wasn't the one calling me.'

'Still too loose to be paying them a visit. We need to be rock solid.'

She shakes her head. 'Nah, Jaxon's placed Mel at the scene. Trespassing. That's enough for me to want to talk to them.'

'It dobs Jaxon in though. Mel will know he can't trust him. Maybe Jaxon can be useful to us? Pick up some gossip from Mel. Judging by the look on Thomas's face, the boy's in big trouble.'

'You're looking to use a sixteen-year-old boy as a spy?'

Busted. 'Yeah, you're right. Bad idea.'

'That's not what I said.'

At the gates of the Lodge, there's activity. The digger we saw on the way up is munching away at the road. A woman with a Stop/Go sign waves us down.

'What's going on?' I ask through the window.

'Traffic calming.'

The logo on the vehicles and work uniforms belongs to one of the many private companies subcontracting for the council and roads ministry. 'Seriously? This is Wakamarina Road. It doesn't get any calmer than this.'

'Just doing my job.' She gestures at a bloke talking on a mobile. 'Feel free to speak to the boss.'

'Back in a sec,' I say to Latifa and she turns off the engine. The boss notices my uniform and finishes his call. We shake hands. 'Must be a good phone, you don't normally get a signal here.'

'Great isn't it?' He's as bouncy as Tigger. 'The folk in the Lodge put up their own relay tower. Sweet as.'

Yeah. Sweet as. 'And did they request the traffic calming?'

'Word from on high, priority.' Nose tap. 'They must be well-connected.'

'On high where, ministry? Council?'

'Both. Fast-tracked apparently.'

'It's a joke. No way this is a priority. Half of the South Island roads closed down due to earthquake, the rest potholed from overuse, and this is what they put you on?'

'Ours not to reason why. Money talks, eh?'

'Rationale?'

He shrugs. 'That's a nasty sharp bend just there, maybe it's encouraging people to slow down.'

'That can be done with a sign. It looks to me like the road is being narrowed down to a single lane.'

'And a speed bump.'

'Unreal.'

'Should be finished by tomorrow, or day after, all things being equal. Anything else I can do for you, officer?'

Latifa is fuming when I get back in. 'Typical. Money talks? Too right it does. Maybe they should try spending some of their own.'

'Hmmm?'

'Money. Getting us ratepayers and taxpayers to cough up for whatever it is they're planning.'

Yes, that's annoying. But my mind is jumping from Charlie Evans' reports of what sounded like automatic or semi-automatic gun fire to a scenario where, with a strategically narrowed road, we'll have even more difficulty getting a tactical assault vehicle in there. Methinks they're preparing for a siege.

And who's going to listen to a crackpot conspiracy theory like that?

10.

There's nothing we can do about the Lodge. All they're doing is home renovations, basic infrastructure: a firing range bulldozed into Charlie Evans' property, a mobile phone signal booster tower, reinforced gates, and the latest as I drove past this morning, two vicious-sounding bull mastiffs chained to the gateposts. None of it criminally illegal – Charlie would have to argue the boundary change in a civil court – and some of it even council sanctioned, courtesy of the ratepayers. I feel like one of those tiny neighbouring countries watching as China built those military bases out of reclaimed sand in the South China Sea. Gaslighted at first by accusations of paranoia, and then left only with the cold comfort of being able to say "see, told you so" once it all goes pear-shaped. But so what if those nutcases believe in the Second Coming and want to turn their property into Fort Knox? They can stay behind their tall gates, play with their guns, read their bibles and we can all get on with living in the real world. Except I just know that one day soon they will surely drag the rest of us into their delusion. Until then I've got stuff to do.

Like the mysteries of Karel Havelka, Gelder's plumbing jobs, and whether or not I was involved in the latter's death. Gemma will be coming back at me soon if my DNA is connected to the victim. Do I come clean about my lost hours and trust all to the investigative process or batten down the hatches? At the office, Jessie James from the *Journal* is patiently waiting outside on her Vespa, scrolling through her phone.

'Morning,' she says.

'No comment.'

'Funny, ha-ha. I'm not after anything for the murder in the Four Square, somebody from Christchurch is on that, like it's too big a story for little me.'

'So?'

'So what's happening with that body you found up at Butchers?'

'Nothing much. You need to talk to the guy in charge of the investigation. He's down at the town hall.'

'DSS Maxwell just puts me through to the media department and they seem to have a policy of only ever speaking to the media when it suits them.'

'I can't help you, sorry.'

An early wintry blast sweeps up the main drag. Jessie zips her puffer jacket up tighter and adjusts her specs. 'Is it true there was bad blood between you and the Four Square victim, Gelder?'

'I thought you were interested in the Butchers Flat story?'

'I'm interested in everything that happens around here. That's why I'm a small-town reporter with no plans to go anywhere fast.'

'Can't help you. Maybe try the police media department?'

'Nick.'

'Sergeant Chester to you.'

'Jeez, you're not easy to be friends with.'

This from somebody who tried to fry my career just eighteen months ago. 'Jessie, I really can't help you. Both investigations are ongoing and of a sensitive nature. You need to speak to the people duly authorised to talk to you. Meanwhile I need to get on with my day.'

'Heard anything about those new people at the Lodge? A Doomsday sect they reckon. Like Jonestown or Waco.'

'No, nothing. But feel free to look into them if you want. We only have so many resources.'

'Ah.'

'What?'

'A reaction. Finally. You don't like them, do you?'

'To the best of my knowledge they have not committed any illegal acts.'

'Good enough for me.' She nods. 'I can usually count on your grudges to deliver me a story.' She revs up the Vespa. 'Thanks, Nick.'

Steve is out on traffic duty. Flick on the kettle and drop a bag into a mug. It was probably wrong to set Jessie James sniffing after Cunningham and his cronies. Maybe even negligent, they're shaping up as a dangerous and ruthless bunch. I call her mobile but she's out of range. Leave a message, she says. How to put this?

'Jessie those guys at the Lodge shouldn't be messed with. Feel free to look into them online or whatever. But you shouldn't approach them personally. Okay?'

She calls back a few minutes later as I'm squeezing my teabag out. 'They really have got you wound up, haven't they? Tell me more.'

'I can't. But trust me, this isn't a joke and they don't play nicely.'

'Okay,' she says, voice sober. 'Noted. Thanks.'

Duly warned, maybe she'll use her journalistic skills to uncover something we might not otherwise have found. That reminds me, Keegan said she'd find out what the spooks had to say about Cunningham.

'Somebody's getting back to me later today; an old colleague from Porirua. She went into SIS until she decided motherhood was more useful to society than being a secret agent.'

'Whatever you can get would be great.' I fill her in on the latest, including the traffic-calming, and lay out my conspiracy theory for inspection.

'Bit far-fetched don't you think?'

'I'd love to be wrong about them.'

'Generally I trust your instincts, Nick. However cockeyed. If there's any substance to this we'll act on it, believe me.'

'Okay.'

'Meanwhile that Havelka execution. I was telling you it reminded me of something?'

'Yep.'

'You've heard of the Whakakitenga Community?'

'West coast religious sect? Kind of Amish meets the Taliban. Been some scandals over the years?'

'That's the one. Loosely translated from *te reo* it's something about prophecy and revelations apparently. Mainly run and populated by white dudes. I investigated a homicide over that way a few years ago, five, six maybe. A Wellington-based mum had abandoned her family and run off to join the sect the previous year. She was found raped and stabbed in a motel in Westport.'

'What's that got to do with Havelka?'

'That's the thing. Six months later, the motel owner was killed, kneeling with an execution-style shooting in the back of the head. Nelson detectives caught the case. No arrests in either. I'll send you the database access codes and references for both homicides so you can check them out.'

This sounds even flimsier than my conspiracy theory. 'You think there's a connection?'

'Who knows? The timing and MO are strikingly similar. What do you think?'

Gift horses, who am I to be choosy? 'I'll follow it up. Thanks.'

'My pleasure. All of this could be at your fingertips if you joined us over here, Nick.'

Sometimes she has a way of saying things that can heat the blood. 'I'll bear that in mind.'

Shuffling and tapping noises at her end. 'Just got a text message from my Porirua friend. She's cancelled coffee. Looks like there'll be no news on your crackpots today. Watch this space.'

By now my tea has gone lukewarm. Sip, grimace, and open up the restricted database files on the west coast murders Keegan mentioned. Seven years ago, thirty-one-year-old Lucy McLernon, from a well-to-do Wellington family, had left her lawyer husband and their one-year-old son to join the Whakakitenga Community on the north-west coast of the South Island. Just over twelve months later she was found by housekeeping staff on a blood-soaked bed in Pine Lodge motel in Westport, eighty-odd kilometres away. Subsequent tests would show she'd been raped and stabbed. The wounds were notably vicious, a virtual gutting according to the pathologist. Lucy had run away from Whakakitenga six weeks earlier alleging instances of abuse. Whakakitenga had, in turn, alleged that she had been expelled for mental instability. For some reason she hadn't returned to her family in Welly's Oriental Bay. A local Westport GP confirmed that Lucy presented with bipolar symptoms, had been taking prescription anti-psychosis medication, and was due to see a psychiatric specialist in Christchurch the week following her murder. No arrests to date.

Six months later: winter in Westport and storms whipping the ocean. While photographing a spectacular sunset on Carters Beach, an Israeli tourist stumbled across the half-buried body of a middle-aged man. The unusually high tides had washed away the sand. He was facedown and there was a wound in the back of his head. The tourist, doing his OE gap year after army service, knew he was looking at a murder. The victim was Darren Robertson, manager of the Pine Lodge motel, reported missing by his wife two days earlier. From entry and exit angles the pathologist posited an execution scenario with Darren kneeling, shot, and then covered with sand where he lay. No arrests to date.

What connects the two Westport murders apart from coincidence? What, if anything, might connect Robertson's murder to Havelka's, apart from method? Stories from the past, other times and places. It all feels like a diverting sidetrack. Instead I call the number that was left on the bat savers' whiteboard and arrange to meet the volunteers coordinator at Pelorus Bridge for lunch. It more directly concerns Havelka, his pastimes, and his associates. In the meantime, back to the list of plumbing jobs Bruce Gelder was doing in the weeks before his grisly death. Try as I might, nothing returns to me for that Monday night at his shack. I recall a hypnotist we consulted once in Blenheim to try and retrieve a lost memory. Are things that desperate yet?

Dripping taps, burst pipes, wayward spas, tick them off. Nobody unduly pissed off with Gelder – sure he missed an appointment here and there but usually because he was tied up by a complication on an earlier job. He never overcharged his hours or fabricated unnecessary repairs. Some people found him personable, others could have done with less chat, and others more. Whatever got Gelder killed, I'm concluding, it wasn't his plumbing work. My mobile goes. DSS Maxwell.

'Reckon you could pop by for a chat, Nick?'

'Sure. What's up?'

'See you in five. I'll get the kettle on.'

Walking into the town hall is like walking into the saloon in Dodge; if there'd been a piano it would have stopped playing. Eyes track me across the big room, up the steps to Maxwell's backstage office. He and Gemma are waiting for me with a pot of tea, a plate of bikkies, and a printout of a forensics report.

'White and none. That right?' says Maxwell pouring.

'Cheers.'

'Have a Ginger Kiss.'

I take two. Might not be eating again for a while. 'What's new?'

'Hoping you can shed light on something for us.'

'Fire away.'

'What's your skin doing under Bruce Gelder's nails?'

'Ah.'

'That's it?' says Gemma. 'Ah?'

'The truth is, I don't know. Or rather, I can't remember.'

'Tell me,' says Maxwell.

Okay, here goes. It was sunset and I had pulled into a gateway just beyond the Lodge to brood about Cunningham's sucker punch and to fantasise about how it might have gone if, like Cher, I could turn back time. A few ciders in the Trout will do that. Maybe I shouldn't even have been driving. I was in the family ute on my way home and when Gelder went by he didn't realise it was me. And so, a safe distance behind, I followed. It was obvious where he was going and he had no business going up there on a Monday. His dredging days were weekends. Or maybe he had every right to go and potter in his shack. I couldn't leave it alone though. For sure he was up to something.

'So you had a bone to pick with him?' says Gemma.

'Yes, but I didn't intend to confront him.'

'Yet you obviously did.'

'Keep going, Nick,' says Maxwell, effectively shushing Gemma.

So I do. There's a track to a logging site just back from his block. I went up there and sat and waited for him to leave. After half an hour it was fully dark. Headlights went by. He was gone. I went down to have a look around, see what he was up to. It's a pretty basic place. No electricity or running water – apart from the river of course. A prefabricated shed, a camp fire, a pile of firewood and cleared trees. His dredging equipment, padlocked to a black beech.

'You remember all this from that night?' says Gemma, looking up from her notepad.

'Yes.'

'But you don't remember what happened?'

'I'm getting to that.'

They wait, and I continue. I had my torch. There were maps blu-tacked to the wall of the cabin: the river and the outline of where his claim lay. Photographs of the glory days: hard men with shovels and picks and a river full of detritus. A copy of *Gold in a Tin Dish*, the history of the Wakamarina gold rush, on an upturned milk crate next to a fold-out camp bed. A bar fridge with a few beers in the door, a tub of marge, some cheese going bluey-green. I can't see what he's come up here for, nothing surprises, what couldn't wait? Maybe he left something behind from the weekend: a watch, a mobile, a set of keys. How can I remember this kind of detail but not what happened next? But from around nine p.m. on Monday to early the next morning is a blank.

'Nothing?' says Maxwell.

'Nothing. I don't even know how I got home.'

'I find that hard to believe,' says Gemma.

'Don't blame you. I would too.'

'Let's try and work through it,' says Maxwell. 'To get your skin under his nails he had to come into contact with you. So you must have had an altercation of some sort.'

'Must have.'

'And if, as you claim, you have no memory of the rest of that evening then the altercation must have happened during that timeframe, perhaps at that location.'

'Maybe. Probably.'

'And you had injuries to your hands, knuckles,' says Gemma. 'Still not completely cleared I see.'

I examine my hands. 'Yes.'

'You're not making this easy, Nick.' Maxwell sighs. 'We really should arrest you or something.'

'It's your job,' I concede.

'We'll need to go through your house,' says Gemma. 'Talk to Vanessa and your son.'

'No.'

Gemma looks at Maxwell but he's giving nothing away. 'Your wife has misled the investigation. She knows you weren't home when you and she said you were. We could charge her.'

'Keep them out of this. I lied to her about when I got back and she believed me. Do whatever you want with me.'

'Boss?' she says to Maxwell.

'Get all this statemented officially. Get forensics up to Nick's home and back to this shack of Gelder's. How come we didn't have that place done already?'

Gemma reddens. 'We did. But there was no sign of struggle. No significant traces of others. It must have been cleared up.'

He looks at me. 'Was that you?'

'Might have been. Or it might have been him. Or the murderers. You said there were two, I seem to recall.'

'So where did you keep Gelder during Tuesday?'

'I didn't keep him anywhere. My memory is intact from Tuesday morning. However Gelder ended up in that coldroom in the Four Square is nothing to do with me.'

And that much he does believe. 'We'll have to suspend you until we can clear this up. I'll inform Keegan. You and the family will have to go into a hotel until we've finished with your house. Meantime if you remember anything, call me.' A shake of the head. 'Nick, I really don't need this.'

Who would? 'Can you make sure somebody feeds the animals and collects the eggs?'

Suspended. That probably means I shouldn't keep my appointment with the woman from the Pelorus Bridge bat savers. But I can go and have a pie anywhere I like, and the Pelorus café does good ones. It's hard to choose between the venison or the wild pork and kumara but eventually the latter wins out plus a flat white. I've phoned Vanessa and alerted her to the latest developments and that we're booked into the Havelock Motel.

'Bloody hell, Nick. Are you going to jail or what?'

'Don't know. Hope not.'

'Is there wi-fi at the motel? I need to be able to log on to the school system for marking.'

'According to the brochure, yes.'

'Paulie's going to be out of sorts again. You pick him up today, okay?'

'Sure.'

The bat woman rocks up as I'm scraping my last piece of pie through the tomato sauce. 'You wouldn't be eating that if you'd just cleared a possum trap.'

We shake hands. She's Jenny from Nelson, a sprightly seventy-year-old with a long tightly plaited grey pigtail. She orders a cheese scone and I join her in another coffee.

A polite delay until the food and drinks arrive. Some small talk and then down to business. 'So, Karel Havelka?'

'Bob.'

'Bob?'

'That's what he preferred to be called. People were always mispronouncing his name, deliberately or otherwise. Must have got sick of being called Carol. Besides I think he quite liked the idea of being a Bob.'

'Tell me about him.'

A thoughtful sip of coffee. 'To be honest he wasn't an easy man to like. Quite abrasive and overbearing. The word austere comes to mind. Very competitive, he chose the furthest, longest, toughest trapline and refused to share the load.'

'How do you mean?'

'Normally volunteers share a line and go out every other week or fortnight. Not him. He did his own, week in and week out. He didn't brook dissent, small-talk, or suffer fools gladly. Hell in committee meetings.'

'Bit of a loner?'

'Understating it. The man was an island, a sub-Antarctic one.'

'The day he disappeared, what do you remember?'

'Well that was the other thing. Nobody noticed until a few days later. He never signed in or out, he hated bureaucracy. So nobody gave it any thought until the police came calling.'

'His wife didn't raise the alarm?'

'Apparently not. It wasn't unusual for him to go off tramping in the bush for a few days on his own. Between you and me I'm not sure they got on that well.'

'The police searched along the trapline for him?'

'Yes, them and some Emergency Service volunteers and a few of us too. Nothing. No trace.'

'Did they bring in dogs, choppers?'

'Yes, far as I can remember.' She shakes her head. 'Executed you say? Who'd do a thing like that?'

'That's what I'm here to find out. Is there a map of his trapline? Maybe I could take a look along it.'

She digs one out of her backpack. 'Line M.' Traces her finger along it. 'Follow the fluoro pink ribbons through the trees. It'll take at least three hours.'

'I'll come back and do it another time. I need to get my son from school.'

'Can't imagine what you might find up there after all these years.'

'Me neither, but it's nice to be able to paint a picture.'

'Yes, I can see that.' She bites her lip, unsure of what to say next, or not sure if she should say it. 'Sometimes it seems so beautiful and peaceful in there. And that's what we're trying to protect. But now and again you come across a scene from the Inquisition with a garrotted possum or whatever and you wonder if you've actually become part of the problem.'

'Sorry mate, Mim can't come over this weekend.'

Paulie is upset at the change in plans. 'Why?'

'Like I said, we'll be staying in the motel for a few days. There won't be enough room. It's not a good time.'

'You promised.'

'I know but this is something we can't help. It's just until the end of the weekend, maybe less.'

A surly frown. 'When then?'

'Best to leave it until the weekend after.'

'That sucks.'

'Sorry, mate.'

'Why do the police want our house?'

'They just want to check something.'

'Who'll feed Spongebob and Squarepants?'

'All taken care of. Don't worry.'

'Mim's gunna hate me.'

'I doubt it.'

'That sucks.'

'You said that already.' Change topic. 'We'll have to buy dinner I suppose.'

'Yeah?' His eyes light up. 'Pizza?'

'Sure. Why not?'

Crisis over.

Under forensic supervision I've been allowed to extract toiletries and two changes of clothes for each of us plus Paulie's game console and headphones. Without them it would be a claustrophobic teeth-grinding few days in the motel room. As we come back down the valley road, Paulie is intrigued by the roadworks outside the Lodge.

'What's that for?'

'Traffic calming.' I try to explain what that means.

'Stupid,' he mutters. Fearing a relapse into the bad mood I divert him with pizza talk.

Vanessa is waiting for us when we check in.

'Got the keys already. Number six.' There's a queen bed plus a single shoved into the corner for Paulie. 'Cosy,' says Vanessa over-brightly.

I clap my hands. 'Early dinner and early night?'

'One out of two ain't bad,' says Vanessa, lifting her bag of school books. 'Where to?'

'Pizza,' says Paulie. 'Pub. Dad's paying.'

Vanessa smiles at me. 'Classy guy.'

Halfway through dinner there's a call from Latifa.

'What's going on? I heard you got suspended.' There's an unsaid 'again'. In her experience this is something I tend to make a habit of.

'How'd you hear?'

'They asked if I could come back in early to help Steve.'

'No need for that.'

'Not your call anymore. Spill.'

So I do. Lots of hmmms and yeahs like her colleague getting accused of murder is pretty run of the mill.

'Did you kill him?'

'I don't think so.'

'They'll figure it out. Anything I need to know?'

'Keep away from the Lodge, don't worry about the water-tank sniper, just focus on traffic and routine stuff. How are you feeling? You ready to come back yet?'

'Truth be told I'm getting sick of my mate's whining dog, and her boyfriend's just as bad.'

'Speaking of which, any word on Daniel?'

'Still due back this weekend.' A pause. 'Look, I'm fine, just sort yourself out, okay?'

'Will do.'

Back to pizza with the family. Paulie polishes off the last slice and I head to the bar to pay the bill.

'Officer. Good evening to you.'

It's Brandon Cunningham. He's got a young guy with him. 'Evening. Sorry I can't chat. Things to do.'

'Not going to introduce us to your lovely family?'

'No. See you around.'

He doesn't take the hint. Strolls over to our table and holds out a hand for shaking. He homes in on Paulie first. 'Hi there, big fella. I'm Brandon. What'd they call you?'

'Paul.' He holds out his hand, serious grown-up fashion.

'This is my nephew Melvyn. He's at the same school as you, I think. Say hi to Paul, Melvyn.'

Melvyn obediently says, 'Hi.'

I step closer. 'That's enough, Cunningham.'

'And you must be Mrs Chester. Vanessa? Is that right?'

'How do you know my name?'

'Small towns. Everybody knows everybody. That's why I love it here.'

Vanessa hurries Paulie up out of his seat and brushes past Cunningham in the narrow gap between wall and table. He makes no effort to move.

'Bless my soul, that's the best thing happened to me all day.'

Mel smirks.

We don't need any more dramas and that's precisely what Cunningham is trying to provoke. Paulie suddenly looks scared, like he's caught a whiff of something rotten or dead. 'We going now, Dad?'

'Yep.' I shepherd them out, my back tingling at unseen threats.

'Great to meet you folks,' says Cunningham. 'Until next time, huh?'

11.

It took a while to settle Paulie, and Vanessa was unable to concentrate on her lesson preparation. She woke extra early to head into school and do her work there. Not before she lanced me over her motel instant coffee.

'That guy is a dangerous creep. Really. You need to keep people like that out of our lives.'

'I'm sorry.'

'I mean it, Nick. I don't want him anywhere near us.' And then she surprises me with her vehemence. 'Keep him away.'

I've seen that same look in Latifa's eyes, in Thomas Hemi's, and now Vanessa's. Like an inoperable tumour took root somewhere deep inside and you can taste it in your saliva. After dropping Paulie at school, I decide today is as good a day as ever. Already suspected of murder, I may as well be hung for a sheep as a lamb. Pulling up outside the Lodge I'm aware that the tree camera will be watching. Wind down my window and look directly at it so they can see that, yes, it's me. I haven't handed my police issue Glock in, even though I'm suspended. Maxwell wouldn't expect me to be using it, or maybe he forgot, or doesn't care. It's on the passenger seat beside me. We don't bear arms routinely here in New Zealand, just on an as-needs basis. With Brit gangsters holding grudges against me I was given the nod to keep mine with me at all times. That particular threat might have receded a year ago but nobody has asked me to change my routines.

It doesn't take long. There's a loud buzz and a click and the big gates edge open. Two blokes step out, I recognise them from the hunting party that interrupted the filming at Butchers Flat. They're both wearing camos and sidearms, low on the hip Dakota-style, and they have growly dogs on leashes.

'Howdy,' I say.

'Can we help you, sir?' Crew cut, clean-cut. Got his henchman image from a comic book.

'Just popped by for a chat with Brandon. Is he home?'

'I don't think Mr Cunningham was expecting you.' His friend is a little more wild and woolly. A backwoodsman. A real Daniel Boone.

'That's the thing about the country. We just drop by. I mean we're practically neighbours.'

Daniel Boone's not interested. 'Come back another time, buddy. When you have an appointment.'

'Let him in.'

'A talking tree? Very Middle Earth. You guys are going to fit in well around here.'

They don't like my jokes. I lock my car, they make me chuck my gun in the boot, then they walk me up the steep driveway. One of the dogs turns out to be a softie and gives me a traitorous lick on the hand. Cunningham is waiting on his expansive front balcony. He looks freshly showered and shiny.

'Just been for a run up the hill. Beautiful up there. You can see the whole valley north and south. Coffee?'

'Sure.'

He dismisses the henchmen and invites me into the kitchen, which is big and neat as a pin, with a view of a semi-cleared pine plantation across the river. 'This is a pleasant surprise. I didn't expect to be seeing you again so soon.'

'Didn't you? Wasn't that the point of the stunt with my family?'

'Stunt? I was just being sociable. Sorry it got misconstrued.' There's the sound of gunshots. Individual cracks mixed in with repeated fire. 'Some of the boys over at the range. That bother you?' He pops a pod in his shiny coffee machine. Maybe his concern for the environment and landfill doesn't run so deep after all.

'Not if you've got the paperwork. Particularly for the automatics.'

'Semi. That's what we love about this country. It's nearly as easy to bear arms here as it is in Texas. Want me to get those permits for you, officer?'

'No need, I'm sure it's all in order. You've been pretty careful with the paperwork to date. Besides, this isn't an official visit.'

'Social call? Nice.'

'How about we stop playing games? Who are you people? Why are you here? What do you want?'

'You people?' He slides a coffee my way across a marble bench top. 'Makes us sound undesirable.'

'The visas you came in on, putting millions into some resort out on the Sounds. That's not your money. Sheriff's deputies from Sioux Falls don't make that kind of cash.'

'Done some research I see. So I don't seem classy or smart enough to have that kind of money? I never figured you for a snob.'

'If you did have that kind of money surely it would be better spent on your daughter's medical bills? Leukaemia in the States would cost a pretty penny.'

I've finally got his attention. 'Cards on the table, huh?'

'Yep.'

'I can't keep calling you "officer" if we're laying our cards on the table.'

'My name is Nick.'

'Do you believe in God, Nick?'

'No.' The coffee is good and strong but the cups are too small. Petite and pernickety, not unlike their owner.

'Me neither. I stopped believing when he didn't answer my prayers.'

So his happy-clappy act is just that. 'Your daughter?'

'Chelsey. She passed on last year.'

'I'm sorry.'

'Yeah? Why? I get the impression you don't like me.'

'I don't. But losing your child like that, it would be terrible.' The big kitchen is echoey. 'Chelsey's mother?' I venture.

'None of your business.'

'Okay. So we've agreed that we don't believe in God and that having our kids die is a terrible thing. It still doesn't explain why you're here.'

He refills my little coffee cup. Another pod for the landfill and I'm beginning to buzz like it's Christmas morning and I'm six again.

'Do you like Neil Young?'

Do I like Neil Young, do I believe in God? All these huge questions. The answer's the same. 'No.'

'That song of his – "After the Gold Rush". There's a group of really, really rich guys who buy into his "silver seed" line. They don't believe they should have to die like all the rest of us. They're the Chosen Ones.'

'Doomsday preppers? Survivalists?'

Cunningham nods. 'They don't sit in the woods with tinfoil hats and rave about chem trails but they may as well. Silicon Valley tech wizards, Wall Street bankers, masters of industry and commerce. They've made their fortunes patenting algorithms that can reach into the souls of men and squeeze a last dollar or vote out of them.' Outside, the hounds are barking at something. Maybe there are intruders at the Gates of Hell. 'But when they look in the bathroom mirror in the morning all they see is a skull with a worm crawling out the eyehole. Climate change, pandemics, the collapse of civilisation, the end of oil, the end of water, the end of broadband. They lie awake at night worrying about that shit.'

'That's what's behind what you're doing here?'

'Cards on the table.'

I didn't expect him to be so candid. Maybe he's very confident of getting what he wants and doesn't give a fuck who knows. 'You're the advance guard. Getting everything ready. Softening us up. For what? Why all this aggro, drawing attention to yourselves?'

'Aggro?'

'Getting in everybody's faces. Pissing people off.'

'Not everybody. Some people up and down the valley like having us here.' He sees I don't believe him and shrugs. 'Besides, why be shy? We're the future. Get used to it.'

'What if we don't want to?' Out the window there's a pause in the target practice. 'It's all boys and men here. Women aren't part of the plan?'

'Sure, when we're good and ready.' He reaches into a drawer and pulls out a file. Pushes it my way. 'Gun permits, building permits, visas, resource consents. All you could ask for, all in there. Your dumb, cute, decent little country is built on paperwork and gentlemen's agreements. Worthless when push comes to shove. Some day soon somebody's going to come along and shake you Kiwis out of your decent complacency.' He folds a paper towel daintily to mop coffee from his lips. 'You should talk to your colleague, the lovely Latifa Rapata. Ask her about the great warrior Te Rauparaha. The guy your rugby players do the haka about. No quarter. I respect that in the original people of this country.'

'I'm not sure Latifa will appreciate you appropriating her culture for your own ideological ends.'

'Not my ends. I'm just a foot soldier. Some rich guy wants to pay me big bucks to help his Noah's Ark fantasy come true, that's fine by me.'

'You don't talk like a foot soldier.'

'Bad guys read too. My daddy was a high school English teacher. He passed on his love of reading to me.'

I hop off the breakfast stool. 'Thanks for the coffee.'

'Not so fast. This was meant to be cards on the table. I've just spilled my guts for you and got nothing in return. Tell me about that crazy accent of yours. Ain't Kiwi, that's for sure.'

'I'm a Geordie, north-east England. We're a stubborn, conservative lot. Don't like change.' I tap my finger on his paperwork file. 'Don't be so cocky about those silly little by-laws and rules and regulations we have here. It was tax returns that brought down Al Capone.'

'Back in the day, sure. But which rich sucker pays taxes these days? You'll need something better than that.' He's already rinsed and dried my cup. 'Face it, Chester, you're already beaten.'

'It's a thing these days, isn't it? Seeing decency as a failing, a weakness. But you and the people you work for, you're the ones running away from something. And look where you've chosen to run to. This dumb, cute, decent little country.' A look into his eyes. 'I think you're still working through a lot of bad stuff and I really am sorry for your loss.'

In another time, place, or life maybe we might have got on. No, that's crap. Mutual understanding doesn't automatically foster love and harmony. It can just as often be another tool for knowing and defeating your enemy. Cunningham's empty-eyed nihilism didn't just materialise when God claimed his daughter. It's been in him a lot longer; maybe honed on some terrified young men or women in a South Dakota police cell. Or maybe he was in the military before that – a turnkey at Abu Ghraib, or perhaps his book-loving father thrashed it into him. It'll take something pretty special to counter whatever he has planned for us and I'm not sure we're equipped to meet it. As long as he keeps skirting the right side of the law, we're powerless. Is that how evil creeps in? Forms completed, permissions obtained?

Target practice has started up again. I head back to my car under the watchful eyes of Daniel Boone, his crewcut friend and their dogs. I give them a wave as I drive away.

Pelorus Bridge is experiencing its midmorning rush; the car park and café are full. Clouds rear from the south-west and a nippy wind ripples the surface of the river. I park in the overflow across the road, shrug on a windcheater and check the map and instructions Jenny the bat woman gave me. Three hundred metres along the Tawa Walk trail, pink ribbons lead off through the dense native forest. I plunge into the unknown.

It must be the green equivalent of the white-out experienced by Antarctic explorers. Or maybe not, as the many shades, smells and textures are a riot of the senses. I can imagine the early settlers and prospectors brushing through this same terrain, feeling the moss spring beneath their feet, the feathery whisper of ferns, smelling the fungus and decay of rotting wood. Flies and wasps floating, the beep of a bird. Before the colonials, Māori would have been through too; gathering food, looking for prey. Did Te Rauparaha lead a raiding party this way?

There's a clearing ahead. Yellow wasp baits on trees, blue plastic funnel shapes – possum traps I assume, wood and wire boxes in the undergrowth – rat and stoat traps? The ribbon trail continues deeper into the bush, up steep inclines. My knees and thighs complain, my lungs and heart work harder; my mind is back on that steep hill where Latifa was snared. Hot, I shrug off the windcheater and tie it around my waist. Take a swig of water, and then another.

More clearings, more traps. Steep climbs and descents, often slippery. Old 'Bob' Havelka must have been a fit, tough piece of work. Up here you can no longer hear the stream of traffic over Pelorus Bridge. Sometimes there's water running in an unseen rivulet or cascade, birds skitting between ancient trees, the hum of insects. At times I need to bend down, hands on knees, suck that thick moist air. What am I doing here? What the hell can this tell me about Havelka's death all those years ago? More gulps of water, more deep breaths.

Another clearing. A possum suspended from one of those blue funnels. Mouth twisted, teeth bared in agony. Half-eaten away by maggots and other insects. Such a scene of horror among the verdant beauty, and a glimpse now of what Jenny meant about the malevolence in this otherwise paradise. But surely that's just the ravings of city folk rarely exposed to the power of nature. It's a possum in a trap, nothing more. Catch a breath. Push on.

In the distance, the whine of chainsaws and the crack and thrump of falling trees. I recall the maps, a pine plantation across the summit of the hill, marking the end of the nature reserve, the perimeter of Eden. This must be the far edge of Havelka's trapline by now and from here it curves back towards base. Nothing here tells me any more about where, how, or why the old man died and at whose hands. Of course it wouldn't. We're talking what, five or six years? Standing still in the centre of the last trap clearing. Listening, looking, breathing in the damp, sweet odours: a hint of cinnamon and fruit around the possum trap, peanut butter, old meat.

And then I see it.

On the edge of the small clearing, a big old tree. Step closer to examine it. Run my fingers along the scars in the bark. Am I imagining it? Another drink of water, a sit down on a fallen branch. Breathe. No, I'm not delirious, I'm not imagining things. The scars on this tree are almost identical to the one where I found Latifa; older of course but still discernible. A metal rope snare for a large animal has been pulled tight here. This, I am sure, is where Havelka died. Professor Bardawi found possible ligature marks on the neck. Was he snared first before being shot? Did the man who killed Havelka plan for Latifa to die the same way? Kneeling to be executed? If so, he was interrupted by my approach. Does that mean he has unfinished business?

None of this makes any sense. How the hell did Havelka's body get from there to Butchers Flat? And why bother moving it? Driving away from Pelorus Bridge, I wonder if I'm losing the plot. Unfit, dehydrated and stuffed. My brain is playing tricks, blanking out my memories, writing new narratives, creating fictions. I ricochet between impulse and reason, order and chaos. Was it always like this? I thought I knew but now nothing seems quite as known anymore. Maybe the neurologist will sort me out. Speaking of which, I should chase them up for that appointment. There have been horror stories on the news lately about underfunded and ill-managed District Health Boards neglecting to get back to patients for months while cancers flourish and diseases take hold. I really don't fancy that.

Midafternoon and it's my job to collect Paulie again. The lowering sun seems extra harsh and blinding. A headache threatens. When I arrive at the school there's a scene unfolding. Mim is crying, Paulie looks on the verge of it, and grandad Michael seems to be in his face. I jump out of the car and join the fray.

'What's up?'

Paulie is trying to step between Michael and Mim. 'Leave her alone. Stop shouting at her.'

Michael turns to him. 'Keep out of it.'

'What's going on?' I ask again.

'The sleepover. You promised and now she's upset. Look at her. I'm trying to explain these things happen but your kid keeps getting in the way.'

Mim lets out another heartbroken wail.

'Enough, Miranda. Don't be silly.' The old man seems embarrassed and agitated to be centre stage. He's not enjoying the attention. He grabs his granddaughter's hand. 'Get in the car. Now.'

'Leave her alone!' Paulie once again tries to step between Michael and Mim.

Other parents and kids are taking an interest. Not much else going on in these parts most days. 'I think we need to calm things down here.'

He straightens and leans in close to me. Spittle on his lips. A low growl. 'Fuck you.'

'Oh, piss off, you silly old bugger.'

'Dad!'

'In the car, Paulie.'

'It's Paul!'

'In the car, now.'

'Bye, Mim,' he says sadly. 'See you Monday.'

'We'll see about that.' Michael gestures for Mim to get in the ute. Under his breath. 'She doesn't need to play with a retard.'

That old red mist descends. I'm over there in three paces and have him backed over his bonnet, my fist raised.

'Hey, hey, hey!' He smiles weakly, holds up placating hands. 'Sorry mate, sorry. I went too far. Sorry. I just get so upset, seeing her like that. Protective, you know? Sorry. Really.'

'Dad! Stop!' Paulie is tugging at my arm. Pulling me back.

Mim, meanwhile, has started giggling.

Some parents and kids are capturing the action on their phones. No doubt I'll be in the *Journal* again sometime soon: Thug Cop Attacks Pensioner Outside School.

It's all over. I don't have anything to say to the nasty old bastard. He certainly doesn't get any forgiveness from me. Driving away, he avoids my eyes but in the back seat Mim forgets her heartbreak and gives me a smile and a little wave.

'He said that?' Vanessa lowers her voice. 'Retard?'

We're back in the motel room and Paulie is plugged into his headphones and an iPad game with a packet of Cheezels for company. I know. It's not good to give kids junk food and too much screen time just because it makes life easier for you. But, you know, it's been a bit of a day. Vanessa is helping me chug a bottle of wine because she's had a funny old day too. Still, that's normal for primary school teachers.

'Aye. He was off his trolley. He was supposed to be calming Mim down but I think he was as upset by the cancelled sleepover as Mim was.'

'Weird. Still you get kids like that at school. Soon as something doesn't go to plan they lose it.'

'Massive overreaction by both of them, for sure.'

'Makes me want to go round there and rip his knackers off. How dare he, stupid old twat.' Vanessa's Hylton Castle accent comes back strongly when she's annoyed. Anybody in Sunderland knows, you never get on the wrong side of a lass from Hylton.

'Makes you wonder if there is something funny going on in that household.'

'Like what?'

'Control-freak grandfather with anger issues, dissociative kid with more mood swings in five minutes than a sitting president.' Head shake. 'I don't know.'

Vanessa glances at Paulie and his Cheezels and video game. Lifts up my still grazed knuckles for inspection. 'Anger issues. Hmmm.' She drains her Montana sav blanc and tops herself up. 'Even if you're right, is it any of our business?'

'If it's affecting the kid then probably, yes.' She passes the bottle to me for a refill. 'Mim seemed to be happy that the old bloke had been pushed around. Gave me a wave as they were leaving.'

A nod. 'So she is affected one way or another.'

'Maybe we should tip off the social workers?'

Clinking glasses, we agree. An anonymous dob-in to the authorities will make us feel much better. Give them that job and keep us, and Paulie, out of it. There's a beep on my phone. DS Will Maxwell – can I pop over to the town hall for a sec? Vanessa flicks her fingers in dismissal and reaches for her bag of marking. Crossing the main drag, my phone goes again. Jessie James from the *Journal*.

'Tell me that was you outside Pelorus School today, Nick. That would make my day. The pics are great.'

'No, it was my evil twin. I was in bed with flu.'

She whoops. 'Can I have your side of the story?'

'He insulted my son. It was a matter of family honour. I was not in uniform, not on duty. I acted as a private individual.'

'Who's private around here?'

'Write what you like. I'm sure you will anyway.'

'Yeah, true. Anyway I'm wondering if you'd like to shout me a beer so I can bring you up to date on my research into the boys in the Lodge?'

'When?'

'An hour?'

'No, I'm on family duty.' And suspended too. It's only a matter of time before that is strategically leaked to her. 'Tomorrow?'

We agree a time and place and I close the call and skip up the steps to the town hall. Nobody seems much bothered by my appearance today, the Dodge saloon piano keeps tinkling, so maybe that's a good omen. Maxwell's backstage dressing room office is packed out. Maxwell is there of course, Gemma as you'd expect, and DC Marianne Keegan all the way from sunny Nelson.

Maxwell nods hello. 'I'd say have a seat but there aren't any.'

'No probs. Need a stretch anyway.'

Keegan gets to the point. 'Forensically it looks like you're in the shit, Nick. There's traces of blood on your bedsheets, on a towel, a torn uniform shirt, and residue in your washing machine.'

'Whose blood?'

'Just yours it would seem.'

'So, what now?'

Maxwell takes over. 'Put that together with your DNA being under Gelder's fingernails then we can be pretty sure a struggle took place between the two of you.'

'That makes sense.' I'm also sensing a "but".

'There was a camp cot in that shack of his. It had been removed before our first forensic run through. Chucked in bushes outside the original perimeter we set. This time we found it and other items. Luckily the weather in-between hadn't degraded them too much. Blood traces on the cot, a pillow, sleeping bag and such, suggest he had a nice lie-down after his fight with you.'

'That's it?'

'No, there are other relatively fresh traces on those items. At least two other people were in that shack apart from you and him.'

'Fellow fossickers?'

'Whoever they were, they were there very recently.'

'Ah. So does that get me out of the shit?'

'It muddies the waters,' says Maxwell.

Keegan again. 'You knew about that shack and about at least part of your encounter with Gelder that night and kept it to yourself. You hindered the investigation, wasted valuable time.'

Gemma leans forward. Is this her moment to shine?

'Can you leave us, Gem?' says Maxwell.

'Why?'

'Sergeant Chester is of a higher rank than you, Constable.' Keegan stares her down. 'He has the right to have this discussion in private without junior officers present.'

'Does he?'

'Yes, as far as I'm concerned.'

Gemma wants to argue but Maxwell signals with a head shake that she better not. If there was room to slam the door on the way out she'd probably do so but as it is it's an undignified squeeze past turned knees and jiggled chairs.

Keegan's got a face like she's dying for a ciggie. 'What a fucking mess, Nick.'

'Sorry.'

Maxwell grimaces, contrite. 'We should still have done a more thorough job on that shack, without Nick telling us. Sloppy work from my end.'

Keegan nods. 'It hasn't gone unnoticed, Will.'

They both look at me.

'Keeping busy?' asks Maxwell.

I tell them about the encounter outside Paulie's school and how it will probably be in the papers soon.

Keegan, to her credit, laughs. 'Fair enough, I would have floored the bastard too.' She and Maxwell exchange a glance. 'Back on board from Monday, Nick. You're not a psycho as far as we can tell. Jerk maybe, psycho no.'

'Gemma won't be happy.'

'Gemma was supervising the search of that shack of Gelder's. I'll be reminding her of that.'

'What about my hindering investigations, wasting police time. Isn't that a disciplinary matter?'

'A lapse of judgement. But a doctor's note would be good. Any news on that?'

'I'm meant to be seeing a neurologist soon.'

'Perfect,' says Keegan.

Vanessa has texted me to pick up some fish and chips from the takeaway. Another night of delicious junk. I call her back with the news that we can probably head home tomorrow.

'Good,' she says in a low growl. 'I'm in need of some angry sex.'

'Mum!' says Paulie in the background. No problem with the boy's hearing.

The chippy is Friday evening full. Steve from Traffic drops by to pick up his order. He's on call tonight and apparently Latifa is over at Daniel's catching up on lost time.

'Good thing too,' mutters Steve. 'Bear with a sore head today.'

'She's been through a pretty rough time.' That reminds me I need to talk to her about my Havelka theory. It still seems too mad and improbable to put Maxwell's way. I'll try and catch her tomorrow before or after my meeting with Jessie James.

'They cleared you yet or what?'

Not the best topic of conversation in a crowded town chippy. 'Back on Monday. You might still be needed though.'

He nods glumly. 'Life is much simpler when all you've got to do is pull over dickheads and fine them.'

'Shame,' says someone behind him.

'Yeah, Tweedledumb, I'm talkin' about you.'

Steve goes and Thomas Hemi comes in with Jaxon. Havelock is like that – a throbbing social milieu.

'Keeping well?' I say, shaking Thomas's hand.

'Well as.'

My order is shouted and I pass over my ticket. 'How about you, Jaxon. Keeping out of trouble?'

'Yes,' says Thomas. 'He is. You in tomorrow?'

'Afternoon, yeah. Got some stuff to do in the morning.'

Aware of eavesdroppers who might want to call him a snitch, he nods. 'Be down with that load of firewood you ordered. See you then.'

'Cheers.'

'Yeah, Tom,' says Tweedledumb. 'Don't cross this copper. Should see what he does to people who piss him off.'

He holds up his camera and there I am on Facebook Live, getting ready to punch an old man named Michael.

12.

Google Earth is a wonderful thing. As are history books. It's all there in those old black and white photos, the diaries of gold rush disappointments, the court transcripts of the infamous Doom Creek murderers and the old gold rush trails they took to escape through the ranges. Cunningham and his good ol' boys in their mule ATV out for a day's hunting nudged my memory and Google Earth backs it all up. Now I know how a dead man from Pelorus Bridge nature reserve – twenty-odd k's by road – ends up what I now see is just a four-kilometre hop over the hill to Butchers Flat. Throw him in the back tray of your buggy like a snipered deer and away you go along those long-forgotten tracks. So that's the how. But why? And what happened to the other half of his body?

A cramped motel room is no place to toss and turn so I slip out the door and take myself off for a walk over to Cullen Point across the water on the road out to Picton. Sitting on a bench looking back from Mahakipawa Hill towards Havelock on this peaceful early Saturday morning reminds me what there is to love about the place. Thin pre-winter sunlight glances off the still waters of the marina and the mudflats. Pukeko and other swamp birds probe the driftwood. The sky is a brilliant blue with wispy white clouds wreathing the hills. Steam rises from the chimneys of the mussel factory and a lone runabout cuts the surface as it motors out into Pelorus Sound for a day's fishing. There are so many mornings such as this to be had around here. But does such beauty and serenity serve only to make the darkness blacker, the poison more toxic, the violence more brutal? Has a taste of paradise weakened my resilience? Murders, violence, bullying were everyday realities for me policing England's tough northern cities. Then I was able to drink with demons and fight hand-to-hand with monsters. Put dinner on the table, nurture my family and sleep soundly at night. Nowadays I see only the fungus on the leaves and the bacteria in the rivers, and I break into a sweat at unexpected touch and sound. Jumping at shadows.

A coffee would be good. By now it's a civilised hour so I text Vanessa to let her know my whereabouts and phone to arrange to meet Latifa at the office. By the muffled sound of things she's not keen to disentangle herself from Daniel in a hurry so I grab a coffee and a bacon-and-egg toastie from the bakery en route. Half an hour later Latifa plonks herself down at her desk and, after making her a cup of tea, I outline my theory.

She frowns and briefly fingers the red weal around her throat. 'Bit of a stretch? I mean, yeah, similar rope marks on the tree but those snares aren't uncommon and hunting is a thing around here.'

'I don't know, I just have this feeling they're connected.'

'Intuition, huh? That's what I like about you, Sarge, you're so in touch with your inner self.'

'There's more.' I tell her about my heart-to-heart with Cunningham and his plan to bring Mother Nature's silver seed to a new home in the sun. Yes, I checked out the song lyrics on Spotify.

She shakes her head. 'White guy delusions. We've seen it all before. Aotearoa was all set to be a privatised Pākehā gentlemen's club two hundred years ago before your government stepped in to colonise us properly first. A little gang of rich white men wanting to turn us into Fantasy Island. Now they want to do it again. What? We're supposed to be this big blank canvas you can project yourselves onto? Give me a break.'

'Cunningham's an admirer of Te Rauparaha. And a bit of a fan of yours in his own sweet way.'

'Gee, that's great. It's so good to have his approval.' She drains her tea. 'Look, Sarge, you mean well and I really appreciate your concern. I owe you big time for getting me out of that snare but ...' She frowns at the floor. 'I don't see it, Havelka and me linked, it doesn't make sense. Focus too much on that and we risk letting a completely unrelated nutter go free.'

'Fair enough, I was just thinking out loud.'

'Maybe, I dunno. Maybe it's time to move on.'

'It's just a few days ago. There's no need to act tough.'

'Isn't there? Ever tried being a non-white woman in a white male workforce like the cops? No? Didn't think so.' She takes a final gulp of tea. 'The neck's healing. Cunningham's a dick. Daniel's home. And you,' she takes her mug to the sink for rinsing, 'have too much going on. You're under a lot of pressure yourself and seeing links that don't exist.'

'Any news from the Nelson Ds? Aren't they meant to be looking for your attacker?'

'They're knocking on doors, tramping up and down hills and rounding up the usual suspects. Nothing so far. I'm figuring it's all a bit too hard for them, poor dears.'

'They need to pull their fingers out.'

'Yeah, but I have low expectations. This is a small country but it's still easy to disappear. Maybe I was just in the wrong place at the wrong time.'

'We'll find him,' I say, more for my own peace of mind than hers.

'I can look after myself. You need to sort yourself out.'

'I'm in the clear over Gelder's murder.'

'Congratulations,' she says. 'Now get back to your family and stop fretting about me, patterns on trees, and those Lodge dickheads. Your cold case will wait until Monday.'

'Any ideas why somebody would move a body from Pelorus Bridge to Butchers?'

'Go,' she hurries me out the door, 'home.'

Latifa is in surprisingly good shape. Or at least hiding things well. She seems to be hauling herself back from a horrific attack and seizing the moment with the love of her life. Maybe that's a simple tough reality for many women who've suffered male violence. Grit teeth, claw back, move on. I should try to learn from that. Next on the list: Jessie James and her research on the dicks up at the Lodge. The Captain's Daughter is an old stone building on the Havelock main drag that wouldn't look amiss in the Cairngorms or the Cotswolds. They've got a cosy log fire and Jessie is waiting for me with a big red drink in front of her.

'Berry cider,' she says. 'Still deciding whether I like it or not.'

I check my watch and am surprised at how much of the morning has slipped away. Vanessa has texted back that she's opted not to check out of the motel as we haven't had confirmation yet that our house is cleared to move back into. It feels like we're on the verge of an argument and fair enough too, I'm being a pain in the arse. Neglectful, obsessive, the usual.

'Bit tight for time, Jessie.' I fill a glass from the water jug. 'Can we make this quick?'

'Typical,' she says, reaching down into her backpack for her notes.

She's got a new tatt on the back of her neck. A red flower. 'I spend hours picking through the innards of the deep state conspiracy and you demand superficial bullet points and sound bites.'

'I'm all ears.'

'Māhana Wellbeing Centre. Heard of it?'

'Out in the Sounds. Cunningham and a few others in the Lodge have invested in it. The basis of their business visas.'

'Well done you. They might be putting in their two mills worth but the major shareholding and the land it's on belongs to a bloke called James Bryant.'

'Good local name. Haven't the Bryants been in this area for yonks?'

'Not in this case. No relation. James Oliver Bryant, native son of Kentucky, is a billionaire of all trades. He sells anything from bottled water to Kalashnikovs to anyone and everyone.' Impressive. It only seems like yesterday that I was questioning Jessie's journalistic credentials and bemoaning her millennial apathy. Now here she is stepping up to the plate. Must be the awards season. She passes me her iPad. 'That's him at a reception held at the NZ embassy in Washington last year, celebrating his newly acquired Kiwi citizenship. Bought and paid for by return of post.' Another swipe. 'And that's him third from left smiling in the background while the American president signs an executive order to repeal some silly environmental protection laws that were getting in the way of corporate profits.'

'So Bryant is the bucks and power behind Cunningham.'

'And the brains too.' More swiping and scrolling. 'Although brains might be a misnomer.' His Facebook page links are a who's who of far-right philosophers, writers and fruitloops through the ages: Ayn Rand, Rees-Mogg, Steve Bannon, Creationism, eugenics, white supremacy, incel, Islamophobia, holocaust denial, apocalypse now, deep state conspiracy theorists, alien abduction, chem trails, anti-vaxxers. 'Take your pick.'

'I already got the gist of this from Cunningham himself, although it's nice to be able to put a name to a nutcase.'

She nods. 'I've already told you about my boyfriend who works on the mail boat?'

'Yep.'

'He's got a mate.'

Here we go. 'The suspense is killing me.'

'Builder's apprentice. One of the few locals working on the Māhana place. Most of them are either from way up north or way down south, or overseas. The locals only got the job temporarily because some other team all got gastro from some dodgy mussels. He had to sign a confidential non-disclosure agreement for the fortnight they had the work.'

'But this mate told your boyfriend anyway who then told you.'

'Non-disclosure my arse. We're talking public interest here. Besides Johnno couldn't keep a secret if you sewed his lips shut. He'd fart it out in morse.'

'Tell me.'

'What would a wellbeing centre need a panic room for?'

As it is, we get the all-clear to return to our home by early afternoon and check out of the motel late. Driving past the Lodge over the traffic-calming speed bump, I'm thinking about that burgeoning sub-group of humanity that exists in some sort of *Westworld* theme park conjured by their own imaginations, remaining impervious to reason and logic, and increasingly cashed up to pursue their dangerous fantasies. It sounds as if I am describing street junkies who just found a wallet but in reality its members are captains of industry, respectable statesmen and women. Movers, shakers all. Sad, and not so sweet, dreamers. Maybe they've always been around but now they seem to be blooming like toxic algae. To hell with them. If Michael Jackson kept a pet chimp and giraffe in NeverNeverLand and Elvis stuck purple carpet on the walls of Graceland, why should I worry if James Bryant wants to waste his money on a panic room at Māhana?

'Does this mean you're in the clear?' asks Vanessa as we round the last bend towards home.

'I suppose so.'

Paulie leans forward from the back seat. 'Can Mim sleep over now?'

The boy is nothing if not persistent. Change the subject. 'Looks like the goats and chooks are happy to see you back. Feed 'em up mate, and we'll unpack and get some afternoon tea together.'

'Wish I could distract you so easily,' says Vanessa, grabbing her bag from the boot as Paulie heads off to the feed bins.

'I'm open to offers.'

She punches my arm in passing. 'Flirtery will get you everywhere.'

A thaw. What else could a man wish for?

Because it's a cop house, the techs have been remarkably diligent about cleaning up after themselves. There are some chemical smells and smudges here and there but a wipe down and the windows open and all is sweet.

While Vanessa catches up on her lesson prep and Paulie hangs out with the livestock, I wander over the farm picking up tī kōuka leaves and enjoying the breeze. Gary drops by; he often does just before he's due to go back out on the trawlers.

'How's the water tank?' I look down and see the bandage removed. 'And the hand?'

'All good. A mate of Marvin's filled it up because he was busy. Said he did all the others too. All on the house, he said. No charge. Community spirit, eh? You've been away a few days?'

'Yeah.' I tell him why the cops have been poking around because that's what he's after, a bit of valley gossip.

'They think you killed the prick with the dredge?'

'They needed to diligently exclude me from their enquiries.'

'Yeah, but did you?'

'No.'

He nods. 'Wouldn't blame you. He had it coming. Wanting to stuff up the river. Rivers are important. Eels, kai and that.'

'Well he won't be able to do it anymore.'

'Wonder who'll get his claim now?'

'What?'

'Maybe that's what he was killed for.'

'A few ounces of gold a year? You're joking.'

'Gold does funny things to people.'

It sure does. I recall Gary's gang links in a previous life. 'Do you know Morgan Hopu?'

'Thomas Hemi's big brother, yeah, kind of. Why?'

'Think he's capable of murder?'

'Morgan?' A laugh. 'Course he is. You don't get anywhere in his game if you're not.'

I lay out the bare bones of the Havelka story for him. 'Think he could have done it?'

'No question he could have. Whether he did is another matter.'

My mind returns to the murders Keegan put me onto. 'Ever hear of

Morgan having any connections to the west coast? Business, property, family, friends, whatever?'

'Probably. Most people have connections everywhere these days, don't they? There's a chapter of the mob over in Greymouth. There'll be friends and associates there, no doubt. Again, why?'

I tell him in the vaguest terms possible.

'Same MO?' he asks.

I nod.

'Bit of a stretch, eh?'

That's the second time today somebody's said that to me.

Gary examines his still swollen hand. 'You should talk to Thomas.'

'Why? It's his brother I'm interested in.'

'Yeah, but I can think of three good reasons you should anyway.' He counts them out on his mangled fingers. 'One, like you, he's no stranger to crackpot theories. Two, he's Morgan's brother so he should know a bit about him. And three, before he found religion he was Morgan's enforcer.'

'Enforcer?'

'Standover man, hit man if needs be. Fearsome fella. We'd even heard of him up on the North Island. World-famous in New Zealand, he was. To us at least.'

Thomas was going to come down and see me this afternoon under the pretext of delivering some firewood we don't need. What was that about? After Gary's revelation, it could be timely. I call and tell him I'll come up there instead.

'Not a good idea, mate. Ruth's got the shits with me. Fancy a beer?'

'Sure. The Trout in half an hour?'

It's late afternoon by the time we take our seats at the picnic table over the road. There's not much daylight left. We probably shouldn't be bringing our drinks so far from the premises but Canvastown can be quite European when it chooses. The picnic area is beside a collection of artefacts commemorating the gold rush days – picks, shovels, other rusty implements and pieces of machinery. There are plaques here and at strategic points along the valley road pointing out spots of historic interest – places where the valley was particularly trashed in the often futile search for an instant fortune. *Plus ça change.* Across the road at the pub a dozen Harleys and other shiny muscle bikes are lined up. The

Sunday afternoon sesh at the Trout is a popular stop-off.

'Don't worry. Just Grandad Groovers, not outlaws.' Hemi takes a draw from his Speights. 'We've got a bit to talk about, I reckon.'

'You first.' My Monteith's cider feels like a mistake. Too cold and gassy. A wind has risen and clouds hang in the south-west. A thermos of soup might have been a better idea.

Thomas reaches into his shirt pocket and chucks a bullet on the table. 'Lapua scenar.' He'd climbed down into his empty water tank to retrieve it. 'Readily available in NZ. Hunters like them. Assume you've got ballistics people who can run tests?'

'Sure,' I say. 'Thanks.'

'I've told my boy to watch himself with his new mate.'

'Melvyn.'

He nods. 'But I thought it might be useful for him to still hang out. Pick stuff up like.'

'Good idea.'

'It wasn't mine, it was Latifa's. Probably yours to start with though, eh?'

'If you ever have any doubts, shelve it. We don't want him putting himself in danger. And we both know these people are dangerous.'

'He's a smart kid when he's not being stupid. He knows he needs to redeem himself. He'll be fine.' Another gulp of Speights. 'Your turn.'

'A little bird tells me you had a colourful past before you decided to go and hide yourself at the far end of a remote dead-end valley.'

'That would apply to half the Wakamarina. Any specifics?'

'Working for your brother? Enforcing?'

His face hardens. 'Those days are behind me.'

'Are they?'

Hemi drains his beer. 'Mate, sorry, you're barking up the wrong tree.'

'Hear me out. Please.' I don't know where that "please" came from, it wasn't intended. But it works. He re-settles and I tell him about the body at Butchers and about the possible link with the west coast murders.

Poker face. 'What's any of that got to do with me?'

'Don't know. I was just hoping you might be able to help. Maybe you know who could be behind the executions. Maybe you recall your brother's interests on the west coast. Maybe there's a link? Anything.'

'And you think I would snitch on my own brother if there was a link?'

It's nearly dark already. The river bubbles behind me and two paradise ducks whoop in passing. A few spots of rain spatter the table. The Boomer bikers have revved up and gone. Only a handful of hardcore regulars left in the Trout now. 'People say you're a changed man, Thomas. You play the part too. But I'm still not sure what that means. Changed from what to what? And why?'

He pats my shoulder as he stands up. 'You want the answer to that, you don't get it for free. You need to earn it.'

'I'm a cop, Thomas. This is my job.'

'Keep at it, Nick. Dig away. But know this: I'm not your enemy.'

13.

Monday morning and I'm back on the job, officially. First, though, Michael Walton and I must go and see the principal and apologise for fighting in the playground.

'He started it.'

She doesn't think that's funny. 'Mr Chester, this kind of behaviour brings the school into disrepute. Parents and caregivers scrapping like hooligans. Front page of the *Journal*. Really.' Lianne Kingi has been good to us and to Paulie. Gone out of her way to make us feel welcome and to help him fit in. I don't want to make her job any harder.

'I'm sorry. It won't happen again.' Unless the wanker steps out of line again.

She looks over at Michael. 'Mr Walton?'

'Misunderstanding. Nothing in it. Water under the bridge.'

'Maybe as far as you're concerned but I need to have confidence that there won't be a repeat performance.'

'Not from me there won't.'

That's about as good as she's going to get from us. We're dismissed. On the way out Michael turns to me. 'Need any pea hay? Got some spare.'

At face value this is what's known as a Kiwi apology. 'Sure. Coupla bales?'

'Six. I'll bring them up later in the week. When suits?'

'Any day after four there's somebody home.'

'Maybe I could bring Paul home with them one day. Save you picking him up?'

Do I want my son in the temporary charge of a bloke who called him a retard a few days ago? 'No need. We have a routine with him. But the hay'd be great.'

'Right.' He holds out a hand for the shaking.

I oblige. We don't need another feud. 'Later in the week, then.'

Back to the station in Havelock. Latifa is waiting patiently, overnight log checked and nothing much for us to worry about. Some skids on the wet roads in the wee hours. Thefts from parked cars in Blenheim. A break-in and vandalism at a bach out on the Sounds. All the remit of Traffic or local Ds.

'And life just got a bit simpler with the disappearance of the Von Crapps.'

'What, all of them?'

'Done a bunk. Steve went to serve one of them with a court order and found an empty house.'

'Foul play?'

'Doesn't look like it. Probably some debts caught up with them.'

'Anything else?'

'There's this one. Right up your street, Sarge.'

A woman from Havelock complaining that her neighbour keeps catching her pet cat in a trap. And a counter complaint from the neighbour.

'This a police matter?'

'She's threatening to shoot the neighbour's dog in retaliation.'

'That escalated quickly.'

'It's gone on for decades, apparently. This is more a flare-up in ongoing hostilities. Think US versus North Korea or Iran.'

I'd rather not. The radio news on the way back from Paulie's school spoke of another tick on the Doomsday Clock. Another step towards James Bryant and his billionaire buddies bolting over here. 'Want to deal with it?'

'I'm still suffering post-traumatic stress disorder.' She fingers the weal on her neck. 'Animals, traps; triggers a lot of bad memories, Sarge.'

'What are you going to do while I'm out there on the front line?'

'Read the OHS circulars. Ease my way back in.'

I give her the bullet Thomas Hemi found. 'Maybe get that over to the labs. See if it can be linked to anything of consequence.'

'Sure. How about we take it a step further?'

'Go on.'

'We've been promising a full inspection of that arsenal at the Lodge and a checking against paperwork. Let's send in the AOS to do that.'

'Run it past DC Keegan. Tell her I'm in favour.'

A grin. 'I'm sure if you're up for it, she will be too.'

Don't take the bait.

The walk down to cat lady and dog woman will do me good. On the way there's a call from Wairau Hospital in Blenheim telling me they've had a cancellation and could I come in for that brain scan on Thursday?

'Okay.' They'll email me a confirmation appointment. Push those thoughts of mortality away. Why am I wasting my time on this neighbourhood dispute when there are two unsolved murders and a violent assault on my colleague requiring attention? Not forgetting a nutso Doomsday cult on my doorstep. The answer is that there are dedicated teams on the Gelder murder and the Latifa attack. Havelka is a cold case that won't be hurried. Sending the AOS into the Lodge for a routine weapons inspection is as good a way as any of keeping everything bubbling along. So it's all creatures great and small for me.

Deidre Brownley is a stalwart of the community association and the quilters club. She's also hard as nails and shouldn't be crossed. Arriving at her weatherboard cottage on the street leading down to the marina I find her around the side gate taunting the neighbour's cat. She's prodding a broomstick through the bars of the trap and making the bell tinkle on the collar.

'That's seven lives now, you fat bastard. Your days are numbered.'

'He's only fat because you made me get him spayed, you sadistic bitch.'

I hadn't noticed Mrs De Voss from next door but I see her now beyond the camellias on the other side of the fence. There's a chorus of yaps from inside the Brownley residence.

'Shush, sweetie. Mummy'll give you brekky soon.'

'Morning, Mrs Brownley, Mrs De Voss.'

They both look like they've been caught doing something untoward, which in a sense is true, and their faces are suddenly transformed into nice little old lady masks.

'Sergeant Chester!' Deidre puts down her broom. 'Come inside, I'll get the kettle on.'

I turn to Mrs De Voss. 'I'll be over to see you in fifteen minutes.'

'It was me who made the complaint. I should be first.'

'I'm giving equal weight to both matters. Bear with me.'

Mrs Brownley's kitchen is stiflingly warm from a roaring log burner and an oven on full-bore cooking something that smells nice. The yapper is a Jack Russell, skidding on the shiny wooden floor, riffling the rug and nipping at my ankles. I'm beginning to see the neighbour's point.

'Can we have the dog out of here while we talk please?'

A refreshing coldness descends. 'As you wish.' She scoops the dog up into her bosom and kisses its head. 'Nasty man doesn't like you, Pip. Go and sleep on Mummy's bed. I won't be long.' And out the door it goes. Only to keep yapping and scratching on the other side.

I politely decline the tea. 'I'll keep this as brief as possible. Those traps are only meant to be used on feral cats and preferably on remote or rural properties. I checked with the SPCA. Mrs De Voss's cat is registered, chipped, spayed and belled. You can't expect any more than that.'

'They're a menace to native birds.'

'That one isn't. It can barely stand up, never mind pounce. Put the trap in your garage and move on.'

'She threatened to shoot Pip.'

'I'll be speaking to her about that.'

She tears up. 'Pip's all I have since Jack passed away.'

'And no doubt Mrs De Voss thinks the same about her pet.'

'Shirley's bloke didn't pass away. He just upped and left and you can't blame him. The cat's not fat because it got spayed, it's fat because she is.'

It's nice to be outside and cool again. 'Don't be wasting any more police time with this nonsense,' I tell Mrs Brownley in leaving.

'And we had such high hopes for you, Sergeant Chester.' The door closes firmly. En route I open the door of the cage but the cat seems quite comfortable where it is and stays curled up on the verge of sleep.

'Did you arrest her?' Mrs De Voss's kitchen is remarkably similar to her neighbour's: hot and stuffy with lots of knick-knacks. It's a pity they can't focus on what unites rather than divides.

'No. And you're not allowed to shoot Mrs Brownley's dog or even to issue threats to do so.'

'Can I shoot her?' She grins out the corner of her mouth. 'Just jokin'. I've made you a coffee so you may as well drink up. It's instant so if it's not good enough, the café's up the road.'

I've decided I like Shirley De Voss more. 'Why does your cat keep going over the fence? More to the point, how?'

'There's a hole down near the back corner. Still big enough for Freddie to get through. He likes rummaging in the compost. The stupid cow shouldn't be chucking her bacon scraps in there, I keep telling her.'

'Maybe if the hole was blocked this would all stop?'

'It's her hole, she should fix it.' She hands me a plate. 'Cake?'

Instant coffee and jam sponge never tasted so good. Maybe it's bringing back fond memories of a Sunderland childhood when life was so much simpler. 'Usually fence or boundary disputes, like repairs, are resolved by the neighbours sharing the costs.'

'But it was her stupid dog burrowing under trying to chase Freddie that did it. On our side we weatherproofed it. She didn't. So it rotted, from her side.'

'I reckon the Menz Shed could sort that out for you in half an hour. How about I talk to them?'

'But if we solve the problem I'll have no-one to talk to will I?'

'What?'

'Arguing with that cow is the only social contact I get all day. You want to take that away from me?'

There it was: a fundamental truth that underpinned so much of my recent experience of life in the Top of the South.

Back in the murder room in the town hall there's been a development. DSS Maxwell has assembled everyone for a briefing, even Latifa for her local knowledge. Gemma tries to give us both the death stare as we take our places but it's plain her heart really isn't in it.

Maxwell taps a spoon on his coffee cup for attention. 'We have a witness who saw a dark-coloured delivery-type van in the Four Square car park at around one in the morning on the day of the murder. Two men were inside. One of them was smoking.'

The witness, an insomniac old guy from the motor camp down the road, was taking his habitual middle of the night stroll to avoid disturbing his wife with his tossing and turning. They'd been up on D'Urville Island in the Sounds since the murder, leaving that very same morning before the discovery of the body and only returning this last weekend to realise he might have something worthwhile to contribute to the investigation.

'No papers, no radio, no internet, no gossip?' asks a young detective, incredulous.

'That's the whole point of D'Urville,' says Maxwell. 'That and the fishing.'

The man could provide only a vague guess on the van make and couldn't provide a rego. The people inside the van were illuminated only briefly by the flare of a match or lighter.

'They'd gone by the time he returned, half an hour later. As they didn't pass him on his walk then the assumption is they headed west in the direction of Nelson.'

Or Canvastown, maybe?

Gemma takes a step forward. 'So we now have a narrower timeline. If these guys were our killers they had finished their work on Gelder by around one-thirty and gone on their way.'

'And if they weren't our killers?' Petty, yes, but I feel like raining on someone's parade and it happens to be Gemma's.

'Then we'll eliminate them from our enquiries,' says Maxwell.

Job lists are allocated: vehicle ownership checks and cross-checks, follow-ups on people living along that road or who might have been on it for any reason at that time of night – logging trucks for instance. Dashcam would be nice. Revisiting any properties or businesses along that route which have CCTV cameras facing the road out.

'I can think of one,' I say. 'The Lodge on Wakamarina Road.'

'Feel free to check it out, Nick.' Maxwell knows I've got an agenda but he's happy to have me out of the way. 'And maybe push on with the plumbing job list, see if there's any crossover with our van?' A few sniggers from those who know I'm on the outer.

'Will do.'

Latifa joins me on the way out. 'Need company?'

'Not sure it's a good idea for you to be in the proximity of Cunningham.'

She rounds on me. 'Would you say that to a male colleague? Would you apply that to yourself? I'm a cop and this is cop business. Let's get on with it.'

Told.

And here we are again. Press the buzzer, wave at the camera, wait patiently for Daniel Boone and Crew Cut to rock up with the guard dogs. The licky one seems pleased to see me – we're talking dogs here.

'Morning.'

'What do you want now?' says Daniel Boone.

'Your help as good citizens.' I explain our business.

'Anything on the video feed is private property. Sorry.'

The speaker goes. 'Constable Rapata! *Enchanté.* Come right in. George?' Daniel Boone looks up. 'I'll be down at the range.'

George asks us to leave our guns in the car. Latifa's ready to argue but I remind her we're all good citizens today. She relents, a little. 'Nobody takes my taser, baton or spray.'

The boys grin. 'Sure ma'am. No problem.'

Up the steep driveway again and Latifa says out the corner of her mouth. 'Looking forward to them trying that with the AOS when they drop by tomorrow.'

'What's that, ma'am?' says Crew Cut.

'None of your business.'

On beyond the house, about another hundred metres down into a wide gully, Cunningham has the whole shooting range all to himself.

'The boys have gone for a run up the hill. If I can do it, they damn well can too.' He smiles and directs his attention to Latifa. 'How may I help you today, Constable?'

She gives him the lowdown. 'So we're looking for a dark-coloured delivery van. Might have been picked up by your camera.'

'George, head on back to the control room, see what we got for that night. Download it on to a thumb drive for the constable here.'

'You sure, boss?'

'Hop to it, soldier.'

A look passes between the men. Cunningham isn't used to being questioned by his subordinates. George could be in for a roasting after we leave. That's a bonus. I admire the range. Three sides of it are rammed earth, bulldozed high to catch the stray bullets. At the far end half a dozen targets spaced about three metres apart. Standard targets, silhouettes and bullseyes, nothing ideologically incorrect.

'Want to try?' Cunningham offers me a semi-automatic Bushmaster.

'No thanks.' A gesture at the range. 'Did you get a resource consent for this?'

'What do you think, Sergeant?'

'I think paperwork is your forte. But from what I can see, the fence line has been changed. Did you consult the neighbour about that?'

'You're digging deep here, Chester. Getting desperate. And I thought you were here asking for my help as a good citizen?'

'Of course. I'll butt out.'

'Funny isn't it?' says Latifa.

'What's that, Miss Rapata?'

'Fences, boundaries, borders. All around the world you and your kind are making a big fuss about how important they are but you're the last people to respect them. You bulldoze your neighbour's fences, you come here with your guns and your "free speech" nut jobs demanding the right to go anywhere you like and whip people up.'

George returns with the thumb drive and hands it to Latifa. 'Ma'am.'

Cunningham lifts the gun, sights it, and lets rip a few rounds at the targets. Turns back, cradling it in his ropey forearms. 'Miss Rapata, did the sergeant here tell you I'm a great admirer of your people, especially Te Rauparaha?'

'You're not pronouncing it right.' She shows him how. 'Yes, he did. He also told me you want to set up your own little utopia in our country.'

'Absolutely. A proud warrior land, civilised by God-fearing, hard-working Scottish folk. That's some pedigree, don't you think?'

'Like to keep things simple don't you?'

'Focused.'

'A rarefied atmosphere on Planet Brandon, eh? Pick and mix your beliefs?'

'Sorry, ma'am. I don't quite follow.'

'Just down the road from here, Tuamarina, north of Blenheim? That warrior you spoke of kicked Pākehā ass. The history books call it the "Wairau Affray".' She finger quotes the last two words. 'Bunch of whities thought they could just wander in and take over. Be warned. Nobody should take us for granted.'

'Oh Lordy, Miss Rapata, you have exactly the kind of genes we're looking for in our brave new world.'

'Slow down, Latifa.'

'Leave the driving to me, Sarge.'

'He's just winding you up. Don't let him.'

She eases off the pedal and we take the next hairpin at a sedate seventy. 'Here's hoping the AOS inspection tomorrow gets under his sweaty white skin.'

'I think it'll take more than that to faze him.'

She pulls over into some space at the roadside and kills the engine. Takes a few deep breaths and angrily wipes a smudge of tears on her cheeks. 'It's funny, I've punched out bigger jerks than him, but he keeps on pressing those buttons.'

'He's well-practised, for sure.'

'Reminds me of a guy at Police College who made it his business to try and bring me down.'

'What happened?'

'I'm still here. He failed.' Latifa focuses on the clouds scudding across the hills.

Maybe she shouldn't be back at work so soon. 'You okay?'

'Yes.' Her tone says back off.

'Cunningham's getting what he wants, eh? Lots of attention from us.'

A determined nod. 'That means either of two things. He's starved of affection or he's intent on distracting us from something else.'

We're both thinking the same thing. 'Fancy a boat trip?'

An hour or so later we're bumping through the choppy Pelorus Sound. The boat skipper, Lizzie, looks like all those perennial outdoors Kiwis: weather-burnished, healthy and slightly removed from the rest of us mere couch potatoes. We've dropped off the thumb drive at the murder room so they can trawl through the Lodge CCTV to find that dark delivery van but I don't fancy their chances. It's a windswept but very clear sunny day. Beyond the spray of the whitecaps we can see the sanctuary of Maud Island and, across from there in a private bay, the wellbeing centre harlequinned with orange and blue builder's plastic.

'Māhana, huh?' says Latifa. 'You know what it means?'

'Warm? Good name for a wellbeing centre I suppose.'

'That's without the macron. *Ka pōrangi ki ngā maunga ki ngā wai matatiki, ki ngā rākau, ki ngā manu: kāhore hoki i kitea he wahine māhana.* "He searched in the mountains, at the springs, in the trees and the birds, but he could not find a wife for himself." Old Māori saying. Change the pronunciation and you have a very different meaning to do with dominance and possession.'

Cunningham winding Latifa up about her fantastic genes. Mother Nature's silver seed. 'Is that what's behind all this? They're planning some kind of post-Apocalyptic fertility farm?'

Latifa squints against the sea spray. 'They'd never get away with it. Surely.'

'Not in a world where rules still apply. But maybe they're looking ahead to when the mushroom cloud disperses.'

'Yuck.'

Lizzie ties up at the jetty. Tells us we'll need to get moving again in another hour with the wind on the rise and the tide changing. Then she gets out her thermos, book and a fishing rod and drops a line in the crystal clear waters.

Almost immediately we're met by a couple of blokes who I may or may not have seen around the Lodge.

'This is private property, sir. Ma'am.'

'And we are police officers doing our job. We've had reports of poachers in the area. We're investigating.'

'No poachers here, sir. I can assure you of that.'

'All the same.' I step forward and the smaller of the two bars my way. 'If you don't step aside we'll have two choppers full of Armed Offenders Squad here in no time at all. If it's privacy you're after, that's not the way to achieve it.'

His mate has a satellite phone. He turns away while he makes a call. A minute later we're waved through. 'You're welcome to walk up our track and use our jetty, but without a warrant you're not allowed to go beyond that fence.'

'We'll decide that,' says Latifa, marching ahead.

'Those are the conditions.' The guy with the phone reaches out an arm to stop her.

'I wouldn't,' I warn him.

Too late, he's on the ground with Latifa's knee on his head and his arms twisted up his back. While Latifa cuffs him I counsel his mate to stay back. When she's finished, she picks up his sat-phone and lobs it into the water.

'You're polluting the environment,' says the boat skipper, frowning.

'What's your name?' I ask of the smaller guard.

'Vernon.'

'Vernon, we're going to be about twenty minutes, half an hour maybe, and then we're gone. Do you want to spend that time handcuffed to the jetty with your friend or sitting in that comfy camp chair over there?'

'We're under orders, sir. This is trespass. There will be consequences.'

'And if you, or your friend, attempt to physically prevent us from doing our job, there will also be consequences.'

'Leave 'em, Vern. Their time will come.'

Latifa crouches down to the man on the ground. 'That sounded like a threat.'

'Read it how you like.'

Vernon takes his place in the camp chair and sulks while Latifa drags his mate over to a jetty rail and locks him to it.

'Fifty minutes left,' says the skipper like she's seen everything. Her rod bends and she puts her book down. 'Yes, you beauty.'

The Māhana Wellbeing Centre is taking shape. It's a two-storey building not unlike the Lodge in its central hexagonal design but bigger and with spoke-like offshoots which put me in mind of the old Strangeways prison in Manchester, a former stomping ground of mine. Māhana is set on a large flat tract of land surrounded on three sides by hills and with an approach possible via air and sea. There's only one road through the hills, currently a track connecting over to Kenepuru Sound. By the looks of the machinery rolling through the distance, that track is being upgraded and bitumenised. There's also an airstrip fit for smaller planes and a helicopter landing pad.

'Could just be one of those super-rich hideaways. They have shit like this down near Queenstown too.' Latifa pushes some windswept tresses back behind her ears. 'But you mentioned a panic room?'

'Let's take a look.'

There are guys painting, plastering, digging trenches and laying pipes. Everything you'd expect from a building site. Except for chat and banter. Heads down, bums up. A chap who could be the site foreman steps our way.

'Help you?'

'Having a look around.'

'Any particular reason?'

'Police business.'

He stabs a thumb towards the two fellas back on the jetty. 'Assume you've got the Yanks' permission then?'

'Assume away.'

'Good as gold. Be my guest. Like us to down tools for a while so you can concentrate?'

'Good idea.'

He lowers his voice. 'Just tell those wankers on your way out you insisted, okay?'

'Okay.' He turns and shouts the orders, waves at a CCTV camera on a pole and points at me. 'Who's watching?' I ask, as if I don't already know.

'Bloke called Cunningham. Remote client supervision. It's becoming a thing in these parts.' He hands us each a hard hat and fluoro vest. 'You'll need these. And I'll have to escort you. OHS. Sorry.'

'No probs.'

We're led around a bunch of rooms that look like they should: kitchens, bathrooms, bedrooms, living rooms; you get the picture. A few of those down one wing seem sturdier with heavier doors and the windows are smaller and higher. Like cells.

The foreman's name is Vince. 'Storerooms, according to the plans.'

'Can we see those plans?'

'Sorry. Above my pay grade.'

Another spoke comprises mainly, we are told, bedrooms, but the layout and ensuite facilities remind me of private hospital rooms. Two others, much bigger than the rest, suggest special purpose. One has all the makings of an operating theatre.

'This is a wellbeing centre, after all,' says Vince. The other, by contrast, has the makings of a control or surveillance room. I've stood in many in my time, same shape, same feel. Platforms in place awaiting consoles. Vince notes my keen interest. 'This mob like their cameras and technology, eh?'

All along the walls and corridors you can see the wires that will link it all up.

'Where's the panic room?' asks Latifa.

'The what?'

'You heard.'

'I'm sorry. Not at liberty to say. We've signed these agreements.' In a whisper. 'And walls have ears.'

'But there is such a thing?' I insist.

A flicker of the eyes. 'Don't know what you're referring to, mate.'

Time and tide's running out so we make our way back to the jetty, free the prisoners, informing them that we made the foreman give us a tour but we found nothing of interest. Vernon is all wet.

'Been for a swim?'

'He retrieved the phone,' says Lizzie the skipper. 'Good on him, too.'

'So what do you think?' I ask Latifa as we bounce back through the chop to Havelock.

'Ever heard of *The Handmaid's Tale*?' I shake my head and she elaborates – a dystopian horror story about man's inhumanity to women. 'I think what they've got in mind is potentially scary as hell.'

But, at this stage anyway, not actually illegal.

It's late afternoon when we get back to the marina and I'm happy to call it a day. By now Vernon and his mate from the Māhana site will have given a full report to Cunningham and he'll no doubt be pondering a response. The AOS inspection is scheduled for first thing tomorrow. Keegan gave her blessing on the understanding that they don't go in like a ninja squad, that everybody stays polite and courteous, and that once all firearms were logged and verified, they would leave the premises.

'We don't need a Waco on our hands, Nick. Got that?'

'Absolutely.' Although a similar scorched-earth outcome might be one way of nipping Cunningham's scary plans in the bud. Latifa and I will keep our distance and leave it to the AOS. We've briefed their techos on the bullet retrieved from Thomas Hemi's water tank. If there's any way of linking it to the weapons they inspect, that'd be great.

Back home Paulie is herding the chooks back into their run. There's no real need. They're the crappest free-range chickens I've ever seen; they just hang around the gate all day hoping to be fed. Maybe they're a metaphor for the way the world is going. Or maybe not.

'Mim's grandad is bringing some hay tomorrow. Said he'd give me a lift home.'

'No need, mate. I'll pick you up.'

'Mum's already said yes. She's got a meeting.'

We really should communicate more. 'Okay. What's mum doing now?'

'The usual.'

'I'll get dinner on.'

'Already on. Roast lamb.'

'Woo-hoo.' We high five. 'Get in.'

Vanessa doesn't see what the fuss is about with Michael Walton. 'Look he's apologised, he's bringing us some free pea hay, he's doing us a favour giving Paulie a lift. Let's give him a chance to redeem himself.'

'After what he said about Paulie?'

'Shitty yeah, but Mim's his first friend since we left Sunderland. We can't afford to hold grudges. Paulie won't thank us for it.'

'Friendship at any cost? Is that what we're teaching him?'

'Ease up, love. Some of the kids do that every day behind his back and sometimes to his face.' She sees I'm stung. 'Yes, children can be cruel and some grown-ups too. For a cop you're a bit fragile at times, Nick.'

'When it comes to Paulie and you, sure.'

She pushes her dinner plate my way for washing up. Gives me a lamb and rosemary flavoured kiss. 'Have faith, sweetie. Look for the best in people.'

14.

Apparently the AOS inspection at the Lodge went pretty smoothly. All the firearms checked with the paperwork and all fitted the guidelines for what is permitted under current New Zealand law. Shame. The techs didn't find any evidence that any of those guns fired the bullet into Hemi's water tank but that doesn't necessarily mean they didn't – they just need closer inspection that's all.

'They searched the place for any unregistered weapons?'

'Cursorily,' says Keegan down the hissing line. Atmospherics, mountains, weather. NZ and cellphones sometimes seem incompatible. 'There weren't any grounds to turn the place over. You got what you wanted, Nick. A show of force. Hopefully they'll pull their heads in. Maybe you should think of doing the same.' She tells me a complaint has been lodged about our conduct out at Māhana yesterday.

'He obstructed us in our duty.'

'Yeah, Lizzie the boatie said he was a twerp and had it coming. It won't go any further, Nick, but dial it down a bit, huh?'

I promise to try.

'Any news on the medical appointment?'

'This for your paperwork?'

'Fuck you, Nick. I'm actually asking after your health.'

'Thursday. There was a cancellation.'

'Hope it goes well. Look after yourself. And yep, a copy of any medical reports would be good for the files.'

Latifa returns from the bakery with two takeaway flat whites and a ginger slice each.

'What's the occasion?' I ask.

'We've named the date, Daniel and me. October twentieth, keep it free.'

'Congratulations.' We have an awkward hug and settle into the ginger slices.

'Any fallout from the raid … ahem, inspection this morning?'

'Nah. All went swimmingly.'

'Bugger.' She brushes some crumbs away. 'The bullet?'

'No match so far.' I tell her Vernon and friend have been complaining about us.

'Sorry, that was my fault. Shouldn't have cuffed that guy to the rail and chucked his phone in the water, eh?'

'For tough guys they seem to have glass jaws.'

She crumples her wrapper. 'Bullies tend to.' She catches me looking at her. 'What?'

'You know there's people you can talk to. Like, about the attack and that. Counselling, whatever.'

'I'm going okay, Nick. I'll let you know if I'm not.'

The landline rings. It's Maxwell from down the road. 'You guys want to drop by? That thumb drive from the Lodge looks interesting.'

'A dark-coloured van heading south along Wakamarina Road at one fifty-two a.m.' Maxwell asks for the image to be frozen. 'Anybody you know up that way with one of those, Nick?'

'Nobody comes to mind. It could have been heading to the campsite at Butchers Flat. Did it come back out again?'

'Not during the timeframe captured for the thumb drive, twelve hours up to midday the following day.'

'We could get the timeframe widened.'

'They still friends of yours after this morning?'

'They respond well to paperwork and warrants. Did your insomniac midnight rambler take a look at this?'

'Yep. Could be the van, according to him. But he wouldn't swear to it.'

'Want me to take a drive up there, ask around, look for it?'

'I think a door-to-door is in order. Maybe you can go along with Gemma and the team to help smooth the way?'

'It won't be needed, this is a murder enquiry, people will be happy to help if they can.'

Maxwell smiles. 'Still, it's the Wakamarina. That reputation as bandit country goes way back.'

'Whatever.' A glance at Gemma. 'Your car or mine?' She waves her key fob in response.

Latifa is sent back to local duties and doesn't look too happy about it. I sidle up to Maxwell on my way out. 'You're wasting a good cop in Rapata.'

'I'm sure she can fight her own battles.'

He's right on that at least. 'She's been through the mill. She deserves better.'

'Point taken. Finished?'

'No. Are the Nelson Ds any closer to finding her attacker?'

'No. They're doing their best, Nick. Trust me.' He's checking his phone. Things to do. 'Tick, tock, mate.'

Gemma is in the driving seat as we head up the valley road. The idea is to check out Butchers Flat at the far end and work our way back while a second team heads in our direction from the Lodge. I estimate we'll probably meet just outside my pretty little red-roofed home.

'You haven't got it parked in your garage, have you?' Gemma slows for a tight bend. 'The boss might have cleared you but I still have my doubts.'

'Persistence. An admirable quality in a detective.'

There's nothing to see at Butchers Flat so we pay Thomas Hemi a visit at the last house in the valley. Ruth is pottering in the vegie garden and Thomas is chopping wood as we make our approach.

'Nick? How's things?'

I introduce him to Gemma and state our business. Ruth goes back to what she was doing. We ask if it's okay for the two Blenheim uniforms to take a wander over the property.

'You think the van's here?'

'Just wanting to check.'

'No need. It isn't here. You have my word.'

Gemma signals the uniforms. 'We'll look anyway.'

Thomas steps forward, axe raised slightly.

I lift my hand. 'No probs, Thomas. I'll take your word for it.'

'What?' says Gemma. 'No way. In you go, guys.'

'We're not here to search. We're here to conduct enquiries.' A nod at the uniforms. 'We've made our enquiry and got our answer. We're going.'

Gemma turns and stalks towards the car. 'We'll be back with a warrant, Mr Hemi. Count on it.'

Thomas has his eyes on me. Over in the vegie garden Ruth is leaning on her spade, checking us out.

'I believe you on the van, Thomas. No other reason you don't want us poking around, is there?'

'Nothing that's any business of yours.'

'I'll take that as a no. Don't make me regret it, mate.'

As far as we can tell, the dark delivery van isn't parked on any property up the Wakamarina.

'So if it didn't return, and we can get extra footage from the Lodge to check that, then where is it?'

Gemma doesn't reply straight away. She's been too busy fuming over her loss of face at the Hemi homestead. 'Let's get warrants for the whole valley. We'll find it.'

'Sure. There's one or two whose words I'd like to verify but it'd be a waste of time and manpower searching every farm in the valley.'

'Your mate Hemi is top of my list.'

'Feel free but I think he's an honest man.'

'I don't know where you got that. From what I hear he has convictions for violence and gang-related activities.'

'Not for a long time. People change.'

'Yeah and pigs fly. We should have been looking into him from day one. A murder in your parish and a thug like him for a neighbour? Whose side are you on, Nick?'

We're back in Havelock by midafternoon. As I haven't had any lunch and the bakery has closed, the choice is a pie from the Four Square or something at the hotel. The thought of a Four Square pie after what happened in their coldroom is too much to stomach. Sometimes it's mind over matter. One pizza and L&P at the hotel later, and I'm fighting fit. Doug is there in his usual seat.

'Found your murderer yet?'

'No.'

'Make it quick. Gettin' sick of having so many strangers in town. You'd think it was summer.'

'Do my best. Know anybody around here with a dark-coloured delivery van?'

'Why?'

'Just asking.'

'Funny that. I was panning up Pear Tree Flat the other day and there was one parked way back in the trees. Looks like it's been there a while.'

By the time we get back up to Pear Tree, it's gone.

'Doug said he was here at the weekend when he saw it.'

'But our searchers never saw it today and they had a good look,' says Gemma, defensively.

'So it's been hidden here since the murder and driven out later. Maybe more footage from the Lodge CCTV will tell us precisely when.'

There are tyre tracks for forensics and, Doug being Doug, we have a more accurate description of the colour and make of the van and he even noted the rego. 'Could have been somebody dredging another fella's claim without permission. Can't have that, can we?'

Maxwell is sufficiently happy with my expert sleuthing over a hotel pizza to not take too seriously Gemma's complaints about my handling of the Hemi matter. It's now early Tuesday evening and while we've been beating around the bush at Pear Tree, a warrant has been served at the Lodge for footage since the weekend. I've brought my own vehicle with me this time so there's no need to go back into town. Gemma has a parting shot before I jump into the ute to go home.

'I haven't finished with Hemi, or you.'

I'm with Doug on this one. The sooner we solve this, the sooner we can all get back to normal.

When I pull into my driveway, Michael Walton's ute is still there, piled with bales of pea hay. It'll be dark soon. If he's been here since just after school time then he's made himself very comfortable – we're talking two hours at least.

'Evening,' he says, standing up from his cuppa at our kitchen table to shake my hand. Over his shoulder Vanessa rolls her eyes and points at her watch.

'You brought the hay, then.'

'And me,' says Paulie, looking up from his homework, a drawing of some sort.

'No Mim?'

'Homework,' say Michael and Paulie at the same time.

Vanessa seizes the opportunity to start rattling some pots and pans in the kitchen and Michael takes the hint.

'Better unload those bales.'

'I'll give you a hand.'

Back outside the sandflies are end-of-day thick but the trick is to keep moving. Michael doesn't seem to notice them; stubby shorts and polo shirt, bare legs and arms, he seems mildly amused by my slapping and waving like a nancy.

'Nice place you have here.'

'We like it.'

'Peaceful, out of the way.'

'Yeah, it is.'

'Missus must get lonely though. Not much social life around here and she's got a bit of spark.'

He gets under my skin like Cunningham seems to get under everybody else's. 'We manage.' The bales are stacked in the corner of the garage and I'll be happy to see the back of him. Maybe a retaliatory dig. 'Your daughter, too. Must be lonely for her out on the farm?'

'Jan? No, she's good. It's been tough since her fella passed away but you keep on keeping on, don't you?'

'She must appreciate you being around to keep a close eye on her and Mim.'

'Yeah. I guess she must.'

A wink and a wave to show he's not going to be baited and away he goes down the valley road.

15.

The van had been stolen in Nelson the weekend before the murder. The owner, hearing about its possible subsequent use, was ambivalent about having it returned if we ever did recover it. The Lodge CCTV picked it up passing midmorning last Sunday, the driver wearing a hoodie and low-pulled baseball cap. Somebody was now chasing any other sightings along that road and others for around that time Sunday morning.

'Stolen from seventy-odd k's away, in plenty of time for the dastardly deed,' says Maxwell. 'So that rules out a spontaneous crime of passion.'

'Masterful deduction, boss.'

'No need to call me boss, Nick. We're a team here.'

'Did Hoodie get a lift up to collect the van?'

'We're working through that. Lots of traffic up and down the valley on a sunny Sunday morning. Could've even cycled over from the Wairau Valley, shoved the bike in the back and gone his way. Endless possibilities.'

Maxwell seems buoyed by developments so I leave him to enjoy his day. Much as I'd love to join the chase, he already has the people he needs. He wants me to focus on Havelka, see if we can find the other half of the body and identify a culprit. Easy as. The hitman thread is the one to follow and I can't help thinking that Thomas Hemi has unresolved secrets in his life: he didn't want us looking over his farm and he took umbrage at me bringing up his past. Fair enough. We all like to think that our home is our castle and that what we were back then is not necessarily what we are now. On the way back up the road to the cop shop my phone goes. Speak of the devil.

'Thomas? How's it going?'

'Okay. Jax told me last night those nuts in the Lodge are pretty pissed off at the AOS raid. They're planning something. Bit of retaliation.'

'He got this from Melvyn, I assume?'

'Just thought I'd pass it on.'

'No specifics?'

'If there were, I'd tell you.' Jeez, he's terse as.

'Thanks, Thomas.'

'I've told him to keep his ears open.'

'Cheers.'

Thomas hangs up. Another set of toes trodden on. It's easy to do around here. Back in the office Latifa has left a note saying she's out on SH6 looking for dickheads. Odds-on, she'll find some. It's midmorning and yesterday's wind has whipped up again. It was my turn to drop Paulie off this morning. As I was pulling into the school car park Mim was hugging goodbye to her mum. I'd never met her before: a striking-looking woman with a strongly defined face and broad shoulders. She smiled at Paulie and at me before getting back into her car.

'Michael double-booked?' I leaned down to her open window as Paulie and Mim went their way.

'Doctor's appointment. You're Paul's dad, I take it. I'm Jan.'

'Nick.' We shook hands. 'Michael brought some hay up to our place last night. Much appreciated.'

Jan nodded. 'He said he was going to.'

'Settling in okay?'

'Getting there, gradually. Takes a while to get to know people.'

'Good. Well, see you around I suppose.'

'Expect so.'

And she'd driven off leaving me feeling slightly short-changed. I'm not sure why but I'd been expecting someone timid, shrunken, brow-beaten. Maybe it's something about Michael's intensity and protectiveness, that vehemence of his when we'd disrupted Mim's sleepover plans. I recall the Māori phrase Latifa had used a couple of days ago about a man searching the mountains and forests for a wife to call his own. Māhana. Jan didn't seem to be the type of woman who would allow herself to be someone's possession. Husband or father. Anyone.

Having revisited the Havelka case, examined the pathologist's report, looked again at the circumstances leading up to the death, I'm inclining to the view that it's Morgan Hopu's handiwork, and that in turn brings my mind back to his once enforcer-cum-hitman, younger half-brother Thomas. Looking at that aerial map and the track from Pelorus Bridge over the hill to Butchers Flat only adds to my suspicions: the Hemi property is less than a kilometre from where the half-body was found. So, is the other half buried somewhere on Thomas's farm and is that why he didn't want us poking around? None of it quite rings true, though. Thomas was at Butchers Flat when the body was unearthed. Not a flicker of reaction. Is he that good an actor? Or maybe it was all just too chaotic that day and I wouldn't have noticed anything anyway. Either way, there are insufficient grounds yet for a warrant so I need to find some. Thomas's charge sheet is a good place to start.

It's remarkably clean for an ex-thug. Most of the convictions are for relatively petty violence in his early gang days. He would have been late teens, early twenties. Skirmishes and turf disputes in pub car parks and nightclubs around Nelson, a drive-by shooting on a house but no injuries reported, the firebombing of a massage parlour. Drug possession, carrying an offensive weapon. A more serious assault over a drug debt left a man in a coma for six weeks. Gemma is right, he was a nasty piece of work back then. But he barely registers after his twenty-second birthday, and he's in his mid-forties now. Two decades clean. Did he get smart or lucky or did he change his ways? There's one blip. Eight years ago he was arrested for being drunk and disorderly in Wellington. He'd got hammered during a pub crawl in the city centre and, shortly after midnight one summer night, the police had been called in response to reports of someone shouting, swearing and disturbing the neighbours. It wasn't something that happened very often around there. The neighbourhood was Oriental Bay. Check the address and a map. A few blocks away from Lucy McLernon's home. Two years later she would be raped and murdered in a motel in Westport and six months after that the motel manager would be shot, execution-style, just like Karel Havelka.

Coincidence? Hemi arrested a few blocks away from McLernon's home. It's like saying a shooting a few blocks away from 1600 Pennsylvania Avenue is an attempted presidential assassination. Hemi could have been in the area for any number of reasons: work, holiday, visiting friends or relatives, a wedding, a funeral. What *was* he doing over there anyway? My understanding is that he has lived on his farm in the Wakamarina for the best part of ten years. Where were Ruth and the kids during this time? He married and started his family nearly a decade earlier, not long after he dropped off those early gang charge sheets. A few residential blocks in Wellington notwithstanding – is there anything linking Hemi to Lucy McLernon? Searching her case file on the database it seems not. Lunchtime, the bakery beckons.

Brooding over a chicken salad wrap and coffee, I map out where to from here. Maxwell needs to be brought up to speed: maybe we should seek a search warrant on the Hemi homestead, and perhaps a visit to Wellington and to Westport is in order. Keegan had mentioned the name of a Nelson D who worked both homicide cases – McLernon and the motel owner Robertson. Scrolling through the emails on my phone, I find his name and number: Nigel Watson. It turns out he's still in the Job but barely.

'Caught me just in time, mate. I retire next month. You the bloke that caused all the fuss last year? Arresting captains of industry, torturing Russian tourists with eels? Fucking the district commander-to-be? Hoped I'd meet you before I left. Nice to put a face to a juicy rumour.' He hasn't got much on today or any other day for that matter and is happy to drive over the Whangamoa to meet here in Havelock. 'Treat me to a pan of mussels and I'm anybody's. Or maybe I shouldn't be saying that to the infamous Roger the Todger, eh?' Hoot.

We agree a five o'clock rendezvous. That should give me enough time to brace for his verbal onslaught.

Phone back on the table and a last slurp of coffee; looking up, I see Jessie James waving on the other side of the window. She invites herself in and joins me. 'Want to buy me a coffee?' Another round ordered while Jessie gets her iPad out and revs it up. 'Been doing a bit more digging on your friends in the Lodge.'

'Great. That warrants a bonus ginger slice.'

'Make it a brownie.' The order goes in. 'Standing Rock and Harney County. Mean anything to you?'

'Standing Rock. Backblocks of America. A year or two ago there was a big environmental protest that got violent. Made TV news around the world. The other one? No.'

'Standing Rock reservation bridges North and South Dakota. It's a few hundred klicks from Brandon Cunningham's neighbourhood. The protests were over an oil pipeline through Sioux sacred grounds and other environmentally sensitive areas. Galvanised a lot of people from right and left, and got pretty nasty at times.' Finger swipe and a new screen. 'Harney County is in Oregon. An armed militia occupied a wildlife reserve in protest at some ranchers charged with arson on federal land. Effectively took over the adjacent town too. Went on a few months and one militiaman got killed at a police roadblock. A lot of he-said, she-said, but the gist is that some believed they were testing the water for an overthrow of the government.'

'All very interesting. But?'

'I trawled through social media looking for any traces from the names I have for those in the Lodge.'

'I already did that. Cunningham's a no-show.'

'Sure but there's this guy Georges, that's George with an 's', French style. Georges LeBlanc, Louisiana native, Cajun as they come.'

She shows me the photo. It's Daniel Boone.

'He heeded the call to arms at the militia stand-off in Oregon and later worked for private security at Standing Rock. If his social media presence is anything to go by, he's one bad hombre. But his name also comes up in connection with some allegations at Standing Rock.'

I read the summary. Then bell Maxwell for a catch-up.

'Look at the injuries.'

Jessie James' research dossier has been printed out in full colour but Maxwell also has the electronic version plus sundry links to supporting news stories, official reports and social media feeds. Jessie also helpfully screen-captured some of the juicier posts in case they mysteriously disappear. It's the Corson County medical examiner's report that we're focusing on right now. The victim was nineteen-year-old Alicia Gomez, a protestor at the Standing Rock site who went missing one night and turned up in a ditch two days later. As well as being sexually assaulted, there were other horrors done to her.

'Secateurs, cigarette burns, snipped extremities, eye gougings.' Not dissimilar to our friend in the Four Square coldroom. Still Maxwell's not buying it. 'Standard gangland or tinpot death squad MO, I would have thought. Horrible sure, but not proof. Anything else?'

'A witness saw her that night heading back to town from the demo. A Trenton Logistics company 4WD was seen following her. That's the company LeBlanc worked for. The same day he'd tweeted a photo of Gomez shouting at him and he made specific threats against her.'

'It says in these reports he was questioned and released without charge.'

'Questioned by guys he probably shared off-duty beers with. Look at the social media feed. He's a big-time hater.'

Maxwell scrolls through. 'Muslims, gays, lefties, women, vegans, greenies, ethnics. Tried reading the comments section of the *Journal* online recently? People like him and views like that are a dime a dozen these days.'

'How come a guy like this gets through Immigration?'

'C'mon Nick, he has no criminal record, and any allegations are just that. His views are deplorable but you get that in a democracy.'

'I can't believe this. Is there something I'm not getting here? Have those guys in the Lodge become untouchable?'

There's the briefest eyelid flicker before he says no.

'What changed?'

'Maybe you should talk to Keegan.'

'You out of the loop, Will?'

There's a flash of anger and a little hurt in his eyes. 'Talk to Keegan. Looks like that AOS raid tipped things.'

A knock on Maxwell's door jamb. Gemma is on the threshold. 'We just found the blue van.'

The car park beside the Renwick sportsground west of Blenheim has become a popular freedom camping spot. The toilets are just fifty metres up the road and the campers for the most part aren't party animals so the site hasn't attracted the opprobrium that others have of late. People keep pretty much to themselves and they keep their curiosity in check. But after two days, the blue van was starting to stink and attract blowflies. You get that when the inside looks like an abattoir apron.

'Assume that's Gelder's blood?' says Gemma.

'Hope so, or we're really behind the eight-ball.' Maxwell waves the forensics team back in and we retreat behind the perimeter tape. 'It'd be nice if something in there linked us to Monsieur LeBlanc.'

'Who?' says Gemma. We bring her up to speed. A tag team, me for, and Maxwell against the emerging hypothesis. 'And who says we can't talk to him?'

'I do.' It's Keegan. She got here so quick I'm wondering if I missed a helicopter landing. 'Nick, Will. Over here.'

Gemma doesn't even frown at the freeze out. Maybe she's watching and learning the Keegan power moves. Instead she gets on her mobile and looks busy.

'It's only temporary,' says Keegan. 'My contact from Porirua has gone all antsy and advised we hold off while she looks further into it. Sirens went off when she plugged some of those names into the internal search engine. She had a late night personal visit at her home from some departmental heavies. Somebody had been jumping up and down about the poor boys being bullied and having their guns inspected.'

'At this stage there's no reason why we should be bothering them any time soon,' says Maxwell.

'You've got to be joking, mate.' Before he can stop me, I introduce Keegan to the mad, bad world of Georges LeBlanc. 'In the absence of any other strong leads, I think we'd be negligent if we didn't have a chat with him.'

Keegan blows out a stream of cigarette smoke. 'Put your case together, maybe wait for the report on this meat truck too, run it past me and, if I like it, in we go.'

Maxwell sniffs. 'Am I still in charge here?'

'Course you are, Will.' She flicks the ciggie away. 'Wouldn't have it any other way.'

Maxwell, still smarting from Keegan's leash-jerk, has told me and Gemma to put the case together against LeBlanc. I guess that means a promotion from the plumbing list. Driving back from Renwick to Havelock, a doozy of a wind is blowing off the Sounds and slapping my car broadside. It's late afternoon, the road is busy and the sun has gone. I've messaged Nigel Watson that I'm running late but we're still set for an early evening rendezvous at The Mussel Pot in downtown Havelock. At home, Vanessa has said she'll see me when she sees me and hung up with a kissy sound.

Nigel Watson looks older than his fifty-five years. He doesn't get much exercise or sunshine but he certainly seems happy enough. His talk is punctuated with chuckles and quips and he's a font of cop war stories, some of which I've heard before as far back as Sunderland ten, fifteen years ago. Global urban myths with names and places interchanged. He's ordered Thai green mussels and I've gone the blue cheese. There's a bottle of local pinot gris to smooth the way but this guy doesn't need alcohol to loosen his tongue.

'What's she like in the sack then? Keegan? Fuck, you lucky man.'

No wonder he's been shunted aside. Voice like a foghorn and subtle as a house brick. 'Shouldn't believe locker-room gossip, mate.'

He taps his nose. 'Right you are, big fella. So what do you want to know about those west coast jobs?'

'Everything you can remember, particularly the stuff that didn't end up in the official record. I've already read that. How about chronological? Lucy McLernon happened first.'

Watson mops some sauce from his chin. 'One of the few I didn't close during my time. Had a better batting average than most of the Black Caps top order.' A truculent slurp of wine. 'Counts for nothing when your face no longer fits and you're up against kids who've been to university.'

I raise my glass in fellowship. 'Old school, mate.' He buys my sincerity and pushes on.

'Nice girl. Good family. Seemed so anyway. But you have to wonder what drives people into these cults don't you? Something amiss behind closed doors?'

'Maybe she was a rebel, or a searcher.'

'Certainly desperate. Not many mothers leave behind their kids.'

It's a balancing act. Cut to the chase, or let him take his own sweet time to get to wherever we're going? 'Were there any suspects from her private or family life?'

'No. Long story short, they all checked out.'

'Old boyfriends, work colleagues? Marriage was obviously shaky if she ran away to join the Jesus freaks.'

'Husband seemed a good bloke. Genuinely upset by her leaving, not upset angry, upset hurt. Same with the news of her death – genuine sad. I think he loved her.'

There's a pause. 'But?'

Watson shrugs. Helps himself to a couple more mussels. 'It wasn't reciprocal. A couple of old girlfriends reckoned the marriage was a sham from day one. A keeping-up-appearances type thing. She was pregnant and the parents put pressure on her to marry.'

'New Zealand in the twenty-first century.'

'More like her family and their judgmental friends in the twenty-first century.'

'Fair point.' He's not such a dinosaur after all. 'So the husband was more like a fling that was made permanent. Was there a one true love in the background?'

'If there was he, or she, didn't have a name. Maybe she craved spiritual satisfaction over base carnality.'

'Very poetic.'

'You taking the piss?' Watson pushes his bowl of mussel shells away. 'Brass tacks. We had no evidence of a previous lover, or family member, or fellow cult member doing the deed. We did have suspicions that the motel manager, Robertson, was a sleazy prick who had convictions and complaints for filming his guests, exposing himself, and such. But no rapes or other violence in his history.'

'And he was able to get a job like that?'

'He didn't own the place, he was a duty manager. Somebody didn't check his references or criminal record. It happens.'

'So do you think his murder was connected with hers? Payback?'

'No evidence found but nothing to discount that as one theory.'

'Other theories?'

'Payback for some other sleaze? Robertson also had drug debts. He was a bit of a party guy.'

'Drug debts would be a more likely scenario for the execution-style killing, yeah?'

'S'pose so.'

There's another 'but' in the air. 'Refill?' The topped-up glass keeps him talking.

'There were no signs of struggle at the motel. No noises heard. The sand on the beach, where it wasn't washed away, the tracks were orderly. Nobody was dragging him kicking and screaming.'

'He didn't see it coming and he knew his killer?' Watson peruses the menu. As it's my treat, he orders himself cheesecake for dessert. 'Make that two,' I tell the waitperson. 'And coffees, please.'

'That stuff is all on the database,' he points out.

'Not the orderly tracks in the sand.'

'Funny. Sure that was in my notes somewhere. Thought I'd inputted it.'

'The tracks. Did they lead back somewhere after the deed? A car park? Tyre impressions? Sightings?'

'Nah. Just the two sets leading in. None leading out.'

'So the murderer came in further up the beach? If the tide is coming in you just walk along the shoreline and it'll be washed away.'

'Looks like it.' The desserts arrive and Watson makes a great show of digging in.

'Thin air after that?'

'Poof!' he says, scooping up some cheesecake.

It's after nine by the time I'm heading back up the valley road. Watson declined my offer of a spare bed and opted to drive back to Nelson. He's probably on the edge of the alcohol limit but not enough for me to insist. He's a big boy. Vanessa is still at her books as I drop my keys on the kitchen table. We snog a while.

'Blue cheese,' she says, wrinkling her nose. 'Nice. Who's your friend?'

'An old-timer from Nelson. Worked a case on the west coast which might link to the Butchers Flat body.'

'Does it?'

'Not so far.'

'As wild goose chases go, a meal at The Mussel Pot isn't half bad.'

'Tough work but somebody's got to do it. All quiet on the home front?'

'Yep, Paulie's still pushing for a Mim sleepover this weekend. Maybe we should oblige?'

'S'pose so. It's a funny set-up there. I'm just as inclined to get out the barge pole.'

'Maybe she'll give something away about what's going on? Call it intelligence gathering.'

'It's sneaky and underhand using a child like that.'

'Yes. Put the kettle on.' Taps her pen on her teeth. 'Your appointment's tomorrow down at Blenheim.'

'Yep.' Focus on the kettle, the switch, the mugs, the teabags.

'I've organised cover for the half day. I'm coming with you.'

'No need.'

'I'm coming anyway. We'll drop Paulie at school and head down there together.'

'Ordinary or herbal?'

'It's going to be fine, Nick.'

'Yeah.'

'Herbal.'

16.

My mate Billy's mum died of brain cancer. He must have been all of seven and she was all of thirty-eight. I remember her fading away those last few months. The beanie and the wig to cover the hair loss. The brave smile. Big eyes. Hollow cheeks. The paleness. The wheelchair. My mate retreating into himself. Billy going through the motions. Billy raging at those around him. Billy staring out of the window and the teacher letting him. Billy moving to another school, nearer to his grandparents.

Billy and his mum are on my mind a lot today. Billy's there when I drop Paulie off at school, hugging him overlong so that he finally and gently pulls away from me embarrassed and a little scared. I see the pale shadow of Billy's mum as I change out of my clothes into the flimsy paper nightgown and lie down on the scanner bed awaiting the hum and click.

'What music do you like?' asks the technician.

'What?'

'You'll be in that tin can for a while. How about some tunes to pass the time? Classical, rock'n'roll, jazz, blues, folk, country and western?'

Maybe some Death Metal. 'Classical? Something calm?'

'I like a bit of Bach cello myself. That suit you?'

'Sure.'

The gown feels as thin as a last breath. I'm not good with doctors, hospitals, health scares, and I always assume the worst. That's me catastrophising again. One of these days my pessimism is going to be spot on and then I'll be sorry.

'All done?' Vanessa's waiting for me when I come out. 'That was quicker than I expected.'

'That's it for now. There'll be an appointment with the neurologist once the results are out.'

'Any ideas when?'

'Results are probably already there waiting to be read and interpreted. It's a matter of when the specialist is free.'

'It's going to be fine, Nick. Really.'

We both agree it absolutely is. I drop her back at school and head to the town hall. Gemma and I are meant to build a case for bringing in Georges LeBlanc for questioning. She'll have been doing more digging this morning while I've been staring into the abyss with that red line moving up and down my face.

'Plenty of Gelder's DNA in the van. Plus others too. Bit soupy, they reckon.'

'No sightings at the Renwick sportsground for who might have left the van there?'

She shakes her head. 'Nearest neighbours think it arrived late at night.'

'So if it was driven out of Pear Tree Flat on Sunday morning, they drove it around for the whole day before dumping it.'

'Or parked it somewhere else for a while. We've got people on car park and street cameras in Blenheim and Picton during that day. Meanwhile I've been doing some digging on your Monsieur LeBlanc.'

Predictably he has police, military and private security history as well as connections to far-right US groups such as the Aryan Brotherhood and KKK. Discharged from the military in 2010 after tours of Iraq and Afghanistan. His police service seems to have been mainly in small-town or county sheriff's departments where references and aptitude are sometimes less valued than loyalty and discretion. Uniformed thugs on the public purse acting with impunity in the American heartland. Who'da thought?

'Where did you get all this?'

'Some links from DC Keegan's contact. Looks like the girls are pushing back against the spooks' boys club.' Gemma is buzzing, maybe she feels part of history in some way. Or at least part of a team.

'And even with this "background", he gets to come here?'

'No criminal convictions. Decorated military veteran. Ex-law enforcement official. On the face of it, a model citizen.'

'No specifics on why the Lodge is supposedly a no-go area?'

'Not yet. That stuff is still classified. What we have here isn't.'

'Any more on the Alicia Gomez case?'

'No.' She enjoys my disappointed frown. 'But we have yet another nasty unsolved death on his watch in a place called Nogales, border with Arizona and Mexico. Abel Hernandez, forty-two, married, three kids.'

'Let me guess, Border Patrol?'

'Nothing so formal and accountable. Once again, private security subcontracted to protect and monitor, among other things, an abattoir known to employ heaps of illegals.'

It turns out that one morning a body was discovered in one of the slaughterhouse coldrooms cable-tied to a chair and tortured to death.

'Similar injuries?'

She nods. 'Very. Same kind of tools. LeBlanc was on duty that night and the victim had been subdued by a shot of ketamine to the neck.'

'But LeBlanc wasn't charged?'

'Nothing specifically pointed to him. Plus the abattoir owner was the sheriff's cousin and a major political donor. Official story was of a quote, "wetback drug-gang feud".'

'Any unofficial stories?'

'Plenty. Unpaid debts, whistleblowing the people traffickers, you name it. The company had recently lost a lawsuit taken out by the union alleging wage theft and sexual exploitation. Abel's name features in some of the news stories.'

'That's enough for me. Is Maxwell around?'

'Yes, I am.' And so he is, right behind me.

'Been there long?'

'Long enough. You're right. We need to talk to this guy and we're going to have to go in hard this time. We want this guy's spit and fingerprints on file.' He stands straight, a man with a rediscovered purpose. 'Early start tomorrow with the ninjas. I'll organise it.'

'All hands on deck?'

'Yep. Even you, Nick.'

Back in the cop shop, I bring Latifa up to speed.

'That's some damning background. Pretty detailed too.' She mutes an incoming call on her mobile. 'Sounds like a power struggle going on in some grey building in Wellington and we're being played.'

'You sure you're just a hick country cop?'

She shrugs. 'Whatever. Let the suits push and shove if it means getting what you need to send those hillbilly fuckwits on their way.'

'Kind of how I saw it too. Besides, the boys in the Lodge are expendable and the guy with the high-level protection is this Bryant fella who owns the properties here and on the Sounds.'

'Maybe he'll find it's all a bit too hard and bugger off somewhere else with his crazy ideas. Aussie, maybe. He'd go down well there.'

'Crackpot, Christian, misogynist, racist, tax-avoider. You reckon?'

'Am I invited tomorrow?'

'Maxwell said all hands on deck so yep, why not?'

Latifa seems happy enough with that and turns her mind to the overnight log and some stats ahead of a scoot out on SH6. 'By the way, we tracked down the Von Crapps. Steve pulled one of them over for speeding last night. Gave a Blenheim address.'

'Good, they're off our patch. Less paperwork.'

'Their old Waka neighbours would agree. Apparently they're jubilant. How'd it go at the hospital today?'

'Just some tests. Pretty routine.'

'That to do with the memory lapse you had with Gelder?'

'Yeah.'

'Be sweet if we can pin this Gelder thing on Georges, get a clear bill for you from the doc, brand new start.'

'Suit me.'

'Maybe I can get up close to that Georges bloke, look into his eyes, see if he was the one that tried to kill me.'

'He ticks all the right psycho boxes.'

'That would be good, eh?'

'Live in hope.'

We retreat into our own thoughts. Hers, I'm sure, dwelling on a slow horrific death in a beautiful native forest. Mine feature hospital waiting rooms, humming machines, X-rays and scalpels. I tamp them down with the distraction of a cold case going nowhere. Nigel Watson lied to me last night, I'm sure of it. He didn't forget to input that vital information about the footprints into the case files. He deliberately withheld it. Did he mean for it to come out last night? Showing off and slipping up? Or was it a deliberate drip-feed?

Opening up the database to check, it's clear I was right. There's no mention of footprints in the sand although it's obvious there should be. Where's the quality control? Crime Scene 101 – any sign of anybody else having been here? Watson was in charge of the locus, and Keegan's predecessor – ex-DC Ford – in charge of the whole case. The quality control buck should stop with him. Maybe he warrants a visit to see how retirement is going. Leaving a message on his brusque voicemail, I'm tempted to call it a day even though it's only midafternoon. Tomorrow's an early start at the Lodge and concentration evades me. There's a throbbing migraine gearing up at the back of my head. Stress or symptom?

'Need to take an early one. I'll follow up on this plumber's list at home.'

'Sure,' says Latifa. 'Nothing much going on. Calm before tomorrow's storm. You okay?'

'Might have a flu coming on. You happy to hold the fort?'

'No probs. Take it easy, Nick.' Latifa rarely calls me by my name and it almost brings me to tears. This is crazy. A massive hypochondriac over-reaction.

My head is pounding as I turn off SH6 at Canvastown to take the valley road. An SMS has come back from ex-DC Ford, plain Dave nowadays, for a catch-up at The Free House in Nelson over the weekend. Sure, there's no hurry and the only thing on my mind right now is a nice lie-down in a quiet dark room. There's a roadblock outside the Lodge. An armed roadblock. What the fuck? A young guy in camos wielding an AR-15 flags me down at the narrowed road-calming speed bump.

'What's going on?'

'Sorry, sir. We're just checking vehicles on this road.'

'You don't have the right.' He can see my uniform, I don't need to explain myself. 'Pack this crap up straight away and go home.'

'Step out of the car, sir. We need to do a body search.'

'Fuck off, you're in New Zealand, dickhead. Clear the way.'

Now the car is surrounded and there are guns being brandished.

'Step out of the car.'

'No.'

'Five seconds.'

'You guys are out of line.'

'Three.'

'Piss off.'

'One.'

The doors open and hands haul me out. I'm pushed over the bonnet of my car. Legs kicked apart, hands patting me down. 'Get Cunningham. Tell him it's me. Sergeant Chester.'

'Sure, man.' Big joke apparently. He gets on a two-way and crackles for a while. The big gate swings open and Daniel Boone, AKA Georges LeBlanc, strolls over, bends to my ear as I'm held down. 'Sergeant?'

My head is ready to burst. 'I asked for Cunningham.'

'Mr Cunningham is busy.'

'Get these jokers off me and off the road or there's going to be trouble.'

'We had trespassers on our property overnight. We're conducting enquiries.'

'Trespassers?'

'Hunters. Poachers.'

It's the same line I used out at Māhana. Payback. 'This is the Wakamarina, get used to it. You can't take the law into your own hands.' The horizon tilting and lurching. 'What you are doing is illegal. You have no right to block the road, no right to stop traffic, no right to be waving those guns around. You're not the police, I am.'

'This road is our property, Sergeant. We checked the records.'

'Bullshit.'

'Absolutely not, I assure you.'

'Get this goon off me.'

LeBlanc's hot breath is on my cheek. There's cigarettes in the mix. Meat. And something chemical. 'You really have no idea what you're messing with, do you?'

He straightens up and signals to the lads to release me and go back inside the main gate. I dust myself down and slide back into the car.

'In the spirit of cooperation.' He grins and slaps the roof twice. 'Enjoy the rest of your day, buddy.'

I think in geo-diplomacy that's known as a show of force. My head is spinning and I'm in no shape to pursue this.

He'll keep.

Vanessa and Paulie aren't home yet. Latifa is ready to send in the troops after hearing the latest but will settle for following up the road boundary issue with the council.

'Get them to check that section on Charlie's land too, where the firing range is.'

'Sure. This is completely fucked, Sarge. They need booting.'

'Tomorrow, Latifa. It'll wait.'

I drop the phone and just make it in time to the toilet bowl before doing a big spew. Cleaned up and a couple of Panadol later, it's bed for me.

It's dark when Vanessa wakes me. She looks worried. 'Love? You alright?'

The headache has gone and I feel like eating. 'Probably just stress. Been a full on few days.'

'Aye. Hell of a day to get a migraine. You haven't had one of those for a while. Have you?'

'No,' I lie. 'All good now though.' A reheated chicken stir-fry and a mug of tea make all the difference. 'Paulie in bed?'

'It's eleven o'clock.'

'I've been out all that time?'

'Cold. I came this close to calling the ambulance but you were breathing fine and just seemed heavily asleep.'

'Must've needed it.'

'Yeah.' She comes up behind, puts her arms around me, leans her cheek against the back of my neck. 'You scared me.'

'I scared myself.'

There are messages on my mobile. Although there's no signal here, I can check them via the internet connection. An email from Maxwell, pissed off that I missed the pre-raid briefing and checking I have my own Kevlar and gun – call time Friday, four a.m. outside the Lodge. Keegan saying she's coming too. Latifa wanting to know if I'm okay after the interrupted call. After the best part of seven hours in bed, there's little chance of me sleeping tonight. Maybe I can work through that plumbing jobs list of Gelder's, finally tick it off.

'And here's me hoping for an early night and a cuddle,' says Vanessa.

'Eleven. S'pose that is early for you these days.'

'We're like ships in the night lately.'

'Goes with our jobs.'

'What an epitaph.' Vanessa shakes her head sadly. 'She was a well-prepared teacher and he was an obsessive cop.'

'Let's not be talking epitaphs yet, love.'

'Do you know why I didn't call an ambulance?'

'Why?'

'Because it's an hour whichever way you look at it, Blenheim or Nelson.

You've got to be really sure it's an emergency before you make that kind of call. And once you are sure it's probably too late.'

'Tomorrow's another day.'

'I mean it, Nick. We need to take a long hard look at ourselves.'

Under other circumstances it could have progressed into a fight but we're both too fragile right now. Vanessa heads off to bed and I dig out the list of Bruce Gelder's plumbing jobs. On it goes, it's too late to be ringing people to check they were happy with his work and didn't hold any festering resentments against him. Wekas shout their warnings from the undergrowth, somewhere a morepork hoots. It's after midnight and even with my seven hours sleep I find myself drifting. Another three or so hours and it'll be time to get ready for the morning raid on the Lodge to bring LeBlanc in for questioning. That show of force was interestingly timed. It's like he has foreknowledge of our impending visit.

I missed the briefing so it's not immediately clear how Maxwell will play it. Ram down the gates and send the AOS in to drag Georges out? Ring the buzzer and ask politely? Both have their merits and their faults. It will be impossible to cover all possible escape routes if he decides to leg it. The property is huge and extends back up the hill into a pine plantation. All will be revealed in the fullness of time.

There it is.

Fourth from last on the list of Gelder's jobs. About a week before his death. Two days of pipe-laying and fittings at a property at Ketu Bay. Listed under the name of the previous owners but I know where it is.

Māhana Wellbeing Centre.

17.

Pre-dawn. Maxwell, Keegan, a team of Ds, some uniform support and the AOS are all assembled outside the Lodge when I get there. They've got floodlights trained on the gates and the Lodge guard dogs are barking themselves hoarse. The AOS tactical vehicle – an armoured car with ramming implements and shields – has already demolished the fence on the property over the road to allow it a run-up. The traffic-calming speed bump has cramped its style, as intended, but it's still revved and ready for the word. A helicopter hovers overhead.

'One of ours,' says Keegan. 'With a thermal camera in case anybody tries to run away.' I can hear other chopper noises approaching. 'News, probably.'

Jessie James loiters down beyond a perimeter tape, trying in vain to make friends with Latifa. You can tell a lot from body language, even from a hundred metres away on a cold dark autumn morning. 'The media seem to be well-informed.'

'Not my doing. I'm suspecting they've been tipped off by Cunningham. He wants plenty of attention and witnesses for this.' I update her on the link between Gelder, Māhana, and the Lodge. 'Even better reason for this circus then.' She seems both emboldened by what she has put in train and yet terrified at how wrong it might go.

Maxwell appears at Keegan's shoulder. 'Ready?'

'With all this noise and light, they should be awake by now. Press the buzzer.'

He does. 'Who is it?' asks a crackly and amused Cunningham.

Maxwell states his business.

'Georges? You want to speak to Georges?'

'Yes.'

'Sure. I'll put him on.'

A few seconds later, LeBlanc asks, 'How can I help you, sir?' There's laughing in the background. They're having a real party back there.

'We need you to come back to the police station with us, Mr LeBlanc. We need to question you in relation to a serious matter.'

'Ask away, bud. I'm right here.'

'At the station, under caution, formally and with a lawyer. You need to come out now Mr LeBlanc or we'll be coming in.'

'That would be trespass.'

Keegan steps forward, nudges Maxwell aside. 'We've got a warrant. If you're not out of that gate in two minutes we're coming to get you.'

'Ma'am, that would be your honourable prerogative.'

There are, as you might expect, differing accounts of what happened next. Certainly the news cameras in the approaching helicopters only caught the tail-end of it and, even broken down later, frame by frame, were next to useless in bringing any clarity to the confusion. Here's what I know. The tactical vehicle, unable to get sufficient run-up in the tight angle, managed only to buckle one of the gates enough to allow a single-file gap for the AOS to squeeze through. It took three attempts to neutralise the guard dogs – kill them, in fact – after the first two guys through the gap took a vicious mauling. Cunningham and his boys were waiting at the top of the hill armed not with their semi-automatics but with buckets of shit to chuck over the approaching AOS. Tempers were fraying big time on our side but Cunningham was keen to keep his guns out of it. That was a fight he knew he couldn't win on this occasion.

The good old boys were having a good old laugh and not even retaliating when the AOS got heavy-handed. After a few minutes the residents of the Lodge were lined up facedown on the manicured lawn and cuffed. Gemma, Maxwell and I checked off each against our list. There were two missing. LeBlanc and the young guy, Melvyn.

'Drop it.'

I remember turning. There, in the glare of the floodlights, was Melvyn aiming an AR-15 at us. He'd been spotted by Latifa and now her gun, and the guns of a dozen AOS, were trained back on him.

'Melvyn,' I said. 'Put it down.'

The boy shifted position, nestling the stock more comfortably in his shoulder. Squinting down the barrel.

'Mate,' I said. 'Please.'

Maybe he imagined himself as a computer-generated figure on a screen. Kill numbers ticking over in the bottom left of the frame.

'Do as he says,' said Cunningham, struggling under an AOS grip to turn his head from a position prone on the ground.

Latifa edged one step closer. 'Drop it.'

But Melvyn kept on pointing the gun and then his finger moved on that trigger.

18.

'What was a fifteen-year-old kid doing among those animals? And armed to the teeth?'

Back in Nelson, District Commander Marianne Keegan has a lot of explaining to do and she's looking to me for answers. Theoretically the chain of command via her and Maxwell should keep me off the hook and it would be possible to force that point. Truth is though, I feel like this has been coming ever since Cunningham sucker-punched me that day in the bakery.

'The paperwork says he was Cunningham's nephew and he had official guardianship of him.'

'Why isn't he at home with his mum and dad?'

'Maybe we can ask Cunningham.'

'Yeah, let's do that. And ask him where he thinks Georges LeBlanc might have gone.'

As far as we can tell, LeBlanc escaped through an old mining tailrace, a narrow four-metre-deep gully hacked out of the bedrock in gold rush days to allow tailings and water run-off to escape down to the river. It had since been adapted to suit their particular needs by being roofed over with material to foil the police chopper thermal cameras. By midmorning the story is on every TV channel and lighting up the internet. Conspiracy theories have blossomed and the US ambassador in Wellington wants a full briefing. It would be fair to say that Keegan might well be fighting for her career. Then again, a kid just died with a dozen AOS bullets in him. One from Latifa too.

Cunningham has the Wellington lawyer Helen Kostakidis with him in the interview room. She glares at me as we take our seats. 'Is my client under arrest?'

'No,' says Keegan. 'And I'd like to take this opportunity to express my heartfelt condolences. This was ...'

'Murder,' says Cunningham. He's remarkably composed for someone who has just lost a family member. It's pretty plain he has me in his sights for that.

I'm happy to front up. 'Melvyn Cody was given a number of warnings to drop the weapon, including from you, Mr Cunningham.'

'He was fifteen. Scared.'

'He was fifteen and holding a semi-automatic assault rifle. As his legal guardian, maybe it was incumbent upon you to assume duty of care.'

'Incumbent, huh?'

Kostakidis taps her pen lightly on the desk. 'What's the purpose of this interview? If it's only to try to justify this tragic shambles we can all go home now.'

'I can assure you there will be a full investigation into the matter,' says DC Keegan.

'Oh yes,' says Kostakidis. 'I'll make damn sure of it.'

Before everybody retreats to their ringside corners for the next round, I try a final jab. 'LeBlanc's disappeared.'

'Has he?' says Cunningham. 'Must've been terrified by your storm-troopers.'

'He knows why we want to talk to him. And so do you.'

'Georges is a good man.'

'No, he's not.'

'Besmirching a guy's name. Need to be careful about that, Sergeant Chester.'

'That sounds like a threat.'

A scraping of chairs. 'We done here? I need to make funeral arrangements for my nephew. Get his body shipped back stateside.'

'Why wasn't he at home with his parents?'

'None of your damn business.'

What's become clear by lunchtime is that Cunningham and his compatriots are going to paint themselves as victims and they will be ably assisted in that by the news media, the conspiracy theorists and, to be fair, the facts. Fact: the record of exchanges over the gate intercom, while showing a degree of playfulness on the part of the Lodge residents, also suggests at best a willingness to cooperate and at worst a lack of promptness in complying. These guys were having a laugh and we lost our patience and went in guns blazing. Fact: our aim was to question one of the residents about a serious crime but our grounds for doing so were circumstantial. Did it really warrant such a show of force? Fact: we failed, the guy disappeared. Fact: we failed, a kid died. Fact: we have history between us, this looked like a settling of scores. Keegan is being lined up to take the fall for this fiasco, unless she can find alternative candidates. That would be Maxwell and me. He's as aware of that as I am and has given me carte blanche on the Gelder case to look into whatever might save our arses.

'Chase all the wild geese you want, Nick. Fill your boots.'

While Keegan and the spin doctors deal with the fallout, all us mere mortals can do is build the case against LeBlanc and person or persons unknown – we know there were, after all, at least two people involved in Gelder's murder – and let the AOS hunt down Monsieur Georges who no doubt has the backwoods survival skills of Daniel Boone himself.

Back in the Havelock cop shop, Latifa is studying LeBlanc's file photo closely. 'I'm pretty sure he's not my guy. The eyes don't work for me.'

'Shame.' I want to ask if she's sure but it won't be welcome. Of course she's sure. She was there.

'We need to go back out to Māhana. If that's the job that got Gelder killed, the answer is out there. You up for another boat trip?'

Latifa closes the photo and logs out. Rubs absent-mindedly at the fading weal on her neck. 'Okay.' She grabs bits and pieces and crams them into her backpack. 'Any fallout from this morning?'

'There will be but so far Keegan and Maxwell are doing their best to manage it.'

'First time I've ever shot anybody and it has to be a kid.'

'You did your job. You, the AOS, all of you. He should have put the gun down.'

'Yeah.' She slings the backpack over her shoulder and turns the door sign from Open to Closed. Pulls the door shut, squints at the sky.

This fucking job can swallow you whole.

The waters are calmer today and we make better time out to Ketu Bay on Lizzie's boat. The two guards, Vernon and friend, are waiting for us on the jetty. I give them a wave. 'Hi guys. All good?'

Vernon answers. 'Mr Cunningham told us to expect you and afford you every hospitality.'

Shit, that means they're already ahead of us and whatever we were looking for has been cleared away. But it also means we're on the right track even if Cunningham knows we are. 'Is Vince the foreman around?'

'He's no longer with us.'

'Dead?'

'Fired. Breach of contract.'

'So which of you fine gentlemen will be our guide today?'

'Both of us. Here ...' he hands us each a fluoro vest and hard hat, 'you need to wear these.'

'What's your friend's name, Vernon?'

'Blake,' says the guy all by himself.

'Is that your first name or family name?'

'My Christian name.'

'I seem to recall you acting in a threatening manner on our last visit, Blake. Can I count on you to behave this time round?'

'Yes,' says Vernon, 'he'll be fine.'

'Great. Lead on, Macduff.'

'The name's Blake.'

'Actually it's "Lay on, Macduff." A common misquote.'

The voice belongs to Lizzie the boat skipper. She holds up the book she's been reading. Collected works of Shakespeare.

'Thanks,' I say.

'Pleasure.'

We get the same tour as Vince gave us. Up and down the halls, through the outhouses. Nothing stands out except for those couple of rooms with extra wiring and drainage.

'We'll be offering a well-equipped medical facility in case of emergencies.' Blake is downright ebullient. He'd make a great tourist guide. 'It's pretty isolated out here and you get some wild weather in those Marlborough Sounds of yours.'

'And the strong rooms? Extra thick, heavy doors and reinforced walls?'

'Storage. Resistant to earthquakes. Neat, huh?'

'You've thought of everything.'

'Not yet, but maybe by the time it's finished.'

'When will that be?'

'Few months maybe.'

'You had some plumbing work done here a couple of weeks ago,' says Latifa.

'What of it?' says Vernon.

'Can you show me where?'

'Just some pipes. They're buried underground now.'

'Still, how about you show me where that is?'

And they do. It's a patch of earth leading off one of the wings and it looks pretty innocent. 'Happy?' asks Blake.

'As.' Latifa is champing at the bit. 'Let's take another look at those medical rooms.'

'Why?' says Vernon.

'Because I say so.'

He turns to me. 'You're the boss. Do you need to see that area again?'

Latifa backs Vernon against a wall while I lift a staying hand at Blake. 'First and last warning, Vernon.' Finger prod to his chest. 'Show some respect.'

'We're a team, Vern. I think you'd better do what my colleague says.'

'Sure,' he says. 'Boss.'

And back we go. One room is shiny, tiled. An operating theatre in waiting. The other longer and narrower but also tiled and with a wide drainage channel running along one wall.

'What's this room intended for?' says Latifa.

'Medical.'

'That's your other room. This one doesn't have the right shape, and less electrical connections you might need for specialist equipment.'

'I'm not the architect, ma'am.'

'You have the plans?'

'No, ma'am. They're held by Mr Cunningham.'

Latifa crouches down, rubs a hand over a patch of tiles. A few steps, about two metres away she does the same. And repeat, two more times. 'What used to be here?'

'Ma'am?'

'These spots along the wall, the tiles have been replaced, they don't quite match the others.'

Vernon puts hands on hips. 'I didn't realise the little lady was a tiling expert.'

'Answer the question.'

'Sorry, ma'am, I can't help you there.'

'Did Bruce Gelder, the plumber, do any work in here?'

'Not that I recall.'

'You sure about that?'

'Positive.'

Latifa gives him a smile. 'Thank you for your cooperation.'

'My pleasure, ma'am.'

'It's all about that room.'

The boat cuts through the still waters of Pelorus Sound and a flock of gannets swoop on some fish near a mussel farm. It's a fantastic day, calm and clear. But I can see Latifa is agitated.

'Tell me your thoughts.'

'These guys are usually the jetty guards. Goons. What do they know about what each tradie is doing on a day-by-day basis? That's Vince the foreman's job. Vernon was adamant Gelder didn't do any work on that room. He was vague about everything except that.'

'Fed the line by his superiors, no doubt. Point taken. Anything else?'

'The fresh grouting. The tiling had been replaced at those spots along the wall. Didn't notice last time we were here because I wasn't focused on it.'

'Expert eye?'

'My dad was a tiler before he retired. He knows all about it. He did all our house himself. Let me help him sometimes.'

'Can't argue with that.'

'But the main thing is, the room just gave me the creeps. Even first time round. Hairs on my neck stood up. No joke.'

I nod. 'We need to go through Gelder's home again, look for any connections, notes, whatever, about this job. Talk to the widow.'

'Marnie.'

'Yeah?'

'I've known her a few years. He was a prize dickhead, she deserved better.'

'I can't see her being too happy to talk to me. Maybe you should follow it up, might be more fruitful.'

'Sure.'

We're chugging into the marina now. The skipper's getting a fair few charters out of us lately. It's nice to be able to contribute to the local economy.

'Send your invoice in, Lizzie. This rate, you might have to get the paintbrush out and write "cops" on the side of your boat. Make it official.'

'Cheers, Nick. The kids will have shoes this winter.'

It's late afternoon. Latifa offers to call in on Marnie Gelder as her end of day wrap-up. That seems like a good deal. There's nothing in the cop shop for us to follow up on and the murder room in the town hall is subdued. Maxwell catches me as I'm ducking my head back out.

'Anything from your boat trip?'

'Maybe.' I elucidate. 'It would be good to find the missing Gelder mobile.'

'We've been through that hut of his and found nothing but if that's what this is all about maybe we should look again. For all we know, it's why he was up there that night when you had your run-in with him.'

'I'll drop by for a nose around on my way home if that's okay with you?'

'Sure, but I'll be sending in a dedicated team tomorrow anyway.'

'I might get lucky and save you the manpower. How's life been on the front line this afternoon?'

'Got to give credit to Keegan. She's taking the hits for the operation and so far not trying to deflect any blame.'

'She was like that with those kid murders last year. Just when you think you've got her figured for a careerist hack, she turns around and does the right thing.'

'Enjoy your trip back up that wild valley road of yours.'

Driving by, I can see that already the Lodge has become a mini-shrine. Flowers, teddy bears, cards; all in memoriam for a kid nobody knew who was part of a set-up that was giving everybody the shits until this morning. A couple of reporters are doing TV stand-ups in the fading light. No armed guards outside the Lodge this evening. No menacing road blocks. The weather and the landscape play tricks on you. Those beautiful calm waters out on Pelorus Sound today serve only to remind you of the *taniwha* lurking beneath. A clear cloudless sky has you expecting a tempest beyond the far hill. And, with the orange glow of sunset over the already wilting wreaths at the Lodge gate, one thing is certain: night will follow day. Something is brewing.

The boy Melvyn had no place in a camp filled with battle-hardened men preparing for their faux holy war. Kids his age should be in school, or kicking balls around, or getting hot and bothered about their first kiss or grope. Guns, death and predation should be the last thing on their minds.

As my car drops down the muddy rutted track to Gelder's hut, I see that someone has been here since the forensics team vacated the scene: belongings strewn on the gravel, knick-knacks broken and tossed aside. I'd take a bet they were looking for the same thing we're after. Of course Maxwell has to be right. The only reason Gelder was up here that night outside of his usual pattern of movement was because he was either looking for something or hiding something. His home would have been too obvious and would have brought unwanted attention and danger to his family. It has to be here. But where?

Replay to that night.

He's up to something. You don't come back here at this time of night unless you've got something to hide. Every trick in the damn book to get around the rules and I'm fucking sick of it. Those wankers at the Lodge, this dickhead here – clowns to the left of me, jokers to the right. Surrounded. I've had enough. His ute's gone so that must have been him driving off five minutes ago. The coast is clear and now it's time to nail the bastard.

Torch. The shack smells of his cigarettes. Something else. Weed? Wouldn't that be a nice way to get him out of our lives. Nothing on the table. Shelves. Lights in the bush. Him? He should be gone. Maybe hunters. It's the Roar. Yell out for a mate and you're dead. Another migraine kicking off. Throbbing away.

Torchlight in my face. Blinding.

'What the fuck. What are you doing here?'

What am I doing here? Good question. This is Gelder's land. I've no business here. Time? Jesus, it's nearly eleven. Where did the last three hours go? 'Nothing. I thought I saw something. Trespassers. Came to check.'

'The only trespasser here is you.'

'I'll be going then.'

'Yeah, you do that.' *He shakes his head, lower lip trembles.* 'Think I need this shit?'

'I don't care what you need.' My head is pulsing. I just want to take some tablets and lie down.

'Do your job, leave me alone. Jesus.'

'So step out of my way.'

He doesn't. 'I'll win this. You'll see.'

'Yeah, yeah.' I push him aside.

He pushes back. And then it's on.

Where did he come from and where was his ute? Maybe that was his vehicle leaving but not him in it. Or maybe it was somebody else altogether. Those lights in the bush – him or them? In what little remains of the day it's easier to see now. A narrow track at the far edge of the clearing. Almost immediately it drops steeply. Black beech and five-finger. Ferns. Vines. Scrabblings in the undergrowth. Rats maybe, or possums. Sandflies fierce in the last biting of the day. Where would you hide something around here and keep it protected from the elements?

After half an hour of bush-bashing I'm none the wiser.

19.

Paulie is a bundle of nervous energy. The long-awaited Mim weekend sleepover is happening today. He woke early and had the chooks and goats sorted while Vanessa and I were still yawning over our first coffee. He's lined up DVDs ready to rock'n'roll, and while Vanessa prepares a selection of culinary treats he's got me raking the driveway and tidying the garage.

'Place is a tip, Dad. You've really let it go.'

It's good to be doing something Zen for a change, and raking leaves on a blustery day is exactly that. Latifa phoned earlier to tell me she called in on Gelder's widow, Marnie, who thought he'd been 'a bit intense' in the few days before he died but nothing especially out of character for a bloke with gold fever. She'd never heard anything about Māhana Wellbeing Centre but recalled he had stayed overnight out on the Sounds for a two-day job and came back with one of his stinking hangovers.

'I might be wrong,' said Latifa, 'but I suspect she won't be wasting much time in mourning.'

'Did she have any suggestions for any favourite hiding places?'

'Not around the house, she was pretty sure of that. She's caught him out having the odd fling before: lipstick on the collar and suspicious text messages.'

'She checked his phone often?'

'Apparently but reckons he might have had a spare.'

Two missing phones now. 'That's it?'

'Except for how did he get to and from his two-day Sounds job and where did he stay overnight? I'm guessing all courtesy of Māhana.'

'They probably supplied the hangover too.'

Latifa will seek clarity on that while I rake leaves.

At noon on the dot, Michael Walton's ute pulls into the driveway and out jumps Mim who waves a brief hello before being whisked off by Paulie to meet the four-legged Spongebob and Squarepants. Michael hands me a backpack, sleeping bag, and an EpiPen.

'Assume you've used these before?' He offers a bashful shrug. 'Nuts and eggs allergy.' That wipes out about half of the culinary treats on offer. 'Mind if I check the windows and doors?'

'What?'

'Mim's mum, very protective. She wants to be sure the windows and doors are secure.'

'Don't worry. They are.'

'I'll check anyway if that's okay.'

'No. It's not. If you don't believe or trust me, feel free to take Mim back home.'

'Dad!'

Paulie and Mim are behind me, each clutching chickens struggling to be free-range again. Vanessa shows up, wiping floury hands on a tea towel. She notices the tension and would roll her eyes given half the chance.

'Michael wants to check all the doors and windows are nice and secure for the sleepover.'

'Sure,' she says. 'Better safe than sorry.'

And so he gets his fucking way.

While Paulie and Mim spend the afternoon exploring the farm, tormenting the chooks and goats, watching cartoons and eating relatively healthy fast food, Vanessa and I potter around doing odd jobs, canoodling and snacking on the leftover treats that had eggs and/or nuts in them. Vanessa is very affectionate and, I'm guessing, she's been thinking.

'I've been thinking,' she says.

'Yeah?'

'The honeymoon's over isn't it?'

Uh-oh. 'I thought we were going okay.'

'Idiot. I'm talking about the farm.'

'You feel that?'

'Don't tell me you don't. We're at war with our neighbours …'

'Not any more. He's dead.'

'There's still those weirdos down the valley. And I notice Thomas is cooler to us these days too.'

'I make enemies wherever I am, love. It's part of my job description.'

'No, it's not your job, it's your choice. And lately you seem to be going at it with gusto.'

'Call it a perk then. Fringe benefit.'

She ignores that. 'And while I like, love in fact, the peace and beauty of this place – violent crime aside – I do find myself going stir crazy now and then.'

'It's not easy to have a social life when you spend most of your free time preparing school lessons.'

'Touché. So it's agreed then, we're digging ourselves into a hole here. Something needs to change.'

'You want to move?'

She shrugs. 'Nelson's nice.'

'And expensive. There's the police house in Havelock. That'll be free after Latifa gets married.'

'She's getting married? When?'

'October.'

'Thanks for telling me. But no, I'm figuring Havelock is still too remote.'

'Remote from what?'

This, I can see from her brimming eyes, is the crux of it. 'Hospital.'

'We can't live our lives waiting for something to go wrong, love.'

'You can talk. That's been us since we got here. Witness protection. The Paulie Fund. Now your brain.'

'You know what I mean.'

'Yes, I do. And the fact is, we need to have a plan. If one of us kicks the bucket purely because we're an hour from medical help then we're being negligent of each other.' A studied pause. 'And Paulie.'

The Paulie Fund – saving up for the rainy day when we're no longer around and he still needs care. That rainy day creeping ever closer. Low blow but on target. 'Okay.'

'Okay what?'

'Let's look at our options.' A cackle from the lounge room. 'Paulie won't be happy. He loves the farm.'

'Good try.' She hands me a plate of chopped-up fruit. 'Here, take these in to the kids.'

They've turned off the TV and taken to doing drawings. Paulie's picture is a simple colourful rendition of farm life: the house, chooks, goats, family and his friend Mim. Everybody smiling under a yellow sun. He'll be forever somewhere between five and twelve and that's how his drawings look. Mim's, by contrast, is a more carefully sculpted rendition of what appears to be a nativity scene. A barn, some animals, a mother and child. Christ crucified in the background. The mother and child sad. It's intricate and detailed, lines of grain in the wooden beams, tools on the stable wall.

'You're good at drawing,' I say, placing the plate of fruit between them.

'Yes, I know,' she replies, not bothering to look up.

After dinner Paulie comes up with a plan for delaying bedtime. 'Can we show Mim the glow-worms?'

I've been fading out and back in again. Head buzzing with random thoughts and rogue fears. Vanessa is looking at me, concerned. Paulie too.

'Dad?'

'What?'

'Yes or no? Glow-worms?'

Vanessa needs to take over the negotiations because I've just been hit by a bolt of lightning. No, not a headache this time, a revelation. There are gold workings all through the hills and riverbanks along the Wakamarina valley. Hacked by pick and shovel, fuelled by fever and lust, they form a geological Swiss cheese of disappointment and broken dreams. Some holes and shafts are the size of houses. Others, like the one down our river track, no bigger than a wardrobe. Ours, and no doubt many others, have become the domicile of glow-worms. Peel back a curtain of ferns after dark and there's a spectacular display of starlight captured in those little niches. And these, I remember now, are the lights I saw in the bush near Gelder's shack that night. A brief peeling back of the curtain as he either went into, or exited, a glow-worm cave on his property. A perfect dry place to hide something. My search of the bush yesterday was too early in the evening to pick it up.

Taking my leave, I trot down the road a couple of hundred metres to Gelder's place. By torchlight there's little sign that Maxwell's dedicated search team has been back today. Maybe it didn't warrant the overtime. Locating the track at the edge of the clearing, I work my way down the steep slope, slippery in places from dew or from moss that never sees daylight and never dries. Turn the torch off, stay still and let my eyes adjust. There are critters and winged creatures out there. I'm told that sometimes those endangered native bats from Pelorus Bridge flit over to the Wakamarina for a change of scenery. The blustery wind that blew my raked leaves earlier has strengthened. Trees creak. I know from our own track that old rotten ones can splinter and break if you so much as look at them.

There. Over to the right. Twinkle, twinkle.

The moon is behind clouds. It's dark as. I carefully pick my way forward with baby steps; for all I know there are other workings here, holes in the ground to swallow a man and never let him go. The glow is brighter the nearer I get and, as far as I can tell, this is the only one that might have been visible to me back in the shack clearing. It has to be the place. Pushing through the ferns, I see that this glow-worm cave is similar in size to ours, little bigger than a cupboard. Switching my torch on, the glow-worms switch their lights off. There's no obvious sign of a hiding place. Running my hands over the damp feathery walls and roof. Nothing. Along the floor. Again nothing. Under that moss the cave is solid rock. It's not as if you can scrabble a hole with your hands and pat it down afterwards.

Shit.

By the time I get back, Vanessa and the kids have done their own glow-worm cave tour, teeth have been brushed, sleeping bags rolled out on foam mattresses in the lounge room, and lights dimmed.

'Should've been there, Dad,' says Paulie sleepily. 'Magic. Eh, Mim?'

Mim lifts her head. 'Yeah, choice. You're so lucky living here, Paulie.'

Vanessa and I exchange a look.

'Paul,' he says. 'It's Paul.'

Screaming.

Mim is screaming.

Vanessa is out of bed ahead of me and Paulie has joined in yelling, 'Mum, Mum!'

The lights go on and while I take care of Paulie, Vanessa attends to Mim. 'It's okay, love, we're here. Everything's alright.'

'There was somebody …'

'A nightmare? Were you having a nightmare?'

'No. There was somebody at the window. A man.'

I rush out on to the balcony. We keep a torch by the barbecue. Flick it on, do a quick scan. No sign. Listen for a moment. Only the river, night scratchings, and the wind blowing through the trees. Back inside, Paulie has calmed but sees an opportunity to get a Milo out of the situation. Mim wouldn't mind one too. On goes the kettle.

'There really was,' says Mim. 'I wasn't dreaming.'

'It gets very dark up here and there's sometimes funny noises: possums, wind.' Vanessa pulls the covers up around Mim. 'Shadows caused by the trees moving. Makes me jump sometimes too.'

'But I saw him.' There's an edge of anger now at not being believed. 'He was there.'

Stir in the Milo and milk. 'What did he look like?'

She jerks like she's forgotten I was there. 'A man. Dark.'

'Dark skin?'

'No, dark clothes.' She thinks for a while. 'A mask on his face.'

'What kind of mask?'

'Scary. A monster.' She brightens. 'Like Shrek.'

'How do you know it was a mask?' Silly question I suppose, but some of the people in this valley could easily be mistaken for Shrek.

'There was light for a moment, then it went.'

'Torchlight? Matches? A car?'

'I don't know.' Then she does. 'A phone. He had a phone.'

'Phones wouldn't work up here, no signal.'

'He was using it like a camera.'

20.

Michael Walton didn't go through the roof when he heard about it on Sunday morning. Mim had finished gabbling her story to him and he just kind of frowned.

'Miranda, what have I told you about …'

'I'm not making it up!' She turned to me. 'Tell him, Mr Chester.'

'It's true.' I recounted the gist. 'Mim is pretty sure she saw something.'

Michael casts a disbelieving glance in her direction. 'Does that happen up this way a lot?'

'Hunters, poachers. Some of them are less respectful of property boundaries than others.'

'The photographing?'

'Weird, yeah. Maybe he was scouting for a burglary. Didn't expect the screaming. Got scared off?'

A shake of the head and he helped Mim pack her stuff into the car. After they left, I scouted around for any traces of our intruder. Nothing. Either he never existed or he covered his tracks well. But if he was there, who might it be? Any number of candidates – Cunningham, I know, has me in his sights for what happened at the Lodge. Would he be so bold? Absolutely. We probably shouldn't be hanging around in such an isolated location for that reason alone – another cross for Vanessa to mark up on her mental balance sheet. It could be LeBlanc who we know is still out there and has so far evaded the crack back-country scouts of the AOS and the helicopter and drone flyovers. Maybe it was Michael himself, keeping a watch and rechecking the doors and windows. It was a bit of a coincidence him making such a weird controlling request and then, hey presto, it comes to pass. Hell, for all I know, my old adversary Sammy Pritchard might have reinstated his fatwa against me from his low-security prison in Yorkshire while awaiting release. My understanding is that he'll be home in time for a merry Geordie Christmas because his manners inside have been impeccable. Maybe I'm his Yuletide gift to himself.

It's a relief to get everybody out of the door this Monday morning and, death shrine aside, even the Lodge seems peaceful today as I drive past. Coming into range there's a message on my mobile from Maxwell to head straight to the murder room. I do so, pulling up behind DC Keegan's Audi.

'What's new?' I accept the coffee and bikkie passed my way.

'Everything,' says Keegan. 'Internal affairs have been sent over from Wellington to investigate the death of Melvyn Cody. Pending the outcome of that investigation, Will here is stepping aside from his role in charge of the Gelder case.'

A glance over at Maxwell, it's clear he's not too happy about it. 'Seems harsh.'

'It's not a demotion,' insists Keegan. 'It's just an administrative precaution. An accountability and transparency measure.'

'Somebody has to take the fall at times like this,' says Will staring at a neutral spot on the wall. 'Justice will no doubt prevail.'

'So who's in charge in the meantime?'

'I am,' says Keegan. 'Will is still on the team but will focus primarily on Havelka. I hear you met up with Nigel Watson recently?'

'Yes. Hard to pin down any connection between the west coast murders and this one, except for similar MO and ballpark timing of around six years ago.'

'And I understand my predecessor awaits your call?'

Ex-DC Ford. I forgot to follow up over the weekend given the excitements of the sleepover. 'You're well-informed.'

'He called me. Stickler for protocol, always was. Wanted to check I was in the loop.' She smiles icily. 'Which I am. Now.'

'So you want me to brief DSS Maxwell on Havelka?'

'You fellas can work it together. It's better you both step away from Gelder for a while.' She refills her coffee from the plunger. 'Until the dust settles.'

This is a polite way of saying that we are indeed taking the fall for the Lodge fiasco after all. 'You'll have an awful lot on your plate, running Gelder and being district commander.'

'Don't fret, Nick. Time management is my forte.'

'Any developments on Gelder?'

'One or two. After the autopsy on Melvyn, his DNA pinged in the system. He was inside the dark blue van as well as up at Gelder's shack.'

'Oh.'

'Indeed. And it turns out that his unregistered rifle was the one that fired the bullet you requested a lab job on. What was that about?' I explain about the water-tank snipings. 'A mischievous kid with a gun and time on his hands in that feral valley of yours,' says Keegan. 'Who'd have thought?'

'Except the snipings seemed to be targeted.'

'The goal being?'

'God knows.' I then outline the possible connection between the water-tank sniper and the attack on Latifa.

'You think a fifteen-year-old boy could have done that?'

'Once the snare is activated, the job's done. He didn't need to overpower Latifa by then. As for what kind of mind can do that? Teenagers are watching all sorts of twisted stuff these days and some of them are very capable of taking the fantasy further.'

'But? You don't look like you believe it yourself.'

I can't explain about the similar snare marks on the tree in Pelorus Bridge. Havelka's tree. It's too long a bow, those snares are in wide usage. The hunters who use them could probably show me a hundred trees with the same marks. 'I don't know. Any news from the team working Latifa's case?'

'Not so far. Have you passed your theory onto them? It could be a nice neat wrap-up. The boy being dead and all.'

'Speaking of neat stitch-ups, it seems weird that if LeBlanc and the kid were the ones driving the Gelder van, that it should be the Lodge CCTV that helps catch them.'

Maxwell is staying quiet. He's staring at his phone. 'Somebody just sent through a photo of me and my family on a picnic from this weekend.'

My phone buzzes with an incoming message too.

'It's a declaration of war.'

Both Maxwell and I have received photos of us, or our homes, and/or our loved ones. In my case, that included our sleepover guest, Mim. Unknown sender but it will turn out to be a pay-as-you-go or stolen SIM.

'It may well be,' says Keegan. 'But we've now been well and truly warned off any further interaction with the Lodge. We can't go kicking their doors down again.'

'On the basis of undisclosed intelligence from the spooks?'

'On the basis of a recent botched raid during which a child died.'

'And we're just meant to sit back and accept this?' Maxwell is grim-faced. 'That's my wife and kids in that photo. Those bastards were following us over the weekend to a school fête for fuck's sake.'

'Maybe you could send your family out of town for a while. A holiday maybe?'

'Sure, and then I hear they've been stabbed in their sleep in a Rarotonga resort. This fucking stinks, Marianne. Find out what we're dealing with here, because if it's a bunch of psychos who have diplomatic immunity, then we may as well pack it in now.'

Will Maxwell is impressive in full flow. I have renewed respect for him.

At that moment there's a brisk rap on the door and a bloke in a suit comes through without being invited. 'Brightwell. Internal.' He nods like he's just done us a favour. 'How's it going, ma'am? Can I have a word with DSS Maxwell?'

'Not right now, Greg. Give us ten.'

'The sooner we clear up this matter, the sooner we can all move on.'

'And the sooner you close the door and go away, Greg, the sooner still.' The door closes. Another knock. 'For fuck's sake.'

It's Latifa. 'Sarge? I just got this weird SMS.' A pic of her and Daniel on their back verandah canoodling.

'Okay,' says Keegan with a sigh. 'I'll headlock the spooks.'

Accompanying Latifa back up the road to the cop shop, I bring her up to speed on the water-tank sniper revelation. So was Melvyn her attacker too?

'The kid?' She thinks about it a while. 'No, it was no kid that did that to me. Those eyes were much older, had seen a lot more.'

'You've never said that before.'

'Yeah, I have. Heaps of times.'

'Not with such emphasis on the "much". How much "much" are we talking here?'

She gives it some thought. 'Much. The more I think about it the more I reckon he was pretty old, like even as old as you.'

Wow. Ancient. 'Forties? Fifties? Sixties?'

'Something like that. Can't always tell with Pākehā.'

'Well that's progress. And, as far as we know, it's not connected to the water tank snipings. You were in the wrong place at the wrong time.'

'What, and he just happened to be lurking there? Bull crap. I wasn't some random tramper he lucked upon.'

'So it still puts somebody else from the Lodge in the frame. LeBlanc maybe. If he and the kid worked the Gelder murder together, maybe they worked the water tanks and targeting of you too.'

We're at our desks now. 'Yeah, but I checked LeBlanc's file photo and the eyes didn't match with him either.'

Keegan's question about the water-tank snipings. To what purpose? Was the kid just letting off steam or was there something else behind it? Everything else about the Lodge suggests ulterior motive. 'Can you look into it?'

'Sure.' Latifa glances up as a shadow appears on our threshold.

It's Thomas Hemi. Eyes bloodshot, face unshaved, hair wild. 'Jaxon's missing.'

Jaxon hasn't been heard from since late afternoon yesterday. Thomas and Ruth didn't start to worry until mid-evening. Spent the precious hours since, phoning, looking, hoping against hope.

'He didn't answer any calls and none of his mates had seen him.' He'd said he was catching up with friends from school. They were going dirtbiking on one of the logging skids over the river. 'Good jumps to be had,' says Thomas, eyes full. 'They're not meant to go there but fuck, some good's got to come out of all that ugly shit.'

'But they didn't go?'

'Yeah, yeah they did but the other kids went home when it got dark.'

'Six-ish?'

'Thereabouts.'

'And you've definitely covered all mates or other possibilities. There's nobody else out there?'

'Nah.'

'Was everything good. No arguments or anything?'

'Nothing out of the ordinary.'

'You've said he's gone off before and done his own thing. He's at that age.'

'Not this time.' A hesitation.

'Tell me.'

'Friday, after school. He came home in a shitty mood. That Yank buddy of his getting shot. Shook him up.'

'Yeah,' says Latifa. 'It would.'

'Told me he got a text from Melvyn on Friday.'

'Melvyn was dead by then.'

'Exactly.'

'What did it say? Did he show you?'

Thomas bows his head in anguish. 'It said, see you soon brother.'

21.

So we've got the AOS hunting LeBlanc, regular police and emergency services searching for Jaxon, and a new round of threats from persons presumably in the Lodge. Meanwhile Maxwell and I are sidelined and nobody is allowed to touch Cunningham and his cronies. Right now there are a number of good reasons for me to go to Nelson: lean on Keegan to find out what the spooks are saying, talk to ex-DC Ford about those west coast cases, maybe even drop by to see Nigel Watson and ask him why he's lying to me. Phoning ahead, I learn that Keegan has skipped over to Wellington on an afternoon flight with the aim, I hope, of lassoing those SIS Ringwraiths personally. Good on her, if that's the case. I'll still head west though; a sense of mission is important to me right now while everyone else does more useful stuff like search for murderers and missing kids. Maxwell has a stay of execution, unofficially running the Gelder show until Keegan gets back from the capital this evening. On that matter, 'Are we still getting the Gelder bush block searched again?'

'Yeah, mate. But we're a bit short-handed right now. Why?'

I tell him my glow-worm cave theory.

'Nice to see the memory slowly returning.' A grin. 'Leave it with me, Nick.'

'It'll all work out, Will. They can't pin this on you.'

A wry smile. 'Watch them.'

Ex–district commander David Ford lives on a five-acre block on Cable Bay Road south-east of Nelson on the way out to the Happy Valley Adventure Park. It's a solid eighty-minute winding mountainous drive from Havelock. We had previously arranged to meet in a pub in the city but appointments are an ethereal concept in this job. Ahead of me there's a minibus full of prospective paintballers, quadbikers and flying-foxers. Across the water in the distance some of the higher peaks in the Abel

Tasman National Park are dusted with snow. Ford is waiting for me on his front verandah like he's got nothing better to do and loves standing around in a snapping wind.

'Keeping well?' We shake hands.

'Very.' He invites me across the threshold. 'Coffee or tea?'

We settle on tea and he'll be Mother. He's got a couple of comfy armchairs facing floor-to-ceiling windows with a view of those snow-capped peaks.

'Stunning,' I say, accepting a chocolate biscuit. 'Thanks for accommodating the change of venue and time.'

He shrugs. 'So what do you want?'

'You were in charge of a murder case about five, six years ago over in Westport. A motel manager name of Robertson.'

'What of it?'

'There's been a similar-style killing on a bloke called Havelka. Half of his body was found up at Butchers Flat recently.'

He nods. 'Keegan gave me the gist. I remember the Havelka disappearance.'

'The only suspect of any worth is Morgan Hopu.'

'Yes, I can imagine.'

'Did Hopu feature in the Robertson case in any way?'

'Is there any mention in the case file?'

'No.'

'There you are then.'

'Nigel Watson mentioned some footprints that weren't included in the case file either.'

'Footprints?'

Blood from a fucking stone; and I thought this bloke kinda liked me. 'Two sets leading in, none out.'

'Watson told you that?'

'Yep, he seemed surprised that it wasn't on the file.'

'It's the kind of thing that should be, isn't it?'

Deep breath. 'You'd think so.'

'Nigel's a funny fella.'

'In what way?'

'Every. More tea?' He tops up my cup. 'Likes his little games.' A car crunches on the gravel outside. 'That'll be Wendy, I'll just help her bring the shopping in. Then maybe we can take a walk?'

'Sure.'

Is this what retirement is about? Stretching out moments, drawing out expectations. Putting the crossword down half-finished so there's something to do later. Shopping unpacked and a warm hello from Wendy, who enquires after Vanessa and Paulie, then it's back outside where Ford steps into his gumboots and I zip up my jacket against the wind.

A dog has appeared at his heel, a labrador: friendly and obedient as Ford would expect of everyone around him. 'Nigel should've been sacked years ago but he's a survivor. Knows how to duck and weave. He'll be picking up his pension soon I expect.'

'A few months, I think.'

'Can't see him needing it. He'll be well set up.'

'The suspense is killing me.'

Ford chucks a tennis ball for the dog. 'There's no mention of footprints in the file because there were none at the scene.'

'So how did the victim get there? And how did the perp get in and out without leaving any?'

'We assume in along the shoreline and out the same way. Robertson's body was at the high-tide mark. Because of the storm it was an even higher tide than usual. Any traces washed away.'

'So what's Watson talking about then?'

The dog's back, dropping the ball at Ford's feet. 'He's a mischief-maker, attention-seeker. Never cut it in the job races, always pipped at the post. Probably thought he should have got my job when I left, instead of Keegan.'

'He didn't seem that bitter and twisted to me.'

'His type never do. But the mischief is one thing, being bent is another.'

'Evidence?'

Ford picks the ball up. Tosses it high and far. 'Never found any but I had strong suspicions.'

'Based on?'

'Leaked intelligence, tip-offs, wasted raids, funny coincidences, that kind of thing.'

'If he's getting handouts where are they coming from?'

'What was that name you mentioned before in relation to Havelka?'

'Morgan Hopu?'

'Good place to start.'

'You said earlier you'd cleared this chat with Keegan?'

'Yep.'

'Does she know you're accusing one of her serving officers of corruption?'

'She worked the other case, didn't she? The girl in Robertson's motel six months earlier.' Ford whistles, summoning the dog.

'Lucy McLernon.'

'Watson was on that one too, if I remember rightly.'

'And?'

'And Keegan's pointed you in his direction for a reason.' The dog drops the ball at his feet again. He picks it up and gives me a grin. 'Fetch!' he says, throwing it out there.

Nigel Watson tells it differently.

'Good try, mate.'

'So have you had dealings with Morgan Hopu?'

'He's a well-known local gangster of long standing. Of course I've come across him in my job. But taking handouts from him? Get fucked.'

Late afternoon. The sun casting long shadows and it's home time for the Nelson office workers. We're grabbing a quick wine in a bar up the top end of Trafalgar Street near the cathedral tower. It's a pretty flash place and so are the prices. 'It's what's being said.'

'Yeah, by Ford, that bitch Keegan, a few others.'

'Why might they be suggesting it?'

'Ask them. Have you checked their bank balances lately? Yeah, I live in a nice house in Atawhai. We save, don't piss our money against the wall, don't have kids to blow it on, and my wife has a good job. Try asking Ford who paid for his country mansion.'

'It all gets a bit "he-said, she-said" doesn't it?'

'But you're happy enough to follow it up if Ford says it first, eh?'

'Ford reckons the footprints weren't mentioned in the case file because there weren't any.'

'So I'm lying. Is that it?'

'Are you?'

'It's a funny little detail to lie about, don't you think? I mean of all the things I could make up.'

He has a point. 'Tell me about your take on the Lucy McLernon murder.'

'What are you after, specifically?'

'You had no suspects at all?'

'Apart from the motel manager, all of the creeps in town, half the blokes in that nutty sect, her husband? Of course we had suspects but none of them matched up enough to pursue. No trace evidence, the key POIs had alibis. What are you getting at?'

'What was your job on the case?'

'Like with Robertson, managing the locus.'

'And Keegan's?'

'She led the enquiry team: door-to-doors, CCTV, collating witness statements and cross-referencing.'

'Big job.'

'She was ambitious. Wanted to control everything. Nothing's changed.'

'You two got on?'

'Did she set you on me?'

'Just asking questions, mate. Trying to find where the truth lies. Tell me about the crime scene. Anything strike you about it?'

'Apart from the presence of a naked dead woman and gallons of blood?'

'Yeah.'

'For such a messy scene there was remarkably little evidence of anybody else being there apart from the victim.'

'Wiped?'

'Professionally I'd say.'

'I don't recall reading that in the case file.'

'Didn't you? Well, well. And you probably missed the bit about a second or third perp too.'

'What?'

'You're right, you missed nothing. That wasn't in there either.'

Watson orders another pinot noir but I'm driving so I'll stick to water. He tells me there are contradictions in the few statements recorded. A witness in a neighbouring motel room recalled hearing several male voices that last evening in McLernon's room although he couldn't be sure it wasn't the radio or TV. Meanwhile another witness two doors down on the other side had stepped outside for a smoke at around midnight just as Lucy McLernon's door opened and a man left the room walking swiftly across the car park to disappear into the darkness. Average height and build, and Pākehā. The smoker's eyewitness account focused the enquiry on a single perpetrator and this wasn't contradicted by crime scene forensic evidence.

'But?'

'There's an industrial cleaning company based in Nelson. Among other things they specialise in rehabilitating crime scenes once the cops have finished their work. Clean the carpets, mop the floors, spray a bit of air freshener – that type of thing.'

I've heard of them – Taurus Cleaning Services. Run by a five-foot-two bundle of energy, good cheer, and dark jokes. 'Tui Kaitu?'

'That's her. Employs a whole load of casuals. Particularly favours backpackers. Likes ordering around the tall blonde Scandi girls. Who wouldn't?'

'So?'

'So she came up to me a few days after the scene was cleared for cleaning and said one of her "Ingrids", as she calls them, had hoovered up a necklace chain, silver, like you might have your crucifix on. Must have been missed by forensics. Thought we should know.'

'Why did she come to you?'

'We've known each other for years. After this long in the job, you get that.'

'So you passed it on to the enquiry?'

'Yep, gave it to forensics and reported it to Keegan. She had it lab tested but it didn't match anybody in the system. Decided it didn't change anything but thanked me for it anyway.'

'But that wasn't the end of it.'

'McLernon never wore such a chain as far as we knew. If the theory is that Robertson circumstantially was the killer and that's why he died later, he never wore a crucifix either.'

'But it could have been left by a previous motel guest or employee.'

'Possible.'

'The chain was entered into evidence?'

'Yep.'

'So what's the problem between you and Keegan on this?'

'I went back to her after the Robertson killing. Reminded her about the chain. Pointed out he didn't wear one. Posited the theory of a second or even third person-of-interest or that maybe Robertson didn't do it. She didn't want to know.'

'An inconvenient truth?'

'Something like that. I still bring it up now and again to anyone who'll listen. I don't think she appreciates it, especially not in her new job.'

'It's not just sour grapes because she got it and you didn't?'

'I never even applied. Is that the line they're pushing? Grumpy old man with a grudge?'

'You wouldn't be the first.'

'I probably won't be the last. Take a look at that chain in the evidence store for yourself. If they've sent you off on a wild goose chase we may as well all get the benefit.'

It's dark heading back over the Whangamoa Saddle. The wind that was tearing into us earlier at David Ford's place has eased. From Maxwell, before leaving mobile range, I heard that neither Jaxon Hemi nor Georges LeBlanc have been found but that DNA from LeBlanc's toothbrush, comb and a pillow seized from the Lodge place him inside the van with Gelder and with the boy Melvyn. So we know who killed Gelder even if we don't yet know why. When I reach the Rai Saddle, it's a maze of traffic cones as the road realignment takes shape. They intend to straighten out some of those tight bends so the speed demons don't have to learn the art of patience and slow down. Literally moving mountains in order to try and appease the unappeasable. Ironing out a hairpin bend in New Zealand seems unpatriotic to me, but what do I know?

On the valley road, rabbits scamper while possums and hedgehogs idle suicidally in the headlights. There's an orange glow out west, another pleasant valley sunset. Late though. The sun went down ages ago but the geography plays tricks around here. Rounding the last bend, I can see now it's not a sunset glow at all.

My home is on fire.

22.

'Vanessa? Paulie?'

Flames fill the kitchen. The doorway is engulfed. No way I can get through there.

'Vanessa!'

The two downstairs bedrooms, including Paulie's, are the same. Smoke. Flames. Blistering heat. What little breeze there is feeds the fire. Popping and cracking sounds. How long before the house collapses? Round to the back balcony, slipping on the gravel. I can't use my mobile to call for help, there's no signal. Not even emergency. Jesus.

'Vanessa!'

The flames, smoke and heat are less intense back here. A hundred metres below me, the river rushes over the rocks. All that water passing by uselessly. The back verandah doors are locked. A precaution after our recent prowler. I hammer on it with my palms. Trying to see through the inferno.

'Vanessa!'

The walls are blistering on the outside. There's a barbecue gas bottle sitting waiting to blow. I disconnect it and hurl it over the balcony into the bush. Grabbing one of the larger rocks from the driveway I smash the back patio door glass and unsnick the lock. The extra oxygen rushes in to feed the furnace. An angry menacing flare like a shove before a fight.

'Vanessa? Paulie?'

A smell of burning flesh and hair. I'm hoping it's just me.

Coughing.

'Vanessa?'

'Upstairs. Paulie is with me. Get us out of here.'

The living room floor is collapsing. Just a matter of time before walls and ceiling go too. And the wooden house supports. The stairs are a wall of flames, fed by the oxygen from the broken window.

'Go to the window on the river side. Above the water tank.'

Either side is a five-metre drop but the tank gives them a chance of breaking the fall. A crash and a huge hole opens up in the kitchen floor, and another in the living room. The roof beams are disintegrating now. Another crash and a yelp.

'Dad! Mum's fallen down.'

There's a sink out on the balcony. I soak my jacket, wrap it around my face and charge through the firewall. That smell of burning flesh and hair is definitely me and I feel it now too. Searing pain. Up those stairs, cracking and collapsing under my feet. Too much smoke, I can't see a thing. My lungs don't want to work. Stumbling, I find Paulie and drag him to the window, push it wide open.

'Jump.'

'It's too high.'

'Do it. The water tank is there.'

'I can't.'

'Do it, Paulie. I need to help Mum.'

He goes. A thump, a crack, another thud. Paulie screaming and crying. Good, he's alive.

'Vanessa?' I can hardly get the word out. Coughing. Gasping. Back to where Paulie was, creeping along the burning floor. More cracks. Clouds of sparks. Another roof beam collapses. I see her now. Eyes wide, she's in terrible pain. The beam is across her lower leg. Smouldering. I lift it off. Drag her to the window. Help her on to the sill. She doesn't wait to be told.

Gone.

In the distance, headlights out on the road.

I jump.

23.

Paulie has a sprained ankle. Vanessa has vicious burns to her lower left leg that will require skin grafts. Mine aren't so serious: blistered hands, arms and head. The house is a wreck and we're homeless.

'Well that's one decision made.'

Vanessa's right. That stunning view out on to the Wakamarina river is no longer an option, for the foreseeable future at least. Vanessa is being kept in the hospital in Nelson for a day or two more. I hug her farewell and though she's putting on a brave face, it feels like she doesn't want to let go. Now Paulie and I are shacked up in the secure suite on the top floor of Nelson cop shop normally reserved for visiting dignitaries. He's been there before, a year or so back, while his mum decided whether or not to leave me and while I waited at home for a Geordie gangster to come and settle some old scores. Paulie's made himself right at home; he has his foot resting on a cushion while he has a banana and watches *Spongebob Squarepants* on TV.

'The goats and chooks?' he says.

'The neighbours will look after them.'

'For ever?'

'We might be able to have chooks in the new place. Not so sure about the goats, mate.'

'Not fair.' Another couple of bites of the banana. 'Prob'ly for the best though.' He's got his mother's ability to move on quickly. He'd gone early to bed last night but then he'd had a scary dream about the Mim sleepover prowler and crept upstairs to be with Vanessa. It probably saved his life. The ground floor bedrooms were the first to go. Vanessa too had dropped off early as she sometimes does after too many late nights finally catch up. Something woke her and she smelled the smoke, by which time things were already out of control.

There's a knock at the door. DC Keegan has brought a bag of groceries and a Tupperware food container. 'Lamb curry. Not too spicy I hope. And a few things to keep you going.'

'Nice of you.'

'Not a problem. My assistant did the shopping. I had a spare load of curry in the freezer; I do a big cook-up every weekend for the coming week.' Keegan never struck me as the domestic goddess type but there you go. 'How are you all doing?'

'We're alive.'

'The fire investigator says it was deliberate. She found traces of accelerant under the laundry.'

'Three guesses who's behind this.'

'Shouldn't rush to conclusions, Nick.'

'Heaven forbid.' As it happens I won't be rushing anywhere today. Paulie needs some TLC and Vanessa wouldn't want me straying too far. Vengeance isn't easy when you have care commitments. 'What did the spooks have to say?'

'James Bryant is untouchable. He has powerful friends both in Washington and Wellington. Until recently he sat on some intelligence committee. Knows stuff. Knows secrets. He's also a generous political donor in his own right, again in both places.'

'But we have a new government now.'

'That's our wriggle room. He picked the losing side this time and while the new mob aren't vindictive neither are they seeing him as a priority.'

'Who's giving us the "hands off" message then?'

'A cabal of young fogey hardliners in SIS. They're in their jobs because of their strong relationships with the far-right cousins in America, Oz and the UK. It's part of a pushback against what they call the leftie virtue-signallers in the new government.'

'So while we get our houses burned down and contend with psychos, these spooks are engaging in some petty culture wars?'

'Seems to me we should just get on with doing our jobs and forget those spoilt private school tossers.' There it is again, that vaguely Scouse class war accent asserting itself just when we need it.

'What's the plan?' I ask Keegan.

'Red card the wankers in the Lodge. Send in the AOS to evict them. Make life so hard they just piss off of their own accord.'

'What if Bryant flexes his muscles?'

'Something solid linking the Lodge to the Gelder murder would go a long way. Plus I hear Bryant's on the wrong end of some presidential tweets of late and being anally probed by a federal prosecutor in Washington. His days of wine and roses are numbered. We can kick him while he's down.'

James Bryant – the man and the money behind Māhana – about to face his own private apocalypse over in the USA. Perhaps relishing the idea of locking himself in his little Kiwi panic room far, far away.

'Maybe we should be careful what we wish for.'

'The police house is yours whenever you're ready.'

Latifa is on the phone. I recall at some point seeing her by the light of the flickering flames coordinating the rescue effort, ordering neighbours around, keeping gawpers away, directing the fire engines through as they arrived just in time to douse the embers. The day has slid by in a blur, back and forth to the hospital, phone calls to insurers, paperwork for the bosses.

'That's your home.'

'I'm moving in with Daniel. We'll be getting our own place anyway after the wedding.'

'Thanks, Latifa.'

'No worries. How are Vanessa and Paulie?'

'Hurting, but nothing terminal. We were lucky.'

'Are we going after Cunningham?'

'All in good time, yes.' Paulie is waving, pointing at his watch. It's time to go back to the hospital to visit Vanessa again. 'Keegan tells me there's still no word on the AOS hunt for LeBlanc or the search for Jaxon.'

'Thomas is beside himself. It's not looking good.'

'No. It isn't.' Paulie is frowning, getting agitated. Promptness is important to him. 'Sorry, got to go.'

'Give my regards to everybody. And look after yourself, okay?'

'Will do.'

School's out as we edge along Waimea Road to the hospital. A phalanx of shiny Audi and BMW 4WDs is drawn up outside Nelson College and I'm reminded of those privileged brats in SIS playing their ideological games while the real world burns down. In a quiet room of her own, courtesy of some Keegan arm-twisting of hospital admin, Vanessa is in a lot of pain and zonked out on medication for most of the visit. Paulie, well out of sorts, is happy to have an early night and some lamb curry. He falls asleep next to me on the couch while I brood and plot vengeance.

24.

Wednesday. Two days since my house burned down. They found Jaxon Hemi early this morning. A mussel boat out in Pelorus Sound came across him during a routine check of the lines. He was attached by cable ties to one of the buoys. He'd been shot in the head, point-blank. Jaxon hung in the water, arms outstretched, in an obscene parody of the crucifixion. On display as a message to all and sundry. Sixteen years young.

'How long are we going to wait before moving on Cunningham?'

'At the moment there's no connection.' Keegan's voice gives it all away. She doesn't even believe it herself. 'Let the process unfold. Forensics. Post-mortem. Who knows, we might have all we need in the next twenty-four to forty-eight hours.'

'Don't count on Thomas Hemi waiting that long.'

'He'd be crazy to try anything on his own.'

'He's a resourceful man and now a grieving father. Assume nothing.'

'Can you talk him down? We really need to keep a lid on this. Do it our way.'

'Bit tied up with things here.'

'What about Rapata? Would she have any influence?'

'Being Māori?'

'Being the village cop. Don't give me a hard time, Nick.'

'I'll talk to her.'

Latifa must have been expecting my call. 'It didn't help that they sent Gemma and some other goon to give him the news. They were lucky to get out alive.'

'He'll be okay with you?'

'Fingers crossed. What can we promise him? Utu's a pretty powerful thing to be bargaining away.'

'No point making promises we might not be able to keep. If the person who did this was one of the Yanks, I can't guarantee he won't just be whisked out of the country.'

'And you want me to tell him that?'

'I don't want to bullshit him.'

'You know what? He might be best left alone to do whatever he needs to do.'

'It could get out of hand.'

'Three dead so far, your house burned down, an out-of-control private militia down the road. Bit late to worry about that.'

'Still.'

A sigh. 'I'll see what I can do.' She has other news. 'The Von Crapps aren't the only people who've left the valley recently.'

'Yeah?'

'The islander house is empty too.' Charlie Evans' farmhand, Israel, and his Vanuatuan compatriots.

'Significance?'

'They were there one night, gone the next morning. One of the redneck neighbours was bragging about it, about how the Yanks were doing our job for us.'

'Tell me.'

'They moved both households on. Jeep full of armed men and some threats. The neighbour's a big fan boy now. Bigot from way back. These Yanks are his alt-right wet dream.'

'Cunningham had said he wasn't pissing everyone off in the valley. Some liked what he was doing.'

'And I did some more digging regarding the water tanks.'

'Yeah?'

'The only delivery Marvin did was to you for the top-up, right?'

'Yeah, Gary mentioned a mate of Marvin's did the others.'

'Marvin knew nothing about it. Word is he was pretty pissed off.'

'So who did the water deliveries?'

'Some bloke from Nelson,' she says. 'Booked and paid for by the Lodge.'

'Them again.'

'Maybe they knew Melvyn had been acting up. Felt guilty. Made reparation?'

'Or they created a problem so they could be seen to fix it.'

'All very Maoist,' says Latifa, hanging up.

After breakfast we get word that Vanessa will be released from hospital later this morning. Paulie's swollen ankle is also on the mend. A beanie covers my singed hair and I'm getting used to the stinging tight feeling in my face and hands. My phone is running hot too; this time it's Gary from out on the trawler, seagulls singing, waves crashing in the background and a satellite delay in his voice.

'Can you hear me, Nick? You guys okay?'

'News travels far and fast.'

'Mate called round to see me, forgot I was away. Saw the fire engines and all that. What happened?'

I tell him.

'Jeez. Look, use my place. I'm never there. And I can stay at Gloria's in Stoke on my week off.'

'Nice offer, mate. Cheers. They've got us in some police accommodation for the foreseeable.'

'Whatever, it's there if you need it. If you miss the valley or need a local base, be my guest.' I thank him again. People rallying around, it's enough to make your chest burst. 'We need to move these people on, Nick. They're no good.'

'Yeah, but there's rules.'

'Might be for you. I know plenty of people who would eat them for breakfast. Just say the word.'

'I'll keep that in mind.' While Gary gets back to hauling in hoki I weigh up the pros and cons of letting slip the dogs of war. Tempting, but first I need to pick up Vanessa from the hospital and arrange for somebody to watch over Paulie – I'm not game to have two invalids in tow at the same time. Trouble is, we don't know that many people over this way.

'What about David?' says Paulie.

Ex-DC Ford? 'You two get on, do you?'

'Yeah, he was here a lot when Mum left you.'

'She didn't leave me, she just needed some time to herself to think things over.'

'Whatevs. He makes yummy banana smoothies.'

'David it is, then.'

Forty-five minutes later, Ford is at the door with a carton of milk and some bananas.

'Ready to get your butt kicked on Crash Bandicoot, Paulie?'

'It's Paul. Milkshake first, then you can try.'

I leave them to it. On my way out, Ford says, 'We'll sort this, Nick. One way or another.'

Driving down to the hospital, I'm thinking what a flimsy and fragile thing the rule of law is. Traffic lights. Pedestrian crossings. Right of way. Truth. Justice. Start to peel them away, ignore them, flout them, negate them and pretty soon you have chaos at every intersection. Is that what they call the End Times?

Keegan is right. Even if we think we know who the bad guys are, we still need to go through due process and collect the evidence. Without that there's nothing. Paperwork is what they hide behind when it suits them but the Brandon Cunninghams, the Georges LeBlancs, the James Bryants of this world hate it being turned against them. That federal prosecutor nibbling away patiently at James Bryant's ill-earned wellbeing. The best way of dealing with dickheads like this is to bore the bastards to death with niggling Kiwi red tape.

'I'd say "penny for them" but I might be short-changed.' Vanessa is sitting on the bed dressed, bandaged, and ready to go.

'How's it feeling?'

'Sore and tight but the drugs are great. Let's get out of here.'

First the nurse gives me a lesson in how to change burn dressings and tend the wound and then we drop by the pharmacy to pick up some supplies. Vanessa is being stoic and me asking about her pain is no-go right now. Instead I tell her about all the offers of alternative accommodation we're getting. 'There's some good people out there,' I say, being uncharacteristically positive.

She's focused on the passing traffic and the windscreen wipers now that a soft rain has started. 'We could have died, Nick.'

'Yes.'

'I told you to keep them away from us.'

'I'm sorry.'

'Yeah, I know you are.' This isn't the best time to tell her about Jaxon Hemi but she needs to know. She shakes her head. 'Poor Thomas and Ruth.' Turning to face me. 'I'm not going back there, Nick. I'm finished with that place.'

Who am I to argue?

'Thomas wants to talk to you.'

The call came from Latifa just after lunch. After checking that Vanessa and Paulie would be okay for a few hours, particularly with ex-DC Ford pottering in the background preparing culinary treats and cuppas, I'm headed back over the ranges and up the valley road while rain drums steadily on the car roof. There's no sign of life passing Charlie Evans' farm and the For Sale notice has gone. Life must be that little bit tougher for Charlie now that Israel is no longer around to help. No doubt I'll get the story later. It's equally quiet at the Lodge: no guards, no dogs, no nothing. Our place is a charred wreck. The chooks are free-ranging over the blackened ruins, scratching the wet scorched earth. The goats chew on grass and brambles like nothing ever happened. Vanessa is right, the valley no longer seems so beautiful and it's hard to imagine living here again.

A few extra vehicles have gathered at Thomas' place including Latifa's and a flash black 4WD. Its owner is on the verandah nursing a mug of something and looking sombre.

'G'day Morgan.' I offer my hand for shaking. He obliges.

Thomas emerges through a doorway, eyes red-rimmed. Latifa is close behind with two mugs of tea.

'Ruth?' I enquire.

'In bed. Sedated.' Latifa hands me a mug.

'I'm sorry for all this, Thomas. Truly.'

He nods. 'You've got your own worries.'

'What are you doing about these people?' says Morgan.

Two brothers, united in grief, both have lost a son. Of course he would be here, now. Ready to serve up justice his way like he did with Karel Havelka. I can see his point. But.

'Following due process, investigating, collecting evidence.'

'Due process?' says Morgan. 'How long does that take?'

'Longer than Karel Havelka got.'

'Him.' A sip of tea. 'Still reckon I was behind that, eh?'

There's a stir inside. Ruth sobbing. Thomas leaves us.

This is no time to rake over old coals, even if it was me that started it. I turn to Latifa. 'You said Thomas wanted to talk.'

'Yep. Best leave it to him.'

Another few minutes and he's back. The rain has picked up and we all edge in further under the verandah roof. There's a real nip in the air and winter feels very close. 'You wanted to see me, Thomas?'

'Latifa told me not to go off half-cocked. Said you'd fix things. The right way.'

'I'll do my best, that's all I can promise.'

'She said these people are connected, have powerful friends. They might even get away with what they're doing.'

'That's a possibility.'

'Doesn't seem fair.'

'No. It's not.'

'What does it take to have that much influence on what's right and wrong? Money? Power? Something to bargain with?'

'All of those things, probably.'

'I don't have much money and I guess to you and them I'm just a brown country bumpkin. Not a good start, eh?'

'All we can do is what's right and hope for the best. It's all we have left.'

'Right in general or right in law?'

'Both.'

He nods. 'I got you here so I can say this to your face. I won't do what you ask, sorry.' He thumbs inside the house. 'Ruth and me, we're hurting. We can't sit back and watch these arseholes trash our world. Like I said to you before, these people believe in the End Times and our rules mean nothing to them.'

'I understand that, Thomas, but ...'

'But nothing,' says Morgan. 'Our law is older and bigger than yours. We'll do what's right in general and in law. Ours.'

I can't stop them, even if I could convince myself I wanted to. As Latifa is backing out in her car and I'm settling into mine, Morgan raps on my window.

'That Havelka guy. You reckon he's whiter than white? Ever wondered why the missus went doolally and the daughter never visits? Do your homework, Chester.'

Before leaving the district I call by the murder room in Havelock town hall. There's plenty going on and it looks like the decision to administratively sideline Will Maxwell has been shelved. He's in the thick of it, running the Bruce Gelder, Karel Havelka and now Jaxon Hemi inquiries while the Melvyn Cody one is handballed to a team flown in from Wellington. Havelka is on the backburner as far as Maxwell is concerned. Everybody in the hall is busy but still able to chuck a sympathetic wave or smile my way. Even Gemma seems to have softened.

'You going okay, Nick?' asks Maxwell.

'All things considered.' I bring him up to speed on Thomas Hemi's state of mind. 'Sometime soon he'll make his move and big brother Morgan is along for the ride.'

'That's all we need.'

'The only way to avoid more trouble is if we get to Cunningham and company first. How's the LeBlanc hunt going?'

'Thin air. The guy knows how to lie low.'

'So we need to clear the Lodge, take away Thomas' targets.'

'Keegan has okayed bringing them all in for questioning. Distributing them around South Island cop shops. North too if we want. Anywhere from Invercargill to Auckland.' Maxwell accepts a coffee from a passing minion. 'Break 'em up, ship 'em out, as she put it.'

'When's this happening?'

'Tonight. A midnight knock.'

'Let's hope Thomas holds off until then.'

'I don't think Cunningham's his man anyway. My money is on LeBlanc. He's the loose cannon, the psycho with runs on the board. Cunningham's a pain but he does seem to have a functioning on-off switch.'

I'm inclined to agree, and figuring the same for the fire at my place. 'I'll leave the raid to you guys. Obviously Keegan and the brass have restored faith in you.'

'Little choice under the circumstances.'

'By the way, Morgan Hopu mentioned something about Havelka having family skeletons. Could be a distraction but what do we know about him? Havelka, that is.'

'Only what's on file.'

'Anybody available to do some digging?'

'To what effect? Clear Hopu? It's not a priority right now, Nick.'

'Yeah, I can see that.' Check the time. 'I'll get back over to Nelson. Do some TLC with the family.'

Maxwell's mobile goes. He scans the screen. 'Message from Keegan. Guess who just flew into Wellington on his private jet?'

25.

'How come he was allowed to travel?'

I've just handed Vanessa another batch of painkillers. She's had an uncomfortable night and her face is pale and pinched. It's heartbreaking. Paulie is working on a journal as part of his absent-from-school curriculum. He's drawn a picture of a red-roofed house on fire and us outside with tears and sad faces. I've got Keegan on speakerphone while I wash up breakfast dishes. Vanessa occasionally snorts or sticks her tongue out when Keegan speaks. Grudge-bearer from way back.

'Bryant's a dual citizen, remember? Kiwi, bought and paid for.'

'And the federal prosecutor still let him go?'

'I don't think he had any say in the matter. It looks like it was all done with a nod, a wink, and a presidential pardon if Bryant stayed schtum on what he knows.'

Money, power, and something to bargain with: Thomas Hemi's take on the whitey justice system. 'So what now?'

'I'm guessing he'll recover from his jet lag and in a day or two will want to inspect his Marlborough Sounds properties.'

'One unfinished and the other abandoned. No way he's ready for Armageddon.' Last night's raid on the Lodge netted nothing. There was no-one at home except Brandon Cunningham, who is now cooling his heels in a cell a few floors below me at Nelson Police HQ. Apparently he's asked to speak to me. 'Maybe they'll put up the white flag and we can all get back to our day jobs.'

'Whatever. Can you get down here and find out what Cunningham's got to say for himself? I've had word that a couple of SIS spooks are galloping our way from Wellington as we speak. If they take over we've lost him.'

So here I am now. Interview Room 3: a table with chairs either side and the recording equipment switched off. Just Brandon and me and four blue walls on this fresh blustery Thursday morning.

'How's the family, Sergeant Chester? Well, I hope?'

'Where'd everybody go? All your merry men?'

He shrugs. 'Gave them the rest of the week off. Been a stressful time lately. They'll be out camping somewhere. Spot of hunting maybe.'

'You asked to speak to me. I'm happy enough just to put you on the next plane out to Sioux Falls. I don't think either of us is here to play yet more games.'

'We can find Georges. We'll take care of him. You don't need to worry about that anymore.'

'Take care of him how? Whisk him back to the US on Bryant's jet or disappear him permanently because he's become an embarrassment?'

'Either way, problem solved for you.'

'Making him go away is not problem solved. Making him pay is problem solved.'

'Money? That's not an issue. Mr Bryant has plenty if that's what it takes.'

'We'll stick to our way of doing things. Anyway, if he's such a liability how come you all went along with him the other night? Why didn't you hand him over then?'

'Band of Brothers, dude. One for all, all for one.'

'Melvyn's happy family.'

His eyes glint at the mention of his nephew's name. 'Cards on the table?'

'Again? Sure.'

'I don't blame you for what happened to Melvyn. Georges is responsible for that. Like he was for the terrible fire at your home. That's why I want him gone. And so does Mr Bryant.'

'It looks like it's Georges against the world, doesn't it? Everybody blaming him for everything. Convenient. What about the threatening photos of us and our families? I can't see him having the wherewithal, or the patience, to bother with such subtleties.'

'Mea culpa. I organised that. A little bit of symbolic chest-beating to keep the troops happy. No real harm done though, surely?'

'And the harassment of Constable Rapata, the midnight calls, vandalism. That was you too.'

'If you say so.'

I suppose I could charge him but with what? Trespass? Stalking? Taking photos without a signed consent form? Slap on the wrist and a fine if you have the right lawyer. 'Anything else?'

'What?'

'You're offering to take Georges out of the picture for us, then it's back to business as usual, I assume. Anything else on the agenda?'

'Mr Bryant is keen for you all to know that he doesn't want to cause any problems here and just intends to live a quiet life and mind his own business.'

'Maybe he does now because he's running out of options and boltholes. Before that he had you beating up on anybody who got in your way. Why? So we'd be distracted and keep our noses out of your business out on the Sounds? That worked well didn't it?'

'Like I said before, not everyone in the valley disapproves of us.'

'Running blacks and welfare recipients out of town? Maybe you could burn some crosses and wear a bedsheet too. Who are you aiming to impress?'

'Our base. Look, bullshit and bluster, disrupt and distract. It's the political strategy du jour. Counter-intuitive maybe, but it works well for some people.' He gives me a wink. 'But not you, huh, hotshot?'

There are footsteps in the corridor: a couple of sallow youths in sharp suits pushing past one of our constables. The Wellington spooks, presumably. They usher me out but not before I get to say, 'No deal, Cunningham.'

Back up to Keegan's office for a debrief. 'There's a lot of noise and distraction. Just when you think you're getting a handle on something it all changes.'

'Classic look-over-there stuff, isn't it? Government one-oh-one: The Dark Arts.'

'It's working on me.' I accept a coffee from her ever-full plunger. 'I just want to run a mile.'

'How's Vanessa? Paulie?'

'Paulie keeps on truckin' but Vanessa's had enough.'

A dip of the head. 'You thinking of chucking it in?'

'Not a good time to be making any rash decisions. Besides I still have a strong will to win.'

She seems pleased to hear it. 'Melvyn Cody and Jaxon Hemi were incidentals weren't they? Sideshows. Gelder's the main game.'

'Because he saw or knew something and Georges LeBlanc needed reassurance.'

'Reasoned negotiation, it's a dying art.'

'We need to find Gelder's phone, or phones. Find out what happened that night he stayed over at Māhana.'

'I'll give Will a call. Pull it up his priority list. You better get back to your family.'

'Where have SIS taken Cunningham?'

'Into one of their safe houses. Awaiting instructions from Bryant probably.'

'I'm still intrigued as to why Cunningham and his troops are based in the valley while the real reason they're all here is that place out on the Sounds.'

'Maybe that's exactly it,' says Keegan. 'The Lodge in your valley is a barracks for Cunningham's hillbilly headkickers. On call for when needed. But really, if you're a man of class and refinement with snobby rich friends dropping in, would you really want such riff-raff hanging around at the bottom of your manicured garden?'

Can't fault the logic of class war. Ever.

Vanessa is snoozing under the weight of another batch of heavy-duty painkillers and I've changed the dressings on her burns. Paulie is trouncing me at Crash Bandicoot and I keep coming a cropper in these crazy Mayan temples. Winter has arrived a week early. It's another rainy day in Nelson and there's a warning out that the Maitai and other rivers in the region could reach flood levels by tonight. The Wakamarina too no doubt, with all that water and mud sluicing off those logged hills in the Richmond ranges. It's foul weather to be out in and I picture Georges LeBlanc, wet and shivering in some abandoned gold workings, plotting his next move.

Those experiments at Stanford University in the US way back in the early seventies suggested that we're all capable of torture under the right circumstances – such as wanting to fit in and aiming to please. We like to think that precious few of us would take actual pleasure in it. Really? Maybe I'm one of them. It's not so long ago that I shoved a gun in a man's face and threatened to kill him if he didn't tell us where a missing kid was. And there was that time with the Russians and the eel. Maybe Georges is just an extension of all of us, occupying his place on society's sicko spectrum. Another brick in the wall of the padded cell.

'Dad! You have to jump the pillars of fire!' Paulie looks at me like I'm not of this world. 'Not run off the edge like a, like a …'

'Useless donkey?'

'Yeah. Donkey.' He shows me how to leap a burning pillar of fire properly. Apt, I suppose, given recent events. 'When are we going home?'

'No time soon, mate.'

'We going to build another house?'

'Hadn't thought about it. Thought we might move into town instead.'

'Havelock?'

'Yeah, maybe. Or Nelson?'

'Too many people.'

'You never said that about Sunderland.'

He jerks on the console and avoids disaster. 'Didn't know better.'

'Prefer the country then?'

'Who wouldn't?'

'S'pose so.'

'Can Mim visit me here?'

'Doubt it, mate. This is police property.'

He nods. 'Mum gunna get better?'

'Sure. Just needs a bit of time. Like your ankle.'

'And your leg after you were shot.'

'Took a while didn't it? And look at me now. Right as rain.'

'Suck at Crash Bandicoot.'

'Don't mock the afflicted.'

Another console jerk. 'Michael got shot too.'

'Mim's grandad? Did he? Where?'

'The war.'

'I meant where on his body.'

Paulie shrugs. 'He lived. Blessing, eh?'

Blessing? Kids, huh?

Thomas Hemi made his move that night as the rivers overflowed, the hills and roads slipped, and the police and emergency services were stretched thin. He got his big brother Morgan to call me from the landline at the abandoned Lodge and invite me up to see real justice in action.

'Come alone,' Morgan said.

With Vanessa zonked out on meds, David Ford has once more stepped into the breach to watch over her and Paulie. He's happy to do so but questions my priorities.

'Think it's wise to be gallivanting off at a time like this?' He nods down the hallway to the bedroom where Vanessa sleeps. 'Your place is here, Nick.'

My mobile buzzes. Somebody sent me a photo. Georges LeBlanc bound and gagged lying on the parapet of what looks like Deep Creek Bridge. Below him, I know, is a drop of around a hundred and fifty metres to rocks and rushing river. I show the pic to Ford.

He shrugs. 'No great loss, I'm guessing.'

'But now it's on my phone it'd be remiss of me to ignore it.'

'Remiss? Call it in. Let Keegan deal with it. Or Maxwell.'

'They've specified they want me and me alone.'

'Let them specify away. Fuck 'em.'

'David? Language.' It's a sleepy Paulie, en route to the toilet. 'Why you here?'

'Be off with you,' he says to me gruffly. 'And when you get back, do some thinking about what's important around here.'

With the rain pounding my windscreen all the way over the Whangamoa Saddle, I try feebly to justify myself to myself. The best I come up with is that if I manage to get Georges LeBlanc back off Thomas Hemi then I can try and prove some point about the rule of law. Who am I kidding? There's something going on and I can't bear to not be at the centre of it.

Deep Creek, just north from my dearly departed home, used to be a thriving community back in the gold rush days. There was a hotel here, a school, a cluster of houses, and down where the creek meets the Wakamarina they attempted to dam and change the course of the river in order to suck up all the gold they thought was there. Another folly worthy of *Fitzcarraldo*. The Deep Creek cemetery, where my mate Steve is now buried after feeling the wrath of a knife meant for me, is also home to several dozen other graves, many unmarked, of those who struggled to make a life here over the years. It's also the last resting place for the victims of those historic Doom Creek bandits. Imagine: weeks and months hacking away at bedrock for a few ounces of the yellow stuff, and some gunslinging lazy wanker is waiting for you behind a bush. Bang, easy money. The cemetery offers free burial for locals, which is a comforting thought in hard times. The journey up here was atrocious. Recent logging and torrential rains turned a bitumenised road into a muddy river. It took all my concentration to keep the ute from being washed into the nearest paddock. Morgan Hopu waves me down with a torch. Thomas is in the background, leaning over a seated Georges LeBlanc who is no doubt relieved to be no longer perched on the bridge parapet. It's pissing down and I'm drenched within seconds of being out of the car. Morgan and Thomas seem oblivious to it. Georges too, by the look of him. He's had a severe going-over.

Thomas stands. 'He's confessed to murdering my son. He says it was for snitching on that kid, Melvyn Cody. He's feeling a bit remorseful now. Wishes he hadn't done it.' He wipes rain from his face and flicks it onto the prisoner. 'Want to ask him about that Gelder fella?'

'I can take it from here, Thomas. Get him back to the station. Get us all home and dry, eh?'

'Home and dry.' He wipes more rain from his eyes. 'That'd be nice.' He nudges LeBlanc with his foot. 'What do you think, Georgie?'

'Fuck you and your dumbass kid. He died crying for his mummy. As for you, Chester. Suck my dick.'

'There's your answer, Nick. Remorseful when it suits him, but the asshole always shines through.' Thomas picks LeBlanc up and throws him over the bridge. There's a sickening snap and a squeal of agony.

Far out. Did he really just do that?

A yell from below.

Thomas leans over the parapet. 'What's that, Georges? Want to go again?' It's then that he shows me the rope attached to the bridge rail. 'Bungee,' he explains to me. 'Not elasticated, I'm afraid. Might have popped a joint or two there.'

I lean over the rail and look down into the darkness. Water rushes below, luminescent white dashing over the rocks. 'Is he still alive?'

A groan, barely audible over the rain and rushing water.

'Guess so. Maybe you could try asking him about Gelder now.' Hemi takes out a knife and starts sawing at the rope.

'Can we hold off for a sec?'

'Make it thirty if you like. Then I'm finished here. And so's he.'

'Thomas, this isn't the way.'

'Twenty-seven, twenty-six.'

'Don't make me take you in, Thomas.'

'Twenty-three, twenty-two.'

'LeBlanc, why did you kill Gelder?' I've never had to shout a police interrogation to a reluctant bungee-jumper in a flooded canyon at midnight in a storm before. It focuses the mind. Especially when his rope is about to be cut. 'LeBlanc?'

'Fuck you, snowflake cuck.'

'Pull him back up.' The voice comes from behind a blinding floodlight perched on the hill leading up to the cemetery. It's Brandon Cunningham.

'What if I don't want to?' Hemi keeps sawing.

'Do it.'

'Do as he says, bro.' Morgan eases the knife out of Hemi's hand. 'I've got an important business meeting tomorrow. Worth a few bob.' Together they start hauling on the rope and in no time LeBlanc is back on the parapet. His left hip looks dislocated. Hemi backs over the bridge to the south side, his side, cradling LeBlanc in his huge arms like an infant. Morgan tags along, a pistol at LeBlanc's head for insurance. 'We'll back up here, you need to turn those lights off 'cause they're hurting my eyes. Wouldn't want to trip.'

The floodlights go off and individual torches come on.

'You come with us, Nick,' says Hemi, quieter. 'You'll be better over here.'

'No need. I'll leave you guys to work this one out.' Yes, I've given up on the noble rule-of-law idea.

Hemi is insistent. 'Really, Nick. That's not the best place to be standing.'

Some ratcheting of shotguns. Cunningham and his men heading my way. 'Choose well, Chester. Keep out of this.'

'Nick, mate.' Hemi is holding something in his hand. A phone? A torch? A metal tube like an EpiPen, a button. His thumb over it.

That's when I see the fresh wires that have been laid along the edge of the bridge. Jesus, he really is going to do it.

'Run, Nick. Now.'

26.

The explosion was precise and loud. Our ears are still ringing. Dust and debris floats from the sky. The bridge is now way down in that deep creek. No people or vehicles are going to make it beyond the nine-kilometre mark on Wakamarina Road any time soon. Thomas Hemi just took out a hundred and fifty years of civil engineering history. Those wild valley rumours about him were true, he would blow that bridge if the balloon went up. Cunningham's commandos stand on the far side of the abyss. Wondering, no doubt, what the hell just happened.

'The Zombie Apocalypse happened, bro.' Hemi gives me a grin. 'And you're on the side of the angels.'

'My family are on the other side,' I point out. 'Those people will go after them.'

'Why would they? Wasn't you that blew the bridge and stole their friend.'

'I don't think they're that discerning.'

'Aren't your folks in Police HQ, Nelson? Can't see it.' Hemi slaps LeBlanc out of his nightmare. 'This is the guy they want. He's our bargaining chip.' Looks up at me. 'Now we're in the big league, eh?'

'Do you realise what you've done, Thomas? This is madness.'

'No mate, this is taking the initiative. Leadership.'

'Mana,' says Morgan Hopu.

'Where did you learn how to use explosives?'

Hemi winks. 'I was in the army reserve for a couple of years.'

'This can't end well, mate. You know that.'

'We all have our lines in the sand, Nick. You too, am I right?'

Of course he is. 'So what now?'

'Better cancel that meeting I had,' says Morgan, heading into the undergrowth. 'Oh, forgot. No phones in the fucken Apocalypse.'

'Shelter would be good,' says Hemi. An engine starts up and Morgan backs an ATV buggy out of the bushes. He nods back over the abyss. 'It'll take them a while to work it out, maybe even send some of them on foot down to the bottom and back up again, but eventually they'll be here. And we need to be ready.' He drops LeBlanc into the roadkill tray and cable ties him to a bracket. 'Hop in.'

A shake of the head. 'I'll walk out.'

Morgan points his hunting rifle my way. 'Hop in.'

'Kidnapping a police officer, Thomas? Really?'

'You're our guest, mate. Duty of care.'

'Why did you bring me in on this? You didn't need me here.'

'True. But I felt I owed you something. The chance to find out the truth about that miner maybe.'

Or maybe implicate me in whatever is planned. An insurance policy?

One last glance towards the gaping chasm and I hop into the mule as requested. How do you replace something like Deep Creek bridge? Having driven down the Kaikoura road since the earthquake, it's clear to me that anything is possible, even moving a fallen mountain. Maybe some army engineers can chopper in a temporary replacement. Maybe they can bulldoze a new road over the hills from Pelorus or Wairau. Meantime the dozen or so households trapped in Thomasland are going to have to learn the value of community. And I need to find a way to bring this madness to a peaceful conclusion.

We bump along a muddy track winding up into a recently logged plantation with the rain almost horizontal and LeBlanc groaning at every lurch. I can't resist pursuing the question. 'Why did you kill Gelder, Georges? You may as well tell me.' A groan. 'Sorry, mate. Didn't catch that.'

'Stop those crazy bastards and I'll tell you.'

'Thomas and Morgan? I can't, Georges. They're in charge here.'

'I meant Cunningham.'

Hemi looks back with a rain-soaked grin. 'Now we're getting somewhere. Let's get you comfy and dry, eh, Georgie?'

Another hour or so later we're in a small clearing beside an abandoned fossicker's hut.

'Came across it out pig-shooting one time.' We carry LeBlanc in while Thomas covers the buggy with branches. The hut has been prepared in advance: camp beds, gas lamps, a stove, food and water. 'Sorry, mate.

There's no wi-fi.' He points to a radio. 'Tranny picks up Magic FM in Wellington when the weather's nice.'

There's even a spare set of dry clothes for everyone. 'You thought of everything.' I hold up a shirt to my chest. 'The right size too.'

'Ruth's a good judge of a man.'

She appears from the shadows. 'Nick. You made it then.' As if this was a dinner invitation.

'It's a big sacrifice for a family to make. You'll all go to prison for this, you realise that don't you? Your youngest still has, what, three or four years left at school?'

'You think having your first-born butchered by these animals isn't a sacrifice already?' Ruth leans over a prone LeBlanc and slaps him none too lightly on the cheek. 'He's the one, Tom?'

'Yep. Had no trouble admitting it, too.'

'Smells like he pissed hisself.'

'Yeah, he's been through a rough patch.'

'There's still time to rescue this, Thomas.' I slip on the dry flannel shirt. 'So far it's destruction of public property and assault.'

'What about kidnapping you?'

Thomas has this presence, I see it now. He should have been the star of that dumb film, not some extra. Is this what Latifa means by mana? Even big brother Morgan, gang leader and successful businessman, seems in awe of him. Ruth, less so. Maybe it's the familiarity of a long-standing marriage. She knows him well enough, knows he's not perfect.

'Misunderstanding. You invited me to take custody of your citizen's arrest. Saved me from getting blown up. We can blame the Yanks for the bridge. We can make this work, Thomas. But it needs to end here.'

By now reports will be well and truly in on the explosion. Emergency services will be scratching their heads on the north side of Deep Creek. Cunningham and his men will have faded back into the darkness and will be fanning out on foot and quad bikes looking for us. Police and emergency helicopters will be in the air. Vanessa will be wondering where the hell I am. David too, has he taken his leave yet? Keegan, Maxwell, Latifa. All wondering what the devil I've got myself into now. Rain pounds the tin roof of the shack and somewhere near there's the sound of rushing and rising water. I'm guessing we're within spitting distance of Doom Creek where it joins the Wakamarina.

'Thomas?' I repeat.

'Ask him your questions,' he says. 'The clock's ticking.' It's no use. The man's as solid and immovable as a Rapanui carving.

There's tea on the go and Georges seems momentarily brightened by it. He's changed into a dry shirt, one of Thomas' cast-offs I'd guess, the way it hangs from him.

'So, Georges, you were going to tell me all about Gelder. Fire away.'

'You haven't dealt with Cunningham yet.'

'Take it as a given,' says Thomas.

'Bring me his head, then we'll talk.'

'What movie you in, dickbrain?' growls Morgan.

'I'm not sure you're in the best position to bargain, Georges.' Thumb over my shoulder. 'Thomas here can turn you over to me or to Cunningham or, if he wants, chuck you off a cliff. You know that already.'

'So I'm a dead man walking and my secret dies with me.'

'You're not dead if you come with me. I can protect you.'

'Doubt it.'

'Cunningham's head is irrelevant if they're that relentless.'

A sly grin. 'A man still likes his trophies.'

'Yanks. They're fucked,' says Ruth. 'The lot of them. Let them kill and eat each other. Put a lid on their stupid country and forget them.'

'One last time, Georges. What did Gelder know about Māhana?'

A calculating pause. 'Read up on James Bryant. Ask yourself what it is the federal prosecutor might have had on him to make him run for the hills.'

That's all he was going to give us for the moment. By now it must be around 3 a.m. so we turn in with Morgan and Thomas on guard duty roster. I offer to share the burden but they decline so I stretch out on a camp bed and fall asleep to the sound of drumming rain and rushing water.

'Shhhh.'

I don't need telling. I heard it too.

Footsteps outside. Multiple. The brushing of foliage and undergrowth. The cracking of twigs. The rain has stopped, wind dropped, and in the grey dawn all that can be heard is birdsong, rushing water and these alien sounds. Whispering and human whistles. People moving into position. Mechanical clicks. Guns being cocked.

'Chester. Hemi.' Cunningham's voice. 'We know you're in there. Send Georges out.'

Thomas looks at Georges like he only just remembered he was there. Lifts his voice to a broken window pane. 'He can't walk. Hurt his hip, I think.'

'So you guys walk out and leave him to us. No guns. Hands up where we can see them.'

'Not sure we can trust you, Brandon.'

'You have no choice.'

'I can't see you hurting us,' says Thomas. 'You don't need that kind of trouble. Really.'

'Accidents happen, it's hunting season. Your government will make it all disappear anyway.'

'Different mob now, mate. Nicer people who mean well.'

'Don't count on it.'

While Brandon and Thomas do their verbal jousting I picture armed men edging ever closer and limiting our options. 'Brandon, it's me, Nick Chester.'

'Maybe you can talk some sense into your Māori friend.'

'Thomas,' I whisper. 'He's right. He doesn't need to slaughter us all to get what he wants. One carefully targeted stray bullet on any of us will do the job. Ruth, Morgan. You want to lose them too?'

'Keep us out of it,' hisses Ruth.

'LeBlanc's a piece of shit. Is he worth that?'

'Do I have a say in this?' asks Georges.

'No, you don't.' I turn back to Hemi. 'Thomas, he's admitted what he did to Jaxon. We know now these guys aren't going to jet him to freedom. He's going to pay. Let them get on with it. Walk away.'

He lifts his chin at me. 'What about your precious rule of law?'

'Greater good.' He looks pensive but already it's in his eyes; he's convinced. I'm not going to give him time to change his mind. 'Brandon? You get what you want and we get to walk away unharmed. This goes no further with us, right?'

'Right, Chester.' A chuckle. 'We're all gentlemen here.'

Can I trust him? Maybe this is one more, one last, mistake among the many I've already made. 'Goodbye, Georges,' I say as we file out, hands in the air, sun glinting through the trees.

There are tears in his eyes but I can't feel sorry for him. There's no remorse, just self-pity, regret that he didn't get away with it.

It's agreed. We'll pin the blown bridge on Cunningham and his mob. They'll deny everything but it'll be multiple versions of the same story and it'll end up being too hard. As for Georges – yes, the traceable SMS'd photo to me shows that Thomas had LeBlanc in custody. But now Cunningham has him – which is true. We made our way out from Doom Creek via a tortuous old prospecting path through the hills and back down to a still-flooded Canvastown, sloshing our way through the knee-deep water in the ATV. The residents of Thomasland, and others flooded out further down the valley, have been evacuated by chopper and accommodated in the school hall ahead of longer-term arrangements. Civil and army engineers are working out what to do with the blown bridge. There are military exercises scheduled for later this year so the Defence department might even chip in for a quick replacement. Maybe billionaire Bryant can match it out of his petty cash. Somebody thoughtfully drove my ute back down the valley for me and left it parked at the Trout with the keys in the glove box. A breeze has sprung up and the school flag snaps briskly against a blue sky.

'This is one cursed valley,' says DC Keegan through a cloud of ciggie smoke. 'And you guys really didn't bump LeBlanc off? Promise?'

'Cross my heart.'

'We've talked to Cunningham and he's saying nothing too. They were all set to hand him over to us. Reckons LeBlanc legged it in the storm.' Not easy, I'm thinking, with a dislocated hip. Keegan eyes me. 'Could have just left him with you if that was the plan, hmmm?'

'Maybe Cunningham doubts my abilities or my integrity. Wanted to make sure LeBlanc was handed over to people he could trust.'

'Understandable in your case. All moot now I suppose.' She flicks her cigarette into a puddle. 'Anyway we'll be winding down the search. Can't see him surviving a night like that.'

'Me neither.'

'Don't suppose you got the chance to talk to him at all?'

'Not much. He's a tough cookie, doesn't give much away.'

'But?'

'But he mentioned something about that place out on the Sounds and hinted that we should be digging more into Bryant and his proclivities. He reckons that's what the Fed prosecutor had on him.'

'Not going to be easy. Bryant's a protected species.'

'But the US media must have got a whisper,' I say. 'FOI and all that.'

'Sure, we can follow it up. But what's it got to do with Gelder?'

'Maybe whatever was on his phone backs up the rumours on Bryant. We can be pretty confident LeBlanc and the kid killed Gelder. All we need to know is why.'

'With both perps out of the picture, the burden of prosecution proof is removed. Maybe the why is no longer so important, Nick.'

'No, but it might give us an idea of what those people are doing here in the first place.'

She shrugs assent. 'That pic Thomas sent you. Ford told us about it. Pretty damning would you say?'

'Worse than it looked. Yes, LeBlanc was tied up but that was only to restrain a dangerous guy.'

'Perched on a high bridge that has since been blown up.'

'Cunningham's a madman. It's a miracle we all got out of there alive.'

'All?'

'Yep.'

'Did Hemi question LeBlanc before you arrived? About what might have happened to his son?'

'You'll have to ask him.'

'I'm asking you.'

'Put it this way, I think Thomas is more at peace now, and you can probably redirect resources from both the Jaxon Hemi and Bruce Gelder enquiries elsewhere.'

'Any reason why I shouldn't arrest Thomas and Morgan?'

'What for? Capturing and losing a wanted man? Some people would hail them as heroes. Wonder about police priorities.'

'This place. Fucking Dodge City, Yanks or no.' She fingers her ciggie packet but decides against another. 'Go home, Nick. Tend to your family.'

Home. Now there's an interesting concept.

Vanessa seems to be on the mend. She's strong enough to be angry with me.

'What goes on inside that thick head of yours?'

Good question. Can I seriously blame my impetuosity on my funny old head, or is it simply a longstanding character flaw? 'I'm sorry but it seemed urgent.'

'And we're not?' A few more salient points from Vanessa and pathetic sorries from me and she can't be bothered any more. 'Brick bloody wall. Honestly.' Back to more important matters than high jinks in the high country. 'The insurance assessor called. They've approved a rebuild on the same site; it'll take anything from six to eighteen months. There's a shortage of skilled labour, apparently. They're all down Kaikoura or Christchurch on earthquake repairs.'

'Interim rental assistance?'

'They'll look at it. And there's a bridging payment for loss of personal belongings due soon.'

'I imagine the department will help out there. And Latifa has offered us the police house in Havelock.'

'We might need it. The assessor was humming and hah-ing about the fire being deliberate and the work of a foreign national, possibly now dead. Wasn't sure his bosses would like the sound of that.'

'We'll leave the lawyers to work it out.' I'm suddenly feeling the lack of sleep, another migraine threatens. 'What a mess.'

'Sunderland is looking good right now.'

'Seriously?'

'It's no less dangerous than here. Maybe it's even safer now with Pritchard inside, Marty dead, and the gang broken up.'

'Sammy's due out soon and I don't trust him to forgive and forget.'

'Worst case scenario? We move back to another place with psychos and crap weather. Least it's familiar ground and I've got friends there who don't say where's your funny accent from? And there's no sandflies.'

Paulie's taken his headphones off. 'Where? What are you talking about?'

A finger prod in my solar plexus. 'Buck your ideas up, Nick. Something's got to change.'

As if on cue a call comes through offering me an appointment with the neurologist to discuss my scan results. Would next Monday suit? First thing? 'Sure. Is it possible to give an indication now?'

'No,' says the receptionist. 'Sorry.'

'Any cause for concern?'

'Dr Copp will explain everything when she sees you.'

27.

Monday rolls around and Dr Copp's rooms, in a quiet leafy street on a hill overlooking Nelson, are awash with sunlight through the large north-facing windows. She has no end of letters after her name, certificates and diplomas on her wall, and a scan of my head on a backlit screen. She has pointed to various white dots which seem to signify or equate with memory lapses – white holes, I suppose you could call them. I'm surprised there's so few. Apparently they're not uncommon and, in this case, not the main issue. Instead there's a dark smudge that worries her. It's been hiding just at the point where my spinal cord meets my brain.

'It's lucky you had the TGA. We might not have seen it in time.'

'What is it?' I ask.

'I don't know at this stage. An MRI scan should tell us. Maybe even a biopsy.'

'Biopsy?'

'We need to find out whether it's malignant.'

'A tumour?'

'Of sorts. Yes.'

For such a petite woman with an equally petite voice she dishes out devastation like there's no tomorrow. Maybe that's not the best simile under the circumstances.

Vanessa is gripping my hand so hard it hurts. 'How soon might we know?'

'I can get you in for an MRI this week, Mr Chester. We'll decide then whether we need a biopsy. Then within about a week of that we should have test results back.'

It certainly puts everything in perspective. Cunningham, Gelder, Havelka; none of them matter a jot. Outside the sun still shines, the birds tweet, and the Maitai river still tumbles over the rocks.

'One day at a time, love.'

'Yes,' says Vanessa.

Because that's all we can do – tamp down the cold, hard fear and push on. One day at a time. Vanessa winces as we walk slowly to the car. She shouldn't really be up and about with her burn still so raw but she wasn't to be crossed on this matter. It's been a flat, often tense, weekend. We're homeless, out of sorts, in pain, and scared. Some people, I know, live a large part of their lives like this and I'm in awe of their ability to hang it together and keep going. Of course they have no choice.

Back in the safe apartment, after thanking the carer and seeing her on her way, my heart wells when I see Paulie again and I try to reassure him that the medical appointment was nothing to worry about. Tears are not far away for both Vanessa and me.

Christ. It's going to be a long dark road ahead.

We've changed Vanessa's wound dressing and she's having a lie-down. Paulie's sprained ankle is on the mend and we're looking to send him back to school tomorrow.

'Mim will be happy to see me.'

'Yep, you'll have plenty of news for her. And for everybody.'

'Lot going on,' he concedes.

And how.

We settle down and watch *The Incredibles* for the umpteenth time. Yes, I know, this kid gets far too much screen time but guess what, it doesn't matter so much right now.

My phone buzzes in my pocket and I check it from time to time. Latifa wants to know how it's going. Keegan too. Maxwell. They can wait. Gary's back in mobile range. Some port down south. None of it is urgent. Nigel Watson, a text.

Busy?

Yes

Got some news. Let me know when suits

Will do

Why did I do that? Why not just tell him to talk to Maxwell, he'll run with it.

'You're missing the film, Dad.'

I hug him close. 'Love you, Paulie. Do you know that?'

'Yeah, yeah. And it's Paul, remember?'

By evening we're all going stir crazy. The kitchen in the safe house is fully equipped but we're still living, for the most part, on takeaways and convenience food. Paulie needs to be back at school, we all need to be back under the cosy duvet of routine. Vanessa tips me the nod and I make the call.

'Can we take you up on the offer of the police house?'

'Sure,' says Latifa. 'When do you want me out of here?'

'Tomorrow suit?'

'Far out. Mind if I pack first?'

'Make it snappy.'

But she's more than happy to help. Being back in Havelock gets us much nearer to Paulie's school and we can begin to settle in to what will probably be our home for the long haul.

If I'm around for it.

The downside is that Vanessa won't be so near the care she was getting at Nelson hospital, but she says she'd prefer the long and winding commute over what we have right now. 'It's like living in a pressure cooker.'

'I'm not so sure moving house is going to ease that, love.'

'Anything to distract us, keep us busy.'

It's heartfelt and I'm not about to argue. Another text: MRI, Wednesday. The day after tomorrow. 'That's handy.' I waggle the phone. 'It's the same day as your appointment with the burns specialist.'

'Two birds, one stone,' she says grimly.

It's surprisingly good to be back in Havelock. Are we so low in resilience these days that even Nelson gives us the big city blues? I know it's not as simple as that but one glimpse of the Sounds and those hills, logged or otherwise, and I do feel a lifting of the spirit. Paulie's at school, Vanessa is resting at home, making a list of what she wants to change about the police house, and I'm shopping for groceries at the Four Square, recently redecorated after the unfortunate incident in the coldroom. I'm happy to pay the small-town inflated prices and accept the good wishes of fellow citizens.

Doug bails me up. 'This mean those Americans have gone?'

'Not yet.'

'Not easy to go panning up at Pear Tree Flat since they blew up that bridge. Silly fuckers.'

'Some people, huh?'

'Indeed. Good to have you back, Sergeant. We need a sheriff in town.'

He salutes a farewell and starts rummaging among the vegies. Ruth is at the far end of the aisle, examining the dairy produce like she's not just been Bonnie to Thomas's Clyde.

'You guys got somewhere to stay yet?'

'A friend down the valley has a hut but they reckon the temporary bridge should be ready any day now. Then we can go home. At least collect some stuff.'

'What's Thomas up to?'

'Organising the tangi for Jax. It's the day after tomorrow, at the marae. You're invited.'

I tell her I'll be there, hospital appointment permitting.

'Nothing serious I hope?'

'Just some tests.'

She nods, eyes filling. 'I don't think we'll survive this, Thomas and me. He's, I don't know. Unhinged?'

'One day at a time, Ruth. He's a good man. Have faith.'

'Faith?' She nods. 'S'pose so. Without it we're nothing, aren't we?'

It wouldn't do to have both of us bawling by the soft cheeses so I head for the checkout.

Breathe deeply.

The next few days are a numb blur. While Vanessa has her burns checked and some grafts scheduled, I'm wheeled along a corridor into a theatre with space age machinery, beeping screens and murmuring professionals, waking up several hours later to groggily receive the news that a little bit of my head has been sent to a lab somewhere. Whatever they saw on the scan warranted closer investigation. I've missed Jaxon Hemi's tangi and I envisage tears, songs, maybe even the odd sad joke, and finally a haka for a proud young man taken way too soon.

It's Friday morning before I'm in any fit state to get out of bed. A tag team of carers has been in the last few days tending to Vanessa, cooking and cleaning, and supervising Paulie. There's umpteen missed calls and messages on my mobile. Paulie is at school and Vanessa still looks exhausted and worried.

'How are you feeling?'

'Wobbly. You?'

'Same but for different reasons.'

During the day things pick up remarkably quickly. Apart from a dressing behind my ear to cover the keyhole, you'd hardly know I've just had a bit of brain surgery. On his return from school, dropped off by none other than Michael, Paulie is delighted to see me up and about. He remains blissfully unaware of the significance of my hospital stay and we intend to keep it that way.

'Mim's invited me for a sleepover. This weekend.'

'Sure. Maybe I can check their doors and windows first. 'You up for it, with your sore ankle?'

'Sure.'

Vanessa thinks it's a great idea under the circumstances and I'm not about to argue. In the evening we heat up one of the half-dozen casseroles left for us by concerned citizens and watch something diverting on TV. My phone is buzzing like billyo but it can wait.

28.

I begin to glimpse why Nigel Watson is on the way out. Johnny No-Mates. Really. Once somebody pays him some attention he doesn't want to let go. I must have had two dozen texts or voicemail messages over the course of this week since that earlier one saying he had some news. The tone has deteriorated sharply in the last forty-eight hours towards the accusatory and abusive. Quote, treacherous dogbreath cunt, unquote. I really don't need this right now. Saturday morning with clouds hanging over the top of the south I decide to put him straight.

'I've been in hospital, mate. Serious personal stuff going on. What you're doing doesn't help.'

'Yeah, well. Sorry. Nobody told me.'

Like it's my fault. 'No excuse for abuse like that. You're lucky I don't come round and knock your block off.'

'Not a good idea in your condition. Do you want the news or not?'

'Jesus. Go on then.'

'The silver chain missing from the McLernon evidence? I found it.'

It takes a moment for me to work out what he's on about. It's been a while. 'I never realised it was missing. You said it was entered into the store.'

'I thought it was. It should have been but it wasn't. I checked after I told you because I knew you'd never get around to it.'

'So where did it turn up?'

'In the Robertson box.'

'The motel manager? How come?'

'Exactly. It was found at the McLernon scene in the motel room but ends up in the evidence store for a murder committed six months later and elsewhere.'

This is giving me a new headache. 'Somebody is pissing about.'

'Spot on, and it's not me.'

'What made you look there?'

'They're related. I was worried, with the chain missing, that maybe the Robertson stuff had been tampered with too.'

'There would be in-out logs for each, computerised and hard copy. Showing dates of evidence entry and who by. It's not so easy to tamper these days.'

'You'd think that, wouldn't you?'

'Tell me, I know you're dying to.'

'Cold-case review. Just over a year ago, not an official one. No logs entered or records kept. All internal and informal as part of a handover.'

'Handover?'

'Outgoing Commander Ford and incoming Commander Keegan tidying up loose ends on their shared unsolveds.'

It's not my fight. Really, it isn't. If Watson wants to go up against Keegan and Ford over some old cases or old grudges, he's welcome. I'm not even investigating the McLernon and Robertson murders. They're tangential to the Havelka case and there's no discernible link so far. Until I get an all-clear or a dive-dive-dive from the neurologist I'm not really interested in Havelka either. Nigel Watson is beginning to suspect me of being in on some conspiracy and he's welcome to that as well. He needs a nasty disease or a posting to the remote Kermadec Islands to get his priorities reformulated and his empathy retuned. To think I bought the wanker a bowl of mussels too.

Aware that neither Vanessa nor I are in good condition for driving, Mim's mum calls to collect Paulie for the sleepover. While Mim helps Paulie get his act together and Vanessa issues reminders to him not to forget this and that, I chat on our threshold.

'Jan, wasn't it?'

She smiles. 'Still is. You lot have had some dramas. How's it going?'

'Getting there. Thanks for having Paulie over.'

'Our pleasure. He's a great guy and easy to please.'

A sudden gust of wind catches her hair and blows it across her face. I fight the urge to brush it aside. 'You guys are gradually settling in then?'

'Yep. Just taken delivery of some chickens. Mim and Paul can compare notes.'

'Did you have a big block in Nelson?'

'Nelson?'

'That's where Paulie said you'd moved from.'

'Maybe Mim's making things up again. She's got quite an imagination.'

'So where?'

'West coast. Near Greymouth.'

'Mim's dad?'

'Yes, he's from there too.'

'Is?'

'Was. Ah, here they come, finally.' Bundling them into the car, Jan gives me a parting wave and it's clear she's glad the interrogation is over.

After lunch Vanessa takes a nap and I hop online. I'm restless and disturbed. Nigel Watson is messing with my brain, as if it didn't have enough to worry about. So it's back to the McLernon and Robertson cases. What is it about them that would make Keegan and Ford take an interest as recently as last year and not deem the disclosure of such recent interest worthy of a mention to me? Something rings a bell, DC Keegan had said to me. Too bloody right it did.

Logging into the database and following the links, I can see there's definitely no official mention of a cold case review. So why the interest and how come Nigel Watson was aware of it? There's a headache nagging in my rear cortex and I don't like to think what's behind it. Warding off the impending migraine, I slam down a couple of Panadols and hope for the best. The police computer system is confused by my unusual log-in location and my erratic and irregular access of late. It decides to block me from going much further until I'm properly back on duty, in uniform, clean-shaven, and re-vetted by the IT department – it doesn't fancy the look of me one bit.

Google it is then. The archives of the local Greymouth scandal sheet enjoyed a lurid few days reporting on the rape and murder of former Whakakitenga community member Lucy McLernon in a motel up the coast at Westport. They called Lucy a Wellington 'socialite', given her upper-class background, although there is little evidence of her gracing any social pages previously. Speculation of a fall from grace, drug and sex abuse allegations at the commune, bikie links, a whole lot of colour and noise but nothing substantial to add to what was already in the official files.

The same journalist, a certain Ollie Harper – their dedicated crime scribe apparently – ran with the Robertson case six months later. Again, nothing substantial to add to what is already known from the files: the man was shot execution style and found on the local beach. The photo shows an eerie-looking place with sand as black as that at Kaikoura. Robertson had an unsavoury past with allegations of hidden cameras and backpackers being sexually pestered where he worked. Did he commit the McLernon rape and murder or did somebody suspect him of it? Either way, same result: an overdue and extreme comeuppance. Or was it just a drugs thing with the inevitable bikie connection – Morgan Hopu and his hitman, little brother Thomas? Both murders remained unsolved. A small postscript. Just over a year ago Ollie Harper reported from an unnamed police source that Nelson detectives were reviewing the case files of the two unsolved notorious west coast murders and that a number of officers had serious misgivings about those investigations. In particular, the family of Darren Robertson welcomed the review as they believed Darren had been unfairly tainted by certain allegations and they were keen to clear his name posthumously. Outgoing Tasman District Commander Ford was unavailable for comment.

The words blur. The headache wins. I spew in the toilet then retire to a dark room for the rest of the afternoon, my skull pounding.

Recovering in time for dinner, I find Vanessa in the kitchen zapping leftover casserole in the microwave and cutting up bread to dip in it. Her fingertips glide across my brow as she gives me a welcome kiss.

'Hungry?'

'Ravenous.'

'How's the head?'

'Better.' We keep our fears to ourselves and eat. Changing the subject, I recount the conversation with Mim's mum.

'So they're from Greymouth instead of Nelson. No big deal. I've got kids in my class who make up much bigger fibs than that. Imaginary parents, grandparents, siblings, pets. Births. Deaths. You name it, and sometimes their living truth is a lot worse than the fib.'

'Guess it's not important. I just wonder about Paulie being exposed to that fantasising.'

'As opposed to the real life crazies you bring home with you?'

'Good point.'

The news is on. Another mass shooting in the US. They're so commonplace these days that it's hard to maintain the sorrow and the outrage. They certainly don't seem to want to do anything to stop it. Those same military style assault rifles in the hands of the men at the Lodge, and all perfectly legal in New Zealand. What will it take to change that? Relatively sane societies hopefully learn from their mistakes: Dunblane, Port Arthur, you get my drift. Meanwhile, in other news, Kiwi cows have come down with some devastating plague: a kind of bovine Ebola that requires mass exterminations to deal with it. Maybe Godzone is not immune to the Apocalypse after all. My mind turns to Cunningham and to the recently arrived James Bryant. Things have been quiet for at least a week now and Georges LeBlanc, wherever he rests in peace, is buried so deep he'll never be found.

'Do you remember once I asked if you'd stay if I wasn't here, or Paulie?' Vanessa has that look on her face. Big talk time.

'Here being the valley, as I recall.'

'Yes, although now I'll extend it to New Zealand generally.'

'Yeah, I remember.'

'You were noncommittal at the time.'

'That'd be right.'

'How about now?'

'Things are different now.'

She purses her lips. 'No shit.'

'The answer is no, I wouldn't.'

'Where would you go?'

'Back home.'

'Sunderland?' She seems surprised at the idea.

'S'pose so. Somewhere for support for Paulie.'

'Same for me, if you weren't here.'

'I'm not dead yet.' I try to smile it away as a joke.

'Might be soon, though.'

'Better book your tickets then.' There's an edge of spite in my voice and I immediately regret it. 'Sorry.'

Her eyes brim. 'What a pair, eh?' She stands up, grimacing at the pain, and hobbles towards the kitchen. 'My turn to do the washing up, I think.'

'Leave it. You should just sit down. I can do it.'

'It's two bowls and two spoons, Nick. I can manage. I need to keep moving or it'll seize up.'

'Okay.'

'Maybe you can get on to Webjet. See if there's any flight deals.' Raises a teary smile. 'Joke.'

Is this the way of things for the next however long?

Back to work on Monday, I can't fucking stand this.

Sunday morning Latifa knocks at the door with some news.

'Charlie Evans is dead.'

I've lost track, what is it? A week, more, less, since I went by and saw he'd taken the For Sale notice down and there was no sign of life around the farm. Nobody to help out too since he lost his farmhand. I was going to follow it up but never did. 'Tell me.'

'Some prospector found him. A young bloke, cold-calling to see if Charlie fancied a goldmine on his land, noticed the alpacas and chooks seemed a bit frazzled. Obviously hadn't been fed for a while. Charlie was hanging from a beam in his hay shed. Been there some time.'

I slump into my seat. 'Forensics and crime scene?'

'There now. First indications are that it's suicide. Plain and simple.'

I can believe it. Charlie was a lost soul when he came to ours for dinner that night. 'Need anything from me?'

'No, it's all in hand. Just passing on the news. How are you going?'

'We're all hanging in there.' She winces. Poor choice of words under the circumstances. 'Thought I might pop in to work tomorrow.'

'Your call. Mind if I collect a few more things while I'm here? I left some boxes of stuff in the shed.'

'Sure. We really appreciate this.'

'No probs. Careful what you wish for though. The office is only ten paces that way. Not always easy to take time out and some of the punters will come knocking anyway, day or night.'

'Beggars can't be choosers.'

Vanessa waves hello from the laundry as she fills the washing machine and Paulie does likewise from his homework in the lounge room. His sleepover at Mim's was blissfully uneventful apart from one of Mim's new chooks leaving a deep scratch on the back of his hand. Jan, a trained nurse, had given him a choice of cool coloured bandaids and kissed it better. Jan and Mim had dropped him off an hour ago on their way to church. Latifa takes two boxes and I take one because I'm a weak sook and we wander out front to her car. Havelock is Sunday-morning quiet and mist drapes the surrounding green hills. It's a beautiful morning to die.

'Don't hurry back to work, Sarge. There's really no need.'

'There is for me. I need the distraction.'

A nod of recognition. 'If Charlie had stayed around, he might have got an offer on his place after all from that prospector.'

'I don't think money was his main worry. He still loved the land too much to let any wanker dig it up. Beattie would have had his guts for garters.'

'Well, if you believe any of that stuff, they're together again now.'

'Amen.'

'Maybe see you tomorrow then.' She slams the boot and jangles her car keys.

29.

On the understanding that I'm just a few paces away in the cop shop if she needs me, and with Paulie at school all day anyway, Vanessa ushers me out the door to work. It's hard to tell which of us is more relieved. Latifa is already there along with Steve from Traffic, and they'll be doing any outreach as I need to stay close. There's hardly enough room for the three of us but with a bit of goodwill and furniture rearrangement we rustle up a spot for me to shuffle papers for the day.

'Any more news on Charlie Evans?'

'No suspicious circumstances,' says Latifa. 'It looks like he wanted out and did it all by himself.'

'Good job that young fella found him,' says Steve, jiggling teabags at the sink. 'The rats and mice were taking an interest.'

'Spare us,' says Latifa.

'Maybe now he's gone that mine can go ahead. Bit of work for the locals.'

Latifa snorts. 'You kidding?'

'A job's a job,' says Steve, mischief curling the side of his mouth. 'The consortium have lodged a claim over the whole district. Got to be gold somewhere under that red ink.'

'Consortium? I looked them up. They're petty fossickers. Clueless bottom-feeders. They want to trash the environment for a quick buck. Anything but get a real job.' Latifa is effortlessly rising to Steve's bait. 'If our lot put in a Treaty claim over the area, people would be jumping up and down about the threat to their backyards. These jokers? Nobody bats an eyelid.'

'White,' I say in reply to Steve's teabag query. 'None.'

'Fucking right,' says Latifa.

My mobile goes. It's Will Maxwell. 'Noticed you were up and about when I drove by this morning. How's things?'

'Well as can be expected.'

'Fancy some fresh air and a cuppa tea? I can meet you in the bakery. Save your legs.'

I've hardly touched the one Steve just made but duty calls. The bakery is still within that five-minute radius if Vanessa needs me. 'Sure.'

A few spots of rain dot the footpath as I head down the hill, and more threatens. The wind snaps at the masts down at the marina and the water is starting to churn. Will has bought us tea and a date scone each and waits at my favourite table by the window.

'I'd like to be able to say you're looking well but you're not.'

'Thanks.'

'Keegan told me about the head. Fingers crossed, eh?'

'Yep.' I pull my tea mug closer. 'You wanted to see me?'

'With the Jaxon and Gelder jobs losing their urgency, I was able to put some people on Havelka.'

'And?'

'We asked our colleagues down in Dunedin to talk to the daughter. Lisbet.'

It turns out she hasn't spoken to, or seen, her parents in nearly twenty years. I attempt to do the sums. 'Havelka would have been about sixty-five by now. His wife early sixties. Twenty years takes them back to their early forties. Lisbet must have left home at a young age.'

'Fifteen.'

'Did she say why?'

'None of our business, apparently.'

Janeen's date scones are on form today. 'Any social services records?'

'Nothing.'

'Any conclusions you'd like to jump to?'

'Domestic abuse is a perennial favourite. Drugs. Wayward teenager. Take your pick.'

'Doesn't get us anywhere really, does it?'

'Except that your mate Morgan Hopu seems to know all about it. Why would he?'

'Why indeed.' I brush some crumbs away. 'Are you going to ask him?'

'Thought you might, when you're feeling better. He seems to have taken a shine to you.'

'It might be a while.'

'No rush. Havelka's been dead five years now. A few more days or weeks won't harm.'

'Any news on Gelder's missing phones?'

'Nothing.'

'Cunningham. Bryant. Any movement?'

'Quiet as church mice.' Maxwell takes a final sip of tea. 'You heard about Charlie Evans then?'

'Yep. Tragic.'

'You settling in okay at the police house?'

'Fine.'

'Family?'

'Yeah, we're all good.'

He stands. 'Hang in there, Nick. We care about you. You're more appreciated than you think.'

He'll never know how close I come to sobbing into his shoulder.

I'm tired of paperwork and fielding calls for Latifa and Steve. Rain has settled in properly now, driving against the office windows, and our combined body heat is steaming the place up. I pop out to check on Vanessa, who is now able to change her own dressings thank you very much and seems brighter and better off without me.

'You happy to pick up Paulie from school?' she says, looking up from a sudoku.

'Sure.'

'Another casserole do you tonight?'

'Yum.'

'I reckon I can get back to work after this week.'

'Great.'

She chucks the newspaper aside. 'We need to stop tiptoeing around each other, Nick. You're scared, I'm scared. Paulie is too but he doesn't know why yet. You can cut the atmosphere with a knife.'

I kneel down and hug her. Tears streaming down my face. Hers too. 'This sucks.'

'Big time,' she agrees. 'But this is no time to be cutting each other off.'

Dismissed. I'm at the school early and so is Michael. He's outside the ute, smoking. It comes as a surprise but then again, why? We've met, what, half a dozen times? I don't know a damn thing about him or his personal vices and I can't totally rely on his daughter's or granddaughter's versions of events.

'Afternoon,' he says, stubbing out his ciggie. 'Won't do to be seen with these outside the school gates and Mim hates the smell.'

'The sleepover went well, I hear.'

'Yeah, they kept themselves to themselves. Hardly a peep.'

'How was church?'

'You that interested?'

'Sorry. Just making conversation.'

'A happy-clappy congregation over in Blenheim. Jan's the one needs it more than me. I go along for the ride. Keep her company.'

'Fair enough.'

'You must see things in that job of yours. Make you question your faith in humanity.'

'There are good days and bad.'

'Young Paul said you had a lot on your mind. Lot of worry?'

I get this a lot. People digging for war stories. Dig away, mate, you'll find nothing. 'The house fire knocked us back and Vanessa's still in a bit of pain.'

He nods. 'I was in the tail end of the Vietnam thing. Brought up Scots Presbyterian but waved goodbye to all that after a few months in those rice paddies. Learned the meaning of "God forsaken".'

'You survived. Can't have completely forsaken you.'

'Yeah, few bits of scrap metal in me to keep the airport detectors beeping.' He taps his right hip. 'Otherwise, good as gold.'

So at least Mim's story about a war-wounded grandad holds up. The siren goes and the kids start streaming out. I can't resist plucking at the loose threads.

'Mim mentioned something about living in Nelson?'

'Did she? Kids say the darnedest things, as the song goes.'

'But Jan said you used to be on the west coast. Greymouth.'

'She'd be right.'

'Nice out there, eh?'

'When it's not pissing down.' He nods, staring into the wide grey yonder. 'And you reckon the sandflies are bad around here?'

'Not your cup of tea?'

'Nah. Again, Jan made the running. She's a searcher.'

'Searcher?'

'The way, the light, the truth. The hereafter.' He straightens up. 'But who am I to tell her it's just a big fucking meaningless void?'

Speaking of meaningless voids. It's as we're driving back to Havelock with Paulie chattering non-stop and the sinking sun glinting off the Pelorus Sound mudflats that a call comes through from Nelson hospital. Dr Copp would like to see me tomorrow. Would 11 a.m. suit?

'That was quick. I didn't expect the results back so soon.'

'It's about a week since your procedure isn't it?' says the receptionist. 'Dr Copp must have had you prioritised.'

Which of course, in my current default state of catastrophisation, translates into bad news. Maybe even the worst. 'I'll be there,' I say numbly.

'Will Mrs Chester be accompanying you? Dr Copp recommends it.'

Call closed and phone back in the cup holder. Wordlessly we drive into the edge of town.

'Who was that?' wonders Paulie.

'Nothing, mate. All good.'

I tell Vanessa about tomorrow's appointment. Can she make it? Sure. Chop vegies. Set the table. Stare through the window at traffic and people drifting by on the main drag. Load the dishwasher. Another evening of tiptoeing around the subject. By the end of it we climb into bed exhausted by the tension and Vanessa spoons tightly into me while we both fail to sleep.

30.

'We need to get that out of you as soon as possible.'

So that's the plan. A bit of radical surgery, some chemo and radiotherapy and fingers crossed. Apparently we've caught it reasonably early so there's cause for optimism.

'Will it be a dangerous procedure?'

'Digging around in the human brain is not without risk,' she says. 'Some faculties might be impaired. But this is about saving your life and we're pretty good at what we do.'

'Faculties impaired?'

'Best to remain positive and realistic.'

'Which faculties?'

'Motor, sight, speech, memory. Senses. All up for grabs, but we're optimistic.'

Are we? 'When do we do this?'

She consults her computer calendar. 'Next Wednesday. How's that sound?'

Soon. Real soon.

We're driving back over the ranges from Nelson, they're enveloped in mist, our doubts and fears have been replaced by a reckless euphoria. 'She seems to know her stuff.'

'And she's not hanging about,' agrees Vanessa.

Impaired faculties. 'Out of our hands now, eh?'

She squeezes mine. 'Always has been, love.'

Maybe it's a false dawn and everything will come crashing down any moment. In the meantime I might just beat this and that's worth holding on to for as long as possible. We stop off at Rai Valley for a raspberry ice cream and enjoy the ice-cream headache for all it is – just that, nothing more. Picking up Paulie on the way through we arrive home to find the insurers have deposited some funds in our account for household expenses. Although the police house comes fully, if simply, furnished and Latifa has added her own touches, this feels like another sign of things moving on for the better. We can buy stuff and make this place ours. No more limbo, no more stasis. We forego the stockpile of casseroles and dine out at The Mussel Pot. Fish and chips for Paulie, blue cheese mussels for me, Thai style for Vanessa. And a Marlborough sav blanc and L&P.

'Cheers.' We clink glasses.

In the morning the euphoria has dissipated but the determination to nail this bastard remains. Vanessa and I even had sex for the first time in a while – a delicate and clumsy affair given her bad leg and my funny head. Still it's nice to get reacquainted. There's work to be done and questions to be asked but I need to stay near Vanessa and driving the winding roads of the top of the south with a tumour in my head wouldn't be a good idea.

'Can I buy you a coffee, Morgan? Over here in Havelock?'

'Don't ask much do you? Make it a tea.' That was surprisingly easy as I fully expected a 'get fucked'. Morgan Hopu chuckles. 'I was coming over anyway. Heard there might be some property going cheap in the Wakamarina.'

Charlie Evans' place, I'm guessing. 'Didn't see you as the farming type?'

'Make that a piece of cake, too. Something nice. See you in an hour.'

Apples for Charlotte, opposite the Four Square. Wacky name for a café, sure, but I'm hoping that the plethora of chintz, china and lace might curb Morgan's instinct for violence. Besides they do nice cakes too.

Morgan perches on a delicate ornate chair with a rose-embossed china cup in his fist. Is it my cancerous imagination or do all the swirls in this place seem to complement his moko? He's poking his little finger out and enjoying the joke. 'Earl Grey. Choice.'

No beating around the bush. 'How come you know so much about Havelka?'

'I made it my business. He killed my boy. The cops wanted to charge me after he disappeared.'

'Who was your source? There's nothing untoward in the official record.'

'Old girlfriend. She was a social worker, asked around. What's on the files isn't always the same as what people think.'

'So what, precisely, did they think?'

'They observed that the daughter, Lisbet, was losing the plot at school after being a good kid before that. They had a chat with the parents and observed a mother in denial and scared to death and a father controlling everything and everyone.'

'And what did they conclude?'

'Nothing. The kid was moved to another school. The family moved to another suburb. The social worker went on maternity leave and they slipped back under the radar.'

'But?'

'But nothing. It's enough for me to know he wasn't the squeaky-clean churchy old man they made him out to be.'

'That's it?'

He refills his china cup from the matching teapot and drizzles in some milk. 'Mate, I'll come clean. I had every intention of doing the fucker either once he got jailed for manslaughter or if he got off. But I'm smart enough to wait, keep things arm's length. The simple fact is, somebody got to him before I did and that's fucken tragic.'

I find myself believing him. 'How's Thomas going? Ruth told me he's doing it tough.'

'She's right.'

'Is that your interest in the Evans' place? Want to be closer?'

'Partly. We lost touch for a while. It's good to be family again.'

'Anything else?'

'Nah. Nothing for you to worry about.'

'The Evans property neighbours the Americans. You're not figuring on a war of attrition, are you?'

'Perish the thought.'

We part ways and Morgan strides off up the street, shakes hands with a local real estate agent, and they head west in convoy to Canvastown.

'That who I thought it was?' Jessie James has sidled up to me.

'Who'd you have in mind?'

'Well-known Top of the South identity and scary dude, Morgan Hopu.'

'He's a big softie when you get to know him.'

'I heard it was him and his brother blew up Deep Creek bridge. Not the Americans.'

'Who'd you hear that from?'

'The Americans.'

'Fake news.'

'They asked me to pass a message on to you.'

'Is that in your job description?'

'Want to hear it or not?' I give her the nod. 'The honourable James Bryant requests the pleasure of your company. Would you like to join him for a Sounds cruise?'

'When?'

'The weather is set to fine up this afternoon apparently. Lucky you, I'm not invited.'

Vanessa doesn't need me anymore and Paulie will be dropped off by Jan and Mim after school. I don't like the idea of being summoned to Bryant's gin palace but Commander Keegan is encouraging.

'Can't harm. See if you can work out what they're up to. When they're leaving et cetera. Maybe they'll confess all about Gelder.'

'Maybe they'll tie me to a lump of concrete and drop me in Pelorus Sound.'

'I doubt he'd be so unsubtle but we've all got to go sometime, Nick.' She realises too late what she's said and mumbles an apology. 'Foot in mouth disease. Family trait.'

I bring her up to speed on the Havelka gossip and my belief that Morgan Hopu is not lying when he says he didn't do the deed.

'Go get 'em, cowboy. And enjoy your pleasure cruise.'

Prospero. It's a catamaran berthed at the posh end of Havelock marina. I'm reminded of the one owned by logging magnate Richard McCormack, graffitied with the name change from *Serenity II* to 'Smaug'. McCormack still graces the financial pages these days fighting a succession of bankruptcy lawsuits as his share float failed and he made some poor life choices that brought the creditors circling. This catamaran is a well-known local charter vessel. James Bryant is on board to greet me looking very like his website photo – well-fed, blond, Christian.

'Nick. Fantastic to meet you.' He has a fine set of teeth. Brandon Cunningham is looking busy down in the cabin. Preparing canapés maybe.

After a falsely warm handshake we take a pew at the back of the boat. The weather has indeed cleared and thin rays of sunlight beam down through the clouds like God himself is smiling on us. 'Nice day for it.'

Cunningham appears with a tray of drinks and nibbles and acts like he's never met me before.

'Thanks, Brandon,' says Bryant, handing me a champagne flute.

As I'm on restricted duty and might die soon anyway I cast caution to the wind and accept. 'Cheers.' A sip. Pricey stuff. 'So what's this all about?'

The boat slips out through the channel and high on my right Cullen Point is garlanded in wispy cloud. Brandon Cunningham has retired to the cabin kitchen to prepare lunch or sharpen his knives, whatever. The skipper is also familiar. Last time I saw him he was facedown on the lawn at the Lodge being frisked by AOS a few moments before young Melvyn Cody was shot. Maybe Keegan is wrong and Bryant doesn't do subtle. Maybe there's a pair of concrete boots back there in the galley with my name on them.

'We all got off on the wrong foot and I'm keen to make amends. Firstly let me apologise for any inappropriate behaviour by my employees which may have caused upset in recent weeks.'

Recent weeks. A mental tallying of the time elapsed since this all started. A month? Two? Either way, we're into June now. Will this be my last winter on the planet? 'At least three people dead, a fourth missing. Arson, assault, vandalism. Yes, it has been a tad inappropriate and upsetting.'

'The more serious incidents were the work of a rogue operator. We've taken steps to deal with that problem.'

'You knew Georges LeBlanc's history long before you recruited him. He was a thug.'

'As I say ...'

'He tried to kill me and my family.'

'I'm deeply sorry and I do feel some element of responsibility. I'd be very happy to look at a compensation package for you, for your loss of property.'

'Fuck you. I'll be the one who decides what and how you'll pay.'

This probably isn't what Keegan had in mind when she encouraged me to be diplomatic and try to get some gen on Bryant's intentions. To hell with it. This has been a tough few weeks and finally there's someone of consequence to take it out on. Concrete shoes? Go for it, I feel invincible today. Fearless.

'Maybe this wasn't such a good idea, Mr Chester.'

'Hell no, we're out here now. Good time to clear the air.' I lift my glass.

'*Garçon, encore de champagne, s'il vous plaît.*' Brandon obliges, resisting the temptation to smash the bottle over my head and shove the jagged ends in my face. I stuff a cracker and cheese in my gob. 'So why are you here, Bryant? Apart from the fact there's a federal prosecutor halfway up your arse?'

'You need to watch your mouth, Chester.'

I look at Brandon. 'Or what?'

'Okay guys, let's take a breather.' Bryant flicks his fingers. 'Brandon, maybe you can go and prepare lunch. Leave the bottle and a bucket. We'll help ourselves.'

I'll say one thing for him, Bryant doesn't give up easily on the deal-making. He's determined to get a result out of today, no matter how hard I make it. Brandon, on the other hand, glowers at me from the galley. It begs a question.

'How did you guys meet?'

'Hmmm?'

'You and Brandon. You, the top end of town international mover and shaker. Him, the sheriff's deputy from Hicksville, South Dakota.'

Bryant smiles from behind his champagne flute. 'South Dakota has the most liberal tax system in the US. If you're filthy rich and want to hold on to your hard-earned, it's the place to be. A good patriot like me has no need of tax havens like the Caymans. Instead I have a *pied-à-terre* in Sioux Falls. Our paths crossed fortuitously.'

'Yet here you are when you could be patriotically sunning yourself in South Dakota.'

'This is a beautiful country. Why wouldn't I be here?'

'You have no choice. America doesn't want you any more. Hell, you're practically a refugee. But before that choice was taken away you had plans for the supershack bolthole on the sounds. Māhana. That's where we're headed now, right?'

'I understand you've already had a good look round.'

'Panic rooms, private air strips, weird paranoid shit. That's your business, but that wasn't what got Bruce Gelder killed.'

'Who?'

'The plumber.'

'Not sure what this is about but I'll look into it.'

'Māhana isn't a wellbeing centre. I'm not sure why you're hiding its real purpose. You could just say it's your own private residence and you'll design it however the hell you like. Maybe obfuscation is second nature. What is it the Feds have on you?'

'Lies, smears and, in the end, nothing.'

'So you can go home, then. Be with your family.'

'You're not showing that renowned Kiwi hospitality.'

'What is it you want from me, Bryant?'

'I don't want anything. On the contrary, I may be able to help you.'

By now we're approaching the jetty at Māhana and the same two goons, Vernon and Blake, are there, except they've smartened up since last time.

'Make your pitch, Bryant. I don't need another tour, I've got stuff to do back home.'

'How is Mrs Chester? On the mend, I hope?'

'None of your business.'

'It'd be nice if you could call me James or Mr Bryant. I'm tiring of the aggression.'

'Tire away.'

'Bear with me, hear me out. This won't take long and it will be to your advantage.'

To tell the truth I'm tiring of my aggression too. Maybe I need to shut the fuck up and see if he trips on his own words. 'The floor is yours.'

We start the grand tour with Cunningham and the goons a few steps behind. Bryant straightens, as if he's shrugging on a suit jacket ready to address a shareholder's meeting. 'You're right. Obfuscation does come easily in these troubled times. You grow to expect the worst in people. Dig moats instead of building bridges. This isn't a health and tourism venture as promised. It is my home and I'm looking forward to moving in.'

'What are you waiting for? It's pretty much finished.'

'Indeed. I've got a couple of Wellington's best interior designers mapping out their ideas as we speak. I'm thinking a month or so and it'll be all systems go.'

'Lovely.'

We head down a familiar corridor with tiled rooms and plenty of wiring. 'You'll have already guessed this is the medical wing. It'll be state-of-the-art. Better equipped than your local hospital I believe.'

If we're talking the one in Blenheim, that's not saying much. Still I offer my coolly impressed face. 'This adjoining room with the drainage channels and the replaced tiles?'

'A morgue.'

'Why?'

'In the event of a pandemic or nuclear or biological incident we need to be able to perform post-mortems to ascertain accurate cause of death so we can take appropriate measures.'

'We?'

'Me. And my team.'

'Better to be safe than sorry,' I acknowledge. 'And where's the panic room?'

'I prefer to call it a safe room.' Bryant nods at Cunningham who presses one of the tiles. On the opposite wall a panel, maybe a metre squared, slides open. 'Be my guest.'

I crouch down and poke my head through the hole. Simply another room, perhaps a little larger than the proposed morgue. 'That's it?'

'Heavily reinforced and practically undetectable. In time it will be adequately furnished and resourced.'

'Who or what are you thinking of panicking about?'

He shrugs. 'Sundry evildoers.'

'People with Ebola or some such?' I venture. 'Thirsty or hungry peasants trying to survive a nuclear winter? That kind of thing?'

'You get the drift. It isn't illegal. I could have my Wellington designers create a perfect reproduction of a Spanish Inquisition torture dungeon and that would be entirely my business.'

'As long as you don't put it to use.'

'No immediate plans, I assure you.'

I stand up and dust myself off. The panel slides shut again. 'Yeah, fascinating but tell me about the replaced tiles.' I crouch down by one and scrape the grout with my fingernail. 'They're what this is all about.'

The door closes behind us. The goons are outside. It's just me, Bryant and Cunningham in a white tiled room with great drainage.

'It's the minor details that do it. Every time. Right, Nick?'

'Right.'

He shakes his head. Cunningham takes a step forward and I brace myself. The increased stress is playing havoc with the alien lump inside my brain. Vision blurring. Nausea rising. A pounding at the base of my skull. Is it my imagination or is there something trickling out of that keyhole wound under the dressing behind my ear?

'Mr Chester, are you okay?'

I steady myself. Palm on the cool tiles. 'Fine.'

Cunningham has his hand on my shoulder, he's staring into my eyes. Seems amused. 'You don't look well, Nick. All this time, I wondered. Mortality, it's a powerful thing, right?' He's pressing me down to the floor. 'Take the weight off, buddy. Time to relax.'

A sigh from Bryant. 'Do it. Let's get this over with.'

Brandon reaches into his pocket.

31.

'Gelder's missing mobiles.' Maxwell is impressed. 'Nice one.'

The wife, Marnie, had them all along. Unbeknownst to her, Gelder had secreted them in her car taped to the underside of the driver's seat, battery and SIM removed. He'd cloned the footage onto both phones and left a third decoy phone, containing the offending material, up at the shack to try and throw LeBlanc off the scent. The decoy was among LeBlanc's stashed possessions when they disappeared him. He'd thought it was mission accomplished but Cunningham was more thorough and hunted down the copies.

'You have something that precious, you want to hold it close, right?' Cunningham had been very pleased with himself.

'So why'd they give them to you?' wonders Maxwell.

'Let's watch and learn.'

We retire to Maxwell's office with the door closed. A tech has downloaded the photo and video contents of the phone onto a thumb drive and we press play.

'*What's down here?*'

The voice is Gelder's, behind the wobbly vision heading down that same corridor at Māhana towards the medical rooms. Blank walls yet to be plastered. Loose wires. Wrappings and building debris on the floor.

A voice off. '*Room one-oh-one, man. Your worst nightmare.*' LeBlanc's Cajun drawl.

Gelder. '*One-oh-one? Fuck's that?*'

LeBlanc steps into vision now. Turning the door handle and waving Gelder inside. '*You never read Orwell? After you, ignoramus.*'

'*Got any more of that blow?*'

'*Swap you.*' The biggest spliff in Christendom appears on screen in exchange for a half-drunk bottle of Wild Turkey.

Inside the room. Acres of white tiling. Gelder's voice again. *'Call this scary? My auntie's front room is scarier. Doilies everywhere.'*

'Look there.'

The phone camera tilts, bounces around and settles on shiny steel rings embedded into the tiled wall. *'The extra wide pipes and drains you put in today, Brucie? That's the reason.'*

'Not with you, brother.'

A giggle. *'Neither are they. Yet.'*

'What?'

'The dusky maidens. Jewels of the South Seas. Call them what you will.'

'You for real?'

'Oh man, once you get the taste for it, there's nothing better. We're gonna make us some warrior babies for the Rapture.'

'Fuck you on about?'

'But for disposals, well, I could have told them. You need abattoir drains for that shit but they wouldn't listen to the likes of me.'

'What?'

'Ignore me, Brucie bro. I'm drunk.'

The video closes in on the drainage channel. Follows it to the outlet at the far end. Zooms in on a clump of dark hair.

'What you doing, Brucie?'

'Nothin'. This place gives me the creeps. You're one crazy motherfucker, Georges. Let's go and finish that whiskey somewhere.'

'We're brothers, right, Brucie? I can trust you?'

'You got me the job, mate. I owe you.'

'That's right, man. I need to piss.' And he unzips and does so right there in the drainage channel.

'Gross,' says Gelder. *'No class, you Yanks.'*

'Pussy.' LeBlanc zips up. *'Easy. Once you're done you just turn on the hose and flush it all away.'*

And that's what he does.

The line is that the steel rings were LeBlanc's idea. He had them installed and as soon as Cunningham found out about it he had them taken out. We've invited Brandon into the town hall to explain himself. Maxwell lets me do the running but it's hard to get a word in edgeways.

'Like your man Gelder said, Georgie was one crazy motherfucker. He got a taste for abusing migrant women at that abattoir he worked at in Nogales. Treated them like just another piece of meat. Kept them shackled, hosed them down. Disgusting. When one of the union guys confronted him about it he killed him.' Cunningham shakes his head in disbelief at how low humanity can go. 'Loco, huh?'

'But still you hired him.'

'Yeah, but we didn't know he was like that until too late. He had plans for your Miss Latifa too.'

He knows that's guaranteed to rile me, press my buttons. 'You're the only one who's showed that kind of interest in her. Maybe you're projecting?'

'Harmless. Pure gamesmanship on my part. To stir things up.'

It's bullcrap. Nobody arranges to have steel rings installed in their employer's new house and hopes to keep it a secret. 'I'm not convinced.'

A shrug. 'Prove otherwise. Once I confronted Georges about the rings, he knew he was in trouble. That's why he went after Gelder. He remembered enough from his night on the booze to know there was footage that might make him look bad. He went too far and involved my nephew in his sickness.'

'Hell of a place to be raising your nephew, among all those sick violent men and their guns, far from home.'

'Plenty of men and guns back home too.' Cunningham picks out a spot on the wall behind me. 'His mama's hooked on crack and pappy's in the hospice waiting for lung cancer to finish him. I thought I could save Melvyn.'

And in his own twisted way, maybe he really did think that. 'But Georges took the boy under his wing?'

'We realised LeBlanc was a problem and we intended to deal with him. Pity he ran away and fell down that mineshaft.'

LeBlanc was in no state to run anywhere. 'Which one?'

'Forget. Sorry.'

'You should have left him in our custody. That was our job.'

'What? With those two mad Māori? They were out of your league, Chester. You had no control over them. Anyway, by bringing Georges to your country we contributed to the problem. It was our duty to end it.'

He's making this up as he goes along. Couldn't give a shit what we think. 'Very noble.'

'You're welcome.'

There's more to it. There has to be. 'It wraps things up pretty neatly and keeps us away from Bryant.'

'If you say so.'

'The clump of hair in the outlet pipe. The blocked drains. Did LeBlanc test the facilities for himself?'

A shrug. 'You might need to look at your missing persons files.'

'We might need to dig up Māhana,' says Maxwell.

'Be my guest.'

'Don't need to. I'll bring a warrant.'

I can see from the expression on Maxwell's face that's well and truly on the agenda. 'On the recording LeBlanc suggests others knew about it.' I press play as a reminder. *But for disposals well, I could have told them. You need abattoir drains for that shit but they wouldn't listen to the likes of me.* 'Who's them and they? What "shit" is he talking about?'

'His own weird shit. Who listens to anybody like him?'

'Warrior babies for the Rapture? I've heard as much from you too.'

'They're only words. Don't worry about what people say. Look at what they do.'

'But the big wide abattoir drains are in there now. Courtesy of Bruce Gelder. It's done.'

'Some plumbing. Arranged and paid for in cash by Georgie for his own crazy reasons. He's no longer anyone's problem so what's the worry?'

'Still seems extreme, doesn't it?' I venture. 'If LeBlanc really was a rogue male, then all you had to do to fulfil your moral responsibility was to hand him over and allow justice to run its course.'

'Maybe we were hasty but our intentions were good.'

'And maybe you didn't want him shooting his mouth off about what he knew.'

'As a former law enforcement officer, I understand your scepticism. It goes with the job.'

That's about as far as it goes with him today. Night has fallen and I need to be getting home. Maxwell claps me on the shoulder as I'm leaving. 'You've done well, Nick. Wrapping things up nicely.'

'Too nicely. I think LeBlanc knew something that got him killed. Him being a bad guy was convenient in the end but he was originally hired for his badness.'

'The useful idiot. Where would we be without them?'

At home, the last of the donated casseroles awaits me in the microwave.

'What are we going to do when these run out?'

'Have another crisis?' offers Vanessa. 'Stock up on frozen pre-cooked?'

She's moving more easily although still obliged to pop strong painkillers every now and again. A quiet resolve has set in. Vanessa intends to get through this. Somebody has to.

'Any gossip?' I ask, after giving her mine.

'Jan and Mim dropped Paulie off today. Jan seemed a bit cool and distant. Did you upset her in any way?'

'I just mentioned that we thought, from Mim, that they used to live in Nelson. They didn't. Apparently it was Greymouth.'

'Yeah, I remember you saying. Funny thing for her to get huffy about.'

'Takes all sorts.'

Vanessa sniffs. 'Another Top of the South feud in the making no doubt. Came from nowhere, goes nowhere. Ten years later you're still bricking each other's windows and can't remember why.'

'That's a universal, love. Used to happen in Hylton Castle all the time. Not Fulwell, though. We're more civilised.'

'My arse.'

'G'night.' Paulie gives us a wave on the way from the bathroom. He's hardly acknowledged my existence since I got home.

'Something I said?'

Vanessa shushes me. 'He and Mim had a falling out. Same reason Jan's acting funny.'

'So he thinks I'm to blame?'

'It'll blow over. Leave it.'

While Vanessa says a proper goodnight to Paulie, I polish off the casserole and check my unread messages. A whole bunch more from Nigel Watson wanting to know if I've confronted Keegan and Ford with his insinuations. The man needs a good talking to, face-to-face. So far those west coast cases are not my concern and he shouldn't be using me to fight his battles. I can conjure up plenty of my own feuds without being drawn into other people's, thank you very much.

I send him a reply text to that effect:

It's not my fight, leave me out of it

Another one comes through. A photo this time. Three men in a pub: Darren Robertson, one man I don't recognise, face half-obscured by a raised hand holding a glass. Another man I do recognise – Karel Havelka.

A message.

Check out the silver chain on the Czech's neck

32.

'Interested now?'

Nigel Watson offered to come over to Havelock but I insisted on making the trip to Nelson. I probably shouldn't be driving but this head thing comes and goes and, what the hell, you only live once. We're on a park picnic bench by the Riverside swimming pool overlooking the dancing current of the Maitai. Ducks catch the rapids and joggers pound the path behind us. It's a cool sunny day. There's takeaway coffees on the go in plastic-coated cardboard cups – more landfill in the making.

'Where did the photo come from?' I tossed and turned all night much to Vanessa's disgust. This feels like I'm being played.

'Ollie Harper, local reporter down that way.'

'You'll be his unnamed police source, I'm guessing.'

'No comment.'

'Where did he get the photo?'

'I prodded him in the right direction. Tipped off by you, I asked him to see if he could find anything linking Havelka to events over that way.'

I bring the pic back up on my phone. Enlarge it with my fingertips. 'What's the occasion?'

'Social pages of the *Greymouth Gazette* six years ago. Top of the South Volunteer of the Year awards, held in Nelson. This is about a month before the Lucy McLernon murder. Havelka was nominated for his work as a boxing coach with a youth club for troubled teens in Blenheim. The newly established girls boxing team was his "groundbreaking initiative". The latter delivered with finger quotes. 'Robertson gave a lot of his spare time preparing and delivering food parcels to destitute and dysfunctional single-parent households on the bleak west coast. More vulnerable teenage girls. Spot a pattern here? The other bloke? Some do-gooder from Nelson or somewhere. But you can see where I'm going with this, can't you?'

'Havelka was involved with Robertson in the rape and murder of Lucy McLernon?'

'That chain around his neck is a ringer for the one at the crime scene. Bet it matches his DNA too now we have his corpse.' Watson prods the photo. 'And they're in each other's company just a few weeks before the deed. Partners in crime.' He brings some pics up on his iPad. 'Did some background digging on your Havelka case while you've had other things on your mind. Lucy McLernon in her prime. Lovely, eh?' He swipes another pic into the frame. 'Havelka's daughter, Lisbet. Could be twins, you reckon? Maybe he was able to project some of his domestic fantasies on to poor Lucy.'

'You and Morgan Hopu been talking?'

'Funny you should mention it. He got in touch, out of the blue.'

Who's playing who here? 'How did he know you'd be interested?'

'I guess he's a finger-on-the-pulse kinda guy. Makes it his business. He'd made the same enquiry to the journo Ollie Harper – any Havelka links to Robertson – and Ollie put him on to me.' Watson smirks. 'A confluence of interests.'

'So whoever did Robertson on that beach did Havelka too. Same fashion. Same motive. That's your theory?'

'Makes sense.'

'And Hopu insists he had nothing to do with it. Somebody else got in first.'

'I'm inclined to believe the sly old rascal. He told me he'd been looking forward to doing Havelka. He was spittin' about not getting the pleasure.'

'So who are we looking at?'

Watson bats away an overattentive duck with his foot. 'Fuck knows, but commanders Keegan and Ford have some explaining to do about tampering with the Robertson/McLernon evidence. Don't you think?'

I can't argue with that any more.

Nigel Watson doesn't get off scot-free. That's why I insisted on coming to Nelson. I'll set the meeting up because odds-on they wouldn't give him the time of day. Watson can front up to Keegan and Ford himself and I'll tag along for the ride.

'I've got my pension to think about,' he grumbles.

'Haven't we all. Man up, mate. You can't keep getting other people to fight your proxy wars.'

Ford is none too pleased to be summoned in from his Happy Valley home to explain himself to a bottom-feeder like Watson and it's written all over his face. Keegan on the other hand seems mildly amused but is no doubt storing it away in her Day of Reckoning ledger. This could backfire badly, for both Nigel and me.

'Nick and Nigel. Good to see you guys hitting it off.' We're sitting in Keegan's office in Nelson with its third-floor view out over the streets and trees, the botanic gardens, river and the Centre of New Zealand monument atop a nearby hill. She flips her hand in an over-to-you gesture. 'Something you want to say about these west coast cases?'

Keegan's looking at me but I defer to Watson. It's plain to see why his career stalled while others younger, prettier and, let's face it, better than him sailed by. He stumbles over his collection of random facts and innuendo. Unable to draw it together into a meaningful narrative. He's all web, no spider. Lacks coherence, is awed by Ford's glare and Keegan's cool competence.

'Nick?' she says at the end. 'Anything to add?'

'I think Nigel's central tenet is that evidence he clearly recalls belonging to the McLernon case – the silver chain found at the crime scene – ended up in the Robertson collection even though it was clearly logged in to the former. He's questioning how and why it got moved and why you and Commander Ford took an interest in these cases as recently as just over a year ago.'

'How about you?'

'Me?'

'Are you raising those questions too?'

I explain the photo, the Havelka link, and the silver chain around his neck. 'So, yes, I'm interested too.'

She nods. Purses her lips. Turns to Ford. 'David? Any comment?'

'As a civilian retiree? Off the record?' A nod in reply. 'Fuck yeah, this useless little prick has been sniffing around me ever since we first passed him over for promotion what, two decades ago? As part of the handover at my retirement, you and I reviewed these cases because that dickhead Westie reporter, briefed and prodded by fuckface here, was yet again digging into Robertson and McLernon. Yes, they remain unsolved but no way was Robertson innocent of his involvement in Lucy's death. He was a sleazebag, no matter what his compensation-hunting low-life rellies say. We reviewed the files and evidence for due diligence and concluded no action necessary.'

'How come the silver chain ended up in the wrong box?' I ask.

'Human error. A misfiling. Stuff happens. I had a lot on my plate back then and Watson here wasn't helping with his shit-stirring.'

'We both wore rubber gloves and everything was kept in its original sealed pouch. The chances of cross-contamination are and were negligible.' Keegan turns to Watson. 'I'm glad you spotted the error, Nigel, and brought it to our attention. Good work.'

Watson looks ready to leave it there, starstruck by a rare compliment from Keegan. I'm not so easy. 'So when you first brought my attention to the cases you alluded to something pricking your memory from way back when. But it was a lot more recent and more significant than a mere prick wasn't it?'

She shrugs. 'It was an unsolved. In some eyes,' a glance at Watson, 'a blot on my career. I didn't want to highlight that. In playing it down, I hoped you might approach it with a fresh view, maybe even close it for me. It's a compliment to your abilities, Nick.'

As with many conspiracies, this bears the hallmarks of fuck-up rather than ill-intent. Ford's haste and lack of concentration compounded by Keegan's penchant for manipulation and gamesmanship. Throw in Watson's festering grudges and bingo.

'So, nothing sinister?' I conclude.

'Apart from weasel, here,' growls Ford.

'Thank you for assisting me with my enquiries.' I stand and hold out a hand to Keegan.

'No problem, Nick. Keep me in the loop with your progress. You seem to be knocking them down like skittles.'

'Sir.' I shake Ford's hand too. There's a glint in his eye like the fury is all for show and he's quite enjoyed his day out.

'Named the day for your retirement yet, Nigel?' says Keegan as we file out. 'We'll have to make sure you get a good send-off.'

Is that all there is to it? Nigel Watson's relevance-deprivation syndrome generates a swirl of innuendo to keep his life interesting ahead of retirement. A one-man school of red herrings. I'm choosing to side with Keegan and Ford on this; they may be many things I don't like but they are not time-wasters. I leave Watson to his empty scheming and go in search of Morgan Hopu. Ringing his mobile, I learn he's at a gym ten minutes down the coast at Tahunanui. On a day like today with blue skies and a glass-flat sea the drive along Rocks Road is spectacular. Paddle boarders skim the surface between me and the island, and snow glistens on the peaks in the far distance.

The gym has lots of chrome and mirrors and crap music, and the air is thick with sweat and competing hormones. Morgan steps off a running machine. He's in pretty good shape for a bloke in his fifties who's lived a reckless life.

'Can't keep away from me, Nick. Must be my charisma.'

'Are you buying Charlie's farm, then?'

'Put in an offer but the agent said there's some question about whether or not it's still on the market. Apparently there was a late amendment to the will.'

'How late?'

'Last week. Just before he topped himself.'

I make a mental note to take a closer look at the Evans suicide. 'You, the journo Ollie Harper, Nigel Watson. You make quite a team.'

A grin. 'Enquiries progressing?'

'I don't recall mentioning to you that I had an interest in the west coast.'

'Didn't you? I must have heard it somewhere. Through the grapevine maybe.'

'I'm wondering if you have a pretty good idea of who it was that got to Havelka before you.'

'That's quite a stretch.'

'You're going above and beyond the call of duty. All you needed to do was deny any involvement and try to sound convincing. And by yesterday you had. Now I feel like I'm being pointed in a certain direction. Why's that?'

'Suspicious mind. Maybe I'm only trying to help and I'm sufficiently resourced to do so.'

'Got a number for Ollie Harper?'

He sends it through to my mobile. 'Say hello from me.' Morgan skips back on to the machine, slips some headphones on and focuses on the video screen above him. A hip-hop artist in downtown Auckland.

Morgan Hopu has taken the initiative on the Havelka investigation while Brandon Cunningham has cleared up Gelder and Jaxon Hemi for me. Maybe I should follow Nigel Watson into retirement. I'm about as useful as a chocolate fireguard around here.

Midafternoon back over the Whangamoa. It's good timing for me to pick up Paulie from school on the way home. I message Vanessa to that effect and she zaps back a thumbs up.

'What you doing here?'

'Hi, Dad' I say. 'Great to see you. How was your day? Oh good thanks, Paulie. How was yours?'

'Paul. Told you before.'

'What's eating you, grumblebum? Something I said?'

'Mim hates me. Your fault.'

'How come?'

'Her mum told her off for making up stories.'

'I was just chatting with Mim's mum. I didn't know it was all made up.'

'Why d'you have to talk to her?'

'Blaming me for Mim telling fibs is silly, mate. If she's in trouble she brought it on herself and has no right to be angry with you.'

'You don't understand.'

It's a grumpy silence the rest of the way home and I'm happy to lob him on to Vanessa and get the hell out. Late afternoon and the shadows are long on the main drag as I pop my head around the door of the cop shop. Latifa looks up.

'What's new?'

'Coupla murders solved and progress on another. A day in the life of ace detective Nick Chester.'

'Only you're not a flash detective, you're a hick cop in a small town.'

'Thanks for reminding me.' I give her the update. 'So Cunningham's not going back to Dakota any time soon.'

'And the progress?'

Same with Havelka – a potted history.

'Well done you.' Her mind is ticking over. 'If your long-ago wacky theory is right, the same person who killed Havelka also attacked me, if the rope marks on the tree are anything to go by. Right?'

'Right, but I was clutching at straws then.'

'And following through the logic, that same person has also killed this Darren Robertson on the west coast.'

'Yep.'

'So if the theory is that the perp is somehow avenging the death of Lucy McLernon, how come this supposed avenging angel then attacks another woman, namely me?'

Fair point.

'Two competing scenarios.' I lay them out for Maxwell while Latifa looks on. 'An avenging angel for the death of Lucy McLernon, which means we should focus back in on her inner circle.' Tick, he nods assent. 'But if the rope marks on the tree link the Havelka murder to the attack on Latifa then we're looking for an accomplice rather than an avenging angel. A falling out among pervs.'

'Or something else entirely,' says Gemma from the spare chair.

'Always worth keeping an open mind,' I concede. Back at Maxwell. 'How do you want to run it?'

'Rope marks on a tree? That's the basis of your deductions?'

'One of them. Faith, Will. I'm on a roll. Knocking them down like skittles, according to Keegan.'

This is not good timing for Maxwell. With the Bruce Gelder and Jaxon Hemi murders all but resolved and pinnable on LeBlanc, the town hall incident room is being wound down and people and resources reassigned.

'I was looking forward to getting back to Blenheim and not having to commute,' he says.

'Bummer,' says Latifa.

He gets her drift. She has unfinished business. 'Sorry. Yep, let's do this.' He lifts his eyes to Latifa. 'How you going?' Waves weakly at his neck. 'Clearing up?'

'Better every day, boss. Appreciate you asking.'

Gemma and a colleague will be dispatched to the west coast to interview the journalist and do further digging. Way down south, the Dunedin detectives will be requested to reinterview Havelka's daughter Lisbet and try to convince her to be more forthcoming about her father. Likewise local social workers and her old school can expect a knock soon. Latifa is pleased to get the nod for that job along with one of Maxwell's regular investigators.

'That religious community out near Greymouth.' I check my notes. 'Whakakitenga. Is it still in operation?'

'I believe it's under new management since the scandals,' says Maxwell. 'Why?'

'Lucy ran away from there. We should put them under the microscope too.'

Maxwell needs to augment the west coast team but he's running short on numbers. 'Fancy a trip, Nick?' He grins at Gemma. 'You can carpool.'

Finally, Wellington detectives will be asked to further probe Lucy's family and inner circle. At last the Havelka/Robertson/McLernon cases are getting the attention they deserve.

'This isn't good timing for you either, Nick.' Gemma has left the room and Latifa hovers on the threshold. Maxwell taps his temple. 'Don't want to exacerbate things.'

'It's good to keep busy.'

Walking back up the street, Latifa tuts disapprovingly. 'Vanessa isn't going to like this one bit.'

33.

Latifa was right. Vanessa went through the roof.

'Are you mad? Five days away from brain surgery and you want to go tramping off over the west coast on a case?'

'It's an overnighter. I'll be back in no time. We'll have the weekend together.'

'The specialist told you to take it easy. There's a course of tablets. Some pre-op stuff to do.'

'It'll still be done and I'll keep taking the pills. No stress. Just a few questions then back home again.'

'Don't you think we should be staying close at a time like this?'

'When I might be dead soon, you mean?'

'Fuck you, that's not fair.'

'If we're right, the person behind all this could be the one responsible for the attack on Latifa. Aren't they worth putting out of circulation?'

'Of course they are but it doesn't have to be you that does it.'

What else could I say? 'It's what's holding me together, love.'

'And me, Paulie, we're not?'

'That's not fair either.'

'No.' She shook her head. 'I suppose not. But maybe you're wrong, maybe there's no connection to Latifa and this person *is* an avenging angel. Can you live with locking them up for taking two nasty creeps out of this world?'

That's the question that occupies my mind as we cross the churning brown waters of the Buller Gorge on our way south-west. I don't get out this way much and that's a pity because the Buller is spectacular, big, powerful. Blasting through steep rock gullies and filling the countryside with its roar and spray. Many of the hills are covered in native trees instead of pine so that's a pleasant change too. Fuck, it knows how to rain here though.

At Greymouth cop shop, I drop Gemma and her colleague Graham, a nice enough lad who spent most of the journey ignoring the scenery and watching surfing videos on his phone. They'll borrow a car from the local plods and go their merry way while I head inland to Whakakitenga. Greymouth seems to me a flat and colourless town tourism-wise; if it wasn't for the snow-capped Alps rising up in the east and the Tasman Sea crashing on the driftwood-covered beach, I'd be inclined to shoot through. Then again I'm not one to talk having been up to historic and spectacular Lindisfarne on the Northumbrian coast with my teenage mates and not even getting out of the car. Back then I was like young Graham, wouldn't have known nice scenery if it jumped up and bit me.

It's a forty-five minute drive from Greymouth and the road narrows and winds through lush vegetation. It's so green here it hurts your eyes. Whakakitenga: the name loosely translates from *te reo* Māori into, in this context, Old Testament–style prophecies or revelations. I'm not sure what to expect of a remote scandal-plagued sect headquarters: fortified compounds and be-robed muscly young men with scimitars? Weeping and wailing and gnashing of teeth? Children with glowing red eyes? I almost miss the turn-off, a narrow gravel track overgrown by an arch of native trees. I didn't phone ahead, figuring on the element of surprise. Besides, they weren't in the directory. A hundred metres on there's a gate across the track, locked with a chain. I leave the car and clamber over. Gumboots would have been a good idea, and waterproofs. The track continues another hundred metres on to a clearing. The rain is relentless, I'm soaked through and ankle-deep in mud. Tui and other native bird sounds echo through the forest. Somewhere nearby there is rushing water, both a river and a waterfall, if the roar is anything to go on.

'Welcome.'

A tall, middle-aged woman with a striking face and grey hair tied up in a bun. Gumboots and anorak. One moment she wasn't there, next she is. Did she wriggle her nose like Samantha from *Bewitched* and magically appear from nowhere?

'Hi.' I introduce myself.

'I'm Beth. You look like you could do with a towel, a nice warm fire, and a cup of tea.'

American accent. Not more *Apocalypse Now*. Please. 'Sounds great.'

I follow her into a modest weatherboard shack. It's freshly painted, colourful, and cosy as toast with a crackling log fire.

'Ordinary or herbal?'

'Ordinary please.'

She waggles a milk carton at me and gets a nod. 'There's a towel on the drying rack there in front of the fire. Help yourself.' Steam begins to rise from my sodden shirt and jumper. 'I'd offer you dry clothes but I'm not sure we share the same taste or size.' A playful smile. 'Unless I've got you wrong.' She hands me a mug and puts a plate of chocolate bikkies between us.

'Sorry for not calling ahead.'

'Cops tend not to.' She hands me a business card. 'But feel free next time you visit.'

'Reverend Bethany Hart. You're in charge here?'

'I'm part of the management committee. We're a collective.'

'I didn't notice many others around.'

'Look out the window. You'll see them.'

I do. Dotted here and there, wreaths of smoke from chimneys, flashes of white in the bushes. Weatherboard cabins melting into the landscape. 'It's not what I imagined.'

'What did you imagine?'

'I don't know really. Stalag Luft fourteen and a big prayer hall. Maybe a large garage with half a dozen Mercs. A temple with a huge gong and flaming torches.'

She laughs. Natural and disarming. 'That's when the men ran this place. We expelled them after the scandals.'

'Can't have been easy.'

'It was remarkably easy. They couldn't look people in the eye anymore. Happy to get the hell out. Excuse the profanity.' She sips from her mug. 'That's why you're here, I assume? Some remnant from the bad old days?'

'Lucy McLernon.'

'Ah, yes. Lucy.'

'You were here then?'

'Yes, I've been here for ten years.'

'What do you remember?'

'Lucy was a very troubled girl.'

'Girl? Wasn't she nudging thirty at the time? Couldn't have been much younger than you then.'

'Thank you for the compliment but she was still at least twenty years younger than me. But more than that, she seemed girlish. Acted like it. If you'd told me she was only fifteen I would have believed it.'

'The scandals as you call them. How aware were you of what was going on?'

'Shamefully, and perhaps to some extent intentionally, ignorant. The men involved played a very tight game and exercised huge control over what went on. Some of us had suspicions and fears but we buried them for too long. Some couldn't stand it and left. Whatever was going on I felt duty-bound to see it through and do my best to try to protect those that stayed.'

'Was there a particular individual or group you recall at the centre of all the suspicion?'

Beth rattles off a few names, some she knew of and some she'd just heard of. They don't ring any bells but I plug them into my phone for future reference. 'Any idea where they are now?'

'Don't know, don't care as long as they're nowhere near.' She shudders. 'Some of those guys, the way this place was set up at the time, the access, the hierarchy. The first time you might meet them would be when they turned up in your bedroom. I was lucky, I arrived too late in life to be of interest to them.'

I show her the photo of Robertson, Havelka, and the other bloke in the pub in Nelson. She doesn't recognise any of them, although the pullover of the semi-obscured man behind the raised glass looks vaguely familiar. Budget department store pattern. Maybe he was one of those names she'd heard of but never got to meet? Maybe she's just seen jumpers like that before.

'Are there any documents or photos from back then that might help?'

'I don't think so. Before they were expelled the men made good use of the shredder. There were financial as well as sexual irregularities.'

'There's no office, no filing cabinet? Somewhere you keep lists of next-of-kin in the event of emergency? Tax receipts? Rates and insurance, power bills?'

She points to a lever arch file on a shelf next to some jars of chutney. 'Go for broke.'

I flick through but there's nothing of merit. 'You travel light these days.'

'Some of the residents are afraid of leaving a paper trail and for good reason. This is their shelter from the storm.'

'So there are only women here now?'

'Yes. Most of the younger ones have moved on. As have those who need or want male company, or have sons.'

'It works well?'

'The occasional squabble but nothing serious.'

'And you all uphold the original beliefs from when it was set up. The prophecies, revelations, whatever. The Māori stuff thrown in?'

'Pretty much. There are Māori wahine among us now since the men left. Not so much of the cultural anomaly anymore. A white male-dominated enclave appropriating indigenous culture was doomed to fail one way or another.'

'Pity it took so long.'

'Five years. Ten. A generation. A millennium. It's all relative isn't it? There's much to be learned from Māori spirituality. Fuse that with some of our more traditional Christian beliefs and it seems to work for us. We're looking after the land better now, for sure.'

I suspect that Latifa might have something to say on the matter. Or perhaps not. 'Here's my card. If anything comes to mind.'

'Sure. It would be nice to bring some peace to Lucy's spirit.'

Amen to that. Some small talk 'Your accent?'

'Colorado.'

'It's near the Rockies isn't it? Nice there?'

'In places, yeah. It's a strange mix of do-gooding liberals like me and absolute gun-loving nut jobs. Try not to judge us all by the crazy few.'

'Why'd you leave?'

She notes my accent too. 'Why did you leave your home, Mr Chester?'

'Running from a violent man who wanted to kill me.'

'Snap.'

They were hardly put under the microscope as intended but, naïve as it might be, I have faith in the Reverend Bethany Hart. Whatever Whakakitenga was in the bad old days, it isn't now. The rain has eased by the time I pull up at Greymouth cop shop. In the waiting area, Gemma and Graham are updating their social media status. We adjourn for a late lunch in a local café and compare notes.

'Ollie Harper says hello.' Gemma scans the menu, unimpressed, and we give our orders to a server.

'He doesn't even know me.'

'He seems to know about you, though, courtesy of his colleagues in Marlborough.'

That would be Jessie James. 'Did Harper have anything useful to say?'

'He's a dirt digger and enjoys his work. Wasn't fazed by the idea that Morgan Hopu and Nigel Watson might have been playing him for their own ends. Happy to oblige for the quid pro quo.'

'The photographs from the volunteer awards night?'

She spreads some printouts on the table ahead of our lunch arriving. 'Here's the rest plus the original article with photo captions of those present.'

The previously unnamed third man in the photo with Robertson and Havelka is one of the names Beth Hart gave me. 'Stuart Batty. An elder from Whakakitenga.'

'We ran his name already,' says Graham. 'Died five years ago. Hunting accident.'

Bad luck, avenging angel, or an accomplice tidying up loose ends?

'Any other names from the article flagged?' A shaking of heads. Lunch arrives: pie, pide, and soup of the day. 'What about these other two?' I show them the ones Beth gave me and Graham keys them into his tablet.

'One dead, the other no trace.'

The dead one is Francis Stilton, aged thirty-six, suicide. The photo seems familiar but I can't place it right now. 'Dropping like flies.'

Gemma puts down her pie and refers to Beth's list. 'Which leaves this other untraceable fella, Robin Walker.'

'Not untraceable,' says Graham, dipping some sourdough in his soup. 'Just untraced.'

'He's not necessarily our man. Let's not jump to conclusions.' But try as I might I just can't help it.

Next stop a hundred klicks north to Westport, with a big wind battering us from the Tasman. Not sure what we'll find here after so long. The tide has long since ebbed and flowed on the black sand where Darren Robertson was found face down with a bullet in the back of his skull. The blood-soaked room where Lucy McLernon was discovered six months earlier has been refurbished and re-painted several times over. Still, Darren Robertson's family live here. What, apart from the distant prospect of possible financial compensation, makes them believe Darren's already seedy reputation has been further traduced? And what do they know of the company he kept?

It's now late afternoon. Light is fading and dark clouds loom on the horizon as yet another winter front sweeps in off the ocean. There's a warning out for damaging winds, flash flooding and king tides. We've taken rooms at the Top 10 Holiday Park at Carters Beach across the road from where Darren was found. Robertson's widow and brother have agreed to meet us at a pub in town and we're shouting dinner. No expense spared.

Robertson's younger brother Kevin sports an All-Blacks beanie and four days' growth. He's a doppelganger of the deceased – that same dead-eyed jowly entitlement. Widow Robertson is still wearing her road-crew fluoros from traffic duty on some damaged interior route. The orders are in: steak and chips for him, schnitzel for her, plus two Jack and Cokes.

'Gettin' anywhere?' enquires Kev.

We've sent Graham off to play pool with the Westies. We don't want to crowd the Robertsons and we're figuring if Graham can emerge unscathed from the pool room he's earned the right to eat at our table. Only later. Meantime we need to woo Kevin and Zara Robertson.

'We are, as a matter of fact. Wondering if you could help us? Fill in a few gaps? There's a possibility Darren might have fallen in with a bad crowd. Maybe got set up.'

'What's that fucken weird accent? You Scotch or something?'

I explain my proud Mackem heritage to Zara and then I show them the awards night photos from the newspaper. 'Recognise any of these people?'

She leans forward. 'About time somebody listened.' Plants a nicotine-stained finger on Havelka. 'Funny accent, like you. Russian or something?'

'Czech. You met him?'

'A few weeks before that silly rich bitch got herself killed at Darren's motel.'

'No need for that, Zaz. Not her fault was it?' Kevin's empathy surprises me.

His sister-in-law relents. 'S'pose.'

'The Czech?' I prompt.

'Yeah, musta been between the awards do in Nelson and the thing at the motel.' Her face freezes. 'Come to think of it, fuck, it was just a day or two before. Was it him, the sick cunt?'

'We're investigating the possibility.'

'I knew it! Knew it wasn't Darren.'

Let's not get ahead of ourselves. 'Recognise any of these others?' I show her the photo of Stuart Batty, Whakakitenga elder, since killed in a hunting accident.

'Yeah, yeah. Him and Daz went pig shooting sometimes. Never met him, lived out bush somewhere, but Daz had a picture in *Pig Shooting Monthly* with this bloke and a big boar. It's on our fridge still. You can have it if you want.'

'Yes,' says Gemma. 'That'd be fantastic. Thanks.'

'This fella?' Francis Stilton. Suicide.

The dinners arrive. Steak, two schnitzels – I couldn't resist one for myself – and a pasta for Gemma. We all dig in. Graham casts a glance our way from the pool table. He seems to be on a roll and some of the young fellas over there look antsy. I wouldn't put it past him to deliberately lose so he can get a feed quicker.

Kevin and Zara examine the photo of Francis Stilton. 'Nah.' They shake their heads. 'Who's he?' asks Kev.

'Just some bloke. You've definitely never seen him?'

They insist they haven't.

'The fellas in these pictures,' says Zara through a mouthful of chips. 'They the ones that really did it? Set Darren up?'

'It's a theory,' I concede. 'What do you think?'

Clearly nobody from our side has ever asked her that before. 'Like I told the reporter, Ollie. It had to be a conspiracy. Darren just wasn't like that.'

Kevin keeps his eyes on his food.

'There were allegations before that,' Gemma points out. 'Darren has history.'

'Those Danish sluts. They knew the camera was in the shower. They were part of it. Played up. Nobody proved that Darren installed it.' She prods her fork at the photos. 'Could have been these guys. Playing the long game to set him up.'

'Anybody else you remember? Somebody we might not be looking at? A mastermind maybe?'

She likes the sound of that. 'Darren didn't really hang around with masterminds but I'll give it some thought. Get back to you.'

'Does the name Robin Walker mean anything to you?'

'Sounds like a dick,' says Kevin plucking some meat from between his teeth. 'Who is he?'

'Somebody who came up in our enquiries.'

'Nah,' they say. 'Never heard of him.'

'Does this mean somebody's going to pay up for the damage to Darren's reputation?' Zara polishes off her chips. 'The hurt and injury and all that. The distress we've suffered?'

'We'll keep you posted.' Gemma offers a business card. 'If you think of anything.'

There's a commotion at the pool table. Some pushing and shoving with Graham at the centre of it. In one swift move he has the offender facedown over the green baize with an arm twisted halfway up the back while showing the rest of the crowd his police ID. Smooth as.

'That deserves a schnitzel.' I place an order on Graham's behalf.

34.

The overnight rain flooded the roads and the wind lifted roofs and brought down trees so it takes longer than expected to get back to Havelock. Before we left Westport we asked the local plods to dig out anything further on Stuart Batty's pig-hunting mishap and Francis Stilton's suicide. Late afternoon, Gemma and Graham drop me at home before pushing on to Blenheim and their respective home bases to salvage what's left of the weekend.

Vanessa's no longer pissed off and just seems relieved to have me back in one piece. 'Mission accomplished?'

'Hardly.' I bring her up to speed on the additional pieces of the jigsaw. 'Any gossip at this end?'

'My leg's feeling better and the graft operation is scheduled for a couple of weeks. Going to try returning to school on Monday but on the understanding I can pike if it's not working.'

'Are you up for it?'

'Don't know yet but I'm going nuts here. I don't make a good invalid.'

Paulie comes out of his room with Mim in tow. 'You're back. Where you been?'

I tell him and Mim nods sagely. 'Nice over there, isn't it? So green.'

'Beautiful in parts. Whereabouts were you?'

'Dad,' Paulie warns. 'No cop stuff, remember?'

'Just chatting. That right, Mim?'

'Yeah. Can't remember the name of the place. We left when I was about six.'

'And that's when you moved to Nelson?'

'Dad!'

Mim is unfazed. 'I was at boarding school in Nelson while my mum was in hospital to stop her crying. I don't tell fibs, Mr Chester.'

Maybe she wasn't fibbing after all. Just telling a different version of the truth. 'Good to see you guys hanging out again.'

'When's tea?' says Paulie, looking daggers.

'Not long.' Vanessa winks at me. 'We'll have an early one then get Mim home, okay?'

'Sounds like a plan. Anything I can do?'

'Sure. Cook dinner while I have a glass of wine.' She grabs a bottle from the shelf. 'Frozen pizzas do you?'

'Twist my arm.' In some ways I'm enjoying the new model lazy-trollop Vanessa but if it wasn't for the fact that I'm a few days off brain surgery I'd feel obliged to take my dietary health into my own hands.

She raises a glass while I crumple up plastic wrappings and program the microwave. 'Lechayim. To life.'

Chin-chin.

After dinner, Paulie and I drive Mim home. The rain has eased and it's dark by the time we get to Dalton's Bridge. Jan is there waiting under the porch light rugged up against the cold. She greets Mim with a hug.

'Did you have a good time, love?'

'Yep. Paul's dad went over near where we used to live.'

'Really?' She takes Mim's bag. Gives me a distracted smile. 'Where?'

'Greymouth. That area.' There's a pounding at the base of my skull. Another migraine threatens. 'Well, better get going.'

'I told him about boarding school, Mum. In Nelson, remember? After daddy left us and you got sad.'

'Not now love.' Jan shakes her head. Kids, eh?

Next thing I'm down on my knees and the stars are exploding. Everything is whirling and won't stop. Paulie is yelling, and so is Mim. My head is in Jan's lap and I've just puked pizza onto her jeans. Her cool palm rests on my brow.

'Sorry.' I'm groaning. 'Sorry.'

She strokes my face. 'Poor thing. It's going to be all right.'

'Sorry,' I say, over and over.

She's looking down at me, searching my face. As if trying to recognise me from way back. 'What have they done to you?' Disconnected. Fraught.

I'm too busy spewing to question her logic. I'm content to let her empathy wash over me. 'Sorry.' Again.

'It's not your fault. It never was.' Tears roll down her face.

In time, it passed. Jan found the medication in my jacket pocket and gave me some. Between them, she and Michael in convoy dropped me and Paulie home to a worried Vanessa. Michael driving me and Paulie in my car and Jan and Mim in their back-up. Michael sizing me up while Paulie fretted in the back.

'Been out and about I hear. Can't be good for you, gallivanting in that condition.'

'Just a migraine. All sorted now.'

'Powerful medication for just a headache.'

'Yeah.'

'Jan got a real shock.'

'Sorry about that.' Last thing I want is for my brain tumour to upset your daughter.

'She's had it tough. Still not over everything, you know?'

No I don't and I've got too much on my own plate to care. I'm dying, I realise that now. I must be.

'Here we are,' I say, relieved to be home. Vanessa takes up the relay baton. Helping me into the house as Michael drives away with a stare. 'I'm fine. Really.'

'He vomited on Mim's mum,' adds Paulie, helpfully.

'Poor thing.'

'She was really good about it.'

'I'm talking about your dad.'

'Oh.'

I spend the rest of the evening being fussed over by Vanessa and even though the symptoms have eased, I give in to it and let her limp around taking care of everything. Hang in there. The day after the day after tomorrow they'll cut open my head and sort everything out once and for all.

35.

'There's nothing in the drains.'

Maxwell was true to his word, showing up at Māhana over the weekend with a warrant, an excavator, pneumatic drills and angle grinders.

'The tuft of hair we saw on the video was nothing more than that. No bones. No chopped up human flesh. No red flags in the missing persons files.'

For all sorts of reasons my brain isn't working too well this morning but, for the most part, I'm inclined to put it down to lack of sleep. I lay awake in the early hours fretting about mortality, the future for Vanessa and Paulie, the questions that remain unanswered and the things that don't fit. Paulie and Vanessa are back at school today. I find myself storing images of their little gestures away in my memory, not knowing if they'll be retrievable after Wednesday. Impaired faculties.

'So why did Gelder have to die?'

Maxwell offers me a coffee from his plunger but my tastebuds are playing havoc today. Even a glass of water sets alarm bells ringing. 'Maybe LeBlanc knew from Cunningham that he was in trouble for installing the steel hoops, remodelling the drains off his own bat and getting drunk with the servants. He couldn't remember what he might have said on the video, wanted the incriminating material back and went into default psycho mode to achieve his aim.'

'A tad extreme.'

'This guy is. Look, we know the type. He'd spoon your eyes out to know where you hid his Easter eggs.'

I'm far from convinced. 'Why would he pay out his own money to have the drains widened and steel hoops put in for no good reason?'

'Did he? Do we know that?' Maxwell closes a window against the chill. 'I crosschecked Gelder's bank account. No trace of any unofficial deposits from LeBlanc, unless it was cash of course as Cunningham suggests. But how would he know about such a transaction if it was cash?' He pushes a printout across his desk. 'But there is a payment from Māhana under the name of JBNZ Trust.'

A quick scan. 'Whatever Gelder was doing there was on the books and, we assume, with the full knowledge of Cunningham and, possibly, Bryant.'

'Cunningham is dissembling.'

'Not very well,' I say. 'We've nailed his lie pretty quickly.'

'It's a thing these days, heads of state look straight down the barrel of the TV camera and let you know they're lying, they don't care, and there's not a damn thing us mere mortals can do about it.' Maxwell draws his eyes away from an incoming on his computer. 'He's wasted our time and resources looking for a non-existent body in their drains. Now we're left with a tidy-up bill.'

'Maybe that's the message. Don't go digging up stuff that doesn't concern us or perhaps doesn't even exist. But we do know the steel rings existed, we saw them on video.'

'Bryant told you that room was going to be a morgue. Post-mortems. Stuff like that?'

'Morgues don't need those hoops in the wall. Dead people don't need to be tethered.'

Maxwell shrugs. 'They're gone now.'

'The morgue is also the place where you access the panic room.'

'Panic room?'

'They're another thing these days. Every mansion has one. Check out *Grand Designs.*'

Maxwell shakes his head irritably. 'We've got enough to wrap LeBlanc up for Gelder and Jaxon Hemi. Maybe we should walk away from this.' Right now that's fine by me. I bring him up to speed on the west coast trip. 'This Robin Walker is a person of interest then?'

'He's the only one not accounted for. The plods over that way are looking into the supposed hunting accident suffered by Whakakitenga elder Stuart Batty. Unless he tripped and fell on his own gun we assume somebody was there and saw what happened. Likewise I'm interested in Francis Stilton's supposed suicide.'

'So we'll put out a national alert for Robin Walker and keep chipping away at whatever we have. Avenging angel or accomplice. Which way are you leaning, Nick?'

Good question, but I find myself leaning towards the latter.

That theory lasts until about lunchtime. I was enjoying a quiet cuppa with Latifa who had been telling me that her enquiries at social services and at Lisbet Havelka's old school proved inconclusive.

'Behaviours consistent with being abused but it never got to the next level of investigation.' Latifa grimaced. 'It happens a lot.'

Gemma barges through the door and slides a photo across the desk to me. 'Nine years ago. A restaurant in downtown Wellington. Birthday celebration for an old but not so loyal friend of Lucy McLernon's. Check out the handsome guy with the big smile and his arm around Lucy's shoulder.'

'Oh fuck,' says Latifa.

Thomas Hemi.

'Look cosy, don't they?' Gemma is jubilant. 'Now we know why he didn't want us sniffing around his property.'

'He and Ruth were married by then. Two kids.' Latifa shakes her head. 'Maybe it's not what it seems.'

'Not according to the old friend. She had the hots for Thomas herself and was spittin' that he and Lucy were, as she put it, going at it like bunnies.'

'And about a year later Lucy herself was married and pregnant.' That drunk and disorderly report I read on Thomas. The first blemish for years in his changed life. From gangland enforcer to family man to cheating lover, and then back to family man. Was Thomas our avenging angel?

'Let's ask him,' says Gemma.

The Hemi family have returned home. They must be the only people still living beyond Deep Creek where access is via the temporary bridge installed by army engineers. There's a weight limit on all traffic and it feels like we involuntarily hold our breaths and suck our stomachs in as we pass over the long drop. We, being Gemma, me and Latifa. Gemma wasn't happy about the latter being there but I pulled rank and waved the cultural sensitivities card.

'Latifa will be an asset,' I insisted.

'Fuck asset,' Latifa had whispered under her breath on our way out to the car. 'I just want to be a fly on the wall when it goes down.'

It's a nice day and there's a pang of something like nostalgia driving past our burnt-out ruin. I can't see us returning and I'll miss that stunning river view. Our chickens and goats have been adopted by Thomas and roam freely in his side paddock as we drive through the gate. Thomas is chopping wood again and Ruth is back working in the vegie garden. Their youngest will be at school.

'This looks serious,' says Thomas, resting his axe.

'It is,' agrees Gemma. She shows him the photo. 'That is you, isn't it?'

Ruth is taking an interest. She's put down her shovel and wipes her hands on her shirt as she approaches. 'What's up?'

'Nothing, love.'

Gemma slots the photo back into her file. 'Will you tell her or will I?'

It's like watching a slow-motion train crash. I should stop Gemma but I'd be playing this pretty much the same way if I didn't know or care about Thomas and his family. Eggs. Omelettes. It's part of our training along with empathy, cultural sensitivity and target practice.

'Can I have a moment alone with my wife?' He looks both at Gemma and me. 'Please?'

'Sure,' I say, overriding Gemma. Maybe it's my own impending doom but empathy suits my purposes today.

They walk back to where Ruth was working in the vegie garden, speaking in low and increasingly urgent voices. A gasp from Ruth. Then she turns and strides into the house.

'Ready now?' says Gemma on his return.

Latifa offers to go and be with Ruth and Thomas acquiesces.

'We first met on this – I don't know what you'd call it – spiritual boot camp thing on the Kapiti coast. I'd been searching for years. Looking for some kind of meaning. I was sick of the gang stuff, the senseless violence. Going nowhere.'

'Weren't you already out of it by then? Teamed up with Ruth?'

'Yeah, trying to make it work. I hadn't been in trouble for a while but it's hard to make a clean break. Always somebody wanting a new favour or calling in old ones.'

'What about Lucy?' asks Gemma. 'What was she there for?'

'Escape her folks I guess. They controlled her, she said. Always judging, expecting. Treating her like an infant.'

'Must have been tough for her,' murmurs Gemma.

'Fuck you,' says Thomas. 'Want to hear me out or not?'

I cast Gemma a warning glance. 'Go on, Thomas.'

'We sparked. At first I admit I was flattered by all this attention from a rich, beautiful Pākehā wahine. But it went deeper than that.'

'Did it?' says Gemma. 'According to her friends, you were Lucy's secret love. Her parents never knew, only selected friends. She wasn't fully committed, was she?'

'Guess not.'

'But you were and you still carried a torch for her.' She takes another sheet of paper from her file. 'That's quite a while after, eh?'

'The drunk and disorderly.' I give him the date and location. 'That was you, wasn't it?'

'She'd just texted to let me know she was getting married.'

'Then she gets pregnant, then she runs away to, what's it called?' Gemma checks her notes. 'Whakakitenga. Is that how you say it?' A nod. 'Then she runs away from there. Ends up raped and killed.' Hemi flinches. 'Must've eaten you up, something like that.'

'Yeah. It did.'

'And so you hunted them down: Robertson, Havelka, Batty. Whoever else. Polished off your old skills. Got your utu.'

'Great little story. Can you prove it?'

'If we dig up your property will we find the other half of Havelka?'

'Who?'

'Why did you refuse us access last time?'

'Because you're Pākehā and this is my land.'

Gemma knows she's not going to get any further today without hard evidence. Or trying once more to press a few buttons. 'What happened with Ruth?' she says softly. 'Not got that fire you're searching for?' Gemma packs her stuff away and stands, casting a glance back to the house. 'You threw it all away for a little rich white girl who denied your existence to those that mattered to her. Now you've lost it all: Ruth, Jaxon. And it looks like you're going to spend the rest of your life in jail.'

His eyes fill and he hefts his axe again. We tense but he heads for the woodpile. 'You know where to find me.'

The return drive is sombre, each of us locked in our own thoughts. I'm wondering how Thomas could know where to look after Lucy died, but then again he had access to his brother Morgan's excellent intelligence network. If Havelka hadn't crossed Morgan's path for other reasons he'd never have entered the frame for Lucy's murder. Thomas Hemi – avenging angel? No.

'I don't buy it.'

'What?' says Gemma.

'The coincidence. Havelka being responsible for the death of one brother's son and the other brother's lover. Ridiculous.'

'You need to get out more, Sarge,' says Latifa. 'New Zealand is a village masquerading as a country.'

'And then Thomas somehow gets to know and kills him before his brother can exact his own revenge? Nah, it's crap.'

'Not going to be easy getting an excavator over that bridge,' muses Gemma. 'Maybe we can borrow that one of Thomas's?'

'Are you listening?'

'Nick, I know you and Thomas have this bromance going but it's clouding your judgement. If it was anybody else in that photo, you'd be in like Flynn.'

Would I? What are the chances? Thomas is invited to the station at Blenheim tomorrow to submit to DNA and other testing and a formal interview. It's the start of a long process and we're far from having the goods on him so there's no hurry or cause for arrest just yet. Is he a flight risk? Something tells me not. 'What did Ruth have to say for herself?'

Latifa leans forward from the back seat. 'Right now she doesn't care if we lock him up and throw away the key.'

'There you go,' says Gemma. 'Even his wife's on my side.'

Maxwell is more gung-ho. 'You should have just brought him back. Kept him locked up, ready for tomorrow.'

I look to Latifa for reassurance. 'I think Sergeant Chester is right, sir. Thomas and his family have been through a lot lately. He's not a violent, or desperate, or unpredictable man.'

Hmm, I'm thinking. You should have seen him on Deep Creek bridge the other night.

'I hope you're right,' says Maxwell.

'And if it is him,' says Latifa, 'I can categorically say he's not the same man who attacked me.'

'Which lends weight to the avenger theory then, doesn't it?' says Maxwell. 'And the assault on you remains a separate matter. Rope marks on trees being the only connecting factor.'

So if Thomas is our avenging angel responsible for the deaths of possibly three men, we need to now lock down a timeline, establish or refute alibis, make links, join dots. We need witnesses and forensics putting Thomas with those dead men.

'Any news on the hunting accident or the suicide?' I enquire. 'Or Robin Walker?'

'Stilton was found by his wife in their barn. He'd taken an overdose. She'd tried to resuscitate him. Too late. Tragic.'

'Evidence of foul play?'

'None. There were whispers of him being involved in scandal at that Whakakitenga place you mentioned. Maybe he couldn't stand the shame of exposure.'

'Batty and the hunting mishap?'

'No witnesses. He was on his own. Had the gun propped against a rock. It slid, went off, took the top of his skull with it.'

'Filthy luck.'

'Isn't it just? No news of your Robin Walker. He hasn't gone through immigration in the last however many years since it was computerised. Or touched his bank account, paid tax or claimed any benefits or been to a doctor.'

'Family?'

'Not known if he had one. Every chance it's not his real name and Whakakitenga took him at face value. Like the French foreign legion.' And later the boy's club burned or shredded whatever trace of him there was. 'Maybe Thomas Hemi took care of him.'

'Or maybe he's our killer.'

'All these maybes.' Maxwell grins. 'And it's still only Monday.'

In the remaining few hours of today we attempt to draw a timeline and hopefully a net around Hemi. Darren Robertson, Karel Havelka, Stuart Batty and Francis Stilton all died within about a six-month period during which Robin Walker also disappeared off the radar. Stilton was the first to die and, on the face of it, by his own hand. Was his remorse and guilt a trigger for the revelation of who was involved and what was to follow? Next came Robertson, a month later, executed on a black sand beach near

Westport. Then Stuart Batty cops it in a freak hunting accident inland from Greymouth heading up towards Arthur's Pass. Last of the known dead is Karel Havelka a few months later, again executed, this time in a forest glade at Pelorus Bridge. Thomas Hemi relentlessly tracking down those he believed implicated in his secret lover's appalling death. Is he capable of such wrath and vengeance? Sure. I saw him in action against LeBlanc. He's capable of cold-bloodedly throwing a man off a high bridge.

If you believe in the End Times then the only rules are the ones you write yourself.

36.

Back from an early morning trip to Nelson hospital for a pre-op shakedown. I've lost nearly a kilo since last weighed but my blood pressure is slightly elevated. Funny that. After the anaesthetist had finished his interview with me, Dr Copp got out her iPad and explained in great detail what she planned to do. I nodded bravely when what I really wanted to do was close my eyes, plug my ears and sing 'I'm not listening, la-la-la.' My fate is not in my hands. That's what these Doomsday preppers don't get. When it's time, it's time. Even Mother Nature's silver seed must wither and die eventually. Nobody escapes. We are all doomed.

Thomas Hemi has submitted to a few tests of his own and now we have his spit, hair, and fingerprints on file. He's brought a lawyer with him. I half-expected him not to but this is serious stuff. Her name is Melanie and she does lots of work for the iwi. Apparently Thomas has been spending more time down at the marae since Jaxon was killed. He seems to be reconnecting with the community he once rejected. I get to watch the proceedings on video in an adjacent room at the Blenheim cop shop while Maxwell and Gemma do the honours. Gemma looks tired, like she's been putting in the hours. DC Keegan has come over from Nelson and is taking an interest too. We sit shoulder to shoulder, takeaway coffees on the go. Keegan brought her keep cup.

Formalities finished, Maxwell leads the charge. 'You understand why you're here, Mr Hemi?'

'Yes.'

'We have some questions regarding your whereabouts over a period of approximately six months around six years ago.' He gives the precise dates.

Melanie leans in. 'For the record, my client has not been charged and is here of his own volition to assist you with your enquiries and is free to leave at any time. Right?'

'Correct,' says Maxwell. 'Should anything change you will be the first to know.' He then invites Thomas to account for himself.

'Six years ago?' He leans back in his chair, hands behind his head. 'That's a long time. I was probably around the farm, doing jobs, or hunting, delivering firewood. I really can't remember.'

'Try,' says Gemma sliding an A4 printout of the dates his way.

Thomas looks at the dates. Twirls the paper with his fingertips. Makes a show of trying to think. 'Nah, sorry.'

'Maybe we can help.' Gemma brings up an image beamed from her iPad to a screen on the wall for all to see. 'An ATM camera on the main drag of Westport. That is you isn't it?'

'Looks like me.'

Gemma's been busy. Trawling through whatever evidence was collected at the time. Old CCTV and other stuff which didn't trigger anything, then suddenly dings a bell. 'You'll notice the date and time.' She reads it out for the record. 'Less than forty-eight hours later, Darren Robertson was found shot dead less than a kilometre away.'

Thomas shrugs. 'Got any pictures of me shooting the prick?'

'We talked to Robertson's wife, Zara. She reckons she saw you in the pub the same night you went to that ATM. Taking a lot of interest in Darren.' Gemma reads from her notes. 'Watching him all night, he was. Thought he fancied him or something. Pervert.'

'From what I hear, Zara doesn't see too well after a few Jack and Cokes.'

'So you do know who Zara is then? Know her habits?'

'After Lucy died, I took an interest. Lucy meant something to me even if not to the cops. They were getting nowhere. Word was already out that Robertson was a sleazebag. Obviously I was looking at him.'

'Did you kill him?'

'No.'

'Why not?' asks Maxwell. 'I would have if he'd done that to the love of my life. Raped, gutted.'

'Sergeant, please.' Melanie puts down her pen. 'That language is designed to inflame and distress.'

'So, Mr Hemi. Why were you stalking Darren Robertson?'

'Gathering evidence. Doing the cops' jobs for them.' Keegan snorts into her coffee. 'And you know what? I don't think Robertson did it either. He might have been there, or led them to her. But he's a panty-sniffer, not a killer.'

'Them?' says Maxwell.

'You know their names already.' Thomas prods the dates sheet. 'Looks like, what, three or four of them?'

'You tell us who they are.'

'Fucked if I know. The ones you mentioned yesterday. Whoever they are, if they're dead that's fine by me.'

'You really don't know their names?'

'No, apart from that Havelka bloke. I was there when you found him. Remember?'

'So what made you give up the chase?' asks Gemma, who seems to be running out of steam.

'Robertson was my only lead. With him gone there was no point.'

'And you expect us to believe that?'

Melanie starts to pack her papers into a briefcase. 'Let us know if you have any further questions or if the samples my client has voluntarily supplied show up at any of the crime scenes. In the meantime ...'

'So we'll keep on digging and we'll run Hemi's prints and DNA against the trace evidence.' Keegan is disappointed but not surprised. She's used to the long haul.

'That's not going to be easy,' I say. 'Given the killings were all outdoor and there were no signs of struggle.'

'Due diligence.' Maxwell shrugs.

'It's interesting that Havelka was last and he was the only one where effort was made to properly hide the body. Chopping it in half. Burying it deep.'

'Thoughts?' Keegan stops checking messages on her phone.

'It makes me think Havelka was more significant than the others. Perhaps also harder to knock off. Required more planning.'

'His army background?'

'Maybe.' Thomas was there at Butchers Flat the day of the earthquake. The day Havelka was discovered. He didn't bat an eyelid. If he'd killed him and buried him there he'd have to be one cool bastard to not react when the body was unearthed.'

'Plenty of people could attest to Thomas being one cool bastard,' says

Gemma. 'Isn't that what you love about him, Nick?'

'Play nice, kiddies.' Maxwell shrugs on his jacket and turns to Keegan. 'Boss, I'd like to authorise an aerial scan on the Hemi property to see if there's any bodies been buried there in the last few years. Might be expensive but getting a digger over that bridge will be dicey and I can't see Thomas lending us his.'

'We could requisition it,' says Gemma.

'Won't go well in court.' Keegan gives Maxwell the nod. 'Broaden the scan area in case there are any more out there. May as well get our money's worth.' She catches my eye. 'A word, Nick?'

Outside the sun is shining and fluffy white clouds scud across a blue sky. It's lunchtime and Keegan invites me for a bite at Ritual Café down the road from the cop shop. We admire the retro kitsch while we wait for our filo and salad.

'Your operation is tomorrow, isn't it?'

'Yep.'

'So everything is in hand, Nick. There's no reason for you to be at work.'

'No problem. The distraction is good.'

'Vanessa phoned me this morning, first thing. She told me about your attack over the weekend.'

'A migraine, that's all.'

'You must know how hard it would have been for Vanessa to phone me, of all people, and ask for help.'

The woman I cheated on her with? Yes, sure. 'Help?'

'She wants me to order you to go home and be with your family. How sad is that, Nick? For fuck's sake.'

Lunch arrives but I leave it untouched.

En route I try to ring Vanessa. She's at school but it's lunchtime so she should be able to answer. The call goes through to voicemail.

'I'm sorry, love. On my way home now.'

A few minutes later a text comes through saying great, can I get Paulie and put the dinner on. Microwave something from the freezer.

She follows up with a call. 'I shouldn't have had to talk to that cow. Jesus, Nick.'

'I'm sorry.' My voice chokes. 'I'm scared, Vanessa.'

'We all are.' A pause. 'This is stupid. Me at work, Paulie at school, you anywhere but where you should be. We need to be together. Face this together.'

'Yep.'

'See you in a while. Let's make tonight good, eh? For Paulie. For us.'

I need to pull over until my eyes have cleared. A logging truck screams past and the car shudders. The hills are vivid green. So beautiful it hurts. There's still a couple of hours until Paulie finishes so after taking a lasagne out of the freezer and chopping some vegies I drop in to the Havelock cop shop to catch up with Latifa.

'You won't take a telling, will you?'

Let's guess. Vanessa's had a word with her too. 'All quiet on the western front?'

'Yes. Go home.'

'No developments? No gossip?'

'Enjoy the weather while it's here. Another big blow coming in a few days.'

I probably won't know much about it once I'm under the knife. 'If Thomas was our killer why would he cut Havelka's body in two and bury the top half just down the road from his property?'

'You tell me.'

'Nothing culturally significant I'm missing here? No ritual I need to know about?'

'I'm not your ambassador for Māori affairs. Go home!'

'So the answer is no?'

'To the best of my knowledge.'

'It's bullshit isn't it? Thomas isn't our man.'

'He's definitely not the bloke who snared me, that's for sure. But even if the two things aren't connected, I still don't see it.'

'Why?'

'Apart from Robertson, all the deaths look sneaky. Hiding bodies, pretend accidents. Thomas doesn't do sneaky. Except for having an affair of course.' She nods towards my computer. 'There's a more detailed report from the Westie cops about the Stilton suicide. Pretty convinced that it's genuine and to the best of their knowledge Thomas and he never met.'

'Still no trace of Robin Walker?'

'He warrants a mention in the suicide report. He formally identified the victim, the wife was too distraught. Probably his job as one of the community elders.' Latifa shakes her head. 'Have you looked in a mirror lately?'

I run a hand through my crew cut and try a smile. 'Not good?'

'Skinny, pale, rings under your eyes. Clothes hanging off you.' She comes from around her desk and gives me a long warm hug. 'You need to start looking after yourself, Sarge.'

Jan is waiting there as I pull up outside Paulie's school. I bow down as she opens her car window.

'Last time we met I'd just spewed all over you. Once again, hand on heart, I'm sorry.'

A curt nod, like we've been over-intimate and she regrets it. 'Feeling better?'

'Lots.'

'That's good.' She drums her fingers on the steering wheel. 'I hear you're going to hospital soon? Paul mentioned it to Mim.'

'Tomorrow. Paulie doesn't know the full circumstances.'

'Right. It must be difficult.'

'Yep.' The siren goes. 'Here they come.'

'There is a God, you know. He watches over us and those we love.'

'It's a comforting thought.' If you believe that stuff but I'm too polite to say so. Although she did rest my head in her pukey lap after all, and stroke my brow with her smooth, cool hand.

'We'll pray for you.' She rests that hand on my forearm and squeezes it.

'Thanks.'

Mim and Paulie skip up to Jan's car.

'Feeling better, Mr Chester?' says Mim.

'Much. Thanks.'

'See you tomorrow,' says Mim to Paulie.

'See you.' He slings his bag into the back of my ute and climbs in.

Something nags at me but I can't grasp it. 'Bye, then.'

Jan gives me a sudden smile, so warm it feels like a blessing. 'Bye, Nick.'

The lasagne goes down a treat. We all watch some *SpongeBob SquarePants* together, much to Paulie's delight, and he goes to bed without trying to stretch things out.

'Night, Dad,' he murmurs sleepily and I hug him close.

'Night.'

Later, after stacking the dishwasher and packing my hospital bag for the morning, Vanessa and I snuggle on the couch.

'You going okay?' she asks.

'Yeah. As well as.'

'The surgeon is good. I asked around. It's going to be fine.'

'Yep. I think it is.'

'Promise?' Her eyes are shining with tears.

'Promise.'

In bed we hold each other tight. The side gate bangs with a gust of wind and soft rain patters on the tin roof. Just as I'm dropping off I feel a shudder pass through Vanessa and realise she's weeping.

'What if this is all there is? What if it really is all just nothing? Why the hell do we bother?'

'We have to, love. Or we'll go mad.'

And she eventually drifts off to sleep while I'm left staring at the moonlit shadows of wind-whipped trees on my bedroom wall.

It's not your fault …

I jolt awake. Checking my phone, it's around 2.30 a.m. The wind has dropped and the rain ceased. That night I dropped Mim off at home and collapsed into Jan's arms on her rainswept porch.

What have they done to you? … It's not your fault … It never was.

She's not talking about me puking on her. She was searching my face for a memory, a flashback, her relived trauma.

I was at boarding school in Nelson while my mum was in hospital to stop her crying. I don't tell fibs, Mr Chester.

Slip out of bed. Dress and down the path into the office. Latifa was right. How can you relax living this close to your workplace? Inside and switch on the computer. Bring up the Francis Stilton suicide report.

Found by his wife lying in a pool of his own vomit. An overdose. A note pinned to his shirt. 'Sorry.'

The wife's name, Jennifer.

Sorry, I said. Over and over from my pool of vomit. No wonder she was triggered.

It's not your fault …

The daughter, six years old at the time. Melissa.

*I can't remember the name of the place. We left there when I was six …
after daddy left us.*

Jennifer Stilton had to be sedated and was later admitted to a mental
hospital. Paralysed with grief. It would be six months before she was fit to
face the world again. The clincher is a photograph of the scene in the barn.
It's no nativity like in Mim's drawing, but the wooden beams and grainy
detail are the same. Some tools hanging on the wall.

Jen becomes Jan. Melissa becomes Miranda becomes Mim.

If Robin Walker was the man who formally identified Francis Stilton's
body then Jen, or Jan, knows who he is and what he looks like. But of
course it's even closer to home than that. I check the signature on the
form: R.M. Walker. M for Michael.

Jan's a searcher, he'd said. *But who am I to tell her it's just a big fucking
meaningless void?*

Latifa will meet me there. I haven't woken Vanessa to tell her my plans.
Instead I've left a note on the kitchen table. 'Sorry', it begins.

It's obvious now the special bond between Michael and Havelka. Both
army veterans. Tough men. Battle hardened. Maybe they share other
things too – a predilection for rape and murder. Michael, if indeed it
is him, is a force to be reckoned with so Latifa and I will connect a few
hundred metres back in the nearest lay-by and approach together on foot.
We've called out the AOS too, the nearer Blenheim contingent are tied up
in a drug raid down near Kaikoura but the Nelson squad can be with us in
forty-five minutes via the winding roads of the Whangamoa. No chopper
unfortunately; it's down on that drug raid in Kaikoura.

It being around 3.30 a.m., there are no lights on at the Walton homestead.
Jan's Subaru is in the driveway but I can't see Michael's old ute. It could be
in the garage under cover which would make sense if he has stuff in the
tray he wants to keep dry from the ever-changing weather.

'Are we going in or what?' Latifa is loyal to me but unhappy at being
snatched from Daniel's warm bed. She's only here because of the photo I
sent her from the database. 'Or do we wait for the ninjas?'

'We should probably wait for them.'

'I can do that. You don't need to be here.'

'Yes I do.'

'Why?'

What do I say to her? Impaired faculties. Condemned men get a last meal. All I want is one last fucking win and to know how that feels. Selfish? Stupid? When was I ever not? Ford's words: *And when you get back, do some thinking about what's important around here.* Vanessa's constant entreaties: *Why is our family never enough of a priority*? They say that some people have a terrific life force that drives them to survive and succeed. Mine must be a death force. I admit it: I'm terrified and in denial. Clinging to a crazy irrational belief that if I keep on doing what I do then I can hold the inevitable at bay. And here's me sneering at people who have religion.

Latifa sees something in me, a need that won't give way. 'Pity you didn't show me Michael Walton's driving licence yonks ago. I'd have known those eyes anywhere.'

'Why would I? He didn't figure.'

'Well whether or not he's your murderer, I definitely want a word with him.' Latifa has taken the shottie out of the boot and I have my police issue Glock. 'Walton has two guns on his licence that we know of. A hunting rifle and a shotgun.'

'And we're assuming he also has the handgun he used for the executions of Robertson and Havelka.'

'Probably the same one he held to my head.'

I'm beginning to have my doubts about this. 'Maybe you're right. We should just leave him to the AOS.'

'Too late,' she says. 'He's on the move.'

The porchlight has come on. 'He knows we're here.'

'How could he?'

'Maybe he doesn't sleep. Maybe he's been expecting us.' Then I see it rigged in the tree above us. A camera, not so flash as the one outside the Lodge, but still enough to do the job. Probably infra-red, night-vision, the type usually used to spot wildlife. He probably has a few strategically placed. Planning for the day we'd catch up with him. An alarm system connected to a PC in the bedroom or to a mobile. Easy as.

The garage door opens but instead of the ute, it's a quad bike that emerges. He shoots out straight across the road and up what I know to be a steep track into the back hills and pine plantations.

'Shit.' Latifa puts down the shottie and gets her phone out to call in the reinforcements urgently. 'What's he think he's doing? This can only end one way. Dickhead.'

Michael must see it differently. 'He knows a way out. A way through. He's been up there before. He's figuring on disappearing again.'

'The only way we're going to catch him is with a mule of our own.'

There's a dairy farm half a kilometre back down the road and odds-on there will be one there. Latifa rushes off to get it with a squeal of tyres on gravel. A light has come on in Michael's house and I'm guessing Jan is awake. She seems unsurprised to find me on her threshold in the middle of the night.

'How long have you known about him?'

'He's not what you think he is.'

This isn't the time to discuss the blurred lines of morality and family loyalty. I nod towards the uphill track across the road. 'Any idea where he's headed?'

'No.'

She's lying. 'He's killed four people that I'm aware of. Attacked another. We need to stop him, Jan.'

'He did what he thought was best.'

'What? Sexually assaulting and trying to kill my colleague was a good thing?' Her eyes widen. This is news to her. 'Maybe Michael isn't what *you* think he is.'

'You're wrong. He couldn't. Wouldn't.'

Latifa screeches up in a bright yellow ATV. 'Sorry about the colour but beggars can't be choosers. Let's go.'

'Last chance, Jan. Is there somewhere particular he's headed?'

She turns and shuts the door behind her.

The track is muddy and steep, so steep it sometimes feels like we're about to roll backwards head over wheels. We have the headlights on full beam but there's no sign of lights from Michael's buggy. Maybe he's too far ahead or has veered off on a side track.

'So far he's left a trail for us.' Latifa points to the fresh tyre marks in front. 'Breathe deep and count to ten, Sarge. We'll get him. You need to keep your blood pressure down for your op in ...' she checks her watch, 'five, six hours?'

It doesn't bear thinking about. But I do, as we climb and slither on the still wet terrain. We shouldn't be here. This is wrong for so many reasons.

Suddenly there's a blinding light upon us.

'Stop there and get out. Leave your weapons in the vehicle and turn your headlights off. Hands high where I can see them.'

He went nowhere and came from nowhere. The tree cover is broken here. We must be near the top of the hill. We do as we're told. Latifa hesitates.

'You know what I'm capable of.'

'Yeah,' she says. 'I do.'

'What's your plan, Michael?' I blink into the cab-mounted floodlight. 'Surely you're not thinking of harming us? Things look bad enough already.'

'So what's two more?'

'Good one, Sarge,' mutters Latifa.

'If it stops here, you could argue you were doing the world a favour with those killings.'

'Except he wasn't.' Latifa lifts her chin, squinting at the light. 'Were you?'

'No.'

Latifa flares up. The prospect of imminent death won't stop her from saying her piece. 'You should have kept your hands to yourself, Michael. Dirty, sad old bastard.'

A gunshot and Latifa drops.

Jesus.

'Turn around,' he says to me. 'Kneel.'

So this is it.

The squelch of approaching footsteps through mud. The barrel of the gun pokes the back of my head, fitting snugly round about where the tumour is. Down on my knees. Head bowed. The bullet should exit just above my forehead. Maybe it's for the best. Who wants to live with impaired faculties?

'Go ahead,' I say. 'Do it.'

'You should have left well alone. It was all history.'

'Until the earthquake. Havelka. Did you point Mim in the direction of my son? An excuse to stay in contact, nose around?'

'No, your timing is out. Mim and Paul were friends before the earthquake. Mim genuinely likes the young fella. Didn't need pushing.'

He's right. My timing is out, fuzzy logic. 'But it must have been useful to you anyway.'

The gun barrel prods deeper. His spare hand is on my left shoulder. 'Shhhh.'

'Something about Havelka linked him to you. That's why you took more care with his disposal.'

I've now realised where we are. Just over the hill, maybe a few hundred metres away, is where Latifa was found in the snare. That's why he attacked her. He thought he'd been discovered.

'The rest of Havelka. He's somewhere around here isn't he?'

'All those people thinking he was a good man. You can't serve in places like Angola or Vietnam and stay good.'

'What came first, the bullet or the gutting?'

'The bullet. He was a comrade of sorts.'

'Brothers in arms, huh? That's why you couldn't resist copping a feel of Latifa? You had her completely to yourself. Not like Lucy, eh?'

'Life isn't black and white. Quiet now.' The gun barrel shifts, I squeeze my eyes shut. Bracing.

'Stop, Dad.'

The pressure eases. 'Jen? Go home, love. Stay out of this.'

'You told me all this was to honour the memory of Francis. But it wasn't, was it?'

'Whose idea was it to pin it on Francis?' The throbbing has started up at the base of my skull. I must be under stress or something. 'Yours? Havelka's? Batty's? It wouldn't have been Darren the Dupe for sure.' Take a guess. 'Havelka, I reckon, but you were happy to go along with it.'

'Dad? Is that true?'

'You shouldn't be here, Jen. Go home. Be with Mim.'

'You'll be wanting to keep Mim away from Grandad in a couple of years, Jen. Seriously.'

I'm pushed facedown into the mud. 'Is this how you want to die?' He snarls. 'A dog in a ditch?' He's got a strong grip. All that time on the land, setting snares, gutting prey. My arms flail uselessly and I'm drowning in a three-inch puddle.

'Dad. Stop.'

Muddy water in my nose and throat. Head pounding. Stars burst behind my eyes. These migraines. I'm weak as a baby.

'Dad. Please.'

'Yeah, Michael. Give it up.' There's the tearing of velcro. An exhalation of air. Latifa loosens another strap on her Kevlar vest. She took advantage of his distracting temper tantrum to make her move. I can't see but I imagine she has the shottie at Walton's ear.

It doesn't bother him. The grip on the back of my neck is as firm as ever. He's stepping into that big fucking meaningless void he talked about and taking me with him.

'Michael,' Latifa says. 'Stop. Now.'

But he doesn't and I can't struggle anymore. It's all gone: Vanessa, Paulie, all our cares and worries. I relax into his grip. Those stars in my skull settle and fade. The fireworks have finished and all that's left is sweet release.

'Dad.'

'I'd never have touched her, Jen. Never.'

'I know.'

He drops his weapon and lets me go.

37.

The aerial GPR scan is postponed until the weather clears. There'll be all sorts of bodies buried out there. Miners from the gold rush too poor to warrant a headstone. Maybe other victims of the infamous Doom Creek bandits. Word is the film will be released this summer with a special preview screening at Canvastown community hall. So far the response is underwhelming; real life seems to be providing more than enough melodrama for most folk in the valley. The GPR will probably pick out plenty of pig and deer carcasses. No doubt Georges LeBlanc too. And I'd bet my last dollar on the bottom half of Karel Havelka being unearthed on the far side of the hill behind where I used to live. The track from Pelorus Bridge over to Butchers Flat branches off north past our place where, if you climb a hundred more metres, you'll be in a great position to shoot out the neighbourhood water tanks. And it branches off south and west past Butchers Flat to connect with the Doom Creek Loop and the Wakamarina track over the Richmond Ranges to Wairau Valley.

We don't know for sure yet but we think Havelka merited special treatment in his disposal because he was the ringleader of the three men who preyed upon Lucy McLernon. Maybe he and Michael knew each other in a previous life. Fiends reunited in a war vets chatroom, maybe, and leaving faint traces of their relationship in cyberspace. Whatever. It was Havelka's idea to try to divert suspicion onto Michael's son-in-law, Francis Stilton, an otherwise blameless, devout and good man. He was on the verge of exposing the cabal's misdeeds at Whakakitenga and bringing too much scrutiny upon them all. Francis was framed by his own father-in-law with some help from Stuart Batty. Too innocent, weak and naïve to fight it, he took his own life. Forced into a devastating family tragedy by his own complicity, Michael went about righting some wrongs and covering his tracks. But Havelka must have known his accomplices were dropping like flies and that his days were numbered. Had he been keeping a low profile in the intervening years?

'Maybe that's why he punched out Morgan Hopu's son,' mused Latifa. 'Prison must have looked safer.'

Or maybe it was pure coincidence and he just had a temper on him. News of the incident alerting Michael as to Havelka's whereabouts.

Havelka was no pushover but Michael's black ops work with NZ special forces in Vietnam would have given anyone pause for thought. As a raw, keen twenty year old he used his Kiwi back-country hunting expertise to snare and gut the enemy, spreading fear where he operated and creating a buffer zone of relative security for his compadres. 'I was good, even if it didn't warrant a medal,' he'd told us on the way to the cells at Blenheim. Then one day he came across a young female Viet Cong fighter caught in one of his snares and something in him went from bad to worse. 'Never looked back after that,' he said. He'd recognised a kindred spirit in Karel Havelka, a mercenary veteran of the Angolan civil war who'd partaken in whatever atrocity was going. Now Michael's daughter knows the truth about him, he's happy to be buried alive in the New Zealand prison system.

'Happy to oblige,' said Latifa. She's agreed to some professional counselling for his attack on her. She doesn't want anything clouding her prospective marriage to Daniel.

There's snow on some of the higher peaks today. I can see it from my window on the top floor at Nelson hospital. They've put the operation back a day. My blood pressure was up even further, I'd had another migraine, and broken the fast by accepting a warming cup of coffee and a bacon sandwich when we handed Michael over. Above all, though, I was two hours late for the surgeon's knife, and doctors of her high regard hate to be kept waiting.

While in here, Maxwell phones me to say that we've closed the book on Bryant, Cunningham, the Doomsday militia and Māhana Wellbeing Centre.

'We've got a result on Gelder and Jaxon,' said Maxwell. 'Keegan wants to call it a day. In return nobody is pushing too hard on the shooting of that kid at the Lodge.'

'No FOI on what the US prosecutor has on Bryant?'

'Nothing, but unofficially via Keegan's contacts there are whispers of unexplained disappearances of migrant workers from some of his Californian fruit plantations. Mainly young women. Nasty goings-on in the packing sheds. Maybe witnesses or victims will be brave enough to speak up one day. Maybe not.'

'I'd lay a bet those steel rings were Bryant's idea all along and that's what LeBlanc had on him. You won't need to dig too deep. Look at the online company he keeps: eugenics, misogyny. Look at the Balkan Wars. Look at Islamic State and the Yazidi. They're going to use that place for sex slavery. We need to boot those freaks out.'

Maxwell sighed into the phone. 'Any weird shit Bryant and Co might be dreaming up out at Māhana isn't illegal right now. It might be their fantasy but they're not acting on it so far. If they do have sinister plans for after the Apocalypse it'll probably be too late to worry anyway.'

It's a vision of hell but by then hell will be a relative concept. Doing it by the book really isn't ever going to work with these people. I shook my sore weary head. 'Fingers crossed for a happy ending, eh?'

Speaking of which, it turns out that Morgan Hopu couldn't buy Charlie Evans' farm outright because he'd left it to Denzel Haruru, the young helper who once worked there to make up for shooting one of the old man's alpacas. But Denzel likes being a bricklayer and is happy to onsell to Hopu, figuring he and Cunningham deserve each other as neighbours. He'll donate the proceeds to the iwi. Charlie probably would have seen the funny side. Latifa certainly does. She can't stop laughing. 'Morgan Hopu over your back fence. That's what I call restorative justice.'

No such good fortune for Thomas Hemi. Ruth has packed her bags and gone, taking the youngest with her. For her their marriage was always an article of faith which she cherished. Faith no more. Thomasland, on the wrong side of the broken bridge, population now just one. I can't help but feel for him. God knows I've made some pretty stupid decisions in my life too.

Vanessa comes into the room. Leans down and gives me a kiss. 'How are you feeling?'

'Good as gold.'

She examines the bed frame. 'I suppose I could always handcuff you to the bed to stop you gallivanting.' A wicked grin. 'There'd be other advantages too.' She's happy to have me with her for at least one more day. We don't know what tomorrow will bring. We'll prepare and hope for the best and let the worst take care of itself.

ACKNOWLEDGEMENTS

The first draft of this novel was written before the horrific Christchurch mosque shootings on 15 March, 2019. Rather than rewrite to take account of these events, I chose instead to foreshadow the inevitable consequences of toxic ideology and the ready availability of military style weapons. Living in rural New Zealand, you can't help but be aware that guns are everywhere but, unlike the US, there does not seem to be the unhealthy fetish around them. For the most part they were, they are, tools plain and simple. But somebody sometime was going to take advantage of that. It is to New Zealand's immense credit that politicians and community alike have united to deal with the problem, to change the ownership laws, and to set the global standard for how to respond to acts of hate with genuine compassion and resolve. Now that I'm back living in Australia again, I'm acutely aware of the cultural and political differences between the two countries. Suffice to say I miss NZ big-time.

The translation of the old te reo Māori saying: *Ka pōrangi ki ngā maunga ki ngā wai matatiki, ki ngā rākau, ki ngā manu: kāhore hoki i kitea he wahine māhana* was sourced from Māoridictionary.co.nz/word/15039.

As always a huge thankyou to my editor Georgia Richter for her guidance and words of wisdom along the way and to the team at Fremantle Press for continuing to have faith in me. Thanks also to my agent Clive Newman and his ongoing efforts to promote me to the world at large. Thanks also to readers Tracy Farr, Amanda Curtin and Gaby Brown. Special mention to the indefatigable Craig Sisterson, a true champion of Kiwi 'yeahnoir' crime and of antipodean crime writing in general.

Finally, of course, my wife Kath – muse, early reader and love of my life, without whom none of this would have been possible.

ALAN CARTER'S CATO KWONG

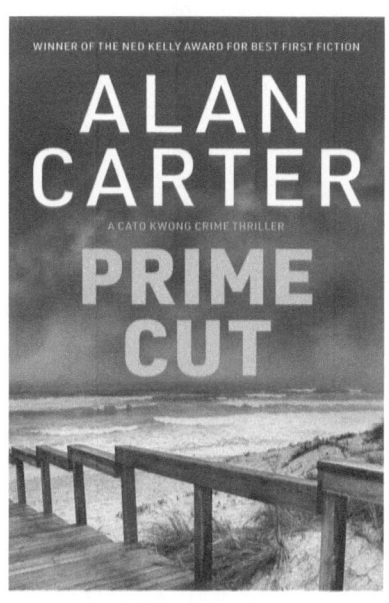

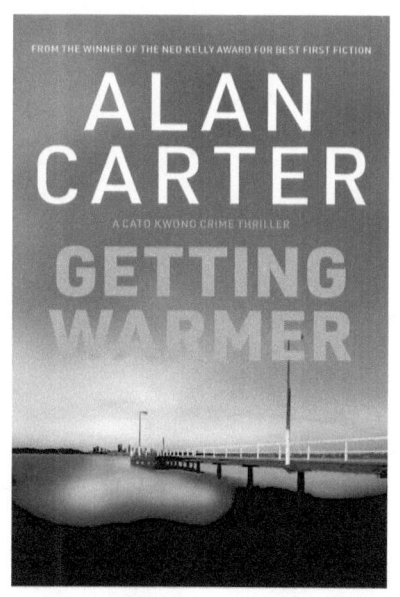

AND FROM ALL GOOD BOOKSTORES

www.ingramcontent.com/pod-product-compliance
Lightning Source LLC
Chambersburg PA
CBHW020843020726
47497CB00005B/1239